MW00576030

A PLACE OF SHADOWS

DAVID LAFFERTY

ISBN: 978-1-54395-125-7 (print)

ISBN: 978-1-54395-126-4 (email)

Dedication

Since so much of this story is about a boy saving his mother, it only seems appropriate that I take the time to recognize mine. I've had the amazing good fortune to have four of them, one biological and three hardy volunteers who not only welcomed me into their lives and families, but who were always there to offer support, advice, recognition when I did well, and a verbal kick in the pants when I didn't. In order of when I met them, these ladies can each take a good portion of credit (or blame, as the case may be) for how this wayward son turned out:

Mary Lou Lafferty
Mary Sue Heitz
Sandra Lafferty
Bobbie Hovey

Thanks, Moms. I love you more than I can say, and this story is for you.

Now what's for dinner?

ONE

I'VE ALWAYS KNOWN THINGS. AS FAR BACK AS I CAN remember, I've always been able to tell when people around me are angry or sad or excited, where car keys or important papers have been set aside and forgotten, when the phone is about to ring or someone is going to knock on the front door. Sometimes I can even sense when something important is going to happen. Maybe not always *what,* exactly; more often it's just a feeling that something is on the way—like how you can smell rain on the wind before a storm.

I never gave it a second thought when I was little. I just figured everyone else knew those things, too. But, by the time I was four or five, I began to realize the funny looks people sometimes gave me were because they *didn't* know. It even scared some people, though back then I was darned if I could see why. "It's because you're special," Mom told me at the time. "They just don't understand how you can know these things, Benny, and people can be very frightened of what they don't understand."

I knew her words had been meant to make me feel better, but somehow they hadn't. "Special," she'd called me, but even back then I knew that special meant different—and different meant weird. It put a whole new spin on things, and right then and there I decided to make sure no one had any reason to believe Ben Wolf wasn't just like everyone else. Sure, maybe there was nothing I could do about the stray feelings and insights that found their way into my head, but I could certainly keep them to myself. All I had to do was learn to hide them. Except from Mom, of course. She saw it as a gift—my sixth sense—and was never scared or acted like she thought I was strange. But at least I could go to school every day without everyone *else* knowing I was a freak.

It was hard at first, and sometimes I forgot and let something slip without thinking, but eventually I got the hang of it. After a while, I even figured out ways to use my ability without people finding out, like the time in the fourth grade when I pulled Kenny Hovey aside to ask about the math homework, keeping him out of the crosswalk long enough for an out-of-control pickup truck to screech through the intersection. Or last spring when Janelle Deveraux was in tears, certain she'd left the research paper she'd been working on for two weeks on the cross-town bus. All I had to do was suggest that maybe she'd left it backstage while working on sets for the school play, and Janelle had been so relieved when she found it that she'd hugged me. How's that for cool? At times like that, having my own private window to things no one else could see was great. It was like I had a secret identity—Clark Kent without the blue suit and cape under my clothes.

At other times, though, it wasn't so great. There was the rainy February afternoon in history class when I looked over at my pal Johnny Moore, suddenly aware that his dog had just died. Lady was twelve and a half, and had passed away while napping in the kitchen at Johnny's house. At times like that, there was nothing I could say, and no way at all I could help. It twisted my insides into knots, making me wish I really *was* like everyone else.

But by the time Mom and I moved north—when all the really weird stuff started—I was fifteen, almost sixteen, and really didn't give it much thought any more. I'd gotten used to the way things worked, and the thoughts and feelings that used to be so loud and distracting had faded to background noise. It was like the music they play in department stores. You can pick out the tune if you stop and listen, but most of the time you hardly even notice it's there.

"...long now."

I looked over toward Mom, who was driving with her window rolled down and the wind tossing her ash-blonde hair. It was midmorning, and June smelled fresh and green. She had turned thirty-eight a couple of months earlier, but she looked a lot younger. Slender and tanned, with a smile that lit up her face and faint freckles crossing the bridge of her nose, it struck me (and not for the first time) that Connie Wolf could be a model—not the frilly kind in slinky dresses and jewelry, but definitely for outdoorsy stuff: hiking shorts, flannel shirts, that sort of thing. "Sorry, what?" I asked.

"Tune in, Benny-boy," Mom said, turning to grin at me from behind her sunglasses. "I said it won't be long now." She pointed through the windshield. "See? We're almost home."

I looked in time to read "WINDWARD COVE—11 MI" just before the road sign disappeared behind us. *Home is Vacaville, Mom,* I wanted to say, and then felt guilty for even thinking it. After all, it wasn't her fault that Aunt Claire had made all those conditions in her will. If it weren't for the old lady, we would still be living in our small, two-bedroom apartment and getting by on what my mother could make waiting tables, selling the occasional painting, and teaching her art classes at the community center. Just the same, I couldn't help but feel resentful, even bitter. All my friends were in Vacaville, and now I would have to start high school in the fall not knowing anybody. It didn't seem fair that a great aunt I barely even remembered could uproot us like a potted plant just because she'd died.

Life sucks sometimes. Even when all of a sudden you're rich.

The two weeks before had been a blur. While I had been wrapping up my last few days in school and saying goodbye to my friends, Mom had spent much of the time on the phone—first with Mr. Travers, the lawyer in San Francisco who had called to break the news that Claire Black had passed away, then with a whole string of relatives, most of whom I'd had never even *heard* of, let alone met. One minute it was just Mom and me, and the next we had an infestation of family. That was something else that bugged me—the way we'd never even been worth a Christmas card from all those assorted aunts and uncles and cousins until it came time to divvy up a rich relative's stuff. *Then* all of a sudden they wanted to form a support group, but I figured the real reason had a lot more to do with curiosity over who got what. My suspicions were more or less confirmed when Mom came home after the reading of the will and all the phone calls stopped right away. I wondered briefly if that meant the money and property that Aunt Claire had left us was a big deal and the other Black relatives were jealous, or if the old lady had tossed us some scraps no one else thought were worth worrying about. Then I decided I really didn't care.

We had left the morning before, having packed nearly everything we owned (except furniture, which went to charity) into boxes and somehow making it all fit into our station wagon. The car was an old Ford LTD, a land-yacht from the 1960s with faded yellow paint and wood veneer along the sides. It had been old even before Mom bought it, back before I was even in preschool, and somehow it kept running despite oil changes and tune-ups that were always too few and far between. I wondered how long it would be before Mom got around to buying a new car, but part of me hoped it wouldn't be too soon. It had been with us a long time. We'd driven until dusk and spent the night in Eureka, staying at a run-down motel even though we could now afford better, and I figured it would be a while yet before Mom got used to the idea that money wasn't going to be a problem anymore.

I slouched in the passenger seat, trying not to feel sorry for myself, and watched the seemingly endless forest of redwood, cedar, and costal cypress blur past the window as the car wound its way up Highway 101. We had been driving for so long that it felt like we must be halfway across Canada by now, even though I knew we were still an hour or two south of the Oregon border. I'd lived my whole life in California, only forty minutes or so southwest of Sacramento, but I had never been this far north and couldn't believe how different it was. I was used to the open, rolling hills around my home town, the gentle slopes dotted with oak trees and covered with thick grass baked golden by the sun. This was a different world. At times the highway ran along the shore, the Pacific Ocean looking huge and blue, with seagulls and pelicans hovering in the air as they rode the coastal breeze. At other times Highway 101 wound through forest that seemed almost primeval, the giant trees creating a phantom twilight as they blotted out the sky above, with lush ferns, snarls of blackberry, and occasional pockets of mist huddled around their bases. It was pretty, but I still missed home.

"Can I ask you something, Mom?"

"Sure, hon. Ask away."

"Why do you think Aunt Claire put us in her will? The last time we saw her, I hadn't even started kindergarten yet."

Mom smiled. "To be honest, it surprised me, too. But she was very wealthy when she passed away, and I imagine she just wanted to make sure the whole family was taken care of."

"Yeah, but didn't you say that she didn't really like us?"

"No," she corrected, "I said that she and *I* didn't get along. She liked you just fine." She glanced over at me. "Do you remember her at all?"

I shrugged. "A little, I guess. It was a long time ago. I remember Uncle Martin a lot better. Wasn't he the man with the train set?"

Mom nodded. "Model railroading was his hobby."

I had to smile. I didn't remember much about my great uncle (great-*great* uncle, I guess he'd have to be, since Aunt Claire had been my great-grandfather's sister). But I did remember the basement of their San Francisco mansion that Uncle Martin had converted for his mammoth railroad, complete with cities and factories, farms and forests, even lakes and mountain ranges with tunnels. Uncle Martin had been a big kid at heart, and I offhandedly wondered what the kindly old man had seen in my stern, uncompromising aunt. We had read *Rebecca* in my seventh-grade English class, and it occurred to me that I'd pictured the character Mrs. Danvers as looking like Aunt Claire.

"Mostly I remember being scared of her," I went on, getting back to the subject. "She hardly ever smiled, and she was always telling me to stand up straight, but she gave me lemon cookies and asked me lots of questions."

"What kind of questions?"

"I…don't really remember." It wasn't a lie—not exactly, anyway—but what little I did remember of those long afternoons in the mansion made me uncomfortable. "I just remember sitting in that room in her house, keeping my mouth full of cookies so I wouldn't have to answer her and waiting for the clock to chime so I could go." I shifted in my seat, tucking one leg beneath me as I turned toward her. "So how come the two of you didn't get along?"

"Aunt Claire and I..." Mom hesitated. "Well, she and I just didn't see eye to eye on a lot of things, that's all." Even without my gift I knew there was a lot she wasn't telling me, but I could tell by her tone that the subject was closed. "But hey, she must have thought we were both okay, right?" Mom added, brightening. "After all, look where we are now!"

I said nothing, turning to face forward in my seat. I knew she was watching me out of the corner of her eye, and I concentrated so I could sense the mixture of her emotions. Doing this is sort of like reaching out with an invisible finger, brushing lightly against the feelings that radiate from people, like the way a dragonfly can touch the surface of a pond while barely making a ripple. She was both nervous and excited over what lay ahead, I realized, but a little sad, too, probably because she knew I hadn't wanted to leave Vacaville. It made me feel guilty again, but I couldn't help asking questions—not to argue, but just so I could get it all straight in my head. "It's great that she put us in her will," I pressed, "but if Aunt Claire liked us so much, how come she made us move all the way up here?"

Mom shrugged. "She felt that the property should stay in the family, and for whatever reason she picked you and me. She had it put in her will that we had to live there until you were eighteen—a legal adult—and that part of the money she left us would have to go into restoring the place. After that, we can do pretty much whatever we want, but if we decide to sell the property, it can only be to another member of the Black family."

"I still don't see why it was such a big deal to her," I grumbled.

"Windward Cove was founded by her grandfather—or was it her great-grandfather? Anyway, it was back during the gold rush," Mom explained. "It's where Aunt Claire was born, and she lived there until she was a teenager. After she moved away, she had the house and inn boarded up, but she never sold the property. She hired caretakers to keep the place from falling apart, and even tried leasing it to people who wanted to reopen the inn, but she only went back there three or four times herself."

"I still don't get it, Mom. If she never went there, and if the place needs so much work, she must not have cared about it very much. Why didn't she just sell it off and forget about it?"

It took a long time for Mom to answer—so long that I had begun to think she wasn't going to. "I asked Uncle Martin that same question once," she said finally.

"Yeah? What did he say?"

"He told me that Windward Cove was probably the only place in the world where Aunt Claire had ever been really happy. But something bad happened there—something that changed her. She never told him what. She loved the place, but...."

"But?" I prompted.

"Well, according to Uncle Martin, Windward Cove broke her heart."

TWO

HIGHWAY 101 HAD MEANDERED TO THE EAST A COUPLE of miles by the time we pulled off at the Windward Cove exit, and Mom swung the station wagon left to cross an overpass, heading west. "There's a sheet of paper with directions on it somewhere in this mess," she said. "Dig it out, will you?"

I went through the road trip garbage that had accumulated on the front seat, sifting through gas receipts, a map that hadn't been refolded correctly, some potato chip bags and candy bar wrappers before I finally found it. "It just says to keep following the road and then hang a right half a mile past the town."

Mom nodded, obeying traffic signs as she dropped the car's speed to forty miles per hour and then twenty-five as we rounded a bend and got our first look at Windward Cove. It wasn't much to speak of. The road we were following dropped down through a wide cleft between wooded hills, continuing for another mile or so to where it ended at a wharf where a few tired-looking fishing boats bobbed and rocked in the swells. Between us and the wharf was maybe a quarter-mile's worth of buildings that clustered along both sides of the road like beggars, forming what passed for a downtown, with a sprawl of old houses and mobile homes crowded into secondary streets on either side.

"Careful, Mom," I teased, trying to keep the disappointment out of my voice. "Try not to get us lost."

"Two thousand comedians out of work, and *you're* trying to be funny," she quipped back.

We drove through town without stopping, and I only had time to note that there was one gas station, a single-screen movie theater, a supermarket, a bank, a hardware store, a couple of used bookshops, and a pizza place. I would have to do some exploring to really see the rest, but so far my hopes weren't high that Windward Cove would be offering much in the way of stuff to do.

The turn we were looking for was right where the directions said it would be, and Mom swung the big car onto a gravel drive that lay in a gap between two sections of low stone wall. Next to the road was a tall pillar made of the same stone, at the top of which a sign reading *Windward Inn* hung from a rusted metal arm. A piece of old fence board had been nailed diagonally across the sign, with the word *CLOSED* written in paint so old and faded that it was barely readable.

The drive climbed the hillside in a series of switchback curves, the pavement sometimes concrete, sometimes gravel, sometimes just ruts in the dirt. Blackberry bushes crowded on either side, with tendrils occasionally reaching out to brush the side of the car as we passed. We reached a small plateau about halfway to the top and stopped at a fork in the road. To our left, the drive continued to wind up toward the top of the hill, while the right-hand fork made a gentle descent to the northeast. "Which way?" Mom asked.

I looked at the sheet with the directions again, shaking my head. "It doesn't say."

Shrugging, Mom turned left. The drive continued to climb for another quarter mile or so before we broke out into sunshine at the top of the rise. A pair of stone pillars flanked the road, a rusted chain sagging between them and secured by a padlock. *PRIVATE PROPERTY—KEEP OUT* was lettered on a board attached to the chain, but like the sign back at the road, the paint had faded almost to illegibility, making the warning seem tired and halfhearted. Mom stopped the car, shifting the transmission into park. "Will you look at *that*," she half-whispered, looking at what lay beyond.

"It's really something," I agreed.

And it was. Even with the windows boarded up, the grounds overgrown with bracken and blackberry, and weeds forcing their way between the stone pavers of the drive, the Windward Inn was still impressive. The central part of the place was shaped in a big oval, with rectangular wings branching off to the right and left, all of it rising in three stories of gray stone. Four chimneys rose from each of the two wings, sprouting from a roof of slate tiles that swept down into wide, overhanging eaves. The center roof was more steeply pitched, rising well above the other two and topped by a tarnished weathervane shaped like a sailing ship. Wood trim had once been painted in ebony and white to accent the stonework, but the paint had faded and peeled, making the edges of the inn look tattered. Towering cypress tress draped the grounds in shadow, their trunks and branches sculpted by offshore winds to loom eagerly, almost hungrily, toward us. Sixty feet behind the inn, the grounds abruptly fell away in cliffs overlooking the Pacific Ocean that stretched out to a faint line on the horizon where the water met the sky.

We *owned* this place? Wow!

I could feel my pulse quicken with a mixture of excitement and unease as Mom shut off the ignition. "The house must've been the other way," she mused, "but as long as we're here, we might as well take a look, right?"

"Sure," I agreed, and got out of the car.

We ducked under the chain and walked wordlessly up the drive, which made a wide sweep to the front porch and back in a shape like a big teardrop. I saw stone planter boxes surrounding a three-tiered fountain at the center, but the fountain was dry and half-covered in lichen, and the rose bushes that had probably once been carefully looked after had gone feral with neglect, fighting with one another in a ferocious tangle, their bases black with age and covered in thorns like shark's teeth. An offshore breeze made the cypress branches creak above us, whispering through the brush and making the foxtails that grew between the pavers bob and nod restlessly.

My sense of unease grew as we climbed three wide steps to the porch, but I tried to shake it off as I watched my mother move to a window just to the left of the massive double doors. "This place is *amazing*," she said excitedly, trying to peek between the boards. "I wish we had the keys —I can't wait to see inside!"

I was doing my best to share her interest, but a sense that something was wrong was making my skin crawl. It was nothing I could put my finger on, exactly, and the rational part of my brain argued that this spooky old place was just giving me a case of the heebie-jeebies. Nevertheless, my arms had broken out in gooseflesh, and sweat had begun to gather on the back of my neck. I couldn't explain how, but it felt almost as if the Windward Inn was somehow aware of our presence. It wasn't a threatening feeling, but more a sense of quiet watchfulness, like the place didn't necessarily mind us poking around for the moment but was waiting to see what we would do next.

Mom tried the door, not seeming surprised to find it locked, and then turned back toward me. "C'mon, Ben," she said, grinning. "Let's see what's around back!"

I followed her down the steps and felt that creepy unease begin to dissipate in the wake of her excitement. The fact that the Windward Inn didn't seem to bother her confirmed that my imagination was getting out of hand, like the way watching old horror movies could still make me squirm even though I knew Dracula was just Christopher Lee with teeth and Frankenstein was Boris Karloff with a lot of makeup. Kid stuff, I reminded myself, and I pushed my silly fears aside. Almost, anyway.

We walked around the south wing, wading through tall weeds that hid tree roots for us to stumble over and getting foxtails stuck in our socks. We turned the back corner to find a wide patio running across the entire western side, bordered by olive trees that had grown into a wall of dusty grey-green and had dropped fruit so long that the last four or five feet of the concrete was stained black. Wisteria ran unchecked along the wall and sent tendrils way up into the eaves, almost as thick as a python at its base and having squeezed the trellis that had once contained it into splinters of bleached wood. A second fountain stood in what had been a wide pool surrounded by benches, centered on the arc of wall between the north and the south wings. The pool was choked with dead plants, and whatever water was left in there gave off a swampy, rotten odor.

"Whatever the kitchen is serving doesn't smell so great," I joked.

Mom wasn't listening. She had hurried to the middle of the building, where sheets of plywood covered floor-length windows that ran completely along the bottom story. She had spotted a gap where one of the edges had come loose and had reached in to pull it further back so that she could poke her head in and look through the glass. A spider scuttled out from the darkness just above her left hand, but it disappeared into the gap on the far side before I could warn her, so I shrugged and closed my mouth instead.

"Oh, Ben...you've *got* to see this!" she exclaimed, her voice slightly muffled behind the wood.

"See what?" I asked dubiously.

She pulled her head out and stepped aside, holding the sheet of plywood back for me. "Just look!"

Sighing, I stepped obediently forward, first checking to make sure Mr. Spider hadn't left any friends or family behind. Satisfied, I turned to see that the window was separated into a lattice of ten-inch-square panes, and I saw that Mom had rubbed a peep hole through the years of dirt caked onto the glass. I cupped my hands around my face to see inside.

It was a ballroom, I realized, when my eyes adjusted to the gloom. A parquet floor stretched fifty feet to the far wall, where a fireplace was flanked by tall double doors on either side. Dark wainscoting rose partway up the walls, above which the room had once been painted white or pale yellow but was now dingy with age and showing darker patches where paintings had once hung. A large bandstand dominated the south wall, opposite a long bar that swept along the north, both covered in a thick layer of dust. In the center of the high ceiling hung a massive chandelier, its crystals shrouded in cobwebs and winking in the dagger of sunlight that pierced the room from where I stood.

My uneasiness returned in a rush. It felt as if the room had been waiting, dark and silent, and our peeking inside had been an intrusion, like opening a crypt. I pulled my head out hurriedly, trying to paste a smile on my face that I knew probably wasn't very convincing. "Wow...pretty cool," I said, but that wasn't convincing, either.

Mom didn't seem to notice and was now craning her neck to look up at the third-story windows as she continued north along the wall, and I had to hurry to catch up with her. I exhaled a thankful sigh when she didn't stop to try any more doors or windows, following a half-step behind her as we continued around to the front of the inn and made our way back to the car. My uneasiness was still cranked up to high while Mom reversed in a U-turn, and I craned my neck around for a last look at the inn.

The Windward watched us go.

We went back down the drive, passing the cutoff back to the main road and dropping into a wooded area on the inland side of the hill. Looking through the window behind Mom's head, I caught a brief glimpse of the inn's weathervane through a gap in the trees above and was relieved when it was obscured by the terrain. *At least we won't be living right next door,* I thought.

The house was tucked among a stand of tall elm trees at the edge of a clearing. To the north, a big field of overgrown grapevines sprawled in a jungle of green behind a dilapidated fence, while to the west a cleft in the hillside peeked out at the ocean. The house was small compared to the Windward Inn but just about as inviting. It was a rambling, two-story Victorian that had probably once been painted blue but had faded over the years to a drab, chipped gray. Tall, narrow windows gazed sternly down at us, and a single chimney rose along the southern wall to point at the sky. A small, eight-sided room straddled the peak of the steep roof, the top two-thirds of the walls all glass. I could make out the silhouette of something up there—a triangular framework or maybe a ladder—before we ducked beneath the elms and came to a stop by the front porch. Mom turned off the ignition, and for a long moment we sat listening to the engine tick to itself as it cooled.

"What do you think?" she asked finally.

"Didn't Norman Bates live here?"

"Oh, come on. It's not really that bad. You could at least *try* to make the best of it, Benny."

I sighed. "You're right. Sorry, Mom."

We got out and climbed the front steps while Mom dug through her purse for the key that had been given to her after the reading of Aunt Claire's will. It was the heavy, old-fashioned kind made of brass, but the tumblers in the lock rolled back without a struggle, and I followed her into an entry hall. "Hey...this really *isn't* so bad," I had to admit, feeling genuine interest for the first time that day.

Before us, a wide staircase climbed to an open gallery on the second floor, while a living room with a twelve-foot ceiling sprawled off to the left. The one room was almost as large as our apartment back in Vacaville, and I whistled, the sound echoing off the hardwood floors. A light fixture clung to the ceiling, and I reached over to flick a wall switch on my left. Nothing happened.

"The house has water and gas, so we can cook and take showers," Mom explained, "but otherwise we'll be roughing it for a few days. The wiring is probably original, and I didn't want the power turned on until we got an electrician to check the place out."

We crossed back through the entry hall, passing into a large family room with a fireplace. A door on the left concealed a tiny bathroom tucked beneath the stairs, followed by an archway that opened into a dining room that was probably large enough to seat ten or twelve people. Antique furniture was scattered here and there, leftovers from a different time, most of it the kind with spindly legs that looked like it would collapse if any real weight was put on it. But at least the place had been dusted, and I remembered that Mr. Travers had arranged to have a cleaning crew sent over.

The kitchen was in the back, made cheerier by windows overlooking the meadow. A gas range that had probably been new back in the 1940s squatted in the corner, and a butcher block stood on stout legs in the center of the room, not far from a small kitchen table with three chairs. There was a walk-in pantry with stairs leading down to a full basement, and at the rear of the house were two small bedrooms separated by a bath and sitting room—almost like their own apartment, complete with a narrow stairwell that slanted up to the second floor. "These would have been servants' quarters, I guess," Mom said.

"Servants? For real?"

"Yep."

We returned to the main staircase and climbed to where a circular window five feet in diameter overlooked the abandoned vineyard. Three bedrooms opened off to the left, and a bathroom and master suite to the right. There was also a room with ceiling-high bookshelves that I took to be a library. At the end of the left-hand hall, a small door revealed the servants' staircase rising from below, then continuing up to the attic. Mom and I exchanged a brief glance and then wordlessly climbed the stairs.

The attic was huge, a shadowy realm of old furniture and boxes, dusty steamer trunks and crates of books, odd shapes and shadows that I couldn't quite make out. I wanted to look around, but a final narrow staircase caught my eye instead. "Where do you think that goes?" I asked.

"The cupola, I imagine," Mom replied.

I remembered the glass-walled octagonal room. "The little room on top of the roof?" I asked.

"Uh-huh. Come on."

I followed her up the stairs to a door, halting while she fumbled with the knob. "It's locked," she said.

I frowned. "That's kind of weird, isn't it? Do you think that's where they stacked all the dead bodies?"

She shrugged in reply, bringing out the key again and using it. She had to shake the handle before the bolt reluctantly rolled aside, the door swinging open on stiff hinges and sending a shaft of sunlight down into the attic. Five more steps opened into the room above.

The cupola was maybe fifteen feet in diameter—larger than it had appeared from the ground. The floor was set below the roofline, with low shelves lining the base on all eight sides. The only thing in the room was the biggest telescope I had ever seen, a monster of steel and brass standing on a metal tripod, its bore easily ten inches in diameter and positioned by hand cranks. It was pointed north, toward the vineyard and hills beyond.

"Look!" Mom cried excitedly, gazing at the surrounding area as she turned a slow three-sixty. "You can see the town from here—and the ocean, too! Isn't this great?"

But I didn't think it was great at all. In fact, all I wanted to do was turn and run back down the stairs as fast as I could. Despite the sunlight streaming through the windows, which should have made the room seem like a greenhouse, the air was freezing cold—so cold that I wondered why I couldn't see my breath. Didn't Mom notice? I crossed my arms over my chest, shivering as a feeling of utter despair and loneliness settled over me. Suddenly, I was more depressed than I'd ever felt before—worse than I'd felt about leaving Vacaville, worse even than the day Mom told me dad was never coming home. It was as if all the joy had run out of the world and my life was empty, meaningless. My throat felt tight, and I had a sudden urge to curl up on the floor and cry.

"Mom…?" I tried to whisper, but nothing came out.

She was experimenting with the cranks on the telescope, grunting softly with effort, and a faint shriek of disused metal came from the gears as the lens slowly swung toward the ocean. The sound made the hairs on the back of my neck stand up, like fingernails drawn across a blackboard. "You can see darn near to Japan through this thing!" she said after a moment, looking through the eyepiece. "Is this place cool or what, Ben? What do you say we make this your bedroom?"

I was horrified by the idea, and when I didn't answer her for a few seconds, she looked back at me, curious. "Ben? ...*Ben!* What's wrong, hon? You're as white as a sheet!"

She reached out and touched my arm, and suddenly it was all gone. My depression lifted like it had never even been there, and the chill in the air dissipated at once. It was warm in the cupola now, almost stuffy, though I imagined the tall elms and sea breeze kept it from getting too bad, and it would even be nice with a window or two open. I staggered backward a step, dizzy at the change, and caught myself on the shelf behind me. "I'm okay," I managed after a moment. It was getting easier to breathe.

"Are you sure?" Mom asked, her brow furrowed with concern.

I nodded. "I'm fine…just got a little dizzy there for a second." *What was that all about?* I wondered.

Mom watched me closely for a moment and then gave me a tentative smile. "Well, okay. If you're sure."

"I'm good, Mom. Really. Just getting hungry, I guess."

"Well, we have sandwiches in the cooler. What do you say we have some lunch and then unload the car? I'd like to get at least partway unpacked before dark."

I gave her a smile—the best one I could manage, anyway. "Sounds great," I replied.

She led the way down the stairs, and I pulled the cupola door firmly closed behind me. My spirits rose as we crossed the attic floor, my earlier cold and depression fading like the dreams that never seemed to stay with me longer than the first few seconds after I woke up. We were almost to the second-floor stairwell when I stopped, looking back over my shoulder as I caught a sound at the edge of my hearing: a faint shriek of disused metal.

The sound the telescope made when turning on its tripod.

THREE

IT WAS LATE IN THE AFTERNOON BEFORE WE WERE FINished, and I sat on the butcher block in the kitchen, absently swinging my legs as I watched Mom stack our small collection of mismatched pots and pans in a lower cabinet. She stood, rubbing her back as she turned to face me. "Did you pick out a bedroom?" she asked.

I nodded. "The corner one—you know, the one with the built-in bed with the drawers underneath."

"It's called a captain's bed," she told me. "Do you need anything else in there?"

"There was a little desk and a chair I dragged in from one of the other rooms, and I thought I'd haul one of those bookcases down from the attic. That should do, I guess."

"Are you all unpacked?"

I shrugged. "More or less. I put my clothes away and made the bed, but I still need to put my posters up, and there isn't much more I can do without the bookcase. There's no hurry, is there?"

"No, I suppose not." She filled a water glass from the tap and drank it. Well, it looks like we've got some time to kill. What do you say we get cleaned up and then look the town over? I want to pick up some things at the grocery store, and we'll need some candles or flashlights to use at night until I get the power turned on."

"And pizza," I added.

Mom shook her head. "No way, pal. I know we give the nutrition plan a break on road trips, but the last couple of days have involved too much grease already. You're getting some vegetables tonight."

"But we only got here this morning," I argued, grinning, "so technically it's still a road-trip day. Besides, we can get veggies on the pizza."

"Ben," she began.

"Ben…need …piiiiizza."

Mom closed her eyes, shaking her head in feigned disgust. "Fine—you win. Enjoy your last night of hedonism, 'cause we start unclogging our arteries tomorrow, understand?"

"Yes, warden."

She made a shooing gesture with one hand. "Just hit the shower, bub, and save the wisecracks for someone who thinks you're charming."

Twenty minutes later, freshly showered and dressed in clean clothes, I stopped to study my reflection in the bathroom mirror. It wasn't something I normally did (I usually just give myself a quick once-over on my way out the door), but something that afternoon made me meet my own gray-eyed gaze. "Some day, huh?" I asked softly.

Yeah, my inner voice agreed, *especially the part where you freaked out upstairs. What was* that *all about?*

"It wasn't anything," I told myself, combing my dark hair back with my fingers. It was getting shaggy again, and it wouldn't be long before Mom started dropping hints about a haircut. "Too much going on at once, that's all. Aunt Claire dies, and less than a month later I'm moving into a house straight out of a Vincent Price movie. *Anybody* would be a little skittish, right?"

My inner voice might have made some uncomfortable arguments to that—some involving freezing cold that only I could feel or sounds coming from empty rooms—but it was nice enough to drop the subject for the time being. Before heading downstairs, I offered my reflection a lopsided smile and a wink, and I felt better seeing my reflection smile and wink back.

I wandered outside while Mom was getting ready. I had left my mountain bike leaning against the railing at the base of the front steps, and I figured I ought to find a place for it. The sun felt warm through my T-shirt, the air cooled by a light breeze whispering through the grass, and I liked the combination. I walked my bike around the side of the house to where the drive ended in a wide garage. It took me a second or two before I realized the doors swung outward, and when I poked my head inside, I was surprised to see horse stalls lining the walls. It wasn't a garage at all, I realized. It was a carriage house, and it struck me again how old the place was. I left my bike in one of the stalls.

There was still no sign of Mom when I pushed the door closed behind me, so I continued around to the back of the house, my hiking boots whickering through the dead grass. A deep porch spread across the rear of the place, opening off a set of double French doors that I must have missed while we were exploring inside, and a small access door that was slanted against the base of the wall opened to steps leading down to the basement. A weathered barn stood almost hidden in the trees a hundred or so yards away, but I figured that could wait. I made my way to the edge of the vineyard instead and stood resting my hand on the splintered remains of what had been a gatepost.

The rows of overgrown grapevines were bigger up close. A *lot* bigger. They rose in great tangled mounds ten to fifteen feet high, the vines twisting and arcing together to form tunnels I could have walked through. The ground beneath was a deep, spongy carpet of rotting leaves, dappled here and there by patches of sunlight that found their way down through the living roof above, but for the most part it was pitched in shadow.

I was thinking how cool it would be to walk around in there when I heard a low giggle. It sounded like a little kid—probably a girl—but I couldn't tell for sure. It was a playful sound, almost mischievous, like a kid playing hide-and-seek and not being able to keep quiet. It came from somewhere in the tangle in front of me, but I couldn't tell exactly where or from how far away.

"Hello…?" I called. "Is somebody back there?" I held my breath, listening, but the sound wasn't repeated. I glanced over my shoulder to make sure Mom wasn't looking for me and then took a few steps into the shadows. I had to stoop slightly at first and brushed away the end of a vine that reached out to tickle the base of my neck, but once I was between the rows, I found I could stand up straight. It was noticeably cooler, like stepping into a cave, and I crossed my arms over my chest for warmth.

The giggle sounded again, this time from somewhere off to my left, and I hunkered low, craning my neck around to look for the owner. It occurred to me that the vineyard would be the ultimate warren for games of tag or spook, and I wouldn't have been surprised if kids from all over town played there. "Okay, kid!" I called out, smiling. "You win! Ally-ally-in-for-free!"

A bird or small animal rustled in the leaves somewhere close by, and a crow cawed faintly off in the distance. Nothing else. I concentrated, trying to use my gift like radar to get a feel for whoever was out there, but I came up empty. It was just me and the grapevines, which would have been fine if it hadn't felt so much like I was being watched.

"Ben!" Mom called from back at the house, and the sudden sound made me jump.

"Coming!" I hollered back, but I stood there for another second or two, still trying to see where my little friend was hiding. At last I shrugged and turned for the gate. "You got me fair and square," I called back over my shoulder, "but just wait 'til next time!"

The sun was headed for the horizon when we got back to town, dropping behind a cloud bank that had gathered out over the ocean to turn the sky orangey red. Mom bought flashlights and a couple of electric camping lanterns at the hardware store and then dragged me through the small market while she shopped for enough food to see us through a couple of days until she could have a refrigerator delivered. "Are you starving already, or do we have time to look around before dinner?" she asked after we loaded the stuff in the car.

"I'm okay for a while," I assured her. Mom had been eyeballing some of the antique stores and cutesy souvenir shops clustered along the main drag, and I knew she was itching to spend an hour or two poking through shelves and not buying anything. It was just her way. "Is it okay if I look around on my own and catch you at the pizza place later?" I asked. Knick-knack shopping wasn't my thing.

"Sure." She glanced at her watch. "It's 5:40 now. How does 7:00 suit you?"

"It works for me. Happy hunting."

Mom reached out and ruffled my hair affectionately, something she's been doing for as long as I can remember. I pretend that it bothers me, but it doesn't really, and I would miss it if she ever stopped.

I spent the next ten minutes or so strolling to the east end of downtown, but there really wasn't much to see. There was a coin-operated laundry I hadn't noticed when we'd first driven through, as well as a couple of mom-and-pop cafes, a Mexican food place, and a bakery. A tiny motel called the Ebb Tide Inn offered private cottages with air conditioning and cable TV, but the parking lot was empty despite the neon "Vacancy" sign that glowed hopefully in the office window. The rest of the storefronts seemed to be geared toward serving tourists, but I couldn't see why anyone would want to waste a vacation in Windward Cove. There was a place that sold homemade jams and jellies and others that sold polished shells, salt water taffy, carvings made from driftwood—that sort of thing. The few people I saw all appeared to be locals—an old man with white hair reading a newspaper while sitting on a bench, a lady who nodded pleasantly to me while straightening a shelf full of old books just outside one of the secondhand shops, and three kids idly practicing skateboard tricks on a homemade wooden ramp they'd set up in an alley. I crossed the street at the end and walked back along the other side, but aside from a realty office offering coastal properties and vacation rentals, it was just more of the same.

I glanced down an alley just past Pirate Pizza and saw a guy about my age struggling to balance a big cardboard box while trying to open the side door of Tsunami Joe, a coffee house that was the next business over. He was slender, almost skinny, with a shock of black hair that was long on top and trimmed short on the sides. "Dude… hold on!" I called, trotting over. "I'll give you a hand."

The kid took a step back and turned toward me with a smile. "Thanks…dude."

She was a girl! The short hair had thrown me, not to mention her black jeans and flannel shirt, but there was no mistaking her now. Her face was narrow, with dark brown eyes and high cheekbones, and now that I was closer, I was able to see the purple highlights in her hair and three piercings in each ear. My face grew hot with embarrassment. *Way to go, big guy,* I thought. *Ben Wolf, village idiot.*

"Hurry up, will you?" she said. "This is getting sort of heavy."

"Oh…right," I said, pulling the door open for her.

"Thanks. There's another door just through here. Do you mind grabbing that one, too?"

I squeezed past her in the narrow hallway beyond, pulled the door open, and followed her into the coffee house. Tsunami Joe was set up in a building that had been nearly gutted by fire at some point in the past. The brick walls were blackened by soot, and the rafters two stories above were charred at the edges. A mismatched assortment of upholstered chairs were scattered around, their cushions sagging and upholstery worn threadbare, amid tables and chairs positioned completely at random. It was like the place was furnished out of secondhand stores, but the effect was both casual and oddly inviting. Framed photos, most of them black and white, covered the walls with the same disregard for order, and alternative rock issued softly from speakers hidden somewhere in the shadows. Half a dozen customers lingered over coffee or iced mochas, ranging from kids about my age to one elderly lady who must have been pushing seventy, most of them sitting hunched over laptop computers while surfing the Internet.

I liked it.

The girl hurried to the service counter on the far side of the room and set the box down with a grunt. I followed her. There was a glass case full of pastries, assorted cookies, and sandwiches, and centered on the back wall was an antique espresso machine—a monster of polished brass and copper that squatted like a gargoyle among shelved jars of coffee beans, teas, and flavored syrups.

"Wow," I said. "Cool place."

"Thanks," the girl replied. "And thanks for the assist." She stuck out her right hand. "Ab Chambers."

"Ab?" I asked, shaking hands.

"Short for Abigail. Three aunts to choose from, and Mom and Dad had to name me after the one I like the least. She never has anything nice to say, and she's driven us all nuts by trying to turn me into Suzy Homemaker since I was five or six. We don't really get along."

I laughed.

"So you're the new boy, right?" she asked. "The one moving into the old Black place?"

"Yep—Ben Wolf," I replied. "How did you know?"

She snorted. "Welcome to small-town life, Wolfman—where your business is never your own. Everyone's been talking about it: genuine relatives of old Claire Black coming to live in the family home. Sorry to hear she died, by the way. Were you close?"

Part of me felt like I should have been annoyed by her blurting it out like that, but I wasn't. I was too distracted. There was something odd about her, though I couldn't put my finger on what it was right away. "No," I told her absently, still trying to figure out what was different. "I haven't even seen Aunt Claire since I was little." Then, suddenly I knew what was wrong! Even though I was standing less than three feet from Ab, I couldn't sense anything from her. No emotions, no insights, nothing.

She was a complete blank to me!

It didn't happen often, but when it did, it always came as a surprise. Usually, I could pick up at least a little something from just about everyone I ran across. But once in a great while I encountered a person I couldn't read at all. It was as if their thoughts and feelings were just pitched a little differently, like a sound just high or low enough to be outside my range of hearing. It made me a little uncomfortable—almost like she wasn't really there—but I shook it off. I was on the verge of making my first friend in Windward Cove, and who knew how many more would come along?

"So," she said, her eyes sparkling with interest, "have you seen any ghosts yet?"

FOUR

"GHOSTS?" I ASKED.

"Yeah," said Ab. "You know, spirits...specters....things that go bump in the night? Try to keep up with the class, will you?"

"You're kidding, right?"

"What, nobody told you? Get with the program, Wolfman. The Pacific coast happens to be one of *the* most haunted places in the whole U. S. of A."

Obviously, she was trying to put one over on the new guy. "Yeah, right," I said, smirking.

Ab frowned. "You don't believe me?" She took my arm, pulling me over to the nearest wall and pointing to one of the framed black-and-white photos. It was yellow with age and showed a man and a woman standing hand-in-hand, with a small clapboard house in the background. "Elijah and Delores Martin, 1874," Ab stated. "Their house is still standing over on Clover Street, though no one lives there now. Elijah's fishing boat went down in a squall, and all hands were lost. After the memorial service, Delores went home, locked the front door behind her, and no one ever saw her alive again. Relatives broke in three weeks later and found her body sitting in a rocking chair in the parlor, her eyes open and staring straight ahead. The newspaper said she died of a broken heart, but since she'd stopped eating and drinking, it probably had a lot more to do with starvation and dehydration. As the story goes, you can still hear her crying when a storm rolls in."

I grinned. "And you've heard this yourself, I suppose?"

Ab shook her head. "Not yet, but I will. I've sat out four storms in the house so far. One of these days I'm bound to get lucky."

I felt my grin fade. *Was she serious?*

She pointed to a photo two feet to the left. "Or here. This is Willis Grade, part of an old logging road about a mile outside of town." The photo showed a heavy wagon pulled by a team of ten mules. Logs were stacked high in the wagon bed, their weight causing the mules to pick their way carefully down a steep stretch of dirt track while the driver strained at the brake. "In 1858, a driver named Big Joe Willis was making his last run of the day, just around twilight, when his wagon brakes gave out," Ab went on. "The wagon was loaded with fresh-cut redwood, and the weight pushed his mule team at a gallop to a curve about halfway down the grade. By then they were going too fast to make the turn, and the whole wagon, team and all, went over the side and crashed at the bottom of a gulch sixty feet below. No one knows why Big Joe didn't jump clear. Maybe he thought he could make the turn, or maybe he just froze in panic. Anyway, every once in a while someone will be out there around dusk and will hear sounds of the wagon rolling down the grade, mules braying and a man shouting and cussing to beat all, followed by a scream and the sound of them crashing at the bottom."

"Wow!" I said. "You're really into this stuff, aren't you?"

"There's not much else to do around here. I figure it's either chase ghosts or let Aunt Abigail teach me to bake muffins." Ab raised her eyebrows. "Which would *you* pick?"

She had a point.

"Or this one here," said Ab, moving on. "This is the lumber mill that made your however-times-great granddaddy his fortune. He moved up here and built it during the gold rush when he figured out he could make a lot more money shipping lumber down to the gold camps than he could by prospecting for gold himself. Things were going great until one day when a boiler valve for the steam-powered saw froze. Before anyone knew what was happening, the pressure built up and the iron boiler exploded, killing four men and seriously injuring nine others. Your granddad brought in a new boiler and got the mill running again, but a month later he had to move the whole operation half a mile north when the workers complained of strange noises, cold spots, and seeing men covered in blood standing by the work stations."

I shuddered, thinking of the strange cold I had felt up in the cupola.

"People have seen lights in our graveyard, we've got a phantom ship that appears every now and then out of the fog, and there's supposed to be at least a dozen ghosts up at the Windward Inn alone. Top that off with all the spirit activity from the time a tidal wave nearly washed away the whole town back in the 1940s, and the place is positively *crawling* with them. And that's just in our back yard. From San Diego to Seattle, this coast has more spooks than anyone has ever bothered to count, and Windward Cove sits at pretty much ground zero."

I looked around, scanning the photos crowding the walls. There had to be a hundred or more. "And how many of these photos have ghost stories attached?" I asked.

Ab grinned. "*All* of them."

I shook my head in wonder, strolling through the coffee house and scanning the walls. "How about this one?" I asked, pointing to a photo at random. It showed a crowd of twenty or thirty men posed in front of a felled redwood tree with a trunk that had to be ten feet in diameter.

Ab walked over. "That's one of the old logging camps from the early 1860s." She leaned forward, pointing. "See the guy second from the left? That's Mike Murdoch, a surveyor for the company. He was part of a team of seven or eight men that would hike around in the woods, sometimes for weeks on end, scouting and mapping the best stands of timber. In March and April of 1866, it rained nonstop for twenty-four days straight, and Mike's team was caught in it. There was nothing they could do but play cards, listen to the rain on the tent roof, and get on each other's nerves. Mike caught cabin fever so bad that he eventually snapped—just picked up an axe and started swinging. He killed three men before the others tackled him, dragged him outside, and hanged him from a madrone tree. Sometimes hikers will come into town and talk about a tiny clearing way out in the woods where they suddenly have felt edgy and scared, and from what I've been able to figure out, that's probably the spot where it all happened."

I nodded, continuing along the wall until I stopped again, my eyes widening as I noticed an eleven-by-fourteen-inch photo that made my breath catch in my throat.

It was the Windward Inn.

The photo was obviously taken back in its heyday. Water cascaded in the fountain out front, and a horse-drawn carriage sat behind an old Model T Ford in the drive. Four women in long dresses were playing croquet on a patch of lawn with a couple of men in straw hats and shirt-garters. They looked happy, unlike most vintage photos I'd seen in which people always wore serious expressions. The inn was a stately sprawl behind them, elegant and lively, and it made me shiver to think of the lonely, abandoned place that now crouched on the hill above town.

"That one's my favorite," Ab confided. "See this chick here?"

My gaze went to the woman she indicated, and I was a little disappointed that I couldn't see what she looked like. Her head was turned toward the lady on her left, and all but the lower half of her face was hidden beneath the brim of a wide hat. She was laughing though, amused by something her friend was saying, and I wondered what they had been talking about in that frozen moment in time.

"That's Sofia LaRue, a stage actress who stayed at the inn for a month or so back in 1914. As the story goes, she fell in love with another guest at the hotel, and they decided to get married. But on the morning of the wedding, Sofia was found strangled in her room. People suspected the fiancée, but he had disappeared sometime the night before and the murder was never officially solved."

I gave a low whistle.

"She's still up there, by the way," Ab said. "One of your permanent guests."

"She probably owes us a fortune in room charges by now." I looked at my watch, surprised to see I was just about out of time. "Listen, this has been great, but I've got to go meet my mom for dinner. You've got me interested, though. Can we get back to this some other time?"

"Sure thing. Tell you what: I get off around noon tomorrow. If you're not doing anything, drop by, and I'll give you the nickel tour of Windward Cove."

I considered her offer. "I'll have to check to make sure my mom won't need me for anything, but I think that'll be okay."

Ab nodded. "Coolaroo. Nice meeting you, Wolfman. See you tomorrow!"

Thump-THUMP...

(...pause...)

Thump-THUMP...

I opened my eyes blearily, at first not knowing where I was and gazing around at the unfamiliar shadows. Memories of the day finally came trickling back, and I realized I was in my bedroom. Not my bedroom in Vacaville, where the streetlamp outside flooded the room in a soft, comforting glow, but my new bedroom, in the place I would have to learn to call home.

I lay there in the darkness, listening to the faint thumping noise that had woken me. A wind had risen in the hours since I'd drifted off, the restless, irregular gusts making the elm trees whisper and creak and rattling the windows in their frames. I figured a shutter had come loose somewhere and was banging against the side of the house. Far off, the lonely sound of a foghorn moaned in the distance, and I wondered how long it would be before I got used to all the new night sounds.

Thump-THUMP...

(...pause...)

Thump-THUMP...

I didn't know what time it was, but it felt late. Reaching over, I groped around on the nightstand until my fingers closed on my wristwatch. I pressed the little button on the side, and the digital numbers were suddenly backlit in bright blue: *03:54.* Too early. I rolled onto my side and tried to go back to sleep.

Thump-THUMP...

Okay, *that* was going to get annoying. I toyed with the idea of getting out of bed and fixing the problem, but it was warm beneath the covers and I didn't feel like wandering around trying to figure out where the sound was coming from. Besides, the house was chilly, and once I was wide awake, it would be a lot harder to drift off to sleep again.

Thump-THUMP...

I frowned in the darkness. *Was* that a shutter? The longer I listened, the more I wasn't really sure. A banging shutter would be as on-again, off-again as the gusts of wind, wouldn't it? But the thumping sound was like a metronome, slow but steady, and for no reason at all, my sleepy mind drifted back to the previous Halloween when my English teacher had us read *The Tell-Tale Heart*. Funny, I'd more or less forgotten about the story, but it sure had creeped me out at the time. That and the other one we'd read by the same guy—the one about the man who tricked his enemy into the wine cellar, chained him to a wall, and then bricked him up alive. Was it Poe? I thought so, but I couldn't remember for sure.

Thump-THUMP...

The cobwebs were clearing from my brain, and it was beginning to irritate me that the more I tried to ignore the thumping noise, the more clearly I was able to hear it. Whatever the wind was banging around was just going to continue until I got out of bed and took care of it—end of story. I listened, doing my best to pinpoint the source before I wasted a lot of time running around in the chilly house. Then I felt my heartbeat increase as I realized the thumping was sounding less like a loose shutter the longer I listened to it. It sounded like, well, *footsteps*. Footsteps of somebody limping.

And the sound was moving.

I began to shake as soon as the idea occurred to me, and an icy sensation made my scalp feel prickly. My mind sifted through possible explanations, but the only idea that sounded even remotely plausible was that maybe Mom was up walking around. But no, that couldn't be it. She generally slept like a corpse, and on those rare occasions when she did get up in the middle of the night, she always turned on lights.

Besides, that didn't explain the limp…

Woah, big guy, I told myself, trying to get my imagination under control. After all, I was just being stupid. Maybe the thumping wasn't a shutter, but it sure wasn't some bogeyman, either. The sooner I got off my lazy butt and saw what was really going on, the sooner I could laugh at myself for being such a baby.

Thump-THUMP...

I threw the covers aside before my nerve gave out, fumbled around with my feet until I found my slippers, and then crossed the room to stick my head out into the hallway. Looking to my left, I could see a darker patch in the shadows that showed that the door to the service stairs was standing open, which pretty much proved that the wind was just playing tricks. Ha! Mystery solved. A window was probably open somewhere in the attic.

I went back for the flashlight lying on my nightstand, and the circle of brightness that appeared at my feet when I clicked it on was as comforting as Obi-Wan Kenobi's lightsaber.

I retraced my steps to the hallway and began to move toward the open door.

Thump-THUMP...

(…pause…)

…Thump-THUMP...

I slowed my steps, my earlier fears returning in a rush. It sounded like someone was on the stairs! But I rolled my eyes in exasperation a second later. *Come on, Ben,* I chided myself. *A few ghost stories from Ab, and next you've got the spirit of Festus from that old show*

Gunsmoke *gimping along beside Marshall Dillon.* I smiled at my silly ideas and stuck my head into the stairwell, aiming the beam of my flashlight both upstairs and down.

Thump-THUMP...

(...pause...)

Thump-THUMP...

The sound was definitely coming from upstairs.

I climbed the risers, trying not to think about the way the thumping sound seemed to move first across the floor, then up the stairs to the cupola. I paused when I heard the creak of old hinges, followed by the click of a door latching shut. Then silence.

I stood still, taking shallow, silent breaths while waiting for something else to happen after that, but all I heard was my own heartbeat in my ears. After about thirty seconds, I exhaled a sigh, feeling relieved that the night's excitement seemed to be over. The window was probably open in the cupola, allowing a draft inside to push things around until the door had finally been blown shut. I grinned in the darkness of the stairwell, feeling like an idiot because I'd wasted perfectly good sleep time for nothing.

I turned, meaning to head back to bed, and even made it halfway back down the stairs when I realized I was still being chicken. After all, if the night's adventures had really been caused by nothing but wind and my own imagination, then there wasn't any reason not to prove it, was there? I paused, turning back around and drumming my fingers on the bannister.

Dude, whispered the detached part of my brain that was still recording details, *do you really want to do this? After all, isn't this the part in horror movies when the curious teenager gets hacked all to pieces?*

I ignored the voice, gritting my teeth and climbing the narrow stairwell before my nerve gave out. Silly fears or not, I knew I'd never get back to sleep until I closed the book on all of this.

The attic was all blackness and hulking, looming shapes around me, but I ignored them and made my way purposefully up the cupola stairs. I twisted the doorknob and had even made it half a step beyond when I froze.

Cold washed over me like a glacial wind, and my breath exited my lips in a puff of frosty white. Feelings of utter sorrow and loneliness hit me in a wave. I sagged, holding onto the door for support as I choked back an involuntary sob. But I knew right away that those feelings weren't my own. I knew it was my gift soaking up powerful emotions from someone—some*thing*—else.

And whatever it was, it was in the cupola with me.

I staggered backward but managed to pull the door closed. I stumbled back down the stairs, my chest heaving, but by the time I was halfway across the attic, I almost had my emotions under control. I turned, shuddering as I pointed the beam of my flashlight back up at the cupola door, the shadows appearing oddly angled and surreal. The door looked completely normal, but something instinctive inside me knew that I wasn't welcome there. The shakes hit me then, and I had to step carefully back down the stairwell to keep from tumbling to the bottom and breaking my neck.

I was still shaking when I crawled back into bed. It was a long while before I finally drifted into a restless, troubled sleep.

FIVE

THE WIND HAD DIED OFF BY THE TIME I WOKE UP, BUT A dreary cloud layer had rolled in during the night to color the morning a somber gray. It seemed as if Windward Cove had decided to skip the summer completely and go right to autumn, but I guessed the cooler weather was just part of living on the coast that I'd have to get used to. Back in Vacaville, the temperature probably would be in the mid-80s by now, and kids would already be thinking about heading for the pool. It made me feel homesick, so I pushed the thought to the back of my mind. The sooner I got used to my new surroundings, the better off I'd be.

I stretched under the covers, not quite ready to get up yet, and thought back on the weird events of the night before. To tell the truth, it all seemed pretty far-fetched and stupid in the daylight. While there was no doubt in my mind that there was something strange about the cupola, I was willing to bet a good portion of what I'd felt when I opened the door was brought on by sleepiness and a lingering case of the creeps left over from Ab's ghost stories. All in all,

I felt pretty silly for overreacting, and when my inner voice started to grumble about me refusing to accept the facts, it wasn't difficult to push *those* thoughts to the background, too.

A hot shower made me feel even better, and by the time I pulled on my jeans, I was whistling and thinking about breakfast. Reaching down, I tried to open the drawer beneath the bed where I'd put my clean shirts, and I frowned when it slid out three or four inches and then stuck. Giving it a good jiggle didn't do any good either. It still refused to open, as if something was blocking it. I slid my hand into the gap, feeling around inside for whatever might be jamming things up, but felt nothing but my folded shirts. Pulling upward on the drawer face didn't work either, but when I pushed down, the drawer slid open smoothly. Curious, I pulled it out all the way, getting on my hands and knees to look into the hole to find out what was wrong.

At first I couldn't see anything, but then I noticed a rectangular shape back in the shadows. It took me a second or two to realize it was a book. I pulled it out, blowing a heavy coat of dust from the cover to read a word inscribed in faded gold lettering:

Diary

Hmm.

The leather binding creaked when I opened it, releasing a faint whiff of old paper. Inside the cover were words written in neat handwriting:

If found, please return to Claire Anne Black
Windward Cove, Calif.

Aunt Claire! Curious, I carried the book across to my desk and dropped into the chair. I gazed around the room with new interest, suddenly aware that it had been my aunt's room once upon a time, and then turned my attention back to riffle through the pages. All of the entries were written in the same neat handwriting, mostly with what looked like an old fountain pen but sometimes in pencil. A handful of photos were paper-clipped here and there or just stuck loose between the pages, most of which were old school pictures of teenagers, along with half a dozen postcards and a pressed flower so dry that it crumbled when I touched it. The margins of the pages were sprinkled with little drawings, assorted shapes, and looping curlicues, and as I looked at them, I suddenly began to feel dizzy. Before I knew what was happening, the room around me began to gray out, replaced by a scene I didn't recognize—someplace with different furnishings and pictures on the walls. For a moment, it looked like a double-exposure on film—my room fading away while the new place came into sharp focus—and I was confused, wondering what I was seeing. But then it hit me. I was looking at my room! My breath caught in my throat as the strong vision filled my mind:

> *A girl—fifteen, maybe sixteen years old—lying on her stomach on the captain's bed. She's pretty, with shoulder-length dark hair and a high, clear brow. She's wearing a dress that would have reached halfway down her calves, but her knees are bent, legs crossed at the ankles and swinging absently in the air. A radio sits on the bedside table, from which a woman is singing* "I'll Be with You in Apple Blossom Time," *but the words are faint and slightly distorted, as if I am hearing them from under water. The singer is named Jo Stafford, and it's the girl's favorite song, but I don't know* how *I know either of these things. The girl's eyes are gray, just like mine and Mom's, and I suddenly realize that I'm looking at my aunt. The diary lies open on the bed in front of her, its leather binding still new, and a dreamy smile turns the corners of her mouth upward as she doodles in the page margin, considering what to write next.*

And just like that, the scene was gone.

I scrambled to my feet, dropping the diary and staggering a couple of steps before I got my balance. I was breathing hard, and a light sheen of sweat made my forehead feel greasy.

What was that? I asked myself.

It wasn't the first time I'd seen something with my gift, but I couldn't remember ever experiencing anything that strong or vivid. Usually, any pictures that popped into my head were brief flashes or vague impressions, nothing like what had just happened, and the raw power of it had startled me. Stooping, I reached for the diary on the floor, at first only touching it gingerly and then picking it up when I was sure nothing else was going to happen.

For now, anyway.

"Ben!" called Mom from somewhere downstairs. "Are you up yet?"

"Yeah, Mom," I yelled back. "Be right down!"

So, big guy, my inner voice asked. *What next?* I didn't answer right away because I just wasn't sure. I knew that Mom would be interested in the diary, but once she saw it, there was a good chance she'd take it away. Even though Aunt Claire was gone, Mom would see it as snooping around someone else's private thoughts. In that light, the idea of reading it made me feel a little guilty, but I was tempted to do it just the same. After all, what harm could it do? I stood there for a few seconds, torn between sharing my discovery and keeping it to myself, and then I finally decided that I didn't have to make up my mind right then. Nodding, I put the diary back in its hiding place and slid the drawer closed on top of it.

Mom kept me busy for the rest of the morning, mostly carrying things here and there, arranging (and rearranging) what little furniture there was in the house to suit her and breaking down our cardboard boxes to eventually take to the recycler. I turned down her offer to tag along while she went hunting for places to buy stuff for the house, quickly wolfed down a ham sandwich, and was on my bike pedaling for town by 11:40.

The ride was fun, especially the steep, downhill curves to the main road that had my heart hammering with excitement and left tear tracks from the wind running back toward my hairline. I took it easy the rest of the way, enjoying the cool air and the smells of evergreen and eucalyptus. Ab was waiting for me just outside Tsunami Joe when I pulled up.

"Good timing, Wolfman!" she said, unlocking her own bicycle from the chain securing it to a post. The bike was an antique cruiser from the 1950s or 1960s that looked like it weighed about a thousand pounds, but the red and white paint looked sharp and the chrome winked even in the gray light.

"Nice bike," I commented. "Very retro."

"Thanks," she replied, smiling. "I found it at a garage sale last year, and you wouldn't believe how bad it looked—just a heap of rusty steel. It took me most of last summer to restore it, but a lot of that time I was trying to find replacement parts on the Internet."

My respect for Ab went up a notch. "You restored it *yourself?*"

"Yep. My dad bought me a book on bike repair, and our neighbor, Mr. Owens, let me use his barn and tools. I thought my arm was going to fall off from all the sanding, but it was worth it in the end. There isn't another bike like this anywhere around here."

"Probably not," I agreed and then changed the subject. "So, where are we going?"

"Everywhere, Wolfman. Follow me!"

As it turned out, "everywhere" in Windward Cove took all of about an hour and a half to explore. What made it interesting, though, was that Ab turned it into sort of a ghost tour of the town.

I had a look at the docks, of course, and a more in-depth tour of downtown, but I also got to see the house where the spirit of Delores Martin still supposedly wept on stormy nights, the graveyard that sprawled on a bluff half a mile to the south, and a condemned house over on Jackson Street where Ab told me a man could sometimes be seen glaring down from a second-story window. She went on to explain that no one knew who he had been, why he glared down at people on the street, or even why he looked so angry in the first place, but the recorded sightings went back to the 1920s.

We then pedaled three or four miles northeast to Silver Creek, the next town over, so Ab could show me the high school where we would both be sophomores in the fall. I had to admit, as much as I had been looking forward to wearing the orange and black of the Vacaville Bulldogs, the maroon and green of the Silver Creek Buccaneers didn't look half bad. The town itself was a lot larger than Windward Cove (it had traffic lights at four intersections, anyway), and among other things, it even had a supermarket, a Sears Department Store, a Home Depot, and a handful of fast-food restaurants. If it wasn't exactly civilization, at least it was a frontier outpost. Ab finally pulled up outside Hovey's, a drive-in that looked like it had been old even before the Beatles left Liverpool. Hand-lettered signs in the windows advertised things like *Corndog Special—2 for $1.00!* and *Try our Root Beer Floats!*

I was starving by then, and the aroma drifting from the place was making my mouth water like an Amazon rain forest. "Please tell me we're taking a break," I pleaded. It felt like we'd ridden all over the Pacific Northwest, and the sandwich I'd eaten earlier was ancient history as far as my stomach was concerned.

"Yep. The grand tour wouldn't be complete unless you got to try the world's best fries!"

She led me inside, and we took seats at a long counter. The inside of the place was all red Formica and chrome, making me think of the old movie *American Graffiti.* There were only two other customers, a boy and a girl maybe a year or two older than Ab and me, sitting together down where the counter made an L at the far end. Half-finished Cokes sat before them, along with an empty plastic basket lined with grease-spotted paper. Their conversation trailed off when we walked in, and they stared silently at us for a moment before picking up their discussion again in lowered voices. Ab glanced at them only once and then seemed to ignore them, but I could feel an undercurrent of tension in the air.

I opened a menu but only pretended to read it while reaching out with my mind to test the emotional water. The guy was feeling anxious and a little uncomfortable, and I wondered why. The girl, though...yikes. There was a lot going on with her: anger, resentment, disdain, and something else, too. Something like attraction, although it was hard to tell for sure—her feelings were too jumbled up. I figured Ab and I had interrupted a boyfriend-girlfriend fight, and it was none of my business anyway. Besides, I was more interested in food.

A man wearing a paper cook's hat emerged from the back and shambled over to us. He was huge, with a barrel chest and tattoos on both forearms that were so old and shrunken I couldn't tell what they were supposed to be. "What'll you have?" he asked, towering over me from the other side of the counter. His voice sounded like rocks grinding together.

"Uh...a burger and a Coke, I guess," I told him.

The man nodded, not bothering to ask how I wanted it cooked or even what I'd like on it, which was probably good since he didn't bother to write anything down, either. "How about you, sweetie?" he asked Ab, his voice warming twenty degrees.

"Hi, Mike," Ab said, smiling at him like he was her favorite uncle. "I'll take a double pastrami burger with everything, a large order of fries extra crispy, and a big chocolate shake."

King Kong patted her hand and retreated to the kitchen.

"So you two are pals?" I asked after he was gone.

"Oh, yeah," she said. "I was barely walking when Mom and Dad brought me in the first time, and I've been coming here all my life." Ab began by telling me how Mike had bought the place after retiring from the Army, and then she moved on through a string of other stories, one after another, that were mostly about the people who were regulars and funny things that had happened there. Local stuff.

I listened without interrupting, using the time to also watch the couple at the end of the counter out of the corner of my eye. The guy was about my size, maybe a little taller, with blond hair that looked like he spent a lot of time on it and wearing a shirt with a designer label on the breast pocket. Beyond that, though, I really didn't notice much about him. I was too busy looking at the girl.

She was amazing!

I would have given odds she was a cheerleader—she definitely had the look. Slender and tanned, with green eyes and a mass of dark auburn hair that fell to her shoulders, she was total Ben-kryptonite. I couldn't take my eyes off her and just about forgot to breathe. Tracy, the girl I'd been nursing a simmering crush over for months back home, faded to a dim memory right then and there.

She glanced over and caught me looking. Her boyfriend followed her gaze a second later and frowned before I managed to look away, my face flushing.

Busted.

"Earth to Ben," Ab said, elbowing me. "Time to get to work."

The burger Mike slid in front of me was enormous—a half-pounder at least—still steaming from the grill and piled high with lettuce, tomato, and onion. Big as it was, though, it looked puny in comparison to the one in front of Ab, which had double patties, thick ribbons of pastrami, and cheese running down the sides like lava. Beside that was a haystack of fries that Ab began to soak with ketchup, and a milkshake so thick it looked like cement.

Lunch was served!

I got through about three-quarters of my burger before I ran out of gas, but Ab plowed through all of hers without even slowing down. I nibbled at a few fries while I watched her (she was right, by the way—they really *were* good) and wondered where she put it all. "I guess riding that dinosaur of a bike must really burn the calories."

Ab looked at the remains of my burger, then back at me. "Sissy," she said, grinning, and then gazed smugly at me while slurping down the last of her shake.

I admit it, I was impressed.

"It's not nice to stare at people," a voice said softly behind me.

I turned on my stool, looking into the face of the blond guy from the far end of the counter. He was standing close and leaning slightly forward, doing his best to be intimidating.

Someone should have told him I don't scare easily.

I looked past his shoulder at the girl, who stood waiting for him by the door. She was looking at me at the same time, and one corner of her mouth turned up in a half-smile. I didn't know what to make of that, so I turned my attention back at Mr. Intimidating instead. I took a quick mental read of his emotions again, and I wasn't really surprised to find out that, in spite of how he was trying to come off, he was more nervous than anything else. I decided to take the polite approach. "Excuse me?" I asked.

"I don't like you staring at my girlfriend," he explained, speaking slowly and smiling like I was some kind of moron. "Or maybe you were staring at *me*, is that it? What...do you *like* me?"

Okay, *that* pissed me off. So much for the polite approach.

"Gee, you caught me, bud," I said, smiling back. "I *was* staring at you. You've got this big wad of something stuck in your teeth, and I just couldn't stop looking. You should do something about that—it's pretty gross."

His smile disappeared as his lips clamped shut. He must not have been used to anyone standing up to him because all he did was glare at me, clearly not knowing what to say. I could see the outline of his tongue, though, probing around behind his closed mouth.

I gave him a wink. "Have a nice day." I turned around to face the counter, my back to him.

He stood there for another second or two and then turned and stalked out the door.

All in all, I was feeling pretty satisfied with how things had turned out, and I looked over at Ab when I saw her shoulders shaking out of the corner of my eye. Her face was all red, and her mouth was twisted shut as she tried to hold back, but as soon as she saw my expression, she lost it and brayed laughter toward the ceiling. "You're alright, Wolfman," she said, clapping me on the shoulder, still chuckling. "You just lost your spot on the football team, but as far as I'm concerned, it was worth it!"

"I don't play football," I told her. "Who *was* that guy?"

"Alan Garrett, your Silver Creek High starting quarterback."

"Oh great. I'm in town a little over twenty-four hours, and already I'm making a good impression."

"Don't take it personally," Ab said. "That wasn't about you, it was about me. Kelly Thatcher and I have been feuding since we were seven."

"Kelly? The girl?"

"Yeah, the one you were staring at. And you *were* staring, Wolfman. Alan had that part right."

"Oh, *please.* So what happened between you two?"

Ab Shrugged. "A bunch of us were at Kelly's birthday party in her backyard. I was next in line to take a swing at the piñata, and when I put the blindfold on, Alan decided to kiss me. It made me all embarrassed and mad, so I beat him up."

I snickered.

"Kelly was jealous over Alan giving me all the attention, so she told me to go home. I thought she'd get over it, but she never did. Alan has been one of her accessories pretty much ever since."

"Oh," I said nonchalantly. "So they *are* going out."

Ab rolled her eyes. "Oh, *gawd.* It's happened already. You're *pathetic*, Wolfman!"

"What?" I asked, feeling indignant.

"This has to be some kind of new record. She didn't have to say a word, and already you're dropping one wing and flapping in a circle!" Ab grinned. "You want her phone number? I think I still have it somewhere."

"No, thanks," I said sarcastically, doing my best to shut her down. "I figure I'll just cut to the chase and get to the *serious* stalking. You know, creep around in the bushes, stare through her window with binoculars, maybe murder the quarterback in his sleep and leave his severed head on her pillow. Now, are we going to get out of here, or did you want to eat another half a cow?"

We split the bill and rode back toward Windward Cove. Ab spent a lot of the time giving me knowing looks and tossing snide comments my way, but I managed to ignore most of it.

Girls. What can you do?

SIX

IT TOOK ME A FEW MINUTES TO REALIZE THAT AB WAS taking us back by a different route, and I pedaled harder, bringing my bike up alongside hers. "Where are we going?"

"There's one more thing I want to show you," she said. "It's a big part of Windward Cove history."

I shrugged noncommittally. After all, Mom probably hadn't made it back to the house yet, and it wasn't as if I had any other plans. We coasted downhill along a winding strip of asphalt shadowed by redwood and cedar trees. Ancient barbed-wire fence paralleled the road just beyond the ditches on either side, posts leaning drunkenly and the strands dark brown with rust. Behind that, overgrown thickets leaked tendrils of early fog that crept slowly inland as the afternoon waned.

We leaned into a right turn around a hillside, and the road leveled out just as Windward Cove came into view. We had emerged a quarter-mile north of town, and Ab veered onto the left-hand shoulder, braking to a stop. A dilapidated barn stood fifty or sixty feet beyond the fence line, looking lonely in the gray afternoon, and at first I thought that was what she had brought me to see. Instead, Ab laid her bike gently on its side, hopped the ditch, and disappeared into a snarl of blackberry vines that had intruded almost down to the road. "Here we go," I heard her call a moment later. "Come check this out, Wolfman."

Laying my bike down beside hers, I jumped the ditch and eased into the tangle, carefully picking my way through the thorny vines. A fat bee droned past my head, and I waved it away, moving up to where Ab squatted beside a four-foot-high pillar of white marble. Moss and dirt clung to the sides, but I could still make out the words etched deeply into the stone:

High-Water Mark
From the Tidal Wave that
Struck Windward Cove in the
Early Morning Hours of
June 23rd, 1946
And Sacred to the Memory
Of the 38 Souls Who Disappeared
Or Lost Their Lives

Below the main inscription was a list of names, but I could only read the first three or four before they were obscured by the moss. All I could do was stand there quietly for a moment. "Wow," I said at last.

"It was the worst disaster to ever hit the town," Ab explained. "The wave was caused by an underwater earthquake centered a hundred or so miles offshore. I can't find any record of what the quake measured, but it was big enough to wake everyone up and cause a fair amount of damage. A fire from a broken gas line ended up burning down the high school, which, by the way, is why you'll be a Buccaneer this September instead of a Windward Cove Sea Lion. Windward Cove only had a volunteer fire department—it's all we still have, in fact—and pretty much the whole town was out trying to help when the wave hit about an hour before dawn. We've got a breakwater out at the mouth of the cove now, but back then there was nothing to stop it. It was upwards of fifteen feet high when it reached the crowd, and no one saw it coming."

"Wow," I said again. It wasn't much, but it was all I could think of.

"Yeah," Ab agreed. "Pretty scary. Anyway, the wave caused some more damage and a couple of electrical fires, and a big aftershock later that morning caused some panic, but the worst was over. Remind me the next time you're in the coffee house, and I'll show you a picture of a fishing boat stuck halfway through the theater wall."

An idea struck me. "Was it one of those fires that burned out the inside of your building?"

"Very good, Wolfman. Before that, it was the Redwood Empire Hotel—the place where people stayed when they couldn't afford the Windward Inn." She nodded toward the marble pillar. "The names of the two people who died upstairs are engraved on here somewhere."

Ab rose to her feet, picking her way back to the road, and I followed her.

I didn't say anything for the rest of the ride to town. Gazing at the surrounding terrain, it was easy to see how a big wave would be squeezed as it swept up from the wharf, growing taller and more powerful as the hills funneled it toward downtown. I half expected to see a tsunami rolling in at that moment, in fact, my imagination being what it is, and I couldn't help glancing nervously toward the mouth of the cove. Seagulls circled above the breakwater, a jumble of rocks and broken concrete forming a gray line about fifty yards out, and I felt better knowing it was there.

We were pedaling through back streets on the outskirts of town when I suddenly heard what sounded like the shouts and laughter of two or three kids, followed by a sharp yip of pain. Ab and I exchanged a glance, and I swung my bike hard to the left, following the noise to an empty lot a couple of blocks off Main Street. The lot was overgrown with tall weeds and strewn with trash, and the rusted-out hulk of an old Dodge pickup truck was perched on cinder blocks in the back corner. Two boys and a girl who were about twelve or thirteen years old were scampering around the truck, occasionally squatting down to peer into the shadows underneath. They all carried sticks and shrieked at one another as they took turns poking at something. The emotions coming off them hit me like a hard slap in the face—excitement and a sort of cruel glee from the kids, confusion and terror from whatever they had cornered under the truck. I caught a brief glimpse of muddy fur and the glint of eyes, and before I even had time to think about it, I was off my bike and running toward them. "Hey!" I hollered. "Knock it off!"

The kids turned at the sound of my voice. One of the boys, the bigger of the two, dropped his stick and looked guilty, while the girl and the other boy just glared at me. The girl even took a couple of steps in my direction and crossed her arms, the stick still in her hand, and I got the feeling she was the leader. "Why don't you mind your own business?" she snapped. "We weren't hurting it!" She had blue eyes and long blonde hair gathered into a ponytail, and she might even have been pretty if her face hadn't been twisted by into a defiant sneer.

"I said knock it off," I repeated, stopping a couple of paces in front of her. "Now get out of here before I tell your folks what you've been up to!"

She made a *pfft* sound. "You can't tell me what to do."

I suddenly closed the distance separating us, and part of me felt cold satisfaction at the way she paled when I grabbed the stick out of her hand. “Wanna bet?” I snarled. Okay, so maybe it wasn’t the smoothest comeback in the world, but I was about six different kinds of mad by then, and it was the best I could do. I wasn’t so mad, though, that I didn’t notice the other boy creeping around to my left, trying to position himself behind me. The boy who’d dropped his stick was still standing in place, looking a little scared now (which suited me just fine), but I had a feeling Mr. Sneaky was going to be trouble.

It didn’t take the girl long to recover, her face going red with anger. “You give that back!”

“Ben!” Ab shouted in warning.

But I was already way ahead of her. I spun, having sensed the smaller boy’s sudden release of tension even as I heard his footsteps in the dead grass, and used the girl’s stick to block his. The little jerk had actually tried to hit me! Just then, Ab stepped up, yanking him back by the collar of his shirt and tripping him over her outstretched leg. He landed heavily on his back, gazing up at me defiantly as I moved to stand over him, pointing the end of the girl’s stick between his eyes. “You done?” I asked.

That more or less put an end to things. The girl and the bigger boy took off, moving past me as they ran for the street. The boy on the ground watched them go and then turned his gaze back toward me to hiss a low threat: “You’re gonna get it!”

I was already cooling off by then, and I stepped back to let him get to his feet. “Yeah, whatever,” I sighed. “Just get lost.” He stalked off, and I watched him go, feeling sad and a little disgusted with myself. Granted, they weren’t that much younger than me—and there had been three of them, after all—but I should have been able to find a better way to handle things. I felt like a bully, and I didn’t like it. I dropped the stick, wiping my hand on my pants as if the wood had left something slimy on my palm.

"Nice job, Wolfman," Ab said quietly, but it didn't make me feel any better. I ignored her, moving over to the truck and hunkering low to gaze into the shadows. It took me a second or two because its fur was dark and caked with mud, but I finally spotted it, lying low on its belly in the weeds and trembling. "It's a puppy," I said.

"Black, shaggy fur, and dirty?"

"Yeah."

"He's a stray," Ab said, squatting down beside me. "I've seen him around town the last few days, sniffing around the trash cans in the alley."

"How do you know it's a boy?"

"It's pretty obvious when he runs away from you. He won't let anyone near him."

I thought I could fix that. "Could you do me a favor?" I asked, turning my head to look at her. "Would you mind running over to the coffee house and getting him something to eat—maybe one of the sandwiches from the cooler? I'll pay you back."

"Sure—and don't worry about money. I'll be right back." Rising, she trotted over to her bike and headed up the street.

"Okay, little guy," I murmured, keeping my voice low. I could see his gaze darting around as he weighed his chances of getting away, and I knew I didn't have much time. "Easy, now," I said, and then began to concentrate, trying to use my gift to send calm reassurance his way. It didn't always work, and it wasn't nearly as strong as using my mind to pick up on the feelings of others, but when I was six, I learned I could sometimes send as well as receive. I discovered it one day after school when a Rottweiler belonging to one of our neighbors had cornered me in the parking lot of our apartment complex. Everyone said he was mean—and he was showing enough teeth at the time to convince me—and I thought for sure I was dead meat. Then, without even thinking about it, I just starting feeling…well, friendly. Almost right away the big dog had stopped growling, and we were buddies less than a minute later. I had tried it a few times since then (and no, it didn't seem to work on girls) but had never really got the hang of it.

I didn't know if it was actually working then or if maybe the puppy had just reached a point where he decided it was time to take a chance on somebody, but little by little his trembling began to subside. He was still confused and lonely, but I could feel his fear ease off as he seemed to understand that I wasn't a threat. After a couple of minutes, he even began to belly crawl toward me. I reached out, palm down, and he got close enough to give my fingers a cautious sniff before retreating backward. I didn't move or make any effort to grab him but, instead, just let him take his time deciding whether or not I was okay.

By the time Ab got back from the coffee house, I was sitting with my back to the fence, the puppy sprawled on my lap. He was bigger than he had looked back in the shadows. At a guess, I'd say he weighed around twenty pounds, and by the size of his paws it was easy to see he had a lot more growing to do. Black fur hung off him in long tangles and covered his eyes. His body was lanky and too thin, and I could feel the ribs under his skin. He tensed, pressing against my chest as Ab eased down beside me, but soon relaxed as we took turns feeding him bites of a turkey and cheese sandwich.

"Looks like you made a friend," Ab commented at last, scratching his head. "So what now?"

I shrugged. "I don't know. I haven't thought that far yet." I took a few seconds to consider the question. "I guess the right thing to do would be to take him to the pound so his owners can find him."

"The closest animal shelter is in Crescent City," Ab informed me, "but honestly, I think you'd be wasting your time. No collar or tags, and he's been here close to a week without anyone stopping by to ask about him. Chances are he was dumped off on the highway and wandered into town."

I frowned. That complicated things.

"But if you think there's a chance, there's a vet in Silver Creek," Ab offered. "If his owners really are looking for him, we could post a notice there."

"Sounds like a plan," I said, "but what about in the meantime? Do you need a dog?"

Ab shook her head. "Bad idea. I've got two big cats, and they're not friendly. Why don't you keep him?"

My reply was automatic. "Can't."

"Why not?"

I opened my mouth to answer and then closed it as I seriously considered the idea for the first time. To be honest, keeping him just hadn't occurred to me, probably because I'd lived most of my life in an apartment complex that didn't allow pets. But hey, things were different now, weren't they?

"Come on, Wolfman. It's not like you don't have the space."

I nodded absently, feeling the beginnings of a smile tugging at the corners of my mouth. She was right about that.

"And he likes you," she pressed. "You're the first person he's let touch him."

She had a point there, too.

"And you like him, don't you?"

I looked down at the puppy in my lap, who was licking the last traces of mayonnaise from my fingers, and I realized that I really did. Comfort and simple happiness was coming off the little guy in waves, and it felt good that it was directed toward me.

"Well? What do you think?"

I looked up at her, grinning. "I think my mom may be in for a shock."

At first I was worried about how I would get him back to the house, but it turned out not to be a problem. He stuck close by my leg as Ab and I walked our bikes over to McKennedy Street. It was as if he was afraid to let me get too far away, but when I stopped to pet him a couple of times, he seemed to understand that I wasn't going to leave him behind. Ab lived in a green craftsman-style house with white trim and a deep front porch, and we stopped at the walk leading to the steps. "Thanks for showing me around," I said. "It was fun."

"Yeah, good times," she said, and then punched me hard in the shoulder. "You're a good guy, Wolfman. See you around!"

I rubbed my shoulder where she'd hit me, watching as she walked her bike around the side of the house, and then looked down at my new friend. "Why do I have the feeling I'm going to have to get used to that?" I asked him. The puppy wagged his tail in reply, panting with what looked like a big doggie-smile on his face. I got on my bike and pedaled slowly toward home, my new friend loping happily alongside.

SEVEN

I KEPT A CLOSE EYE ON THE PUPPY AS I RODE HOME, worried that he'd get tired, but he kept right up alongside me the whole way. He moved in a gangly, loose-jointed trot, awkward with his big feet and legs that looked too long for his body, but showed no signs of running out of steam. In fact, the only time he slowed down was when we were climbing up the drive, me in my lowest gear and panting as I stood on the pedals, and he kept waiting for me to catch up with a "what's taking you so long?" expression on his face. Everyone's a critic. We turned right where the dive split, turning away from the even steeper climb up to the inn, and I was glad for the gentle descent while I got my breath back.

As we dropped down toward the meadow, I saw that there was a strange car parked in front of the house, a BMW showing a lot of dust and bug-splatters from the road. A slender man I didn't recognize was leaning against the hood, arms crossed as he gazed up at the second-story windows. He was dressed in khaki pants and a button-down shirt, and even though I'd only been in Windward

Cove for a day or so, I was pretty sure he wasn't a local. Our station wagon was nowhere to be seen, which meant that Mom still wasn't back from town yet, and I wondered how long he'd been waiting. He turned as I coasted to a stop, smiling at me from behind rimless glasses. "You must be Ben."

"That's right," I said cautiously. "Can I help you?"

"Bill Travers," he said, stepping forward and offering his hand. "I'm your Aunt Claire's lawyer." He frowned slightly. "Or I was, anyway. I'm very sorry for your loss."

I recognized the name. We shook hands, and I began to relax as he bent to let the puppy sniff his fingers and then reached out to ruffle his fur. My skittish new friend seemed to think the man was okay, and even if I hadn't picked up on Mr. Travers' nonthreatening mood, seeing that put me more at ease. Not that he looked like a serial killer or anything, but you never know. "Sorry, but my mom's not here," I told him.

"That's okay," he said. "I've just got some paperwork to drop off. Can I leave it with you?"

I shrugged. "Sure."

Mr. Travers nodded and went to retrieve a fat manila envelope from the passenger seat of the car. "The keys to the inn are in here, too," he explained as he handed it over. "They might not do you any good—it's been years since any of the doors have been opened—but it's worth a try."

"Thanks."

A short, awkward silence passed between us, and then he smiled again. "Well, I guess that's it," he said. "Please give your mother my best and tell her to give me a call if I can help with anything else." He took a business card from his shirt pocket and handed it to me. "Good luck to both of you." With that, he gave me a polite smile one last time and then began walking around to the driver's side of the car.

I glanced at the card, noting the San Francisco office address and phone number, and a question occurred to me. "Mr. Travers...?"

He turned, raising his eyebrows.

"I was just wondering. How come you drove all the way up here? I mean, you could have dropped this stuff in the mail or sent it FedEx, couldn't you? Why go to all that trouble?"

He took a few seconds before answering me. "I guess I felt like I owed it to Claire," he said at last, looking a little uncomfortable. "I have a lot of clients, but your aunt was...well, special. She kept to herself mostly, but she was really something once you got to know her. Sadly, very few people ever took the time, and during the last two or three years, I think I might have been the only friend she had left." He frowned. "At least, I *hope* she considered me a friend. She had a stern nature and a direct way of speaking that turned people off, but there was something about her that I just liked." He glanced up at the house and then shrugged. "Besides, I wanted to see this place one last time."

"One last time? So you've been here before?"

The man nodded. "Twice. The first time was...oh, I guess it had to be about ten years ago, give or take. Anyway, it was right before she changed her will, and she was still getting around pretty well back then. She showed me through the house, and we even walked around the outside of the inn. She had her own driver, of course, and there was no reason at all for her to have her lawyer along, but she asked me to bring her." He smiled a little wistfully. "She never would have said so in a million years, but I think she just wanted the company."

"And the second time?" I pressed.

"Last summer." He frowned again, his eyes seeming to lose focus as he thought back. "*That* trip worried me. Her health was pretty bad by then, and I tried to talk her out of coming. But she insisted, saying she had some final business to take care of, and once her mind was made up about something, there was no budging her. Just between you and me, I think she knew she didn't have much time left and wanted to say goodbye to the place."

"So, what happened?" I asked.

He shrugged. "Nothing much, really. We drove up to the inn so she could have a look, and then we came here. She told me to wait in the car, and then she got out and went into the house alone, leaning on her cane and with that big tote bag she always carried bumping against her leg. She was inside for a long time—long enough that I was starting to get worried—and I was just about to go in after her when she came out the front door. Her eyes were all puffy and red, like she'd been crying, but she was her old self again by the time she got to the car. 'Take me back to the city, Travers,' was all she said, and she didn't say another word until we were in San Francisco." His focus came back as he met my gaze. "That part has stuck with me ever since," he confessed. "Not 'take me home,' but 'take me back to the city.' I think as far as your aunt was concerned, home was here."

I couldn't think of anything to say, so I didn't.

Mr. Travers took one last look at the house and then offered a brief, halfhearted smile before getting into his car and driving away.

I watched him go, absently stuffing the business card into my back pocket and thinking about Aunt Claire. It made me feel sad and even a little jealous that he had known her better than I had. For the first time, I didn't picture her as the grim old lady who used to scare me when I was little but, rather, as the teenage girl from my vision, smiling a dreamy smile while listening to the radio. I offhandedly wondered what it would have been like to really know her and whether or not she would have liked me.

I glanced down at the puppy, who was watching me with his tail swishing lazily back and forth. "Come on, little guy," I said. "Let's see if we can get you cleaned up before Mom gets home."

I'd never given a dog a bath before, but it turned out to be not nearly as tough as I thought. After making an initial circuit of the downstairs and giving each room a good sniffing over, he followed me up to the second floor and watched with good-natured curiosity as I started filling the bathtub. I spread a couple of towels on the floor and left a couple of others within easy reach, and then pulled my shirt off in case he decided to turn it into a wrestling match. "Okay, pal," I said, grinning. "We can do this the easy way or the hard way. Which is it going to be?"

Nobody was more surprised than I was when he jumped into the bathtub, turned around twice, and then sat down, looking at me expectantly.

"Um…okay, then," I said. "Glad we got that straightened out." He was dirtier than I had thought, and the water turned dark brown before I'd even finished wetting him down all the way. I drained the tub and filled it again, and then used up most of a bottle of shampoo getting him clean. I had to admit, he was a good sport about it, sitting there quietly while I scrubbed him down twice, and I figured I had his last family to thank for getting him used to bath time. We were about halfway through the last rinse when we were interrupted by the sound of Mom's voice.

"Don't tell me. It just followed you home, right?"

I looked up, startled and feeling a little sheepish. I guess I'd been so busy that I hadn't heard her come home. "Actually, yeah," I confessed. "He sort of did."

She leaned in the bathroom doorway, arms crossed and a bemused half-smile on her face. "Oh, well," she sighed, shaking her head, "I suppose it was bound to happen sooner or later. Boy or girl?"

"Boy."

"You sure?"

"*C'mon*, Mom."

She held up her hands. "Okay, okay…just asking. It's not like you've grown up with pets. Does this beast have a name yet?"

I glanced at the puppy, whose black bangs hung straight down in front. "How about Moe?" I offered.

Mom nodded. "I can see the resemblance. So okay, here's the deal: you feed him, you make sure he has clean water at all times, you scoop all the land mines he leaves in the yard, and any accidents in the house are yours to deal with. Are we clear on that?"

"Crystal," I replied with a nod. "But you should know he might not be staying with us long. I'm going to post some flyers around town and at the vet's office, and his real owners may be back for him."

"I should be so lucky," Mom said, shaking her head in disgust. I knew she wasn't serious, though—the only feelings coming off her were pleased excitement. "Will you look at the *paws* on that thing?" she complained. "He's going to be *huge!* Jeez-Louise, couldn't you have found yourself a nice toy poodle? Maybe a Chihuahua?" With that she turned and disappeared down the hall. A moment later I heard the front door close, followed by the sound of the car starting and driving away.

Moe liked being dried with the towels, but he liked the blow-dryer even better, and by the time we were finished, he seemed to glow in the late afternoon light. His fur was wavy and soft, hanging over his eyes and falling into a droopy beard that gave him a mischievous look. I was surprised how handsome he was now that all the caked-on mud was gone. It seemed impossible to me that someone would have dumped a puppy this cool, and I couldn't help but think that his owners would come looking for him sooner or later.

We pretty much had the bathroom cleaned up by the time Mom got home, and we hurried to see what she wanted when she hollered up the stairs. I grinned when she handed me a set of stainless steel bowls, a collar, a couple of stuffed dog toys, and a can of tennis balls. "There's a big bag of puppy chow in the back of the car," she told me, "along with some canned food to mix in it. We'll go to the county office and get him licensed if his former owners haven't shown up in a week or so."

I hugged her. "Thanks, Mom!"

She hugged me back. "How about you unload the car while I fix us some dinner?"

The sun was starting to disappear behind the hills when I opened the back of the station wagon, and I saw a stack of sketch pads, an easel, half a dozen blank canvases, and a big bag of paints, brushes, and pencils stuffed in the back along with the dog food. Obviously, she'd found an art supply place during her travels that afternoon, and I was glad. If she'd caught the drawing bug again so soon, it meant she was happy. I lugged the dog food inside and dropped it in the pantry while Mom heated some canned stew on the stove. "I almost forgot, Mr. Travers dropped by while you were out," I told her. "He left an envelope full of paperwork and the keys to the inn."

"Thanks, hon."

"Where do you want me to put your stuff?"

"In the cupola, please."

Cold dread washed over me. For a moment, all I could do was stand there.

Mom glanced over at me when I didn't move, her brow furrowing. "What…a couple of flights of stairs too much for you?"

"No…" I said, stalling while I tried to come up with a reason to keep her out of there. "I, uh, just thought the library room would be better. You know, so you'd have shelves for all your supplies and art books."

"Are you kidding? There's only that one window, and the light in there is horrible. No, the cupola's *perfect.* And besides, there are plenty of shelves up there too, remember?"

"But what about that big telescope?" I tried again, grasping at a straw. "Won't that be in your way?"

Mom leaned against the counter, folding her arms. "What's this about, Benny?"

"Nothing," I lied, the word sounding lame as it hung all by itself in the air. "Just…trying to help."

She watched me closely for a second or two, clearly sensing that there was something more, but then let it drop. "Well, thanks, but it'll be help enough if you can just get all that stuff up there before it gets too dark to see. Besides, dinner's almost ready, so you'd better get a move on."

I nodded and left, not wanting to answer the pointed questions that would be coming my way if she suspected there was a real reason I was stalling. Besides, *I* was the one with the problem—the cupola hadn't affected Mom at all, had it? I hurried, not wanting to get caught up there after sundown, and managed to grab everything but the stack of canvases on my first trip. Moe came along, curious to see what I was up to, but when I was halfway up the cupola stairs, I noticed that he was no longer by my side. I turned to look, and it took me a few seconds for my gaze to find him in the attic's gloom, pressed between an old steamer trunk and a stack of cardboard boxes. "You coming?" I asked.

Moe sank to his belly, nose between his paws.

I tried not to think about what that meant. "Suit yourself," I told him, and then pressed on before my nerve gave out. I held my breath as I opened the cupola door, climbing the last few steps and standing there for a tense moment, but then let it out in a grateful sigh when I didn't sense any weirdness. The temperature seemed normal enough (well, maybe a *little* cooler, but that could've just been my imagination), and for the moment at least, I didn't feel anything but my own nervousness. Okay so far.

Just the same, I didn't waste time, leaving Mom's stuff on one of the shelves and heading back downstairs with Moe trotting alongside me. Back at the car, I managed to wrap my arms around all the canvases at once, feeling the need to hurry as the gray-gold of the sunset was fading fast.

"Dinner!" Mom called as I was halfway up to the second floor.

"Be right there!" I called back down, my heart pounding heavily in my chest. Shadows were taking over the house, creeping slowly out from the corners like water filling a sinking ship, and I could feel sweat gathering on my forehead and the back of my neck. Moe seemed to sense it, too and whined as I hurried down the hall and took the steps to the attic two at a time. He growled when we reached the top, his tail disappearing between his legs as he stared up at the open cupola door. Cold air drifted down toward me like the open door of a freezer. I grit my teeth, pounding up into the frigid air, my spirits immediately plummeting into gloom and sorrow. I could barely see in the cupola now; the sunset was just a coppery line through the gap in the western hills, and I set the canvases down with shaking hands.

Behind me I heard the cupola door creak slowly shut, latching with a click.

For a tense few seconds, all I could so was stand there, my heartbeat and labored breathing loud in my ears. I was afraid to move… afraid *not* to move. There was no denying it—there was definitely a presence in the cupola, although I couldn't pinpoint exactly where. It was all *around* me!

Down in the attic, Moe let out a long, mournful howl.

"Who are you?" I whispered.

Moe was barking now, and I heard him climb the cupola steps to scratch at the door. The sound broke my paralysis, and I walked rubber-legged across the floor and down the steps. I was afraid the door wouldn't open, but it did, and somehow I found the nerve to stop and look back up into the darkness. "Scare me all you want to," I said between gritted teeth, "but you'd better leave my mom alone. You hear me? *Leave my mom alone!"* Saying that made me feel a lot braver, and I left the cupola door open behind me, making myself walk the rest of the way down the steps and across the attic floor. Moe backed down the stairs to the second floor ahead of me, growling as he looked at a point past my shoulder, but I didn't turn around.

In the darkness behind me, I heard the cupola door creak shut.

I fled.

EIGHT

THE HIGH SCHOOL BUILDING IS DOOMED. I STAND AMONG the crowd of townspeople—some looking sad, some looking stubbornly hopeful, but most just looking sleepy and bewildered—as sixty-foot flames reach for the predawn sky. Even the men of our fire brigade knew the fight was over before it ever really began and have turned the hoses of our old and hopelessly inadequate pumper truck on the surrounding buildings, wetting down the walls and rooftops to keep them from catching fire as well. No one will blame them. Everyone was confused and frightened by the sudden shaking of the earth, the surging of which tumbled many of us from our beds, and by the time some had collected their wits sufficiently to realize a fire had broken out, it had already grown well beyond the capabilities of our volunteers.

I can hear children crying all around me, and they're not the only ones. Barney Hanlon, veteran of the First World War, waves people back from the bucket line that he had been attempting to organize, tears tracking through the soot on his cheeks. Margaret Lindsay weeps openly, and my heart goes out to her. She was a teacher long before even I came under her stern gaze as a child. I am somewhat more removed, insulated by my longtime grief, and view my surroundings with a sort of numb detachment.

I step back, as many do, from the heat that still builds in intensity. Yellow and red flames turn the gloom into noonday brilliance, licking hungrily at the western and southern walls and driving back the coastal fog that shrouds the rest of the town at this lonely hour. I notice that smoke and flames also belch from the third-story windows and have all but consumed the roof. Then, as if sensing my very thoughts, the roof peak buckles suddenly and collapses in upon itself, sending a shower of sparks into the black sky and raising a murmur from the crowd.

A hand suddenly clutches at my arm, and I look to see Henry Jacobs standing on my left, staring into the gloom behind us with an expression of horror on his face. At first I'm confused—after all, we're all witnessing a tragedy from which Windward Cove will need years to recover. What else could be stealing his attention? Then I realize sounds of the fire and crowd are eclipsed by a muted roar from the west. I pull free of Henry's clutching fingers, turning around to gaze into the darkness...

Moe barked, and I rolled out of bed, landing on the floor hard enough to knock the wind out of me. All I could do was lie there for a few seconds with my feet still up on the mattress, tangled in the covers. I was shaking, but whether it was from the night air cooling my sweat or just lingering adrenaline from waking so suddenly I couldn't be sure. I took deep breaths, waiting for the room to stop spinning. Moe, a blotch of deeper black in the gloom, stared down at me from the foot of the bed, his head cocked to one side.

"Whoa," I said, my voice sounding unnaturally loud in the stillness. I wasn't speaking to anyone in particular, but hearing a voice, even if it was just my own, made things feel a little more normal right then. I was still shaking, but after a minute or so my heartbeat was more or less back to normal, so I kicked free of the covers and got up to sit on the edge of the bed. Reaching over, I picked up my watch from the nightstand and touched the button for the light: *03:54*. Too early to get up yet.

I shook out the covers and slid back between them, half-surprised to find the mattress still warm from my body heat. I patted the space beside me, and Moe wormed his way up to snuggle his head on my shoulder. His tail thumped the bedspread twice, and he sighed, his breath tickling my ear. It made me feel better.

Part of me wanted to write the whole thing off. After all, it wouldn't be all that hard. Hearing about the tidal wave and seeing the monument had given me a whopper of a nightmare, that's all. A stubbornly rational part of me was even insisting that I'd probably feel pretty stupid about it once the sun was up. Good arguments, and it would have been nice to cling to them, but there was just no getting around it. This time I knew better. The dream was just too real, and I recognized it for what it was: a vision, full of facts I had no way of knowing and thoughts that definitely weren't my own. What I had to figure out was whether it was just a bunch of images—a sort of psychic rerun of the past—or if it all actually meant something.

The only thing I knew for sure was that if I really wanted to sort it all out, I was going to need some help. That complicated things. Ab was the obvious choice, of course. She knew all the weird Windward Cove history. But how could I ask her without telling her about the vision? She would start asking questions—questions I'd rather not have to answer. She was the only friend I'd made in town so far, and the last thing I wanted to do was spill the beans and have her realize that I was a freak.

I tried to get back to sleep, but the images in my head wouldn't let me. The scene kept playing over and over in my mind. Weirdest of all were the little details that kept occurring to me the longer I thought about the images: the smell of smoke and sea air, the heat of the fire baking my face, how different my clothes and shoes had felt. Things that hadn't consciously crossed the mind of the man whose eyes I'd been seeing the vision through. I rolled onto my side, trying to find a comfortable position so that I could drift off to sleep, but it just wasn't happening. After what seemed like a long time, when I noticed that the pitch black of my room was giving way to a weak, gray light, I finally gave up and got out of bed.

I was sitting on the front steps an hour or two later, still mulling things over, when Mom finally found me. "You're up early," she said, her voice raspy from sleep.

I shrugged, watching Moe as he ran around the yard, his tail swishing as he sniffed at this and that.

She sat beside me, forearms balanced on her knees as she held a steaming coffee mug with both hands, and we watched Moe together for a while. It was nice to have her there, feeling the warmth of her through her flannel bathrobe and the smell of her coffee drifting in the morning air. After a minute or two, she bumped me with her shoulder. "You okay, Benny?"

"Hmm?" I asked, turning to look at her. My mind had been elsewhere, and her question caught me off guard. She was watching me closely, frowning slightly with concern and with her hair still mussed from her pillow. "Oh, yeah," I told her. "I'm fine."

"You sure?" she asked, raising her eyebrows, and then sighed. "Look, I know moving up here has been hard on you, but…"

I smiled, returning her shoulder-bump. "It's okay, Mom—I'm good. Really."

She gazed at me for another second or two and then nodded, turning to watch Moe again. She reached over to touch the back of my head, entwining her fingers in my hair, and we just sat there for a while, sharing the morning.

I think it was right then and there that I discovered I *was* feeling pretty good. It was odd, because part of me felt like I should still be sad over having to leave the only home I'd ever known. The fact that I really wasn't all that bothered by it even made me feel a little guilty, like it was some sort of betrayal. But even with the big helping of weirdness that Windward Cove had dished up for me so far, I seemed to be settling in faster that I would have thought possible. I probably should have been scared silly, but I wasn't. I was more interested than anything else, and the thought of that was surprising.

"Uh-oh," Mom said. "Here comes trouble." Moe had seen us sitting together and was headed our way at top speed, his tongue hanging out the side of his mouth. She held her mug safely out of the way while he bounded up the stairs, licking at her face while trying to crawl into her lap. "Easy there, you big moose!" she laughed, ruffling his fur as she tried to avoid his tongue. She finally pushed him back and got to her feet. "So what do you have going on this morning?" she asked.

"No plans," I replied, hugging Moe as he turned his attention to me.

"I've got an electrician coming in around ten, so we've got some time to kill. What do you say I scramble us some eggs, and then we take a hike up to the inn? I'm still dying to see inside, and those keys Mr. Travers left are calling my name."

I felt a shiver on the back of my neck like the touch of an icy finger, but I shook it off. I mean, after what I'd already faced in the cupola, how bad could it be? And besides, no *way* was I going to let her go up there alone. "Sounds fine." I told her.

It wasn't exactly the truth, but it came out sounding close enough.

An hour later we were standing on the front porch of the inn, and Moe and I watched while Mom sprayed WD-40 into the keyhole before inserting the heavy brass key labeled *Front Entrance.* She had to jiggle it and twist hard, but the tumblers finally rolled aside. She grinned over her shoulder. "Cover me—I'm going in!"

I grinned back at her, but my grin turned into a wince as she pushed the door open, the hinges squealing in protest. I followed her across the threshold, and we stood in the wedge of daylight just inside, smelling moldy wallpaper and air that hadn't been breathed in a long time while our eyes adjusted to the gloom.

"Oh, *my...*," she said.

I couldn't have put it better myself. We stood in a wide lobby stretching thirty feet on either side, the hardwood floor covered with a thick, unbroken layer of dust. Furniture covered with heavy tarps stood in shapeless mounds like snowdrifts, arranged for guests who had checked out decades before. Across from us, twin staircases rose on either side of a small elevator with a brass accordion cage half drawn across the dark opening. Empty bookshelves rose to the ceiling along the right-hand wall, in the middle of which stood a darkened archway with a set of batwing doors like the entrance to a saloon in an old western. Half of the left wall was taken up by a second, wider archway leading further back into the inn. Next to that was a front desk that stood before a checkerboard of empty mail slots and room keys that glinted dully from where they hung in neat rows. Daylight slanted in from the cracks between the boards on the windows, the dust motes stirred by our footsteps swimming lazily in the narrow beams.

The air was still, almost expectant, like a pause between breaths.

I was already starting to sweat. The sense of watchful awareness I'd felt when we walked around the place a couple of days before was back, only stronger. And now that we were inside, I could feel other things, too: faint, detached snatches of emotion like distant echoes. I had been ready to deal with the same kind of intense cold and sorrow I'd felt in the cupola, but this was different. For one thing, the emotions weren't as concentrated, probably because they were spread out over a lot more real estate. But they were *everywhere,* too many to count and drifting in and out of my range like whispers in a library.

Moe must have felt it, too, as he whimpered softly and stayed close to my leg.

Mom didn't appear to notice any of it, though, and for the next hour or so she took the lead while we explored the place from bottom to top. The batwing doors opened into a bar, while the archway by the front desk led back to the restaurant and the kitchen, with a secondary corridor that led past the ballroom and ended in a cluster of five or six small offices. Behind the kitchen, we found a door that had swelled shut, and after a lot of sweating and tugging to get it open, we discovered concrete steps leading down into cold blackness and the faint sound of dripping water (luckily, Mom hadn't thought to bring a flashlight, so we got to skip the basement.)

After that we went upstairs. Most of the guestroom doors were standing open, and we saw that the second floor was split between thirty small, anonymous rooms on the inland side—each of them a single room with a tiny bath like you could find at any roadside motel—while the seaward side had small suites with windows overlooking the ocean. The third floor, though, was obviously where the high-rollers stayed. Those were all bigger suites, each of which had two bedrooms and a bath with a separate sitting room and a fireplace. Big windows would have provided sweeping views of the Pacific Ocean if they weren't boarded up. I figured the Windward Inn must've been pretty swanky back in the day, but it struck me as kind of sad. There were pieces of furniture in some of the rooms—a chair here, a brass bed frame there—and a few pictures left hanging in rooms and hallways, but the peeling wallpaper and our echoing footsteps made the Windward Inn feel less like a place for people to gather. It felt more like some ancient tomb where most of the artifacts had already been carted off to a museum.

While Mom gushed over the old bathroom tile and fixtures, furniture, and odd knickknacks left here and there, I was secretly keeping track of my own discoveries. I found four separate places where the air seemed to drop twenty degrees in the space of less than three feet—one in the bar, two on the second floor by the stairs, and one at the end of the third floor hallway. Elsewhere, so many feelings had soaked into the fibers of the place that certain rooms seemed to have personalities all their own. For instance, the kitchen gave off feelings of pleasant urgency, like there was always a lot to do, but mostly it had been a pretty happy place. On the other hand, one of the offices in the back felt petty and spiteful, like somebody mean had worked there for a long time. In other rooms, there were more specific emotions: a bathroom on the second floor gave off sorrow like I'd felt in the cupola (though not as bad), another room almost choked me with intense fear, and there was even one where I had the overwhelming feeling that we were being watched. Worst of all was a suite at the end of the third floor—the only one where the door was closed and locked. It was right next to the cold spot in the hallway, and the feelings coming from the other side of the door were cold, detached, and brutal. I even picked up some stray images while we stood there: the muzzle flash of a gun firing, a spray of blood, and the body of a woman in a red dress being buried in a desert. All of that hit me at once, and I was shaking when we turned and headed back for the stairs.

For the record, at that point, I was willing to believe pretty much anything Ab had to say about Windward Cove. I mean, she could have told me that the ghost of Judy Garland was known to skip down Main Street singing "We're Off to See the Wizard," and I would have asked if Toto was there, too. I'd never had much of an opinion one way or another about haunted houses and such, probably because I'd never been in one. But between the inn and the cupola back at the house, there was just too much emotion—too much *presence* for me to hang on to my skepticism any longer. Mom, Moe, and I might be the only living things walking around the Windward Inn right then, but we definitely weren't alone. Mrs. Wolf's favorite son was officially convinced.

And then it happened.

We were about halfway back from the scary room at the end of the third floor hall when Mom stopped to look at an old painting on the wall. It was a seascape, I noted, but the colors had faded so much that I could barely make them out, and mold had ruined the lower third of the canvas. I barely gave it a glance because I didn't think it was all that good to begin with—you know, one of those unremarkable pictures that hang in public places so that there is something on the wall. Being an artist, though, Mom never passes up an opportunity to look at someone else's work, so she didn't notice the waiter when he suddenly appeared from the dark elevator shaft.

To be completely fair, Moe saw him first. I had reached down to pet him when his ears perked up and he made a soft sound that was half-growl, half-whine. I followed his gaze in time to see the man pass through the closed grating like it wasn't even there, and I felt my eyes go wide as my breath caught in my throat. He was tall and skinny, wearing a white, waist-length jacket, black pants, and a bow tie. I couldn't say what kind of shoes he wore because his legs faded away to nothing just below his knees. The cart he was pushing was the same way, its lower third just empty space as it hovered a foot above the floor. He turned, gliding silently down the hall away from us.

I shot a glace toward Mom, who was carefully scraping at a moldy spot on the picture to see some detail, totally unaware of what was happening. I probably should have gotten her attention, but before I even knew what I was going to do, I was hurrying to follow the waiter instead. Moe hesitated a second and then was right beside me. We moved quickly, closing the distance to follow about fifteen feet behind him. Now that we were closer I could see that he wasn't quite as solid as he had initially appeared. At the center, he looked more or less normal, but he faded to near translucence at the edges. He finally stopped at the door to Suite 301, turning and allowing us to see his face in profile. I cringed, wondering if he would notice us, but it was as if we weren't even there.

He hadn't been a great-looking guy, I decided, with thin, slicked-back hair, no chin to speak of, and a prominent Adam's apple. He adjusted a small bouquet of flowers that sat on the cart beside a silver dome and then straightened his jacket before reaching out to knock silently on the door. Well, he knocked where the door *would* have been—it was already standing open. He waited a few seconds, hands politely behind his back, then smiled with big, crooked teeth and mouthed words I couldn't hear while gesturing toward the cart. After seeming to listen to some reply, the waiter gave a professional nod and then pushed the cart into the room, fading away to nothing as he crossed the threshold.

I hurried forward to peek inside, but Suite 301 was empty. There was nothing but dust on the floor and ragged curtains hanging limply in front of the boarded-up window. A prickly sensation flowed from my scalp to the small of my back, and the breath I hadn't even realized I'd been holding came out in a rush. Moe peeked warily into the room around the door jamb, and then relaxed when he saw there was no one inside.

"Hey, Ben!" Mom called from down the hall, and I whirled in surprise, choking back a cry. "Where'd you go?"

"N-nowhere," I called back, trying to sound as cheerful as I could while my heart tried to hammer its way out of my chest. "Just, you know...poking around." Moe raced ahead of me while I started walking toward her, and it was all I could do to not look back over my shoulder. I moved slowly, giving my shakes time to pass before I got close enough for Mom to notice.

Mom waited for me, ruffling Moe's fur while he stood with his front paws on her thigh, and it didn't take a genius to figure out that she hadn't seen anything. A big part of me wanted to tell her—just blurt out everything Moe and I had witnessed. But I held back instead, afraid that once I started, I wouldn't be able to stop. Telling her about the waiter would lead to telling her about the other things I'd sensed in the inn, which would probably then lead to telling her about my visions and finally to my freaky experiences in the cupola. I didn't want to dump all that on her. Mom had been happy ever since we came to Windward Cove—happier than I'd seen her in a long time—and I didn't want to spoil it. Besides, she was already worried about how I was adjusting to all the changes, and I wasn't about to give her more things to worry about if I could help it.

I was pretty much back under control by the time I reached her, and Mom smiled at me before glancing at her watch. "Whoops... time we started back," she said. "Have you seen enough?"

In spite of everything, the question made me smile. "Yep," I replied, and followed her down the stairs.

It was time for Ab and me to talk.

NINE

I MANAGED TO HOLD IT TOGETHER ALL THE WAY HOME—partly by force of will, but mostly by just refusing to think about what I'd seen. Luckily for me, the electrician was already there when we got back to the house. He was an older guy with silver hair and Coke-bottle glasses who was leaning patiently against a Chevy pickup with "Norm's Electric" stenciled on the doors. He and Mom exchanged hellos and started off together in search of the fuse box while I let out a whoosh of air and sank heavily to the porch steps. Then the shakes hit me again, and all I could do was sit there for a few minutes, trembling violently in delayed reaction.

A ghost… I'd seen a *real* ghost!

Shock made the memory seem unreal, although at this point I was past trying to explain it away. I took deep breaths, pulling myself together so that I could walk without falling down, and then got my bike from the carriage house. Moe ran alongside me as I pedaled for town, initially falling behind as I zigzagged down the drive, but still beating me to the entrance by taking the shorter route straight down the hill. His long, gangly legs carried him at a seemingly tireless run, his tongue lolling out in a big doggie-grin, and after a while I stopped worrying about him being able to keep up.

We were about halfway to town when I noticed a guy stopped by the side of the road. He was about my size but heavier in the shoulders and arms in a burly kind of way. His hair was light, almost colorless, and he wore an old flannel shirt and faded jeans patched at the knees. He squatted beside a mountain bike, holding up the back end with one hand while carefully inspecting the rear tire as it rotated slowly before his eyes. The bike had seen better days, its yellow and green spray paint showing numerous battle scars, and with a noticeable bend in the handlebars. As I pulled up, I could see the disassembled pieces of a fishing rod lashed to the top tube of the frame.

"Having some trouble?" I asked, pulling over.

"Nah, just a flat," he said, looking up to smile at me briefly. I had just enough time to see that he was close to my age before he turned his attention back to what he was doing. "Ha…there you are," he said a second later, stopping the wheel and lowering the rear end back to the pavement. "Do you mind holding this for a sec?" he asked.

"Sure." I reached out to hold his bike upright while he shrugged out of an old canvas backpack he was wearing and began to rummage around inside. Moe sniffed the bag curiously, and the guy chuckled, giving him a friendly pat before pulling out a set of needle-nose pliers that he used to yank a piece of stiff wire that was embedded between the tire treads. "Mystery solved," he said, tossing it well off the road. "Now, if I'd only remembered my patch kit, I'd be back in business." He said it with a rueful smile, not seeming all that bothered, and took the bike back from me as he rose to his feet. "I guess the fish get to live another day."

“Here, I’ve got a tube you can use,” I offered, twisting around to unzip the little pouch under my seat. “I always carry a couple.” I pulled out one of the small boxes and tossed it to him.

“Thanks, man!” he said, grinning, and switched the box to his left hand so that he could reach out with his right. “Leslie Hawkins,” he said by way of introduction, “but folks call me Les.”

We shook hands. “Ben Wolf,” I replied, and then I held his bike for him again while he bent to flip the quick-disconnect lever and took the wheel off the frame. He had the tire off and the tube switched in just a couple of minutes, his big hands working with deft speed, and I passed him the small pump I keep clipped to my frame so that he could inflate it.

“Good enough for now,” he said, handing my pump back. “I can air it up the rest of the way at the gas station.” He stuffed the pliers and the old tube in his pack and then stood, slinging it across his back. “What do I owe you?”

I shook my head. “Don’t worry about it.”

“You sure?”

“Absolutely. Chances are you’ll find me stranded someday, and you can pay me back then.”

“Count on it, dude. Thanks again!”

We rode side by side the rest of the way into town, and he tossed me a wave of farewell as he veered left toward the Texaco station on Madrone Street. Moe and I continued another block or so to the coffee house, slowing as I noticed a yellow, late-model Mustang convertible pulled up at the curb out front.

That’s not exactly true. I mean, I noticed the Mustang all right, but what really caught my attention was Kelly Thatcher in the front passenger seat. She was leaning back, her auburn hair spilling over the headrest as she sunned herself. *Dang*, she looked good! She turned as I pulled up on the sidewalk, gazing silently at me from behind dark sunglasses.

A couple of seconds ticked by. "Um…hi," I said at last. That's me—last of the silver-tongued devils.

Her lips curved upward in a slow smile that made my stomach do little flip-flops, but she turned her face back toward the sun without saying anything.

Hmm, I thought, smiling to myself. *That worked out well. You impressed her so much she's speechless.* Swallowing back a chuckle, I leaned my bike against the coffee house wall and went inside with Moe at my heels.

I could feel brittle tension in the air as soon as I crossed the threshold, and the smile faded from my face. The place was deserted except for a couple of guys talking to Ab across the service counter, and one of them turned as I stepped inside. He was maybe a year or two older than me, with a weight lifter's build and a closely-cropped haircut like a Marine. He nudged his companion, pointing at me with his chin and muttering, "This the guy?"

Alan Garrett turned to look at me, frowning, and I could feel the tension in the air go up another notch or two. "That's him," he replied grimly, and began crossing the room toward me with his pal bringing up the rear.

Moe must have picked up on the bad vibe too, and he stepped in front of me, growling and showing his teeth. I dragged him back, shushing him. If things got ugly, I didn't want him getting hurt. "What's up?" I asked.

"I don't know where *you* come from," Alan spat, stopping bare inches in front of me, "but around here we don't beat up on little kids!" He had his hands out from his sides, clenching and unclenching them, and anger was coming off him in waves so strong that I thought I would choke.

I shook my head, confused. "What?"

"I hear you like playing with sticks!" His hands came up, open palms thudding into my chest and knocking me back a step. Alan's face was livid with rage, with red spots high on his cheekbones. His friend gave me a predatory smile, moving eagerly around Alan like he was anxious to get in on the fun.

Ab came out from behind the counter, shouting something about calling the cops, and then everyone paused to look past my shoulder as I heard the front door open behind me. I risked a look backward and was relieved to see Les standing just inside, taking in the scene with a glance. "Hey Alan…Rick," he said, shrugging out of his backpack and setting it on the floor. His tone was friendly enough on the surface, but there was a dangerous undercurrent to it that was hard to miss. He stepped up beside me, leaning an elbow on my shoulder but keeping his eyes on the other two. "What's going on here, Ben?"

"Not sure," I told him. "We were just getting to that part."

Alan clenched his teeth as if he wasn't sure what he wanted to say. His buddy was glaring at Les, looking like an angry pit bull, but the tension that had dominated the room seconds before was quickly being replaced with confusion and uncertainty. "You know this guy, Hawkins?" Alan asked at last.

Les nodded.

His eyes narrowed. "Then your taste in friends sucks. He scared my sister and her friends half to death yesterday, and beat on Rick's little brother with a stick."

"That's *not* what happened!" Ab snapped. "I was trying to tell you!"

"Hold on a second," I said, finally understanding what this was all about. "Blonde girl about so tall?" I asked Alan, holding my hand at shoulder level. "Lots of attitude? *That* was your sister?"

Alan just glared at me, so I took it for a yes.

"And you—Rick, is it?" I asked, turning toward Alan's pal. "Was your brother the bigger or the smaller of the two boys who were with her?"

Rick glanced briefly at Alan is if for reassurance and then looked back at me. "Scott's the littler one," he answered, still angry, but definitely not as sure about the situation as he'd been a moment before.

"Yeah, I thought so." I was starting to get pretty pissed off myself by then, and I struggled to keep my voice calm. "So here's what happened: when Ab and I got there, those three had my dog cornered under an old pickup, and they were jabbing at him with sticks. Meanest thing I ever saw. I took the girl's stick away from her and then had to knock Scott's stick out of his hand when he tried to hit me from behind. Then they ran off. That's *all*. End of story."

"You callin' my brother a liar?" Rick challenged.

I looked at him. "He told you that I beat on him? Then yeah, he's a liar, 'cause I never touched him." Rick's face flushed dark red with rage, although I'd be lying if I said I cared at that point. "Tell you what," I offered, "go home and have him show you all his fresh bruises. *Then* come back and talk to me if you still want to."

I could feel Les straighten beside me as Rick took a threatening step forward, but Alan put a hand on his arm, stopping him. A few seconds went by, and I honestly didn't know if we were going to mix it up or not. "Is that what really happened, Ab?" Alan finally called back over his shoulder, never taking his eyes from my face.

"Pretty much," Ab snapped. "But he left out the part where Brandi threw a fit because Ben was spoiling her fun! *That* was what I was trying to explain before you decided to go all caveman!"

Alan gazed at me with a thoughtful expression for a few heartbeats and then stepped back, releasing Rick's arm. "I want you to stay away from my sister and her friends," he told me at last. "We clear on that?"

"Glad to," I replied. "As long as *they* stay away from my dog."

Alan frowned but said nothing more as he moved around me and headed outside. Rick stood there for a few seconds longer, smiling that predator's smile of his again, and I waited to see what he would do. Now that Alan was gone, the emotions in the room had gone quiet. Ab was still a blank to me, but I could sense uncertainty from Moe and calm assurance from Les. Rick, though…he was a different story. A sort of eager aggression radiated off him in waves, like a mountain lion focused on its prey, and I was sure for a second or two that things were going to go south again. I tensed, waiting for whatever was going to happen. Instead, though, he circled around us and followed Alan out to the street, purposely bumping shoulders with me as he passed.

I let out a breath as I heard the Mustang's engine start and then fade in the distance as they drove away. "Well," I said after a second or two. "*That* was fun."

Les chuckled, clapping me on the shoulder as he went to retrieve his backpack, and then sauntered over to Ab. "Mornin' buttercup," he said cheerfully.

"Hey, Leslie. Fishing today?"

Les grinned. "It's what I live for."

I shook my head over how calm they both were, as if the last few minutes hadn't even happened. Maybe it was a small-town thing, like an old western in which the locals were used to seeing fights in the saloon. *Next time we'll have to break some furniture,* I thought, and smiled to myself.

As Les leaned on the counter, Ab reached over to unzip his backpack and pulled out a big thermos bottle. It was probably older than all three of us put together, with dents and scratches in the metal that was patterned to look like red and green flannel. She unscrewed the cap and sniffed inside, wrinkling her nose. "Don't you ever wash this thing?"

"Are you kidding? And ruin years of built-up flavor?"

She gave him a disgusted look, filled the thermos with black coffee, and then stuffed a paper sack with four or five sandwiches from the cooler. While Les was loading the thermos and food in his pack, she turned to smile at me. "So what brings you out here, Wolfman?"

"I, uh..." I paused, casting a nervous glance at Les.

"You what?" Ab pressed.

"I wanted to ask you about, you know—stuff." I winced at hearing my own words come out sounding so lame. A couple of seconds ticked by, and all I could do was stand there, feeling like a dork.

"He probably means ghosts, Ab," Les supplied offhandedly, like he was trying to be helpful.

I felt my eyes widen. "How...?"

"How did I know?" he asked, flashing me a grin. "Come on, dude...what *else* does Ab talk about? She's all over spooks like a border collie with a tennis ball." Ab punched him on the shoulder, but Les just chuckled and reached out to ruffle her hair. "Besides, it's not like you could hang around this one-horse town for long without seeing *something*. So, don't freak out. You'll get used to it after a while."

All I could do was stare at the two of them. Les was still grinning, while Ab just watched me with an expression of amused expectancy. "Close your mouth, Ben," she advised after a moment.

I closed it but still couldn't think of what I wanted to say, so the silence continued to stretch out.

"He's still freaking," Les observed calmly.

Ab sighed. "I know. Listen, Ben...why don't you have a seat? I'll get you something to drink, and then you can tell me and Leslie all about it."

I dropped obediently into the closest chair, Moe turning around twice and curling up at my feet. I was shocked that the two of them were taking the whole idea so calmly. I guess I'd been expecting more of a reaction out of Ab. Her taking my news in stride the way she did—not to mention Les not batting an eye about it either—was a bit much. "Does *everyone* in town see ghosts?" I asked.

"Nah," said Les, reaching over the counter and helping himself to a coffee mug. "Just folks who are more aware of their surroundings. You'd be surprised how many people aren't." He strolled over and dropped into a chair across from me, frowning in thought while pouring coffee from his thermos. "Hmmm…how can I put it? Okay, how about this: have you ever been going somewhere while something was on your mind and then realized you couldn't remember who you'd passed on the street? Or spent half an hour searching the house for your wallet, only to find it had been sitting out in plain sight the whole time?"

I shrugged. "Sure. Doesn't everyone?"

"Yeah, and that's exactly my point—everyone *does.* I even know some folks who are that way most of the time, looking at the world without really seeing it because their attention is always turned inward."

"So, what's your point?" I asked.

"My point is this: I bet people see ghosts and other weird stuff a lot more often than they realize. They just don't know what they've seen because they're not paying attention. Think about it: if what they're seeing looks natural enough, it just blends into the scenery. And even if something is out of place, their mind just automatically fills in the details—you know, like the way you can read a word fifty times without realizing there's a letter missing. It looks perfectly fine because it fits in with everything around it." He settled back in his chair, taking a sip from his mug and then shrugging. "That's the theory that makes sense to me, anyway."

"Les is full of theories," Ab supplied, joining us at the table. She slid a mocha in front of me. It smelled rich and chocolatey and was topped with whipped cream. "I want to know what you saw!" Her eyes were bright with interest.

I started off intending to just tell them about the waiter in the hallway of the inn, but in the end I told them everything. I hadn't meant to, but they sort of ganged up on me. One or the other would stop me with questions when I glossed over a detail or left something out, and one thing just sort of led to another. Telling them about the ghost led to telling them about all the other feelings and images I'd experienced in the Windward Inn that morning, and before I knew it all the dominoes had fallen over. I told them about the weird stuff in the cupola, my vision of Aunt Claire as a teenager, and even a more or less full explanation about my abilities—something I'd never shared with anyone but Mom. The cat was out of the bag, and it took me a few seconds to fully realize what I had done.

My voice finally trailed off when I ran out of things to say. Close to an hour had passed, and both Ab and Les were staring at me with expressions I couldn't quite read. Was it fear? Wonder? Or were they just convinced that I was totally full of crap? My heartbeat felt heavy in my chest, and the longer the silence stretched out, the more uncomfortable I felt. I finally dropped my gaze, picking absently at a gouge in the tabletop with my thumbnail.

Way to go, Ben, I thought. I could only imagine what would come next. The laughter. The teasing. The jokes about my future job with the Psychic Hotline. My throat tightened, and my face felt suddenly warm. From two friends to zero in one easy step. Why couldn't I have just kept my stupid mouth shut? I noticed that my hands were trembling, and I pulled them off the tabletop so they wouldn't see, clenching them into fists in my lap.

It was Les who finally broke the silence. "Wow," he said softly. I forced myself to look up, and I was surprised to read genuine interest in his expression.

Ab was grinning openly at me. "That…is…so…*cool!*"

The weight seemed to lift from my heart, and after a second or two, I managed to smile back.

TEN

WE PROBABLY COULD HAVE GONE ON TALKING FOR THE rest of the day, but business at the coffee house was starting to pick up. A husky guy who was probably a senior in high school walked in with his girlfriend, both of them carrying backpacks.

"Hi, Pete...Terry," Ab called, rising from her seat and heading toward the espresso machine. She began making iced coffee drinks for them without being asked, so they must have been regulars. The couple waved while calling out greetings to Ab and Les and then pulled out laptop computers from their backpacks and began setting them up at a table by the front window.

"They'll be here all afternoon," Les informed me in a low voice. "They play one of those online games with all the wizards and dragons and stuff. Ab will have to chase them out of here with a broom at closing time."

I smiled and then turned my head to watch as another customer came in, followed almost immediately by two more. "Must be the lunchtime rush," I said, checking my watch.

"Yeah, looks like the party's over," Les agreed. "What else do you have going on today?"

I shrugged. "Nothing, really."

"Great. Let's get out of here. It's too nice a day to hang around inside." It sounded good to me, so we hollered goodbyes to Ab and went out into the sunlight.

I followed Les to a small cove just south of town. Several bicycles lay on their sides at the top of the cliff, and we left ours with them before hiking a narrow trail down to where the waves churned and foamed along a wide patch of shoreline. Three surfers in wet suits—two boys and a girl—stood warming themselves beside a driftwood fire, while four or five others straddled boogie boards far out in the swells, waiting for their next ride. As I watched, one of the waves must have looked promising, because two of the surfers started paddling like crazy. The swell petered out almost right away, though, and they abandoned it, turning back to rejoin their friends. It made me wonder how often a really good wave came in, and how long they were willing to wait for it. As far as I could tell, the ocean didn't look like it was going to do anything special that day, but they were out there just the same. Was the thrill really worth all the waiting? Or was I missing the point, and was it really about the anticipation and hanging with friends? Maybe I could ask one of them sometime.

"Hey, Ben! Come over and meet the sea monkeys!"

I turned to see Les squatting in the sand near the fire. He'd assembled the two pieces of his fishing rod and was attaching a hook and lure to the line while talking with the guys. The girl sat on her knees a couple of paces off, scratching Moe's ears with both hands while he licked her face.

How about that? I thought. *My dog the ladies' man.*

"Ben, this is Chuck and Vern," Les said when I walked up, "and the hottie over there making out with your pooch is Nicole." Chuck was a head taller than me and a little on the chunky side, with blond hair tied back in a ponytail. Vern was shorter, with a lean, muscular build and ebony skin. He smiled welcomingly when we shook hands, and I liked him right away. Nicole had shoulder-length dark hair and a gold ring in one nostril that didn't do anything to change her girl-next-door looks. Cute. She waved and then laughed and started rubbing Moe's belly as he rolled onto his back, his tongue hanging out one side of his mouth in an expression that was almost embarrassing to watch.

He was *definitely* going to have to teach me that trick.

We all talked for a while. The usual stuff: where I came from, what I thought of Windward Cove, what kind of music I was into—that sort of thing. Vern and Chuck exchanged a brief glance when I confirmed that I was Claire Black's nephew, and that Mom and I had moved into the old house below the inn, but I didn't sense anything beyond interest when I quickly probed their emotions, so I ignored it.

"Are you guys coming down tonight?" Nicole asked, coming over to stand beside us.

"Maybe," Les replied. "I haven't really decided yet."

I looked over at Les, eyebrows raised.

"Most Saturday nights there's a pretty good crowd down here," he explained. "There's not much else to do, so everyone brings an armload of firewood along with snacks and drinks, and we just hang out. Good times—you should come."

I shrugged, doing my best to look nonchalant, like maybe I had to check first to make sure the Swedish Bikini Team didn't need me for anything. But the fact was it sounded like fun. I just didn't want to tell them I'd have to ask my mom for permission.

The other surfers started coming in, shivering with their hair dripping and sand clinging to their wet suits, and I stepped back to give them room by the fire. More introductions were made, but I lost track of most of their names. One guy gave me unfriendly eyes, like outsiders weren't welcome on his beach. A couple of the others were polite but indifferent, but most of them were really cool. There were even two more girls: Monica, whose darker skin and slightly almond-shaped eyes made me wonder if there was some Native American blood in her family, and Kim, a stunning Asian girl who pulled down the top half of her wet suit to display an intricate cherry blossom tattoo that ran from just above her waist all the way up to her right shoulder blade. Sure enough, Moe made the rounds for their attention, and he wasn't disappointed. There was more talk of the beach party while everyone warmed up and got out of their wet suits, and all of them had mastered that trick of keeping a towel wrapped around them while first shucking the swimsuits they wore underneath and then pulling on dry clothes. The conversation didn't last long, though. By twos and threes they grabbed their stuff, tucked their boards under their arms, and drifted away, hiking back up the trail.

We hung out until late in the afternoon, Les fishing in the surf and me just goofing around while watching Moe romp in the shallows and sniff whatever seemed interesting. At one point, he had a starfish in his mouth, but I took it away from him and threw it as far out as I could into the water. I walked along the shore, avoiding the scattered clumps of washed-up seaweed buzzing with flies and taking time to examine tiny shells and sand dollars. Mostly, though, I just relaxed, liking the breeze, the sound of the waves, and the way the pelicans would swoop down and splash into the water like kamikazes.

I spent some time thinking about the party, too and wondered if Mom would let me go. I wondered even more if Kelly Thatcher would be there and what that slow smile of hers might look like by firelight. *Hey, maybe she'll actually open her mouth and say something,*

I thought, smiling to myself. Of course, if she was there, Alan Garrett would be, too. He and I weren't exactly headed down the road to being best buddies, and my trying to get to know Kelly would just make things worse. Besides, even if I didn't like him, scoping out his girlfriend wasn't cool. Bottom line: if I had half a brain, I'd just leave that whole situation alone.

Still, it was fun to think about.

"Had enough of this place for now?"

I turned. Les was standing behind me, his fishing rod taken apart and his backpack slung over his shoulder. "No luck?" I asked.

"Nope. I guess that's why they call it fishing, not catching."

We hiked back up to our bicycles, and Les raised a hand in farewell as I veered off toward home. The afternoon was getting chilly as the sun dropped toward the horizon, and I felt peaceful and at ease. Funny...you would think I'd still be upset about my ghost adventure that morning, but I wasn't. Talking it out with Ab and Les had really helped. Or maybe it had been the laid-back afternoon. Or both. Anyway, I was at about 9.5 on the mellow meter when I leaned my bike against the porch rail and trotted up the stairs into the house.

"Mom?" I called out, closing the front door behind me.

No answer.

A piece of paper was sitting on the table next to the door, and I picked it up, curious. It was an estimate from the electrician, detailing all the work that had to be done to get the power back up and running. There was a *lot*, and I whistled when I saw how much it was going to cost. There was a note at the bottom, though, saying that the kitchen circuit was safe enough to use, so I dropped the estimate back on the table and went back to the kitchen to check. The overhead light came on when I flipped the wall switch, and I grinned. How about that? One step out of the Stone Age. "Mom...I'm home!" I hollered again.

Silence.

The car was still in the drive, so she had to be around there somewhere. I poked around the rest of the first-floor rooms, but no luck. Maybe she'd gone for a walk. If so, that gave me time for a shower before dinner. Moe followed me upstairs, and I was almost to my bedroom when I noticed the door to the attic stairs was open.

I went over and stuck my head into the stairwell, gazing upward. "Mom…?"

There seemed to be more light in the attic than usual, and when I climbed the stairs, I discovered it was because the cupola door was propped open with a broom, allowing sunlight to filter down from the windows above. I noticed that Moe was no longer by my side, and I turned to see him gazing up at me from the second floor hall. "What…you're going to let me do this alone?" I asked.

He sank to the floor, lying with his head just beyond the threshold, looking at me.

I couldn't blame him.

Crossing the attic floor to the base of the cupola stairs, I paused to reach out tentatively with my gift and test the emotional water. No feelings of cold or loneliness seemed to be present —for now, at least. After a moment, I exhaled a thankful sigh and crept slowly up the stairs, ready to retreat if I picked up on anything creepy.

Mom was sound asleep in an old rocking chair that she must have dug out from somewhere among the stacks of junk crammed in the attic. It was an ugly, hulking monster of dark, carved wood and sickly green velvet. The upholstery was worn and faded, and I could see wisps of dingy stuffing peeking out from three or four places where the seams had split. She slept with her legs curled up beside her on the seat, half-turned to one side and facing away from the stairwell.

She'd been busy, I noted, looking around. The windowpanes sparkled, the shelves were freshly dusted, and the floorboards were scrubbed clean and smelled faintly of Murphy's Oil Soap. Even the big telescope gleamed, victim to an attack with metal polish and a rag. Her art books and supplies were organized and shelved, and she'd set up her easel and stool so that she could look out over the vineyard. I still wasn't wild about her turning the cupola into a studio, but I had to admit the place looked pretty good now. Almost inviting, even.

I stepped over to try the hand cranks on the telescope, not surprised to find they turned easily now. Mom didn't do anything by half measures, and she had cleaned and oiled the gears. I spent a few minutes looking at the ocean beyond the cleft in the hills and then swung the barrel around to explore downtown through the eyepiece. I adjusted the lens, and the bricks of the theater wall jumped into sudden, sharp focus. After a few light touches on the hand cranks, I could see people talking on the street, their faces so clear that a lip reader would have been able to follow their conversations. Mom had been right that first day—the telescope was really something. I bet on a clear night you could count the rocks on the moon!

Mom murmured softly in her sleep, and I turned to look at her, noting for the first time that one of her new artist's pads and a pencil lay on the floor on the far side of the chair. I stepped around her to pick them up, tucking the pencil behind my ear and flipping open the cover of the sketch pad. With everything else she'd gotten done, I doubted that she'd had time to do any drawing, and I was surprised to find charcoal sketches on the first three pages. I'd been looking at Mom's work all my life, and I still enjoyed listening to her talk about art, even though we'd both discovered a long time ago that I'd never be any good at it myself, so I was able to study her drawings with a fairly practiced eye.

The first sketch really wasn't much to speak of—just a rough outline of the southeast corner of the vineyard with the barn in the background. I turned my head to look out the window, smiling when I saw that, while the details were rough, she'd captured the angle and perspective just about perfectly. Her second sketch was better: a scattering of leaves frozen as they crossed the paper, as if blown by the wind. Nice details. I turned the page.

Her third sketch was unfinished, but so far it was the best of all. Centered on the page was the dilapidated gate to the vineyard, the weather-beaten post leaning at an angle in the tall grass. Beyond that was the jungle of overgrown grapevines, writhing and swooping in great mounds that created a mazelike warren beneath.

I had bent to look at a particular detail—an odd shape concealed in the shadows—when Mom sighed, murmuring something in her sleep. I turned, closing the sketch pad and squatting beside the rocker, my hand on the wooden armrest. "You awake, Mom?"

She blinked, a sad expression on her face slowly dissolving into a half-smile when she recognized me. "Ben. Hey," she said, reaching over to entwine her fingers in mine. "What time is it?"

I checked my watch. "Almost half past six."

She raised her eyebrows briefly in acknowledgment, not really listening. I could tell her mind was somewhere else, as her gaze was focused in the space between us.

"You okay, Mom?" I asked.

"Mmm?" She looked at me and then smiled that half-smile again. "Oh…sure, hon." She released my hand and stretched lazily, then settled back again with a sigh. "I bet you're starving."

"Getting there," I admitted. "But listen, why don't you let Chef Ben handle dinner tonight? You really did a job up here today. You look pooped."

"Yeah, I guess I am. But I like how things are shaping up in here." She caressed the arms of the rocker. "What do you think of my chair?"

"I think it looks like road kill."

She shrugged. “Nobody’s telling you to sit in it.”

I chuckled. “What do you want for dinner?”

She dismissed the question with a wave. “Well, I sure don’t want any of those awful canned raviolis you love so much, but beyond that it doesn’t matter. I’m not all that hungry.”

“Leave it to me,” I assured her, standing up. “I promise not to gross you out.”

She yawned, snuggling into the chair again and closing her eyes. “You’re a good boy. I guess I’ll keep you.”

I went downstairs to the kitchen and rummaged around until I found a big can of Campbell’s Chicken Noodle Soup. I made a couple of sandwiches while the soup heated, ate one of them while pouring half the soup into a bowl, cut the other sandwich diagonally, and tucked the halves around the base of the bowl on a plate. I grabbed a spoon and napkin, tucked a bottle of water between my elbow and side, and headed back upstairs, balancing everything carefully so that I wouldn’t slosh soup all over the bread.

Mom was asleep again when I arrived, so I set her plate and the bottle of water on one of the shelves. “Wakey-wakey,” I called, touching her arm. “Dinner’s ready.”

She opened her eyes, saw the plate on the shelf, and smiled up at me. “Smells good. Thanks, Benny.”

“You want me to bring it over?”

“No, I’ll get it in a minute. Let me finish waking up.” Her eyelids drooped.

I was starting to get a little concerned—it was unlike her to nap like that. “No hurry,” I teased. “Old people need lots of sleep.”

She opened one eye. “One more old-person joke, and you’ll be right back in the orphanage, bub.”

I grinned. The mischievous glint I’d been looking for was back in her eye, and it made me feel better. “A bunch of kids are planning to hang out down on the beach tonight," I said, changing the subject. "Can I go?"

"Sure, hon," she replied sleepily, closing her eyes again. "Have fun."

I opened my mouth, then closed it again, surprised that she'd said yes right away. I'd been expecting the usual round of questions—where exactly I'd be, who I'd be with, if any adults would be there—followed by back-and-forth negotiations about when I'd have to be home. Skipping that whole discussion felt weird, so I figured I'd better go for confirmation. "You sure?"

She sighed, sounding a bit exasperated. "If I end up with any grandkids out of this deal, I'll disown you."

I grinned again—*that* was more like it! "As long as you'll still bail me out of jail."

She made a shooing gesture with one hand, and I trotted down the stairs, sure at that moment that I had the coolest mom in the world.

ELEVEN

I WENT DOWNSTAIRS AND ATE MY SOUP, SPOONING IT right from the pot while standing at the counter, and then leaning over the sink to drink down the broth. Mom hated when I did that, always calling me a barbarian when she caught me at it, but I never understood why. I mean, why wash a separate bowl if you didn't have to? I got Moe his dinner and went upstairs while he was eating.

I briefly considered taking a shower, but when I looked through my bedroom window and saw the sun already disappearing behind the hills, I settled for just washing my face and pulling on a fresh shirt instead. I pulled my Vacaville Bulldogs sweatshirt on over that, grabbed my school backpack, and trotted back downstairs, going through the kitchen for a couple of Pepsis and a big bag of Crunchy Cheetos. I stuffed them in the pack and zipped it closed on my way out the front door.

Twilight was settling in as I pedaled away from the house with Moe loping along beside me—a patch of darker shadow in the deepening gloom. Stars emerged as the last traces of scarlet bled away, the trees seeming to grow closer and more threatening as darkness crept outward from their bases. I switched on my bicycle's headlight, chasing its yellow glare down the hill to the road.

I wondered if I'd be able to find the beach again, but it turned out that I didn't have to worry. As night fully descended, the flickering red-gold coming up from below clearly outlined where the cliffs fell away to the cove. I left my bike away from the tangle of others lying near the trail head, leaning it against a stunted tree a few yards off where it would be easy to find again.

I smiled as I stood with Moe at the edge of the cliff, looking down at dozens of beach fires burning cheerfully below. The smells of wood smoke and sea air drifted up to me, along with the sounds of music, overlapping voices, shouts and laughter. Smiling, I made my way down the trail with Moe keeping close by my leg.

There must have been over a hundred kids there—probably from Silver Creek and the outlying areas as well as Windward Cove—ranging in age from middle-schoolers to older kids wearing Humboldt State University logos. Blankets, camp stools, and beach chairs were clustered around the various fires, some of which were small, almost intimate, while others blazed five or six feet high. There were coolers and portable stereos, glow-in-the-dark Frisbees arcing back and forth, two volleyball games surrounded by spectators, and even eight to ten guys playing football down by the water's edge. Dogs were everywhere too, chasing one another around or just visiting the fire circles looking for attention or treats. There was dancing of course, some couples were making out, and most of the college kids were drinking beer, but no one was even close to being out of control. As far as I could see, it was just one big party, and everyone was having a good time.

I wandered through the crowd, weaving around fires and clusters of people talking, while listening to rock, hip-hop, Reggae, and even an occasional country tune that drifted in and out of my hearing. I watched one volleyball game in which two girls wearing maroon and green "Silver Creek Varsity" shirts took on four guys who probably outweighed them by forty pounds each. The guys obviously didn't realize what they'd gotten themselves into, and they got creamed 15–3.

"Ben! Hey!"

I turned just as Nicole the surfer girl ran up and caught me in a hug. She broke it off sooner than I would have liked and stepped back, smiling. "You made it! Have you been here long?" I was about to reply when she noticed Moe and dropped to her knees, laughing as he greeted her with a wagging tail and sloppy kisses. "Mo-Mo! I missed you!" They carried on like that for a couple of minutes before Nicole got back to her feet. "Everyone else is over there," she said excitedly, waving vaguely in a direction that could have been either just up the beach or somewhere in Okinawa. Then all at once she gushed, "IgottapeesoI'llseeyoulater!" and was gone.

"Yeah, I made it," I said as she retreated from sight. "No, we just got here…Fine thanks, how are you?" I grinned at Moe, who was looking up at me with what looked like a self-satisfied expression. "Come on, *Mo-Mo*," I said, and we headed up the beach.

We caught sight of Les, Monica, Vern, and Ab all sprawled on blankets around a good-sized fire that was not far from the football game. Moe raced over and started wallowing all over Ab and Monica, and I was headed that way too when I noticed that Alan Garrett and his buddy Rick were two of the players in the game. I tossed a wave toward my friends but then veered left and walked to the sidelines. Not that I was all that interested in the game, but I *was* curious to see how good Alan really was.

His team had possession of the ball. I watched as Alan took the snap, fading back with the grace of a panther and taking stock of each of his receivers with casual precision. At the last minute, he decided on the guy going long and fired a pass that traveled in a controlled arc, dropping neatly over the receiver's shoulder and into his hands. Touchdown.

Wow.

"Do you play?"

I turned at the sound of the unexpected voice and was surprised to see Kelly Thatcher standing beside me, arms crossed as she watched the game. I looked behind her, noting for the first time that a bunch of girls were clustered around a nearby fire—probably the players' girlfriends.

"Not really," I replied. "Well, I mean, sure…during gym class. But never on a school team or anything."

"Oh?" she asked coolly, turning toward me with her eyebrows raised. "Basketball, then? Baseball?"

I shook my head, liking the sound of her voice. It was low and kind of husky—very Demi Moore.

"Well," she said, turning away. "I guess I was wrong—I had you pegged as an athlete."

I didn't know what to make of that, so I let it go.

"So what *do* you do? Band...choir?" She smiled, still not looking at me. "Chess club?"

I shook my head. "None of the above."

"Hmm. So you *don't…do…anything*." Her emphasis on the last three words made it a challenge.

"You should see my butterfly collection."

She turned with an expression of mild surprise. "You're kidding, right?"

"Yeah," I said, grinning at her, "I'm kidding." The verbal sparring was kind of fun. "I'm Ben Wolf, by the way."

"I know," she said, nodding. "Word gets around here fast. I'm…"

"Kelly Thatcher," I finished for her. "I know."

She smiled.

I smiled back. All in all, things were progressing nicely.

"He's really good, isn't he?" she asked.

"Who is?"

"Alan," she said, turning back toward the game. "My boyfriend."

So much for progress. "Yeah, he is," I had to admit, following her gaze in time to watch Garrett evade a tackler easily, then throw a bullet pass to his buddy Rick, who took it another five yards or so before being taken down. "I hear he's the starting quarterback."

Kelly nodded. "Since he was a sophomore. Last year's starter got hurt two games into the season, and the coach put Alan in. They came from twenty-eight behind to win the game, and by the time the season was over, Alan had taken the Bucs to their first league championship in almost thirty years."

I grunted noncommittally, still not liking him, but my respect for the guy had begrudgingly climbed another rung. Damn.

Moe chose that moment to abandon Monica and come over, his tail swishing excitedly. He did a figure eight around and through Kelly's legs, and then jumped up and put his paws on her thigh, nuzzling her hands.

"*Ugh...*" she said, trying to push him away. "Can you call off your dog?"

"Sorry," I said, pulling him back. "He doesn't mean any harm. He just likes you." I watched as she brushed at the leg of her jeans, as if wiping away something gross, and I felt a twinge of annoyance. "Guess you're not much of a dog-person, huh?"

"Oh, they're cute and all," she assured me, looking up. "I just don't want fleas."

My annoyance flared, but I tried to keep it out of my tone. "Moe doesn't have fleas."

"Yeah, but he can *get* them."

"If he does, I'll get him a flea collar," I said, my voice terse. I winced inwardly as soon as I said it. The conversation was going downhill fast, and I didn't know how to salvage it.

We both turned to watch the football game, an uncomfortable silence stretching between us.

After a few moments Kelly cleared her throat, and I sensed that she was as sorry as I was about the sudden awkwardness. "I have birds," she offered tentatively, trying to change the subject.

"I'll get you a collar."

I turned to see her gazing at me with a puzzled expression, but then understanding came into her eyes and her brow smoothed out. "Oh...that was a joke!"

I shrugged. "Not one of my better ones, I guess." But the tension between us had eased, and I offered her a smile.

"No, it was good," she quickly assured me. "I just wasn't expecting it, that's all." She bit her lower lip shyly. Then her eyes glinted with reflected firelight as her lips turned upward into what I was beginning to recognize as her patented We-Both-Know-You-Want-Me smile. "I wasn't expecting you to be this cute, either."

My stomach did the flip-flop thing again as my face grew warm, and I was glad it was dark so that she couldn't see me blush. "Nah," I replied, "I just have a twisted sense of humor."

Her smile warmed briefly, but then she turned back toward the fire where her friends were gathered. "I'll get you a collar," she said over her shoulder, and then walked away.

I watched her go but then turned back toward the game so that I could smile in the darkness without anyone seeing me. I watched the guys run a couple more plays, and then a wad of cold seaweed hit the back of my head with a wet *splat.* "Hey!" I protested, whirling around.

Les sat by the fire, grinning evilly while Ab rolled around on her blanket, cackling. Vern and Monica were chuckling as well, and I began to laugh too, using my fingers to comb the soggy mess out of my hair as I walked over to join them. "Thanks for that," I said, flopping down between Monica and Les.

"Happy to help," Les told me, still grinning. "You looked like you needed a good dose of reality."

"What do you mean?"

"Oh, *c'mon*, Wolfman," Ab said. "We all saw your little audience with the prom queen. How'd it go?"

I shrugged. "She said hi, I said hi, we talked about her boyfriend, and we found out she doesn't like dogs. That's about it—no big deal."

"Maybe not to you," Ab teased, "but you can bet that Kelly's bothered."

"How so?"

"Because you're not following the program," she explained. "See, when Kelly talks to you, you're supposed to roll over with all four paws in the air. You know…chat her up, tell her how pretty she is, that sort of thing. It's what she's used to, but it didn't happen this time. It's going to drive her *nuts!*"

I shook my head, dismissing her theory with a wave. "Don't you think you're reading *way* too much into it?"

"Believe what you want," Ab said. "You'll see I'm right soon enough."

I was still pretty sure Ab was just trying to mess with me, but she exchanged a knowing glance with Monica over the fire, and I wondered.

The conversation turned to other subjects, and we talked until late. I could tell that both Ab and Les wanted to talk more about my weird experiences, but thankfully they didn't bring it up in front of the others. I appreciated them keeping all that stuff to themselves, especially the part about my abilities. After a while, we were pretty much talked out, and we just sat sharing a companionable silence, Vern dozing off and on while we all stared at the flames. I spent the time thinking about Kelly…and trying *not* to think about Kelly. The fire was burning low, and more than three quarters of the crowd had headed home when I finally looked at my watch, surprised to see it was well after midnight.

"I have to go," I told them, scrambling to my feet. "I didn't know it was so late."

Everyone but Ab said goodnight. She said "See you tomorrow."

"I will?" I asked, hurriedly stuffing my trash into my backpack, and then slinging it over one shoulder.

"You will."

"Fair enough. Come on, Moe. Let's go find your jammies."

A light was burning in the cupola. A soft, orange-yellow glow, like a candle or a night light.

My heart sank when I saw it, realizing that Mom had waited up for me and that she was probably angry because I was coming home so late. Not that we'd settled on a specific time or anything, but based on when I usually had to be home (11:00 on a Saturday night, unless it was a special event…and now here it was almost 1 a.m.), I knew that Mom would tell me that we'd had an understanding. And she'd be right.

Way to go, genius, I thought. *After tonight, you'll be lucky if you* ever *see another Saturday night party.*

There was nothing to do but get it over with, so I left my bike by the front steps and went inside with Moe trailing behind me. The house was dark, but enough moonlight filtered in through the first-floor windows for me to climb the stairs and find my way to my room to retrieve my flashlight. Clicking it on, I made my way to the stairwell and climbed up to the attic. I didn't even try to be quiet, and I made my way quickly across the floor, guided by the soft light filtering down from above.

"Mom, I'm really sor..." I began.

The light in the cupola went out. Not suddenly, like a switch being turned off or a candle being blown out. It just...faded away.

I froze, terrified, with one hand on the bannister and my foot on the first stair. "Mom...?" I called softly after a moment.

Silence.

No...not quite silence. I *could* hear something. A faint sound, like the soft intake and release of breath. Someone was up there.

My first instinct was to turn and run, but then it occurred to me that it might be Mom. If she was still sleeping, then something might be wrong. She might be sick, and I was the only person in the house who could help her.

But what if it's not Mom?

I shook off the idea. It's not like I had a choice, and if I kept thinking about it, I'd probably just stand there until I died of old age. My hands were shaking so badly that the circle of my flashlight's beam quivered at my feet, but I slowly climbed the cupola steps, turning as I reached the top.

Mom was curled up in the rocking chair, covered in an old patchwork quilt and taking the slow, regular breaths of deep sleep. I was so relieved that I sat down on one of the low shelves, letting out a relieved breath. I wiped the greasy sweat that had broken out on my forehead, and then I put my hand down into something wet beside me. It startled me, and I looked over to see Mom's untouched dinner, the soup cold and the bread gone stale.

I used her napkin to dry my hand and then rose and went to her side. "Mom," I called, gently shaking her. "You need to wake up now."

She stirred, muttering thickly in her sleep, but I couldn't make out what she said.

"What's that?" I asked, shaking her again.

"Hiding," Mom muttered again. "She's only hiding…"

Still dreaming, I thought, smiling as I pulled pulling the heavy quilt off her. I squeezed her hand while giving it a shake. "Come on, Mom. Time for bed."

That finally brought her around, and she blinked. "Benny…hi," she said sleepily. "Did you have a good time?"

"Yeah, I did, and I'm sorry it's so late. You can yell at me tomorrow. Come on...if you sleep in this chair any longer, you'll wind up in traction."

She nodded, still groggy, but when she tried to stand, her left leg folded and I had to keep her from falling. "Nice save," she said, laughing shakily, and then she winced. "Ow…my leg's asleep. Can you help me?"

"You bet." She put her arm over my shoulder, and I helped her limp down to the second floor and into her bedroom. "You okay now, Mom?"

She smiled, now fully awake and looking a lot more like her old self. "I'm fine…just cold. I don't know where you found it, but that quilt you covered me with was *warm.*"

My scalp prickled as a chill ran down my back.

She limped over to her bed, sat down awkwardly, and then looked back at me. "I said I can manage now, Ben. You go on to bed."

All the moisture had dried up in my mouth, and I swallowed painfully. "G'night," I managed to croak.

"Good night, hon. Sweet dreams,"

I closed her door behind me and walked slowly back down the hall as if in a daze.

The quilt I *covered her with?*

I stopped halfway across the threshold of my room when I suddenly realized that something had changed. The cupola, which had always been filled with bitter cold and sadness, had been peaceful tonight. Whatever lived – okay, *not* lived—up there had even covered Mom with a blanket! And what about that soft glow? It had been soothing, like a night light, keeping watch over her until I came home. There was nothing sad or cold about that, right?

Maybe that was all that the ghost had wanted all along—for someone to move in who loved the place! Was that it? Could it really be that simple? Better still, what if it had been nice as a way to say goodbye? I grinned with sudden excitement and relief. Maybe we didn't have a ghost anymore!

I turned, hurrying back up to the attic and taking the steps up to the cupola two at a time. I was well into the room when I skidded to a stop, my smile fading, my heart seeming to seize up in my chest.

Bitter, freezing cold washed over me. The cold of a thousand January midnights, of broken promises, of lies and nightmares. It seeped into me, seeming to freeze my insides and the marrow of my bones. I stood there, unable to move, and watched as the eye of the telescope, which I'd left aimed toward town that afternoon, slowly swung around to point north, toward the vineyard beyond the night-darkened glass.

Somehow, I managed to get out of there and make it down to my room. I don't remember how. One moment I was in the cupola, the tiny hairs on the back of my neck trying to stand on end, and the next thing I knew, I lay fully clothed beneath the covers of my bed, terrified, shivering violently, and hugging Moe for security and heat. I wondered what it all meant, what to do next, and most of all wondering if I'd *ever* feel warm again.

There was one thing I knew for sure, though: there wasn't just one ghost in my house.

There were *two* of them.

TWELVE

"*TWO* OF THEM?" AB ASKED. "ARE YOU SURE?"

I nodded. "Positive."

It was early afternoon, and we were sitting in a couple of overstuffed chairs inside Tsunami Joe. The Sunday morning crowd had come and gone, and it was looking like the place would be pretty much deserted for the rest of the day.

"How do you know?" she pressed. "I mean, maybe it's still one ghost and it just likes your mom better."

"Already thought about that," I told her. "In fact, I was awake most of the night thinking about it. But you'd be sure, too if you could feel it like I can. Whoever's up there most of the time—the one who makes the room cold and depressing—well, being nice just isn't in him."

"So we're talking about an angry spirit."

I frowned. "No… not *angry,* exactly. Maybe a little resentful, but he feels more…I don't know…heartbroken, I guess. Not just sad, but *desperately* sad, you know? Hopeless. Like someone who just found out his dreams were never going to come true."

"'He,'" Ab said.

"What?"

You said *his* and *him.* Are you sure the spirit is a man?"

I shrugged, shaking my head. "No, not really."

"How about the other ghost?"

"No idea."

"Okay, so what *can* you tell me about the new one?"

I chewed the inside of my cheek, thinking about it, but sighed when I came up empty. "Sorry, but I was sort of distracted at the time. At first, I was so worried about being in trouble, and then was scared silly when the light went out that I really didn't pay much attention to details. Looking back, it seems to me that the room felt peaceful and comforting, but there was too much else on my mind right then, and I'd be lying if I said I was sure."

Ab sighed. "Well…darn."

"Sorry. I'll try to do better next time."

"Hmm? Oh, don't worry about *that,*" she said, dismissing my apology with a wave. "I'm just a little bummed because I was all set to go explore the inn. But that'll have to wait for now while we figure this out first." She rose to her feet, flashing me a smile. "Let's go. I want to see this haunted room of yours!"

"What…now?"

"Sure. Why not?"

I looked around at the empty coffee house. "You can leave just like that? I mean, don't you have to ask your boss first?"

A line appeared briefly between her eyebrows but then smoothed out again when she seemed to make a connection. "Oh…I guess I never told you. *I'm* the boss."

I felt my eyes widen. "For real?"

"Oh, c'mon, Wolfman. How else do you think this place got decorated in Early American Spooky?"

I was impressed. "How did you manage to swing that?"

"It runs in the family. Have you had a chance to eat at Pirate Pizza yet?"

I nodded. "Mom and I had dinner there our first night in town."

"You know Bob—the big guy behind the counter who tells all the dumb jokes? He's my dad. My family owns this building, the pizza place, and the coin-op laundry down the street. They were using this space for storage until I talked them into letting me turn it into a coffee house a little over a year ago. Legally, my folks are the owners and I'm just helping out with the family business, but the project has been mine from the beginning. They loaned me the start-up money, but beyond that, they just help me keep the paperwork in order. All the furniture came out of thrift stores, and there's a place in Crescent City selling used restaurant equipment where I picked up everything else. Windward Cove is too small to interest the big outfits like Starbucks or Peet's, but it's plenty big enough for me. Even on a slow day, we get a pretty good morning rush, and lots of kids come in after school to do their homework, hang out, and surf the 'net. The place has turned a profit pretty much since opening day, and I finished paying my folks back four months ago."

"How do you keep the place open when you're in school?"

Ab looked at me like I was a moron. "*Employees,* Wolfman—duh! I have four stay-at- home moms working here part time," she explained with a touch of pride. "I can't them pay much above minimum wage, but at least I'm saving them from daytime TV."

"Wow," I said appreciatively. "I had no idea. So, someday there'll be a string of Tsunami Joes all over the country?"

Ab shook her head. "Probably not. Right now Mom and Dad have me putting most of the profits into a savings account for college.

Besides, I'd rather get a job tracking down paranormal stuff. *Speaking* of which," she said, raising her eyebrows expectantly, "shouldn't we get a move on?"

"Wow," Ab said quietly, stopping her bike as the house came into view. "It's been a while since I was up here. I'd forgotten how grim it looks."

"Yeah, a cheery kind of place, isn't it?" I agreed, gazing at the severe angles and the tall, frowning windows. "I called it the Norman Bates house the first time I saw it."

"Norman Bates?" she asked, looking at me. "Who's that?"

"You know, the guy from that old Hitchcock movie *Psycho.*"

Ab shook her head. "Never heard of it."

"You're kidding! Okay, then you'd have to say it's sort of like the house in the original *Thirteen Ghosts,* right?"

Ab's expression was still uncomprehending. "What are you? Some kind of old monster-movie buff?"

I had to think about it. "Yeah, I guess I must be," I admitted finally. "A lot of the horror and sci-fi stuff from the 1950s and 1960s is really cool: *Invasion of the Body Snatchers, The Thing from Another World, Creature from the Black Lagoon*. You should check them out sometime."

Ab shrugged. "Maybe. For now, though, Windward Cove already has enough chills and thrills for me."

She had a point, and I pedaled after her as she rode the rest of the way to the house.

Mom came out the front door just as Ab and I were climbing the porch steps. She'd still been asleep when I left earlier, but it didn't look like it had done her much good. Dark circles shadowed her eyes, and her face looked drawn and tired. She seemed to brighten a little when she saw us, though, and offered Ab a smile.

"This is my friend Ab Chambers," I told her. "Ab, meet my mom, Connie Wolf."

They exchanged hellos, and then they were off and running—chattering away like long-lost friends before I even knew what was happening. Mom is naturally outgoing and can have the meanest person in the world eating out of her hand in about ten seconds, and it looked as if Ab was cut from the same cloth. Since it no longer mattered if I was there or not, there was nothing left to do but listen. Ab talked about the town and her family—stuff I already knew—but I also found out that she was a little over three months older than me, that she liked reading Stephen King and Robert Crais novels, and that her two cats were Splatter, a gray tabby, and an orange and black calico named Goblin. For her part, Mom told her how much we loved our new house (I could've argued that point but decided not to), how she and I had been related to Aunt Claire, told her more about *me* than I would have liked, and even referred to me as "Benny" three times—a habit I really hoped Ab wouldn't decide to take up.

Women. Sheesh.

"Whoops…I need to get going," Mom said at last, checking her watch. "The art shop in Silver Creek closes early on Sundays. I'll be going by the grocery store too, Ben—anything special you want?"

"No, I guess not," I said. "Thanks anyway." I watched her lean heavily on the rail as she went down the porch steps and then limp toward the car. "Are you okay, Mom?" I called after her, concerned.

She looked back, giving me a partial smile as she made her way slowly around the front of the station wagon, leaning on the hood. "Oh, I'll be okay," she assured me. "I thought my leg had gone to sleep last night, but I must have a pinched nerve or something. It'll work itself out."

I nodded, frowning, and watched her get behind the wheel and drive away.

"Your mom is really nice," Ab said.

"Yeah, she's the best," I agreed. "Come on—I'll show you around."

I gave her a tour of downstairs, but after a few minutes, she confessed that she already knew what it looked like from taking trips up here over the years and peeking in through the windows. The second floor took a little longer. We were halfway up the attic stairs—me, followed by Ab and a reluctant Moe bringing up the rear—when a funny thought hit me out of the blue. I stopped and turned to look back at her, grinning.

"What?" she asked.

"Check *us* out," I said, starting to snicker. "We're a *Scooby Doo* cartoon!"

Ab glanced back at Moe and then smiled at me while nodding toward the attic above. "Very funny. Just keep moving, Shaggy… before Velma decides to hurt you."

Moe stopped at the top of the stairs, whining softly, and Ab and I paused midway across the attic floor to exchange a glance. "He doesn't like it up here," I explained, trying a smile on for size. It didn't fit, so I put it back.

Ab's face was unreadable. "Animals are very sensitive. There's a theory that says that they can see ghosts even if we can't."

Great. I turned, reaching out with my gift to probe behind the cupola door.

Sullen, brooding sorrow.

I swallowed, my heart starting to beat heavily in my chest. *"It's up there,"* I whispered.

The color drained from Ab's face, but she looked determined nevertheless. "Can you go in?" she asked.

"I…think so. I don't know how long I can stay, though."

She nodded. "Just do the best you can, okay?" Moving past me, she went up the cupola stairs, opened the door, and climbed into the sunlit room above. I followed, shivering as cold and depression settled over me. It was not as bad as it had been the night before, but bad enough. "How do you feel, Ben?" she asked, turning to look at me.

"Chilly," I answered, crossing my arms over my chest. "And sad. So *sad*..."

"I feel kind of jittery," she confessed, "but that could just be because you're freaking me out a little. Do you need to leave?"

I shook my head, still hugging myself but managing to hold it together better that I thought I could. Either the presence in the room wasn't as strong, or I was learning to tolerate it better. "I'm okay for now," I assured her. Just the same, I cast a wary glance at the rocking chair, for some reason not wanting to go anywhere near it.

"No candle or lantern," Ab mused, looking around. "Nothing that could have shed the light you saw last night." She looked over at me. "Did your mom have her flashlight with her?"

"No."

"You're sure? You said you weren't really noticing details. Maybe she had something but took it downstairs before we got here this afternoon."

My eyes narrowed. "You don't believe me?"

"Sure I do," she replied. "But I've made a fool of myself more than once by jumping to conclusions, so I want to make sure we cover all the bases. So...could your mother have had a flashlight or a candle up here that you didn't see and then taken it downstairs sometime this morning?"

I shook my head. "No. I wondered the same thing and came up here after sunrise. Her dinner dishes were still here, but no light."

"Maybe she came up sometime during the night?"

"I was awake—I would have heard her."

Ab nodded and resumed looking around the room.

It was then that I noticed the new pictures.

Mom had been busy. Half a dozen sketches and a watercolor lay spread on top of the surrounding shelves, with a second watercolor drying on the easel, all of which shared a common theme. From a detailed charcoal drawing of a single grape leaf to a sweeping view of the overgrown, tangled acres, all of the pictures depicted the vineyard in some form or other.

"Even with all the sunshine, this place still feels weird," Ab noted from across the room.

I nodded absently, only half-listening. A detail shaded into the grape leaf picture had caught my attention—something that looked out of place—and I frowned as I tried to figure out what it was. Then I recognized it.

It was an *eye!*

Set below and slightly to the right of the leaf's bottom edge, it was there, just discernable in the shadows. Weird. On a hunch, I examined the other drawings more carefully, identifying human figures in three more of them. Or, rather, *one* human figure. I couldn't be sure, but it appeared to be the same person: a little girl.

"Ab, look at these." She came over, and we bent our heads together over the drawings.

One sketch depicted what the vineyard probably looked like back when it was still tended, the vines trimmed into neat rows and heavy with grapes. In that picture, the girl was peeking out from behind a gnarled trunk. Only half her face visible, but her lips were turned up in a mischievous smile.

The second sketch showed only a vague shadow darting between the rows.

In the third sketch, she was just entering the vineyard, laughing back over her shoulder as she disappeared into the foliage. I stared at that picture for a long time, my scalp prickling as I remembered the giggling I'd heard in the vineyard my first day.

"Hey, Wolfman," Ab called.

I looked up to see her gazing at the watercolor painting on the easel. Stepping over, I saw that it was a picture of the girl skipping along the vineyard fence line. Or where the fence had probably *been* once upon a time, anyway. Her face was in profile and not very detailed, and her lower body was obscured behind tall summer grass that rippled in a frozen breeze. She wore a red dress, and her hair was the golden yellow of corn silk.

"Who *is* she?" Ab asked after a moment.

I could only shake my head in reply.

THIRTEEN

A WALL OF BLACKNESS RUSHES TOWARD ME, HIGHLIGHTED by foam and pieces of wreckage swept up from the docks. For a brief, insane moment, I wonder if the earthquake somehow broke Windward Cove off from the rest of California and the town now sliding into the Pacific Ocean. But then the wave hits me and the world turns to chaos.

Shocked by the impact and the sudden, brutal cold, I gasp involuntarily, inhaling seawater as the weight of my sodden clothing pulls me under. I flail wildly, colliding with people and unidentifiable debris in the swirling confusion. Powerless against the force sweeping me inland, I struggle to reach the surface, legs kicking helplessly, my hands clawing at nothing. Even in my panic, however, I'm surprised to discover that I can see. Light from the fire still consuming the roof of the school appears as if behind a rippling curtain—sometimes above me, sometimes beneath my feet, sometimes back over my shoulder—as I twist and somersault in the churning flow. The roar of the wave mixes with screams of terror and pain, gurgles, and cries for help, but the noises are muffled almost to silence by tons of water, sounding far off and making me feel isolated—cut off from any hope of rescue. Then my head unexpectedly breaks the surface of the water, allowing me to hear everything at full volume, and I find that the bedlam of sound is far, far worse than the isolation. I have time for a single, ragged gulp of air before I'm dragged back under, and part of me is grateful for the quiet.

...Grateful that I can no longer hear the sounds of people dying around me.

I sat up, gasping for air as I clutched at my bedcovers, and for a moment didn't realize where I was. I rolled automatically to my side as my stomach clenched painfully, sure that I was going to puke seawater all over the floor. Nothing happened but a couple of dry heaves, though, and after a final shudder, I managed to get myself back under control. Shakily, I groped around on the nightstand, knocking my flashlight onto the floor before I found my watch. *03:54.*

I rolled onto my back, my breathing starting to slow down as I used both hands to wipe the greasy sweat from my face. I felt on the verge of panic, wishing that the awful vision had only been a dream yet knowing that it hadn't. Somehow, I was witnessing the events of June 23rd, 1946—seeing them through the eyes of a man who had been there, feeling his pain, hearing his thoughts as if they were my own. *Who was he?* I wondered. Had he survived the tidal wave? Or was his name inscribed somewhere on the memorial pillar outside of town? And if he was a victim, would I sooner or later be living through a vision of *that,* too—stuck in his mind while he died? I shuddered again, thinking, *And if I'm there when it happens, what will happen to me?*

I knew there was no going back to sleep at that point, so I swung my legs out of bed and put on a pair of sweatpants. Downstairs in the kitchen, I put a kettle on the stove and then hunted around in the cabinets until I found Mom's instant coffee. I'd watched her often enough to know how much of the freeze-dried stuff to put in the mug, and then I added a packet of powdered hot chocolate to make a poor man's mocha. By that time, the water was hot and a few minutes later I was sitting with Moe on the front steps, the mug warm and comforting in my hands as I waited for the sun to come up.

What was I going to do? Between all the ghosts that seemed to be cropping up lately and my disturbing visions, the situation was already feeling out of control and getting more complicated all the time.

I probably would have felt less pessimistic and scared if I'd been able to talk to Mom. She had a way of putting things into perspective that always grounded me. But I couldn't even do that. She'd returned from the art shop the previous afternoon an hour or so after Ab went home. She'd bought four more canvases, along with a fistful of brushes and a couple of dozen more tubes of oil paint in assorted colors, and barely said hi to me before going straight to the cupola. I followed her up, trying to get her to talk about her drawings of the little girl, but she chased me off. She told me she was feeling inspired and wanted to ride that wave as long as she could. Mom promised that we'd discuss it later, but later never came. When I finally went up to check on her around sunset, she was asleep in the rocking chair again, covered with that old quilt. Waking her took forever, and even though her tone was civil enough while I helped her limp downstairs to bed, I could tell that she was irritated with me. I felt badly for bugging her and even worse for wanting to talk about things that might change the way she felt about the place.

I frowned, feeling suddenly selfish for not stopping to consider her feelings. I mean, after all she'd had to do over the years—raising a kid on her own while working one and sometimes two jobs to make ends meet—was I seriously considering doing that to her? I sighed, cupping my chin in one hand while gazing into the depths of my mug. *No,* I decided. She deserved better, and I realized that dumping all that on her was the last thing I should do. *Reality check, genius,* I told myself derisively. *If there's someone who's overdue for life to cut her a break, it's Mom. For the first time since dad died, she's not worried about money, she's living in a house and a town she loves, and she's even painting again. Dude…you are SO not going to kill her buzz with your whiny-ass crap. Just pull up your big-boy pants and deal!*

I nodded, glad that I'd had time to think it over. Okay, Mom was officially out. For now, anyway, and I'd only burden her if things got to the point where it was absolutely necessary. I reached over to scratch Moe as he lay beside me on the porch. "Time to switch to Plan B," I told him.

Moe opened one eye, his tail thumping the floorboards.

Of course, I didn't *have* a Plan B yet, but that hadn't stopped me so far, right?

Ab had the day off, and she thought it would be a good idea for us to research who the little girl in the vineyard might have been, but I wasn't due to meet her until nine. That gave me a lot of time to kill, but just the same, I was anxious to get started with the day. I went back upstairs just as the sun was beginning to peek over the horizon, immediately noticing that the door to Mom's bedroom was standing open. I poked my head inside, saw that her bed was empty, and then looked down the hall and saw the door to the attic stairs was open as well.

She must still be riding that creative wave, I mused.

Twenty minutes later, freshly showered and dressed, I trotted down to the kitchen to see about breakfast. It looked as if Mom hadn't been down yet, and it occurred to me that here was a great opportunity to throw out a peace offering to make up for annoying her so much the night before. Working quickly and hoping she wouldn't come down and spoil the surprise, I scrambled a couple of eggs with bacon, onions, and bell pepper, spooned it between two pieces of rye toast, and then carried the sandwich and a cup of coffee upstairs.

"Morning, Mom," I called, climbing the last steps into the cupola. I was relieved to find that the place felt more or less normal, and I figured that the gloomy spook had decided to take the morning off.

"Hi, hon," she replied absently. She was barefoot, wearing jeans with holes in the knees and a shapeless green tank top. Her hair was pulled back into a ponytail and secured in place with an elastic band. She didn't pause to look over as she gazed through the telescope, adjusting the focus to see some detail in the vineyard below, a sketch pad and a pencil in her free hand.

I stood there for a long moment before I realized that she wasn't going to stop what she was doing. "Here's some breakfast," I offered.

"Mmm?" she asked, finally looking up. She gave me a distracted smile, as if she'd already forgotten I was there, and then noticed the plate and cup in my hands. "Oh…thanks, Benny. That's nice of you." Instead of reaching for them, however, she began scribbling on the open page in her hand, taking quick glances through the eyepiece as she worked.

"I'll just…set it over here, then," I said, my feelings a little hurt, and placed it on the same shelf where I'd left her soup two nights before.

She didn't answer, frowning as she worked on some detail with the pencil.

"I'm supposed to meet Ab later," I added, realizing that she was in "the zone," but thinking it would be best to get all the necessary discussions out of the way. "Is that all right?"

Mom gazed at her sketch critically, chewing her lower lip and appearing not to hear.

"Mom?"

"Fine…fine," she said, looking through the eyepiece again. "Go have fun."

I stood there for a few seconds more, but I couldn't think of anything else to say, so I retreated down the stairs and went outside.

The morning light went from gold, to gray, and then back again to gold as I stepped out from beneath the porch overhang, the sky a jigsaw of clouds drifting on the wind. I could smell rain in the air, and the dry grass hissed and undulated restlessly as the breeze picked up. Moe kept nuzzling my hands, a tennis ball in his mouth, and I threw it for him periodically as I strolled around toward the back of the house. He would run full speed until he caught up to it with a pounce, and then he would trot back to me looking happy and satisfied with himself. I considered riding into town and was even reaching for the handle of the carriage house door to get my bike, but then I thought better of it and turned away. There was nowhere in particular I wanted to go, and I figured I'd just get bored riding around aimlessly until it was time to meet Ab.

My steps eventually carried me to the vineyard, and I stood there for a while, my hand resting on the weathered gate post. I stared into the tangle, watching how the wind made the vines weave and sway hypnotically, as if inviting me into their green depths. After a minute or two, I stepped forward, ducking into deeper shadows and venturing fifteen or twenty feet into the living maze. There, I stood for a while longer, holding my breath, listening for any sounds like those I'd heard on my first visit. Nothing. No hidden, soft giggles; no rustle of movement.

"Are you there?" I called out. I thought doing that would make me feel stupid, but it didn't. My voice sounded loud in my ears, kept close by the surrounding foliage. Moe whined softly, unsure of what I was doing, but probably sensing my expectancy. I put a hand on his head to quiet him and strained my ears, listening. The only reply was the creak and whisper of the wind in the vines, and I quickly began to feel uncomfortable. I turned and retraced my steps, following Moe as he bounded past me toward the ruined gate and feeling better as soon as I was back in the open.

Looking up, I caught a glint of reflected light from the cupola, and I wondered if Mom was watching me through the telescope. I waved but then dropped my hand when I saw no answering movement. I shrugged—maybe she hadn't been watching after all. The breeze blew my hair back from my forehead as I looked around, wondering what to do next.

My gaze finally settled on the barn, a hulking structure of darkly weathered boards leaning tiredly in the weeds maybe a hundred yards off. With everything that had been going on, I hadn't gotten around to exploring it, and I set off in that direction. I stumbled slightly as I drew close to it, my feet finding twin ruts that had been worn into the earth by trucks or machinery a long time before. At last I stood before the big double doors in front, noting that they were made to slide to either side, hung by rusted wheels on an overhead track. The doors were secured by an ancient hasp but no lock. I swung it open before grabbing the handle on the right and trying to roll the door aside. With a squeal of rusted metal, the door moved grudgingly about six inches and then stopped, refusing to budge. The door on the left was a little better, though, and between the two, I managed to create a crack just wide enough to squeeze through. Moe followed as I slipped inside.

At first I wondered if I should have brought my flashlight, but when my eyes adjusted, I found that more than enough light filtered in from the cracks between the boards to allow me to see. On either side were heavy posts supporting a ceiling fifteen or twenty feet above my head, which extended maybe a third of the way into the interior. I moved further inside, discovering that it was actually the floor of a deep loft that was accessible by a wooden stairway off to my right. Beyond where the loft ended, the interior of the barn soared to the cobweb-strewn rafters forty feet above. At a juncture of roof trusses was a large nest where a tawny-colored owl watched me suspiciously.

The barn had been used for farm equipment, I discovered. An ancient tractor sat on flat tires in the center of the floor, covered entirely with rust, and a couple of wooden wagons were parked against the eastern side. I recognized a disc and plow back in the shadows, three or four other farm implements I couldn't identify, and a collection of garden tools hanging from the left-hand wall.

I poked around some, smelling old wood, creosote, and years of dust, and was about to leave when a stack of wooden crates and a metal cabinet in the back corner caught my eye. Curious, I wandered over. One of the crates had been opened, the lid sitting askew on the box and covered in dust. I leaned the lid against the side of the crate, reached tentatively into the packing straw inside, and withdrew the first object I touched—an empty bottle of dark green glass. Only then did I realize that there was writing on the crate, and I stepped back to read it: "Koelling and Sons Glass Works, Santa Clara, Calif." Below that was stenciled "Btls, Grn, 1 Gross."

Wow, I thought, putting the bottle back. *The excitement around here never stops.*

Bored, I stepped over and pulled open one of the cabinet doors, not expecting a cascade of white to tumble suddenly out toward me. I jumped back, yelping in surprise. The owl in the rafters screeched in response, and Moe barked.

Then I laughed, bending over to pick up one of the squares of paper lying at my feet. Hundreds of them lay in front of the cabinet where they had spilled out from a rotted cardboard box that had split down one corner. It was small, maybe three by five inches and spotted with mold. I turned it over to see what was printed on the opposite side, blinking in surprise when I saw a picture of the Windward Inn. There was writing on it too, and I held the paper at an angle to the light so that I could read it. "Windward Cellars" was spelled out above the picture, with "Cabernet Sauvignon" written below, and I realized I was looking at a label for a wine bottle.

I shrugged, a little disappointed, and dropped the paper. No big surprise—a vineyard generally meant there was a winery around somewhere. Not an especially tough mystery to solve.

The owl in the rafters screeched again, clearly upset by our presence and flapping its wings, and I figured it was time to leave. "Come on, boy," I said to Moe, and we made our way back out into the gray morning.

FOURTEEN

I MANAGED TO YANK THE BARN DOORS CLOSED AGAIN, the rusty wheels squealing grudgingly on their overhead track, and I had walked maybe fifteen or twenty yards in the direction of the house before I noticed the empty space beside me. "Moe…?" I called, turning.

He was about halfway between me and the barn, one forepaw raised as if he'd stopped in midstride. As still as a stone, he stood with his gaze riveted on the vineyard. At the sound of my voice, he glanced over at me, his tail swishing in a brief, almost offhand acknowledgment before he returned his attention to the overgrown rows. As I watched, he took three steps in that direction before pausing again, ears perked and head cocked slightly to one side.

"C'mon, boy," I called. "It's time to…"

Moe gave a single, excited bark and then took off at full speed toward the jungle of green. He disappeared between the rows a moment later, his black fur merging with the shadows.

"...Or not," I sighed, and then followed him at a run, ducking into the vineyard a few seconds later. I could only guess that Moe had heard some critter that he'd decided needed to be chased. Whatever it was, I just hoped that it wasn't a skunk. I paused just inside, not really breathing hard yet, and listened to determine where Moe was.

I heard rustling sounds maybe fifty feet ahead and slightly to the left, followed by three barks, each sounding a little farther away as Moe increased his lead. Jeez, he was really moving!

I took off after him, sometimes able to run for ten or fifteen feet, but mostly I had to swerve and duck my way through the tangle, sometimes bent nearly double. I had to keep stopping to listen, the rustling of my own footfalls on the rotting carpet of leaves drowning out the sounds of Moe ahead of me, but after a while, I seemed to be gaining on him as whatever it was he was chasing led him on a zigzag course through the rows.

I heard him cross my path somewhere up ahead, now tracking off to the right, and I pushed myself harder as I adjusted course. "Come on, Moe. Leave it alone!" I hollered, starting to laugh. The chase was kind of fun. I continued onward, following as he crashed his way deeper and deeper into the vineyard, enjoying the springiness of the ground beneath my feet and the cool air in my lungs. A few moments later, I broke out suddenly into an open patch and had to dive to the right to avoid plowing into Moe as he stood in the unexpected brightness. I landed hard, rolling over twice before coming to a stop on my back, and laughing as I squinted up at the drifting clouds above. I lay there for a moment, breathing heavily as my heartbeat slowed, and then raised myself up on my elbows to look over at him. "You done yet?" I asked, still chuckling.

Moe ignored me. He paced restlessly back and forth across the tiny clearing, raising his head periodically to sniff the breeze and whining eagerly. His quarry must have gone to ground, and he was still trying to figure out where it was.

"Hey," I asked, "are you listening to me?"

Moe glanced over at me briefly, turned in a circle to give the air one last sniff, and then reluctantly came over and plopped down by my side, clearly disappointed with the way things had turned out.

"Don't worry," I assured him, ruffling his fur and thinking that some squirrel was probably pretty pleased with itself about now. "You'll get it next time!" We stayed there for another minute or two, me smiling as I stroked Moe's side and watching as the clouds slowly thickened into a gray overcast above.

Then I heard it, and the smile faded from my lips as my gaze swept the shadows. It was the soft sound of a child's voice, humming a handful of notes from some tune I didn't recognize. My scalp prickled, the breath seizing in my chest.

Moe went rigid beside me, and I rolled to my knees, grabbing his collar to hold him in place. So *this* was what he'd been chasing! My heart thudded behind my rib cage as I strained to hear more. The voice belonged to a little girl, I decided, and had been so soft that it was nearly hidden in the breeze. She'd hummed in that slightly discordant way young kids do when they are repeating a song, the sound having a haunting, distant quality like a far-off echo. It had just been a few notes, dying off before I'd had time to pinpoint their direction, but a shiver turned my spine to ice as the tune branded itself into my memory.

Moe strained against his collar, his tail whipping pack and forth as he panted excitedly, ready to take up the chase. I rose to my feet, shushing him as I slowly allowed my fingers to let go. I moved my hand to his back, where I could feel him trembling with excitement. "Easy, boy," I said in a soothing voice, straining my ears for the sound to be repeated. He glanced quickly at me and then grew quiet, all of his muscles tensed in anticipation.

The moments seemed to drag on while we waited, my heartbeat marking every slow second. I took shallow breaths, straining my ears but hearing nothing but the whisper of the breeze and an occasional creak of the vines where they grew gnarled and thick at their base. I had almost given up when the voice came again, softly singing the same series of notes, and ending with the mischievous giggle I remembered from my first day in Windward Cove. Before the sound had time to die out, we were off like a shot, moving together now, Moe glancing occasionally back to make sure I was keeping up as we crashed through the vines.

We followed the sounds for an unknown distance, until I was gulping air and blinking at the sting of sweat in my eyes. Sometimes we heard a giggle, sometimes notes from the song, and we had to adjust our course repeatedly, veering sometimes left, sometimes right, but heading generally north. Several times we had to stop, breathing heavily as we listened for our next clue, and when it came, we would dash off again, moving in tandem as the little girl's voice teased us onward.

We ran… and ran…and ran, until I was sure my heart was going to explode in of my chest like the newborn monster from the *Alien* movies. I was almost out of steam by then, gasping air in great, ragged breaths. I didn't even bother listening for the girl any more—it was all I could do to keep up with Moe as he stayed hot on her trail.

We suddenly broke out into the open on the far side of the vineyard. I felt an odd mix of relief and disappointment: glad to have the confining grapevines behind us, but frustrated because Moe began to pull steadily further ahead of me. I pushed even harder, sprinting along a wide, level stretch of land at the base of steep hills rising abruptly to my right. To my left, cliffs fell away to where the ocean swirled and foamed against the rocks below. I watched as Moe disappeared, cutting right into a wide gap between the hills. All I could do was put my head down, following him as fast as I could.

My steps slowed as soon as I rounded the turn, and I gasped in relief as I came to a stop, dropping to my knees in exhaustion. The gap was actually a box canyon fifty feet wide and maybe twice that distance deep. The surrounding hillsides were nearly vertical—jumbles of rock and loose earth gathered near their base where the sandy terrain had occasionally broken off and slid to the bottom. Shadowed and craggy, the canyon reminded me of a moonscape—nearly barren except for a few stunted, hardy plants clinging precariously here and there.

Noises bounced and echoed between the high walls. I strained to listen for the little girl, but after several long minutes of hearing nothing but the wind and sea, I finally shook my head and gave it up. We were alone. The pursuit was over, at least for now, and it had turned out to be nothing but a wild goose chase. Moe still hadn't given up, though, barking excitedly as he trotted back and forth, trying to figure out where our quarry had disappeared. I watched him as I rubbed the sweat out of my eyes. My heartbeat was slowly coming back to normal, the pounding of blood in my temples easing off. I shivered, as the ocean breeze was stronger now that we were in the open and cold against my back where my shirt stuck to me with perspiration.

Moe trotted anxiously over to me two or three times, whining like there *had* to be something I could do. I chuckled as I watched him and had to call three times before he finally came over and sat down, heaving a big doggie-sigh of disappointment.

I knew how he felt. I guess I'd been assuming the girl had some purpose in leading us around, but when I saw where she'd left us, it seemed obvious that all she wanted was to get us out of the vineyard.

Fair enough, I thought. *She was here first, after all.* If running us ragged before dropping us off in the middle of nowhere was her way of saying, "Hit the road, guys," I guessed all Moe and I could do was take the hint. "And anyway, what would we have done if we'd caught her?" I asked, smiling as I rose to my feet while drying my palms on my jeans.

Moe looked up briefly and then leaned against my leg to scratch an ear with his back foot. Getting outrun by a ghost didn't seem to bother him much.

I glanced at my watch, realizing there wasn't much time left before I was supposed to meet Ab. "C'mon, boy," I told him. "We need to get going."

We exited the box canyon, hiking back the way we'd come. I briefly considered going back through the vineyard to see if our little friend would make another appearance but then decided not to. Trying to navigate through that jungle would just slow us down. We turned left instead, skirting the east side to save time.

Moe took up his usual position by my side as we trudged through the dry grass, and I found myself humming the little girl's tune to the tempo of my footfalls. *Who was she?* I wondered. It had to be the same girl who kept appearing in Mom's drawings, but since I couldn't seem to get her to talk to me, I was on my own to find out for sure.

And what was up with all those pictures Mom drew? Could she actually *see* the girl? My instinct said no. Even as distracted as she had been lately, I was sure Mom would have mentioned something as significant as that, which left the question still unanswered. The only other explanation that occurred to me right then was that the weirdness of Windward Cove was starting to seep in and show itself in her art, but a shiver rose up the back of my neck and I mentally thrust the thought aside. *Don't go all Twilight Zone, Ben,* I told myself firmly. *There's plenty of creepy stuff to go around already; you don't need to start inventing your own.* I knew, though, that eventually I'd have to find a way to get Mom to tell me about the pictures, and sooner rather than later. All the mysteries were starting to stack up.

I turned my thoughts back to the girl. Why was she in the vineyard in the first place? And why did she work so hard to get Moe and me out? She'd become silent soon enough after leading us out the other side, so there had to be *some* reason she didn't want us in there. Was there something she didn't want anybody to find? I stopped, taking a moment to scan the sweeping acres of grapevines that swayed and undulated in the breeze, and then shook my head. I could probably spend a week searching through there and still come up empty.

With a sigh I started walking again. I had too many questions. Hopefully, Ab would be better at figuring out the answers than I was.

Even though we were running late, I took the time to stop by the house to splash water on my face and chest, and then pull on a clean shirt. The door to the attic stairs was standing open (*big surprise there*, I thought), and I stuck my head inside. "Back later, Mom!" I shouted up the stairwell.

I waited three or four seconds for her to answer but was rewarded with only silence. "Mom?" I repeated at last.

"*Yes*, Ben—I heard you," her voice finally came drifting back down, sounding just as preoccupied as she'd been earlier. I detected an undercurrent of exasperation in her tone too, like I was annoying her, and it stung.

I waited but eventually realized that was all she was going to say. There were no inquiries about when I'd be back or where I was going. Uneasiness crept into my heart, but the feeling was eclipsed almost immediately by a sharp stab of resentment. Apparently, I wasn't *nearly* as important as her pictures these days! I toyed with the idea of calling up again to volunteer the information, if for no other reason than to force her to listen whether she liked it or not. Then I remembered how much she'd been turning away lately and ignoring all my attempts to reach out. Resentment won, and I stalked away without another word. *Maybe she'll find a spot for me on her Give-a-Crap List later,* I sulked inwardly. Part of me knew I was being petty, but I ignored the thought before my conscience had time to make a big deal out of it.

Mom clearly had better things to do.

Fine. So did I.

FIFTEEN

MY MOOD WAS STILL DARK AS I SLAMMED THE FRONT door behind me and stomped around to get my bike from the carriage house. Moe must have sensed that something was wrong, as he stuck close by my side, offering an occasional low whine.

"Don't worry, boy," I assured him in a mutter. "I'm not mad at you."

Nevertheless, he remained as close as my own shadow while we rode into town. The overall gloom of the day increased as the blustery morning edged toward noon, and I could smell the salt tang of the ocean and the sour but pleasant odor of damp eucalyptus. The last gaps closed between the clouds above, darkening into a mournful overcast that wept occasional patters of rain that slanted down on the wind. All in all, it matched my mood about perfectly.

As the rain began to increase in frequency and duration, a practical voice in the back of my mind pointed out that I'd be doing myself a favor by going back for a jacket or, better still, just staying home. Of course, by then I had worked up far too much indignation and self-pity to give in to common sense. Deep inside I knew I was being stupid, I but felt an odd, almost vindictive satisfaction in riding out in spite of the weather.

Fortunately, we made it to town ahead of the worst of it. I chained my bike to a post outside Tsunami Joe, watching as the handful of other people on the street headed for cover, and then went inside with Moe trailing behind me.

The place was busy. Across the room, I could see Ab look up as we entered and then frown at the clock above the espresso machine before turning her attention back to steaming milk into hot foam. "Sorry, Wolfman," she called as I drew up to an open spot at the counter. She glanced at me over her shoulder, offering me a brief smile of regret. "Looks like we're going to have to reschedule."

Six people were lined up waiting for drinks, and the woman at the front shot me a glare that was almost hostile, as if irritated that I was distracting Ab. I ignored her, looking around to note that nearly three-quarters of the tables were occupied. "Wow…rainy days must be good for business," I offered, shrugging to hide my disappointment.

Ab snorted. "There's nothing good about *this* rainy day. My afternoon lady called in because one of her kids is sick, so now I have to cover her shift. Plus, I've got a clogged drain that's backing up the sink." She shook her head. "Somebody *please* shoot me."

You'd think hearing that someone was having just as rotten a day as I was would make me feel better, but it didn't. "Want me to take a look at the drain?" I offered. "I'm a whiz with a plunger and a snake."

"Thanks, but Les is already working on it," Ab replied. She turned, kicking at a spot below my field of vision. "Hey, Leslie—say hello to Ben."

"Hello to Ben," his muffled voice came from below the counter.

"Hey, Les," I called back, smiling. I wanted to chat some more but figured they were both too busy. I settled for stepping back to watch instead, hoping for a break in the action, but after just a few minutes, I realized that wouldn't be happening any time soon. Customers continued to wander in as the rain turned into a heavy downpour outside, and there were never fewer than three or four people in line.

Even though Ab worked at a fast, efficient pace, I could see it was all she could do to keep up with the drink orders. Looking around, I noticed all the plates and coffee mugs beginning to stack up on the tables where customers had left them, so I made Moe lie down in a corner out of the way. Stepping behind the counter, I found a square plastic tub and a wet towel and started playing busboy. *Why not?* I decided with an inward shrug. After all, it gave me something to do. And helping out was actually kind of fun, too. If nothing else, it took my mind off all the unanswered questions rattling around in my head.

I caught Ab's eye, and she smiled, mouthing "thank you" when she saw what I was doing. It made me feel good, like I was making a big deposit to my karma account, and I tossed her a wink in reply. Just the same, though, I couldn't help but think about Tom Sawyer getting all his friends to paint Aunt Polly's fence.

I discovered another sink in a small back room behind the service counter, so between washing dishes and clearing tables, I managed to kill the next couple of hours. I settled into an easy rhythm, letting my mind just sort of idle in neutral, and over and over again I caught myself singing under my breath, softly repeating the melody that Moe and I had followed through the vineyard. I still didn't recognize the tune, but it sounded like a real oldie. I kept trying to shake it off, but as soon as I thought about something else, it would repeat itself. It was lodged firmly in my head, like the skin of a popcorn kernel stuck between my teeth, and after a while I gave up and let it stay.

The rain finally petered out around midafternoon, but I could see through the front windows that the storm probably wasn't over yet.

I decided it was time to make a run for home before it started again. By then Les had finished with the drain, and the place was starting to empty out anyway, so I figured Ab could take it from there. Besides, Moe was getting restless and was starting to draw disapproving looks from the remaining customers as he followed me around.

We said our goodbyes and left, stepping out into the cool afternoon where puddles stood in the asphalt and drops of water hung from the eaves like strings of diamonds. I was feeling pretty good by then, my mood having swung back to normal during the intervening hours. As soon as I unlocked my bike from the post, however, the little girl's tune died on my lips as anger made my face feel hot.

Both my tires were flat. It took only a couple of seconds to discover that the tips of my valve stems had been cut neatly away. Gritting my teeth, I unzipped the pouch under the seat, and, sure enough, my spare tubes were missing too.

"Sonofa*bitch!*" I spat, automatically straightening to look up and down the street. Whoever had done it was, of course, long gone. Worse still, I couldn't even call Mom for a rescue. My cell phone, which I hadn't even touched since leaving Vacaville, was sitting conveniently on the nightstand in my bedroom. Mom almost never carried hers, and as usual it was probably sitting forgotten somewhere with the battery dead. And there was no way to call the house, since we hadn't had a phone line installed yet.

No two ways about it. I was walking home.

Seething, I set out right away, pushing my bike by the handlebars while casting apprehensive glances at the clouds looming overhead. I figured that if I hurried, maybe I could make it back home before the sky opened up and dumped on me.

No such luck.

Fat drops of rain were already splattering against the asphalt before I reached the halfway point, quickly intensifying into a heavy shower. I was drenched by the time I finally made it to the gap in the stone wall that marked the mouth of our drive. Wet as I was, though, the rain did nothing to cool my simmering anger, particularly since I had a pretty good idea who was responsible for cutting my tires and steaking my spares. After all, the list of people who didn't like me was pretty short. Sure, petty vandalism seemed a bit beneath a guy like Alan Garrett, but I had no problem at all picturing his buddy Rick stooping that low. It was just too bad there was no way to prove it.

Moe trotted happily alongside me, seeming to enjoy the change in the weather and oblivious to my discomfort. Fortunately, things got better as we climbed further up the winding drive to the house. The trees overhead provided partial cover, and at least the rain stopped blowing in my face as we rounded the leeward side of the hill. Just the same, I was soaked, cold, and miserable by the time the house finally came into view.

I stopped, sighing in frustration. My plans to stand in a long, hot shower faded away as I saw the delivery truck parked out front, "Hawthorne's Interiors" painted on its side. A rocking chair was substituted for the H in the logo, but I had a hard time appreciating that bit of cleverness right then.

Today just keeps getting better and better, I thought dejectedly.

A couple of burly guys wearing the Hawthorne's logo on their coveralls were just coming down the porch steps as I walked up. They both glared at me, looking annoyed. "You live here, kid?" one of them asked.

I nodded.

"You just lucked out, then. We were about to leave. Did you forget you had a delivery scheduled for today? We've been waiting nearly an hour!" He didn't even try to hide the fact that he was pissed off, and his partner looked just as mad.

"How could I forget something I never knew about in the first place?" I snapped back. Normally, I'd never mouth off like that to an adult, especially a couple of gorillas like those two guys, but I just couldn't help it. "Anyway, my Mom's here. That's our car parked right over there!"

He shook his head. "We knocked three or four times. Nobody's home." He crossed his arms over a barrel chest, glowering at me. "Now, do you want this stuff or not?"

I sighed, my anger bleeding away. It had been a long day, and my last outburst had taken what little outrage I had left. I was just too tired by then to keep the fire going. "Look, I don't know why she didn't answer the door," I told him at last. "It's a big house, and maybe she just didn't hear you." Those were lies, of course. I had a pretty good idea why she didn't answer but saw no point in getting into it. "I'm sorry you had to wait," I added, "but if you hang on a second, I'll get the door for you." I watched, and their expressions seemed to ease. I guessed the apology had mollified them at least a little.

I propped the front door open and then trotted down to the rear of the truck where they had rolled up the back door and were pulling out a long loading ramp. "So what have we got?" I asked.

The man who hadn't yet spoken consulted a clipboard. "Most of what's back here is yours," he said. "A sofa and love seat, coffee table, two end tables, an entertainment center, TV, and a refrigerator. Just show us where you want it all."

I cringed, having no idea what Mom had in mind. Maybe I shouldn't have avoided all those shopping trips. "I'll have to ask," I confessed. "Do you mind holding on another couple of minutes?"

The man's eyes narrowed, his irritation returning. "You've got about five while we get the first couple of pieces onto the porch and out of the plastic."

Nodding, I darted into the house, taking the stairs two at a time and racing down the hall to the attic stairwell. "Mom!" I shouted. "There's a delivery truck here with all kinds of stuff! Can you come down and show these guys where it goes?" Silence greeted me, and I frowned, picturing her asleep in that god-awful chair again. Frustrated, I hurried up the narrow flight and was halfway across the attic when I pulled up short.

The door to the cupola swung closed.

The sight made me pause, but only for a second. "Oh, you are *so* not screwing with me today!" I snarled. Maybe the words were directed toward the spirit in the cupola, or maybe toward my mother. I couldn't be sure. It didn't really matter because, either way, a moment later I was hammering on the door. "Come *on*, Mom! Wake up, will you? We both know you don't want *me* decorating this place!"

Frozen air wafted through the crack below the door, the wood itself seeming to radiate cold. I rubbed my arms, shivering, but I thought I heard a sleepy murmur. I pressed my ear against the portal, ignoring the way it felt like an ice cube. "Mom…?"

"She's hiding," came her voice faintly from beyond the door. "Only hiding…"

A sudden chill washed over me. It was far worse than anything I'd experienced in the cupola, because this time it came from inside me. *Who was hiding?* I wanted—*needed*—to ask. Mom had murmured those words in her sleep before, but I hadn't thought much about them at the time. Now, though, I suspected they had real meaning.

"Let's go, kid!" the deliveryman shouted up from below.

I shook my head, turning to hurry back downstairs.

An hour later, I was watching while they wrestled a big stainless steel refrigerator into its space between the kitchen cabinets. They had been happy when I told them to just leave the rest of the furniture in the big empty room to the left of the front door, which worked for me, too because it saved a lot of time. It wasn't just that I didn't feel like guessing how Mom wanted the stuff arranged. My real priority was to see the job finished and get them out of there so I could get back upstairs. I sat on the butcher block, my right leg bouncing impatiently while one of the men installed a T-fitting on the cold water valve under the sink and then ran a plastic hose to the back of the fridge for the ice maker. The whole process probably didn't take more than ten minutes, but to me it felt like hours.

Finally, they were finished, and after signing the delivery form and saying an obligatory thank-you, I watched them climb back into their truck and drive away.

About freaking time!

The late afternoon light was fading as I made my way back upstairs. As usual, Moe squeezed himself into a space among the junk in the attic, hunkering down to watch apprehensively as I exhaled a breath and turned the knob on the cupola door. I had pushed it maybe a third of the way open, steeling myself to cross the threshold, when next I found myself stumbling down the steps.

Something on the other side had pushed back!

I was caught completely off guard, nearly tumbling all the way to the attic floor as the door slammed in my face, but catching myself on the bannister at the last moment. Moe came to his feet, growling as cold air from the cupola washed down the narrow stairs in a flood, as if trying to force me away.

I guess I should have been terrified, but it had been a long day and I'd had enough. "Oh, I don't *think* so!" I hissed, and then grit my teeth, charging back up into the freezing wave of depression. I twisted the knob while hitting the door with my shoulder. It gave a few inches and then was pushed closed. I hit it even harder, this time almost managing to block the jamb with my foot, but I was forced back again. I choked out a sound of fear and rage, the mix of emotions momentarily drowning out the cupola's depressive atmosphere but making it hard to think clearly. "MOM!" I hollered, pounding on the door. "Mom, WAKE UP!"

"...Ben?"

Then I was falling through the doorway as all resistance suddenly disappeared. I landed heavily, bruising my ribs on the stairs beyond, but scrambling back up immediately and pounding up the risers. Both the cold and depression were gone, but I barely took note of the fact even though Moe was now beside me again, a comforting presence by my leg. I stood gasping just inside the cupola, cradling my ribs as I scanned for my mother in the darkness.

"Benny...what's wrong?" she asked.

My gaze detected movement—the slow rocking of that big, ugly chair—but the shadows of the room made details impossible to see. "Why didn't you *answer* me?" I accused. "Are you okay?" There was an edge of panic in my voice that I didn't even bother trying to hide.

"Of course, Ben. I'm fine. Why wouldn't I be?" Her words came slowly, heavy with sleep and sounding slightly confused. "I've been here all the time. All you had to do was call and I would have heard you."

I exhaled a ragged breath, rubbing my eyes with the heels of my hands. "It's this *room,* Mom," I said, trying to keep my emotions under control as the words starting spilling out of me in a rush. "Something's *in here!* This place isn't right. The house, the vineyard... *the whole town!* Won't you *please* come downstairs so we can talk?"

A long pause. No answer.

"Mom...?" I stepped tentatively forward, straining my eyes in the darkness until I could make out her shape curled up in the rocker. She was sleeping again, her breathing slow and regular. Had she even heard me?

I shook her shoulder gently. "Mom... Mom, please wake up."

She finally stirred. “Mmm? In a while, Benny, okay? Just a little while, I promise.” She drifted off again.

I shifted my weight from one foot to the other, wondering what the hell I was supposed to do. There was no way I could leave her alone, although something told me that trying to wake her again would be useless. I stood there for a moment, shivering in my still-damp clothes, and realized I was out of options. Lowering myself to the floor, I sat beside the front corner of the rocking chair, glad that the quilt covering Mom was big enough that I wouldn't have to actually touch the puke-green velvet. I called Moe to me, reaching over to wrap the trailing edge of the quilt around us both. Moe settled down with a sigh, and I began to feel warmer right away.

I stared out into the darkness, listening to the old house creak softly to itself as it settled in for the night.

When Mom woke again, I'd be there.

SIXTEEN

THE WATER AROUND ME GOES BLACK AS I AM SWEPT FURther up Main Street, the firelight from the burning school blocked by the buildings to my left. I continue to tumble and spin in the freezing darkness, no longer able to tell up from down. My foot brushes the street surface at one moment, my shoulder or back impacting it painfully at the next, and I concentrate only on being ready to take my next gasp of air as my head breaks the surface at irregular intervals. I inhale as much seawater as oxygen in those precious seconds, my throat burning from the sour brine. The screams around me are fewer now, and I try not to think about what that means.

I sense rather than see things around me; people and objects caught as helplessly as I in the churning flow. Sudden, frequent impacts threaten to force what little air I have remaining from my lungs, and as I bounce and careen my way up the street, it occurs to me that I'm in as much danger of being bludgeoned to death as I am of drowning. All I can think to do is cover my head with my arms and tuck my knees into my chest. I give myself up to the irresistible force, abandoning all natural instincts to flail against it.

The underwater spinning makes me dizzy, and I clench my stomach, fighting to hold down my gorge. If I vomit, I know my body's next natural reaction will be to inhale, and then I'll be dead. In that respect, the freezing water helps. The bitter cold makes all my muscles contract, while at the same time helping me to remain alert even as a lack of oxygen threatens to steal consciousness from me.

After what seems like hours but in reality can't have been much more than a minute, the momentum of the tidal wave at last begins to slow. The mass of water eases to a slow, reluctant halt, and I find myself hanging suspended momentarily in the freezing void. My heart leaps for joy, and I'm grateful beyond words as my dizziness begins to subside. For the span of perhaps three heartbeats, I can hear only the swirl of water around me. The sound is deceptively calm, almost soothing.

A hand clutches suddenly at my sleeve, and I automatically look in that direction. There is someone beside me in the blackness! The knowledge that I am no longer alone is an incredible comfort, and we clasp hands tightly as our brief moment of stillness comes to an end. The water begins to reverse course, quickly picking up speed as it retreats back to the sea.

My unknown companion, who at that moment has become my dearest friend in the world, stays with me as we rocket back the way we came. We continue to pick up speed at an alarming rate, and now my greatest fear is that we'll be swept past the wharf and into the ocean itself. I grip the hand in mine more tightly, kicking and paddling awkwardly at right angles to the flow as I desperately try to reach something to anchor ourselves against.

Suddenly, I can see again!

We emerge from the shadows back into the glow of the inferno still blazing on the school's roof. At that moment, I make a desperate grab for a narrow, vertical shadow coming up fast on my left, and I recognize it as a street sign even as my fingers close around it. I twist against the flow, barely managing to hook one leg around the stout post before my companion's inertia nearly tears my shoulder from its socket.

Wreckage, debris, and bodies stream past us like leaves in a gale. It's as if the wave has a life of its own, greedily dragging stolen treasures back to its lair. I look downstream and am surprised to find myself gazing into the eyes of Mrs. Lindsay! The old teacher, who minutes before was weeping at the sight of the burning school, now grips my hand with surprising strength, fighting for life with a determination that rivals my own. She is horizontal in the flow, her legs trailing behind her. Her cheeks are puffed with contained air, but as our gazes meet, I can see the corners of her mouth turn upward in a brave smile. The smile seems to renew my strength, and I strain to hold us back against the wave's icy clutches. Mrs. Lindsay always was a tough old bird, and I begin to hope that if I can just hold on for a few more seconds, the two of us may both live to see the dawn.

A massive shape spins past, missing me by inches. I catch a glimpse of a beautiful young girl, smiling invitingly as she holds out a bottle of Coca-Cola. I realize it's the bench from the corner of Main and Cedar, where people would sit to wait for the Greyhound bus that comes through on Tuesday afternoons and Thursday mornings.

I don't hear the thud when the bench strikes Mrs. Lindsay, but the impact vibrates up my arm, nearly tearing me from my precarious hold on the signpost. The bench continues on its way, disappearing in the distance as I look down in horror. Blood flows from the back of the old lady's head, streaming behind her like a crimson pennant. Her fingers go slack in mine as the life fades from her eyes. Bubbles escape from her now-parted lips, and though I strain to keep hold of her hand, I know I won't be able to. Her limp body seems twice as heavy, and I can feel her slipping from my grasp. Still I try, in the vain hope that she is only stunned and I may yet save her.

Against all reason, I release my fingers from the signpost, praying that my hooked leg will be enough, and reach for a more secure hold on Mrs. Lindsay's wrist. Before I can, however, her fingers slide from my grasp and I watch in despair as she is carried away.

My God, *I think as she disappears into the murky gloom.* I'm so sorry, Mrs. Lindsay.

A muffled, repeated booming draws my attention back upstream, and I feel my eyes widen in terror. A massive white shape emerges from the darkness, bouncing and rolling slowly in my direction. It takes me a moment to recognize what it is: Jim Benson's car! The 1937 Packard looks as big as a whale as it bears down on me, although I note that it seems to be slowing as the retreating water begins to become shallow. I freeze momentarily, torn between waiting to see if it will stop before reaching me or letting go and taking my chances with what remains of the wave.

I wait too long.

The car hits the street sign half a second after I release it, breaking the post off at its base. The sheer mass of the Packard blocks the flow of water, slowing it dramatically on the downstream side. I'm still trying to swim clear when the front fender rotates around, pushing my trailing left leg downward and crushing it against the street. I scream, bubbles erupting in front of my face as I vainly try to pull free of the agonizing weight, but the car has finally stopped with my leg trapped beneath it.

At that moment, my head suddenly breaks the surface as the diminishing wave recedes toward the wharf. The water causes my body to roll, and something snaps in my knee as my pinned leg bones grind and crunch. The agony tears another ragged scream from me, sounding unnaturally loud after being under water so long. I finally come to rest on my side, trembling violently with cold and lingering terror, as the last few inches of the wave trickle and slide past me.

Weakly, I raise my head, vomiting seawater through my mouth and nose in great, retching gouts. I see bodies littering the street amid the wreckage, some showing faint signs of life, but most lying in limp, rag-doll sprawls. Scattered screams rise around me as the injured cry out in the darkness, but far too many of my neighbors are beyond help. A moment later, the air raid siren begins to wail, and I'm glad that someone had the presence of mind to alert the surrounding area of the disaster. They'll hear the siren all the way over in Silver Creek.

The world begins to gray out, and I finally give in to exhaustion. The agony in my leg is a distant thing now, almost unnoticeable, and my vision narrows to a pinpoint. My eyelids drift shut as I wait for unconsciousness to claim me.

My wait isn't long, and when the darkness comes, it is a blessing.

I twitched awake, blinking in a soft glow that seemed to radiate warmth and security. It faded as soon as I opened my eyes, leaving me in unfamiliar shadows, and I wondered if it had ever really been there to begin with.

Disoriented, I gazed at the surrounding windows uncomprehendingly, still tasting seawater in the back of my throat and wondering where I was and how I could be sitting curled up on hard floorboards. Only a moment before, I had been lying on Main Street with a car crushing my leg. …Hadn't I?

A hand stroked my hair, and I recoiled, choking back a cry.

"Benny…?"

At the sound of Mom's voice, it all came back to me—I was in the cupola. Moe emerged from beneath the quilt, stretching, and as my heartbeat began to slow, I noticed that while the room was nighttime cool, it wasn't bone-chilling. I reached out with my gift, probing all around for the gloomy spirit, but it was nowhere in range. *It must be off sulking somewhere else,* I thought groggily. I glanced at my watch: *03:54.* I'd been out for hours. *Way to go, Sergeant Rock,* I chided myself inwardly. *Asleep on guard duty. They can shoot you for that, you know.*

"Honey, it's the middle of the night. What are you doing here?"

I unfolded myself painfully, rising to my feet and rolling my shoulders to work out the kinks. "I was waiting for you to wake up," I confessed, turning, "but I guess I fell asleep myself."

A chuckle drifted from the shadows in front of me, warm and affectionate. "Doofus," she teased. In that moment, she sounded more like the Mom I knew than she had for a couple of days, and my heart swelled with love for her.

"Are you okay?" I asked.

"Sure, hon. I just needed to catch up on sleep." Another chuckle. "I guess we both did, huh? Must be the stress of the move."

I didn't think the move had been all that stressful, but I let it go. She was actually talking to me for a change, and I didn't want to break the mood. "You ready to come down?" I asked hopefully.

She might have paused before answering, but if so it was brief enough that I couldn't tell for sure. "I probably should," she replied. "If I don't feed you every now and then, people will start to talk."

I smiled, suddenly realizing that I was starving. "Yeah, Moe won't share his kibbles," I teased back, "but water hasn't been a problem. We just drink from different toilets."

"*Ugh*...gross, Benny. Give me a hand, will you?"

I helped her out of the rocking chair, and we made our way downstairs.

Forty minutes later, the eastern sky was showing a band of pink through the kitchen window as we put together a big breakfast of eggs, sausage, and pancakes. The smells were comforting, as well as our familiar routine of her manning the stove while I fetched, measured, and stirred. I'm good with brainless labor. In between exchanges of easy banter, I found myself absently humming the tune from the vineyard that was still stuck in my head. Visions from my latest dream kept trying to encroach as well, but I purposely ignored them for the time being. I was too tired to think about all of that, and I figured there would be plenty of time to process all of it later. All in all, it looked like things were pretty much back to normal, and I was feeling a lot better as soon as we sat down together and the hot food started to fill the snarling hole in my stomach.

I'd already killed the eggs and was halfway through my stack of syrup-drenched pancakes before I slowed down enough to talk. By then I'd already decided that I didn't want to ruin things by bringing up yesterday's weirdness, so I set out on what I hoped would be safer ground instead. "I've been looking at your drawings the last couple of days," I tossed out casually. "They're really good."

Mom had been staring at her plate with her chin in her hand, but she looked up at my comment to offer me a smile. "Thanks, hon. I'm glad you like them. This place has really inspired me."

"I guess it has—you've been cranking stuff out like a machine." I paused to take another bite, intentionally keeping the conversation at an unhurried pace and using the pause to gently probe at her emotions. Okay so far, but something told me that I should proceed carefully. "So," I continued after swallowing, "what's with the little girl?"

Her gaze hardened almost imperceptibly, wariness rippling her emotional water, and I wondered why. But her feelings and expression eased when I simply looked back at her—Mr. Innocent—and her smile returned. "Nothing's *up* with her, Benny. I just started drawing the vineyard, and something seemed to be missing. It needed a little girl, that's all."

"Oh, so she isn't real?" I asked. Her wariness rippled again, and I quickly put some icing on the question to put her back at ease. "I thought maybe you had seen one of the neighbor kids goofing around in there."

Mom shook her head. "I haven't seen anyone. We're kind of off the beaten track out here, aren't we? No, it's more like that landscape I did up at Lake Shasta last year. Remember how I turned that radio tower into a tree?"

She was being evasive—I could feel it. Substituting a tree for a tower in a single landscape was a far cry from the same little girl recurring over and over again. I wondered what she wasn't telling me and why the truth made her so uncomfortable. I briefly considered digging a bit more but then decided not to press my luck—at least for now. The last thing I wanted was for her to shut me out again, so I just smiled. "Well, like I said, the pictures are great. She's really… lifelike."

Mom smiled briefly back at the compliment and then returned her attention to her plate. I followed her gaze, noting that she'd hardly eaten anything—mostly she'd just pushed the food around with her fork. Come to think of it, I couldn't remember her eating much of anything the last few days, and concern pushed my other thoughts to the background. "Mom…are you okay?" I asked, leaning forward.

"Hmm?" She looked up, and for the first time I noticed that her face was starting to look a little gaunt, her hair hanging limp and unwashed. "I'm fine, Ben—just tired. I'll feel better after I've slept in a bed for a change." Her gaze focused as she studied my face. "I think *you* could use some shut-eye too, Bub. Tell you what: let's leave the dishes for now. They'll keep until after we've had some decent sleep."

Bed sounded good. Between all the bad dreams lately and spending the previous night on the cupola floor, I was beat. I helped Mom back upstairs, listening at her door until I heard her pull up the covers, and then went to my room with Moe trailing behind me.

My eyes began to close as soon as my head touched the pillow, and I wondered nervously if I'd be reliving more of that awful night back in 1946. Sleep came before I had time to worry much about it, though, and there were no dreams.

Maybe pancakes were good for that.

SEVENTEEN

MOE WAS GROWLING.

I blinked, squinting in the brightness and momentarily puzzled as to why the light seemed so different in my room. I was hot, my sheet clinging to me as I lay in a rectangle of sunshine slanting in from my window. It took a few seconds for the memories of the last twenty-four hours to come trickling back, and I glanced at my watch, finally realizing why the sun was so high on my wall. *11:38*. I'd been asleep for over six hours. Wow.

The sound of loud knocking drifted up from the entry hall, and Moe growled again, ending with a muted "*Wuf!*"

I kicked free of the sheet and pulled on a pair of running shorts before making my way to the hall. I rubbed sweat and sleep from my eyes, my footfalls heavy and awkward with drowsiness, and noted as I passed that Mom's door was standing open, her bed empty. Shooting a quick glance back over my shoulder, I wasn't surprised to see the door to the attic stairs standing open. *Back at it again,* I thought. *Terrific.*

The knocking came again, sounding a little insistent now. "Hold on…I'm coming!" I shouted as I hurried downstairs. Moe beat me there, standing with his forepaws on the door and his tail wagging, and I had to push him aside before I could open it. A light breeze drifted in, as cool and refreshing as an angel's kiss.

Ab stood on the porch, wearing her customary black jeans and a maroon *Silver Creek Buccaneers* T-shirt with the sleeves cut away. Her eyebrows rose as she looked at me, lips turning upward in a bemused smile. "Sleeping in a little late this morning?" she teased.

I offered her half a smile in return and almost invited her in, but then crossed the threshold to join her on the porch instead. I moved past her and sat down on the top step, half turning to lean my back against the rail post. The breeze felt great and was helping to clear the last of the cobwebs from my head.

Ab lowered herself down across from me, mirroring my pose against the opposite post. "You okay, Wolfman?"

"Yeah," I began, my voice raspy. Then I frowned, scratching where drying sweat made my scalp itch, and shook my head. "No."

"What's up?"

We sat there for a long while, and I split my attention between idly watching Moe romp around the yard and meeting Ab's gaze as I brought her up to date. Her eyes widened in fascinated interest as I told her about the chase through the vineyard, and by the time I got to the part about pushing against the invisible force holding the cupola door closed, she was leaning forward with her elbows on her knees. I wrapped up my story by recounting my latest dream about the tidal wave and then sat back when I was finished, all talked out.

We shared a minute or two of thoughtful silence while Ab frowned at empty space, mentally digesting everything I'd just told her. I let her take all the time she needed, inhaling the tangy smell of summer-dry grass as I tried to sort out my emotions. I was both interested and scared, I realized, but worry over Mom's odd behavior was mixed in there, too. Toss in feeling overwhelmed by the pile of unanswered questions that kept stacking up, along with my frustration over having no idea about how to begin answering them, and I was pretty much a mess.

About the only thing I knew for sure was that I needed a glass of water.

Ab finally rose to her feet, brushing dust from the seat of her jeans. "Do you have anything going on today, or can you come with me for a while?"

I shrugged. If the last couple of days were any indication, Mom wouldn't even notice that I was gone. "Come with you where?"

"You'll see," she replied. "I want to do some research."

I shrugged again. "Sure, I guess… No, wait," I amended a second later. "My tires are still flat, and I'm out of tubes."

"They sell 'em at the hardware store," Ab said and then headed for her bike. "Go make yourself beautiful, Wolfman—I'll be back in a few!"

I showered and dressed quickly, and even had time to clean up the breakfast dishes before Ab came back. I paid her for the inner tubes, and we worked together to swap them out on my wheels. She was faster than I was—all that restoration work on her own bike had turned her into a pro—and I had to hurry to keep up. "Are you bringing Moe?" she asked when we were done.

I nodded.

"You'll need a leash, then."

I went inside for it and paused at the base of the stairs on my way back out. "Bye, Mom!" I shouted.

No answer…but then again, I guess I hadn't really been expecting one.

We left, swooping down the switchback drive to the road, and I was surprised when Ab veered away from downtown. It took me a minute to realize that we were headed for Silver Creek, and I pedaled harder to pull up alongside her. "So where are we going?" I asked again.

"Someplace where hopefully we can find a few answers," she replied. I tried pressing her further, but that was all she'd say. Shrugging, I settled back to enjoy the ride.

We passed the vet's office on the outskirts of town, and I remembered that I'd never gotten around to posting a flyer there in case Moe's original family was looking for him. It made me feel a little guilty, but after one glance at Moe trotting alongside me, I cruised on by without slowing. *Maybe we'll stop there on the way back home,* I thought.

Maybe.

We rode through downtown Silver Creek, Ab waving and calling out occasional greetings to kids we passed on the street. We made a brief stop at a mom-and-pop market, and I held our bikes while Ab ran inside. She came out a minute or so later with a small plastic sack that she hung on her handlebars before we set off again. A library came up on our left, and I wondered momentarily if we'd stop there, but Ab didn't even glance that way. Research, she'd said. But research *where?*

We were nearly at the outskirts on the far side of town when my curiosity was finally satisfied. Ab cut right, turning into a drive beside a sign that read "Autumn Leaves Residential Care Home."

This is it? I wondered.

It looked like a bunker—a wide, flat-roofed place made of cinder blocks. It was surrounded by poplar trees so old that their roots had cracked the concrete walkways and had rippled the asphalt of the parking lot. Maybe ten or twelve cars were parked on the side marked "Staff Parking," but only three were on the side marked "Visitors." Moe and I followed Ab as she braked to a stop beneath a wide overhang that shaded the glass front entrance. "This is your big plan?" I asked.

"Yep," she replied, and then looked at me with a serious expression. "I didn't know if you'd come if I told you where we were going. Is this going to creep you out?"

"No," I said, and then frowned at her in confusion. "Why would it?"

She shrugged. "Some people get really uncomfortable around old folks, that's all. And I'll be honest: a lot of them are in pretty bad shape. But they're all really nice, and I've been coming here for years. This is the place to go if you want to learn about the *real* local history—which closets have skeletons, who did what and why, and where all the bodies are buried. Every town has its secrets, and if there's anyone who will know something about your ghosts, they'll be here. You up for it?"

"Sure. Just give me a sec." I gave Moe a drink from a hose lying coiled beneath a privet hedge to one side and then tied his leash to a metal post supporting the overhang and hooked him up. He was panting after the long run and stretched out comfortably on the cool concrete.

We pushed through the glass doors, stepping into a tiled hall with a reception desk at the far end. The air was cool, carrying a faint whiff of urine and whatever hospitals use to clean it up with, and elevator music issued softly from speakers in the ceiling. It was a little depressing, really, and I tried to shake the feeling. A chubby lady wearing bright pink scrubs smiled as we stepped up to the reception desk. "Well, hi, Ab! Who's your friend?"

"Hey, Nancy. This is Ben. He just moved to the cove, and I thought I'd introduce him to some of the gang."

The woman frowned slightly. "We served lunch a little while ago, so most are napping now. Carl and a few others are in the day room, though." She gestured down the hall to our left. "You know the way."

We thanked her and walked further into the building. We passed by a nurse's station where another woman and a man called out hellos to Ab, and emerged into a large multipurpose room on the far end. Tables and plastic chairs were placed at random across the white linoleum floor, along with three or four vinyl sofas clustered around an old console TV. Bookshelves loaded with board games, puzzles, and paperbacks lined the left-hand wall, a drinking fountain and shuffleboard table were on the right, while the back wall was all windows looking out on a well-tended flower garden.

Eight or ten people were scattered around the room—most sitting hunched in wheelchairs, and the rest with either canes or walkers beside them. One old man painstakingly turned the page of a newspaper laid out on the table in front of him, while nearby two ladies chatted softly over their knitting. Another man leaned sideways in his chair, his mouth slack as he stared at nothing. I felt sorry for him.

Ab led me toward the sofas, where a paunchy old man who was bald except for a narrow wreath of white just above his ears sat with his hands folded on his belly. On the opposite end of the sofa was a shriveled black woman with her head tied up in a bright yellow kerchief. They were watching an old movie on TV, and I recognized *The Day the Earth Stood Still*—the original, not the remake. A sci-fi classic. I'd seen it about a hundred times.

The old man and woman both looked up from where the alien Klaatu was teaching Mrs. Benson the words that would keep Gort the robot from wiping out Washington, DC with his heat ray. "Abby!" cried the woman.

"Hey there, sugar!" the man said, offering Ab a lopsided grin. "Did you bring any bourbon?"

Ab shook her head, smiling. "Come on, Carl—you know you're not supposed to drink anymore."

"Don' listen to this ol' fool, Abby," advised the woman. "He tryin' to get you in trouble." She turned her attention to my face, studying me closely, and I felt an odd, prickly sensation—like Peter Parker when his spider-sense starts tingling. Without thinking, I reached out toward her with my gift and then almost jumped in surprise. It was like touching a spark! My eyes widened slightly, and I watched as the shadow of a smile touched the old woman's lips.

"How about a pack of smokes, then?" Carl pressed, his eyes twinkling.

Ab snorted. "Oh, right…like I'd ever try *that* again. They didn't let me back in this place for a month, remember?"

"Come *on*, kid. You can't just leave me here dying of nothing!" The old man winked at her. "So who's your boyfriend?"

Ab flushed. "It's not like that. This is Ben Wolf. He just moved into the old Black place. Ben, these are my friends Carl Thielen and Lisette Gautier."

I stepped forward, first shaking hands with Carl and then moving to the old woman. Instead of shaking, though, she turned my hand over, studying my palm through a set of thick reading glasses that were secured around her neck by a loop of bright purple beads. After a moment, she looked back up at me. "You got the sight, don' you, boy? *Hoo…*you got it *strong*." Her gaze was clear despite her age —almost piercing—and her voice was as rich as molasses.

I shifted my feet, uncomfortable under her gaze, and tried to smile. "Sorry, ma'am…I'm not sure what you mean."

The enigmatic smile touched her lips again, and she patted my hand reassuringly before releasing it. "Sure you do, *cher,* but tha's alright. You come back and see ol' Lisette when you ready." She turned her gaze back to the TV, where Mrs. Benson was gravely repeating, *"Klaatu...Barada...Nikto."*

"Lisette is our local psychic," Ab explained. "She moved here with her husband in the 1960s when he took a job at the Pacific Lumber Company down in Scotia. But she was born and raised in the South." She looked past me. "Where was that again, Lisette? And didn't you tell me your mother was psychic, too?"

"New Orleans, *cher.*" She pronounced it *Nawlins*. "Lived with *ma mère et ma grand-mère* before marryin'. Women in my family *all* had the sight."

"Aw, don't listen to Marie Laveau and all that bayou bullshit," Carl interrupted. "Next she'll want to sacrifice a chicken or some damn thing."

Lisette gave him the finger, never taking her eyes from the TV.

"C'mon, Lizzy...show Ben how you got them beads!"

She laughed—a rich, mellow sound. "You *hush,* ol' fool. He not ready for *that*."

They shared a conspiratorial chuckle, and something in their tone made me flush, although I had no idea what they were talking about. Come to think of it, I was pretty sure I didn't want to.

Ab elbowed me, grinning. "Don't let them bother you, Wolfman—these two have been best friends for years. They're like this all the time."

The three carried on like that for another few minutes, Carl and Lisette asking questions about local gossip and people, all of which sounded pretty boring to me. Then again, maybe if I was stuck in a place like Autumn Leaves, even boring news might be better than nothing.

Carl settled back, at last getting down to business. "So what brings you out to the House of the Living Dead? If you're ghost hunting again, you might as well just stick around here. One of us is bound to oblige you any minute now."

"We're looking into something," Ab explained. "Is there anyone here who might know something about the history of the Black house?"

The old man considered the question. "I might be able to point you in the right direction," he said after a moment, and then his eyes narrowed mischievously. "It'll cost you, though."

Ab snorted. "Doesn't it always?" She tossed him the plastic sack she'd brought from the mom-and-pop market.

Carl reached inside and pulled out a bag of butterscotch candies. "*That's* my best girl! Thanks, sugar!" He unwrapped one and popped it in his mouth, rolling his eyes in pleasure, and then passed the bag to Lisette. "Okay, so if anyone would know about the Black place, it'd be Eleanor Markham," he confided. "Her folks worked up at the inn, and she grew up playing on the Black property." He frowned. "You might have to come back, though. She's kind of in and out most days, and this ain't been a good week for her."

"How is she today?" Ab asked.

Carl craned his neck around to look at an old woman slouched in a wheelchair by the garden window. Then he turned back, shaking his head. "Sorry, kid."

"She be alright," Lisette disagreed, still staring at the TV. I could hear the butterscotch clack against her teeth as she worked it around in her mouth.

"Nah, she's broccoli today, poor thing. Maybe tomorrow."

"Give her a candy an' talk to her," Lisette insisted. "She come 'round."

"We'll give it a try," Ab decided, bending to take a butterscotch from the bag. "Thanks."

The movie end credits were starting to roll on the TV. Lisette stirred, leaning heavily on her cane as she came to her feet. "Come on, ol' fool," she commanded, pulling a pack of playing cards from the pocket of her housedress. "You quit pesterin' Abby and Ben. Come play me some gin rummy now."

"For how much?"

Her eyebrows raised. "How much you feel like losin'?"

Ab and I crossed the room as they headed for a table.

Eleanor sat by herself, wrapped in a knitted shawl despite being in a patch of sunlight. She stared straight ahead, her eyes milky and lids at half-mast behind thick, horn-rimmed glasses. Her white hair was thin and wispy, showing a pink scalp beneath, and the skin on her hands was crepe-thin and dark with liver spots.

We dragged a couple of the plastic chairs over. "Mrs. Markham?... Eleanor? It's Abigail Chambers." She smiled sweetly, keeping her voice low and reassuring, and I got the feeling she had a lot of experience with this sort of thing. "Do you mind if we sit with you a while?" She unwrapped the butterscotch and placed it in the old woman's hand.

After a moment, the old woman frowned down at the candy, studying it carefully as if trying to figure out what it was. At last she slowly brought it to her mouth and then returned her gaze to the garden outside.

"How are you feeling today, Mrs. Markham? Has your son Larry been in to see you this week?" Ab went on like that for five or ten minutes, trying to coax the woman into the conversation by talking about the weather, various happenings around town, and specific details that meant nothing to me. She went on to tell the woman who I was and what had been going on in the vineyard and the cupola, asking if she might know anything about it. Still nothing. There was just no drawing her out. I sat there quietly, feeling out of place since I had nothing to contribute, and turned my gaze outside the window as my mind began to wander. The old woman remained unresponsive, sucking the candy while staring ahead and seemingly unaware that we were even there. It was sad and a little disappointing. It looked like we'd come all that way for nothing.

"Ben..."

I turned back to them, raising my eyebrows. "Yeah?"

Ab gave me an exasperated look. "Quit the humming, will you? I think it's bothering her."

I shifted my gaze, noting that Mrs. Markham had turned her head to stare at me, and I flushed. "Sorry," I told them, and then shrugged. Try as I might, I just couldn't shake yesterday's tune from my head. It was stuck in my brain like a tick.

Ab sighed. "It's okay...Mrs. Markham doesn't want to talk today anyhow." She leaned forward, kissing the old lady on the temple before rising to her feet. "We'll come back soon, though, okay?" she asked, but Eleanor's only reaction was to turn back to the window.

We started toward the exit and then stopped a few steps later to exchange a wide-eyed look as softly, haltingly, a voice began to sing behind us:

"Blue skies...smiling at me...

Nothing but blue skies...do I see..."

It was the song from the vineyard.

EIGHTEEN

AB AND I TIPTOED BACK AS ELEANOR MARKHAM CONtinued singing softly, as if to herself:

"Bluebirds…singing a song

Nothing but bluebirds…all day long

Never…" Her voice trailed off, the last note hanging expectantly in the air as she frowned, her eyebrows coming together. She inhaled twice, opening her mouth as if almost remembering the next line, only to close it again when whatever she was thinking wasn't quite right.

The seconds dragged by, and I cleared my throat, searching for something encouraging to say, but Ab stopped me with a hand on my arm. "Don't," she whispered. "Just give her time."

Remembrance then flooded the woman's expression, and she took up the song again, going through the bridge and to the end without pausing:

"Never saw the sun shining so bright

Never saw things going so right

Noticing the days hurrying by
When you're in love, my how they fly
Blue days...all of them gone
Nothing but blue skies...from now on..."

With that, the old woman bowed her head, her shoulders shaking. At first I thought the song had struck her as funny, but a second later I realized she was crying. Ab knelt beside the wheelchair and took her hand. Eleanor raised her head, looking into her face with tears streaking her cheeks. "She died, you know," the woman told her. "Oh, Abigail, she died so *young!*"

"*Who* died, Mrs. Markham?" Ab murmured, bringing her other hand up to stroke her hair.

"Why, Bonnie did," she explained, drying her cheeks with a corner of her shawl. "I'll never forget her—she *loved* that song. But I lost her...I lost my best friend."

I stepped forward, squatting in front of the wheelchair to place myself in her field of vision. "Bonnie?" I pressed softly, and watched as Mrs. Markham's gaze shifted to me.

"Bonnie," she said, nodding as her eyes welled again with tears. "Bonnie Black—Claire's sister."

I straightened, the unexpected revelation rocking me momentarily. It was like having a punch land that you never even saw coming. Ab glanced at me, eyebrows raised, and I shook my head in reply. This was all news to me.

"Claire Black had a *sister?*" Ab asked. "Are you sure?"

"Such a sweet girl, and *so* full of life," Eleanor went on, snuffling, and I wondered if she'd even heard the question. "Precocious, I suppose you'd say, and very much a tomboy too, but everyone loved her, especially Claire."

"What happened, Mrs. Markham?" Ab, murmured, still stroking her hair.

The old woman's eyes narrowed slightly, her gaze seeming to focus on something far off. "The wave," she said. "It rose from the darkness and swept through town like the wrath of God." She shook her head. "I don't know what we'd done to make God so angry, but whatever it was, we all paid the price for it that night. Nearly every family lost someone. Mother was never the same afterward. Nobody was, really."

"And Bonnie?"

"I was only six," Eleanor explained. "I asked afterward, but nobody would tell me anything. It was years before I learned the details. I remember the earthquake, though, and how it shook all my toys off the shelf in my room." The old woman paused, frowning slightly as if replaying the image seen through her six-year-old eyes.

"What happened after the earthquake?" Ab prodded.

"The shaking woke people all over town, so everyone was up when the fire bell rang a few minutes later." The woman's clarity seemed to be improving as she told her story. "Mr. Black went to help, leaving the girls alone at the house. It was the last time anyone saw Bonnie alive. It was still well before dawn, and poor Claire must have fallen back to sleep." The faraway look left her face, and I was surprised when she turned toward me, reaching out to pat my arm. "It really wasn't her fault, young man. Claire was *always* the responsible one. Bonnie must have slipped past her to see what all the excitement was about."

I placed my free hand overs hers and gave it a gentle squeeze. "Did they find her body?"

She shook her head, now completely with us and focused. "Oh, no, but then again, there were so many who were never found. The wave carried away more than it left behind. When all was said and done, less than half of the new headstones that went up in the cemetery had coffins to go with them. Bonnie was just one of many. Of course, after the earthquake and wave and that terrible aftershock, of course, which frightened us all, too—well, there just was so much confusion that it was late in the morning before anyone even noticed that Bonnie was missing." Eleanor's lower lip began to tremble, fresh tears spilling down her cheeks, and I got a little misty myself as her next words were punctuated by hitches and sobs. "By then Claire, bless her…had…had turned the inn into a shelter and hospital. And…after her father nearly…nearly dying, the news that Bonnie was gone… Oh, it just *broke* her." The old woman brought her palms to her face, weeping again. "That poor girl," she sobbed, her voice muffled behind her hands. "That poor, *poor* girl…"

Ab gently rubbed the woman's back while she cried, whispering soothing words that I couldn't make out. All I could do was sit there, staring at the floor while everything soaked in.

Aunt Claire's sister. My Aunt Bonnie.

I looked up when Ab finally straightened. Mrs. Markham had cried herself out and was now slumped in the wheelchair with her chin on her chest, sleeping. "I'll take her back to her room," Ab said quietly. "Why don't you take off? I'll catch up with you later."

"I can wait," I offered.

Ab shook her head. "Don't bother. I'm going to be a while. Now that I'm here, I'll catch hell if I don't make the rounds and say hello to everybody. Besides, I need some time to think, and I can do that better if I don't have to keep introducing you all afternoon. No offense."

"None taken." I nodded toward the sleeping woman. "If she wakes up before you leave, tell her I said thanks, okay?"

"You bet." Ab stepped behind the wheelchair and began pushing it toward the door.

A thought occurred to me a second or two later. "Hey," I called after her softly.

She stopped, turning to look back at me over her shoulder.

"All this stuff you do...I mean, hanging out here and everything." I paused, not quite sure what I wanted to say, and then finally offered up the only thing I could think of. "You're...pretty cool."

Ab grinned and then winked at me. "I know."

Moe was all rested up and ready to go when I exited the building, and he trotted happily alongside me as I pedaled slowly back toward Windward Cove. My brain felt like it was bulging with all the new data that had just been stuffed into it, and I enjoyed the sunshine and fresh air while I gave myself time to digest it all.

The vet's office came up on my left, and after a brief hesitation, I finally gave in to guilt and made myself veer into the parking lot. I'd never gotten around to making up a flyer about Moe, so I settled for explaining things to the lady behind the front counter and leaving my cell phone number instead. Maybe it wasn't as much effort as I'd originally planned, but it was enough to ease my conscience. Besides, it had been days already, and all in all, I wasn't worried. If Moe's family was really looking for him, they would have stopped by before then, right? The lady was nice, writing down all of the information. She even told me that they offered a free initial examination for rescued pets and urged me to call soon to set up an appointment. I promised I would and left there feeling better about dropping by.

My stomach was growling by the time I got to Hovey's, and after one whiff of the smells coming from the old drive-in, I swung into the parking lot. It was already after 3:00, and I had used up my dawn breakfast a long time before. I rode past the only car in the lot—a maroon Jeep Liberty with a "Buccaneers" sticker on the rear bumper—and by the time I leaned my bike against the front wall, I already knew what I'd be having from scanning the hand-lettered signs in the windows.

Mike saw us through the kitchen reach-through when Moe and I sauntered inside and barked at us from where he stood at the grill. "Hold on there, chief—the pooch stays outside! Health code."

"Oh, sorry," I said, Mike's gravelly voice stopping me halfway to the counter. I shifted my weight nervously from one foot to the other, wondering if I could still order something or if I should just take off.

"Take him to the patio out back," Mike offered, his voice sounding a lot less harsh this time. "You know what you want?"

"Your corn dog special and a root beer float."

"You got it. I'll bring it out in a minute."

"Okay, thanks." I did an about-face and headed back through the door, my nervousness easing off. Mike's size and that growl of his still made me jumpy, but he was beginning to seem like not such a bad guy.

Moe followed me while I pushed my bike around to the back of the building, where we found a big cement patio bordered by pepper trees. Redwood picnic tables stood beneath a corrugated metal overhang that shaded the half of the patio nearest the building, while concrete tables beneath umbrellas of rusty aluminum stood in the sun.

I was leaning my bike against one of the support posts of the overhang when a low voice surprised me, making me jump. "Well if it isn't Big Ben," said a girl. "And all by himself, too."

I was still in the sun and had to squint before I saw Kelly Thatcher lounging in the shade. She sat with her legs crossed, her elbows resting on the tabletop behind her. Her teeth and the whites of her eyes stood out against her tan as she smiled at me. "Oh, hey," I said, trying to sound casual. "I didn't see you there." I grabbed Moe's collar before he could jump on her and made him lie down instead. "How's it going?"

Kelly shrugged, the movement as graceful and controlled as some exotic cat. She was wearing khaki shorts and a loose, gauzy blouse unbuttoned partway to show a bikini top underneath. I swallowed, forcing myself to keep my gaze north of her neckline as I sat on the tabletop across from hers, my feet on the bench. "Here for a late lunch, too?" I asked.

"Making a food run," she replied. "Alan's mom and dad are out of town for a couple of days, so he threw a hot tub party."

"Sounds like fun."

Again the shrug. "It's alright," she replied, "but I thought it would be a good idea to throw some burgers to the apes. Most of the guys have been drinking beer all afternoon, and they're starting to get rowdy. Alan hasn't even noticed the way Rick keeps staring at me." She sighed and stretched her legs, still looking at me. "Like I'm a piece of beef jerky or something."

I nodded noncommittally. Much as I wasn't a Rick fan, I couldn't say I really blamed him.

"His girlfriend is getting *super* pissed," Kelly added. "Mostly at me, like it's *my* fault." She frowned, her face going all pouty.

I didn't think it was one of her better expressions, but maybe that was just me.

"You don't think that's right, do you?"

I shook my head. "Absolutely not."

Her pout eased some. "Really?"

"Yeah, you're *nothing* like beef jerky." I paused, frowning at the roof while I pretended to give the issue serious thought. "You're more of a Hostess Sno-Ball."

"A *Sno-Ball?*"

I nodded, giving her my best serious expression. "The pink kind."

The last of the pout dissolved from her face, and she giggled. "You're cute."

I thought so, too—right then, anyway—but Mike lumbered out the back of the diner before I had a chance to prove it some more.

“That’s thirty-two even,” he told Kelly, setting a cardboard box full of burgers and fries wrapped in wax paper on the table beside her. She continued to smile at me, opening her purse and handing Mike two twenties without looking up.

I watched Mike head back inside, and when I turned to Kelly again, I noticed another button was open on her blouse, exposing a flat, tanned midriff below her bikini top. I wondered if she knew it had come undone. *Eyes north!* I told myself, and quickly shifted my gaze back up to her face.

“So…” Kelly said, changing the subject, “you and Abigail. How’s *that* going?”

I shook my head, confused. Had news of our ghost hunting already gotten out? “What do you mean?” I asked.

“You guys seem to be really into each other, that’s all.”

Mike came back out, setting my corn dogs and float on the table beside me before turning to give Kelly her change. She accepted it wordlessly, still staring at me with her eyebrows raised.

“That’s four bucks, kid,” Mike said, turning back my way.

I dug out five singles and handed them over, looking up at him. “Thanks,” I said, grateful for the chance to break eye contact with Kelly. Maybe it was partly because I still had a hard time sorting through the jumble of emotions that came off her in waves, but something in her gaze was starting to make me squirm.

Mike took the bills from me with a nod and then disappeared back inside.

“You haven’t answered my question,” Kelly prompted. She rose, turning to toss her purse on top of the box before picking it up. I had just enough time to see that she looked just as good from that side before she turned back to me with an expectant expression.

“It’s not like that,” I told her, repeating Ab’s words from earlier.

A smile touched the corners of her mouth. “Sure looks that way.”

It was the second time that day that someone had hinted about Ab and I being more than friends, and I wondered what was up with that. It's not like we were going around with our faces mashed together or anything. Considering that the only time she'd ever even touched me was to slug me on the arm, the idea was actually kind of funny.

I gave Kelly what I hoped sounded like a relaxed chuckle. I was still uncomfortable under her scrutiny but decided that maybe playing offense for a change might put me back in control. "What's the rush?" I asked her. "After all, I've only been around a few days. At least give me a week to check out the local talent."

I thought that would make Kelly back off, but her smile only widened. She stepped closer, shifting the box to one arm, and my heart sped up as I suddenly found myself close enough to feel her body heat and inhale the coconut scent of her sunblock. Leaning forward, she plucked one of my corn dogs from the basket and took a bite, slowly chewing and swallowing with a glint of challenge in her eyes. "You won't *need* a week," she said at last, handing the corn dog to me. She turned before I could think of an answer and walked away without a backward glance.

I watched her go around the corner of the building and heard an engine start a moment later. A few seconds after that, I saw the Jeep Liberty on the road heading back toward Silver Creek.

"Careful with that one, kid," growled a voice, and I looked over to see Mike leaning in the doorway, arms crossed. "Her kind is nothing but trouble."

He turned and disappeared inside without waiting for a reply, so I looked down at the corn dog in my hand instead, staring at the end with the missing bite.

Wow. Had that really happened?

I took a bite of my own, relishing the secret thrill of having my mouth where hers had been. A moment later, though, I started to laugh softly, shaking my head as I realized what a complete douche I was being. *Get a grip, Wolf,* I thought. In spite of the monster crush I had on her, it didn't take a genius to figure out that Kelly Thatcher was just messing with me. *What...do you think she's headed off to break up with the football star?* I asked myself sarcastically. *Oh yeah, that's probably it. Just keep holding your breath, big guy —she'll be back any minute now to tear your clothes off.*

I laughed again, feeling a lot more grounded than I'd been a minute before, but part of me was still a little disappointed just the same. At last I pulled the rest of the corn dog off its stick, broke it into pieces, and tossed them to Moe one by one.

It helped.

I *seriously* needed to get my head on straight before I did something stupid. Besides, I had plenty of other things to keep me busy, like finding out more about Bonnie. I bit into the other corn dog and chased it with a sip from my float. Then I grinned, suddenly realizing that I knew just where to start.

It was time to read Aunt Claire's diary.

NINETEEN

MY ROOM WAS STUFFY, AND MOE AMBLED OVER TO A shady corner as soon as we crossed the threshold. He settled on the hardwood floor with a sigh, watching me with his nose between his paws while I raised the window to let in the early evening breeze.

Squatting, I pulled out the drawer of my captain's bed and set it to one side, and then reached way back to grope around in the shadows. After a moment my fingers brushed the leather binding, and I fought back an urge to pull my hand away. I was still a little nervous after what had happened the last time, but I made myself bring the diary out. Standing, I blew off the fresh layer of dust that had settled on it since the last time it had seen daylight, feeling excited and hopeful that somewhere inside would be the answers to some of my questions.

Dropping onto the bed, I stuffed my pillow between my back and the headboard and opened the front cover.

If found, please return to Claire Anne Black

Windward Cove, Calif.

Just reading the words again in Aunt Claire's neat handwriting made the back of my neck tingle. It was like having my own secret window to the past, and I turned to the first page, anxious to get started.

> *Mon, 22 Apr, '46*
>
> *Well, today started out lousy enough. The first day of school after Easter break, and I'm already worn out. I was up at the inn until after 11:00 last night getting the ledgers in order, so I was already tired this morning.*

I raised my eyes from the page, looking warily around, but my room was still my room. *Okay so far*, I thought, and continued reading:

> *Honestly, I have no idea how Lee was able to manage everything Daddy gave him to do and still graduate with high honors. Of course, I'm starting to understand how much responsibility he truly had now that more and more of it keeps shifting over to me. I suppose Daddy was still holding out hope that Lee would be coming home soon, but after his last letter when he dropped the bombshell that he has extended his service contract with the army for another year, I should have seen the handwriting on the wall. I'm sincerely proud of Lee for his service to his country and more grateful than I can say that he lived to see V.E. Day, but for the life of me, I can't understand why he feels so compelled to stay in Nuremberg until those awful trials have finished. You would think that since landing in Normandy he would have seen more than enough ugliness by now.*

A surge of excitement went through me as I suddenly made the connection. She was talking about my great grandfather! Elijah Black (who went by his middle name, Lee) had passed away long before I was born, but I remembered Mom telling me that he had fought in World War II. I shook my head, thinking how cool it would've been to have met him. I continued to read, feeling even more of a personal bond with the girl who had written the entry so long ago:

> *But I suppose I'm just being selfish. It's probably awful of me to have my nose out of joint over being asked to help with the family business. But, honestly, is it so terrible that for me to wish to be like everyone else? To get to go to dances and football and baseball games instead of always making sure the details Daddy can't be bothered with are taken care of?!? I just wish I knew if wanting those things made me normal or the most spoiled, ungrateful girl in the world.*
>
> *Anyway, this morning would have been much better if Bonnie had minded me just this once when I asked her to get ready. I had her green spring dress and slip laid out for her, as well as her bobby socks and white sweater with those lovely pearl buttons, and I thought she was going to be good. When I went looking for her, though, her clothes were right where I'd left them and she was gone. I was so mad I could just spit, but I should have guessed she'd be playing in the vineyard.*
>
> *Even then I couldn't blame her. Not really. She's been so sad, what with all the rain we've had lately. This is the first day of sunshine we've had in nearly two weeks, and Bonnie was bound to make a run for it as soon as she had half a chance. It may be wicked of me to say this, but once again, I wish Daddy would help keep an eye on her. Flora had a nice breakfast of bacon, eggs, and toast all ready and waiting*

for us, but instead I had to chase a six-year-old through row after row of grapevines with my hair in rag curlers. The little wretch thought it was funny!

As always, I couldn't stay angry with her for long, even though we were late. By the time she was in her school clothes and no longer looking like a ragamuffin, we had barely fifteen minutes before the first bell and we had to settle for cold bacon and egg sandwiches on the ride to school.

A shadow moved in my peripheral vision. Distracted, I glanced offhandedly at the girl who crossed in front of the window before my gaze returned to the page.

But, dear diary, the day turned out SO much better...

"Hey!" I said, suddenly realizing what I'd just seen. I scrambled to my feet, holding the diary in one hand with my index finger marking the page.

The room has changed again, reverting back to Aunt Claire's time while I've been reading. Like before, I'm momentarily confused by the change in furniture and pictures on the walls, and I have to remind myself that I'm still in my room. The window, which I had opened for fresh air only a minute or so before, is now closed, and morning sunlight streams between frilly, half-drawn curtains that definitely aren't mine. Outside I can see scattered clouds drifting on the wind. An open book titled Our Hearts Were Young and Gay *lies face down beside the radio on the nightstand.*

I watch as my teenage Aunt Claire takes a rolled pair of socks from the top drawer of a dresser, and I scoot hurriedly out of the way as she sits on the edge of the bed to put them on. She isn't wearing any makeup, and her hair is looped around mismatched strips of cloth like a patchwork wig. "Bonnie!" she calls as she begins to lace on a pair of white and black leather shoes. Her voice still sounds a little distant but has lost the underwater quality it had during my last vision. The part of my brain still recording details wonders if that means anything, but I'm too busy trying not to freak out to give it more than a passing thought. My heart is pounding in my chest, and it's hard to breathe. I'm fascinated, scared, and disoriented all at once, the combination making me shake with a rush of adrenaline.

"Bonnie, have you washed your face and brushed your hair yet?" There is no answer, and after a moment, Claire frowns at the open doorway, looking annoyed. "If you're still in bed after all this time, I swear *you're in trouble!" She stands, smoothing her skirt before hurrying out into the hall.*

After a brief, uncertain pause, I follow her on shaky legs. I can make out Moe where he sprawls next to the wall, reduced to an almost invisible outline by the vision. He raises his head to watch me curiously as I pass and then settles back down on the floor.

For a moment I wonder if the images will be confined to my room, but they aren't. Claire sweeps into the bedroom next to mine and then appears back at the doorway seconds later. "Bonnie!" she calls. "Where are *you?" She hurries downstairs, and I follow her past half a dozen framed portraits hanging in the stairwell that I don't have time to spare more than a glance. Claire never pauses, and as I follow her toward the kitchen, I realize that the place looks a lot better in the 1940s—inviting, even. Area rugs muffle her footfalls, and low, comfortable-looking furniture makes the place feel a lot homier. Until then I hadn't been able to imagine the house as being anything but echoey and aloof, and I wonder if Mom and I will ever make it as nice as this.*

Claire halts beneath the kitchen archway and quickly scans the room. "Have you seen Bonnie?" she asks.

A woman stands at the counter, putting slices of bread into a toaster with sides that swing open from the top like wings. She smiles briefly in greeting and then shakes her head before picking up a spatula and prodding whatever is crackling in a cast-iron skillet.

Seated at the table is a man with a narrow face and prominent widow's peak, and he looks at Aunt Claire over the top of his newspaper. He's wearing a green cardigan buttoned over a shirt and tie, and although I've never seen a picture, I'm pretty sure he's Claire's dad—my great-times-whatever grandfather. "Bonnie?" he asks, and then shakes his head. "No, although I may have heard the front door slam a few minutes ago." He frowned at his watch and then reached over to pour more coffee into his cup from an electric pot near his elbow. "You need to hurry. It's almost time to leave."

Claire turns angrily, and before I can get out of the way, she walks right through *me! I feel a momentary chill, like moving past an open door in January, followed by a slight prickly sensation that makes gooseflesh break out on my arms and sends a cold chill down the back of my neck. Then the feeling passes, and I look over my shoulder at her retreating back before turning to follow her around to the front door and out into the sunshine.*

"BONNIE!" she calls, hurrying down the porch steps. She turns without waiting for a reply, heading toward the vineyard across thick spring grass heavy with dew. I pause, looking beyond her, and am surprised to see the neatly tended rows

of grapevines beyond the board fence that is weather-beaten and barely standing in my time. The gate is standing open, and through it I see a young girl with tousled blonde hair look up. She's barefoot, wearing baggy overalls over a patched sweater. Grinning, she darts out of sight as Claire calls her name again...

And just like that, the vision was gone. Reality came back all at once, as suddenly as the flipping of a light switch.

I blinked in surprise, disoriented all over again while my brain processed the sudden shift from spring morning to summer evening. One moment the sun was bright as it climbed through scattered clouds on my right; the next moment it hung low in the west, turning the sky a deep tangerine. The fence had reverted to a sagging ruin, its missing boards making it look gap-toothed, and in a blink the vineyard was once again an untamed jungle of green.

My legs went all rubbery, and I sat down hard in the dry weeds, hugging the diary to my chest while taking several deep breaths. I shivered, the breeze cold against my damp T-shirt and the sweat I could feel trickling down my scalp. My trembling eased off after a minute or so, excitement elbowing my shock out of the way as I realized how amazing it all was. I had actually seen reruns from 1946!

But how could that happen? Was the diary somehow a connection to the past—maybe some kind of psychic window? Or had Aunt Claire's thoughts and feelings embedded the images into the diary itself, like data on a computer's hard drive?

More importantly, *could I do it again?*

My index finger was still marking the page where I'd left off, so I opened the diary again, angling the page to the fading twilight, and reread a line from that page:

But, dear diary, the day turned out SO much better than it started! Philip Garret actually talked to me. ME! Lunch was nearly over, and I was getting my home ec book from my locker when I looked up and there he was. He asked to borrow my history notes, but he's aces in history, so I think (I hope!) he was handing me a line. We talked for a few minutes, mostly about our favorite Hit Parade *songs, but other than finding out that we both like Nat King Cole, I can't for the life of me remember what we said.*

He walked me to class afterward, and everyone in home ec saw! June and Mary Lou teased me all afternoon, but I know they were happy for me (well, Mary Lou mostly—June has been carrying a torch for him since last year, but she's being swell about it so far, and if she's snapped her cap, it doesn't show.) Everyone says that Philip and Alice broke it off last week. Does this mean he has his eye on me? Why would he give me so much attention if he didn't?

I can't wait for school tomorrow!

As I read, I kept looking out of the corner of my eye to see if the visions would come back, but the world stayed in the present—at least for now. Anyway, it was getting too dark to read any more, so I closed the diary with a sigh. Disappointed, I got to my feet and moved three or four steps toward the house before I stopped, turning.

The vineyard looked blue-black as the twilight faded, and without thinking, I made my way over there instead, pausing just beyond the gatepost. The breeze was picking up, causing the vines to whisper and hiss and creak, and I realized that I could hear the surf too, pounding restlessly off in the distance.

I stood there for a long time, reaching out with my gift but sensing nothing. "Bonnie…?" I called out at last. "Are you out here somewhere?" I held my breath, straining my ears, and for a second I thought I might have heard laughter riding faintly on the wind. The sound wasn't repeated, though, so I'd probably imagined it.

I turned back toward the house, automatically looking up at the cupola, a black outline against the emerging stars. The windows were dark, which meant Mom was sleeping again, curled up in that creepy rocking chair. I wondered if she was alone.

But I knew she probably wasn't.

TWENTY

MY FIRST IDEA WAS TO RIDE RIGHT OVER TO AB'S HOUSE and tell her what had happened, but it was almost fully dark by then and I was tired from all the miles I'd already covered that day. Anyway, Ab would still be there in the morning, and if I could pry another vision or two out of the diary in the meantime, I'd have that much more to share.

Moe was waiting for me in the entry hall, all excited and bouncy like he hadn't seen me in a week, and hugging him seemed to wash away the last of the weirdness. It occurred to me then how fast I'd gotten used to having him around and how great it felt to always have an eager sidekick.

He followed me upstairs as I went to holler up the attic stairwell. "Mom? You hungry?"

No answer, and I felt the familiar twinge of irritation that was happening way too often lately. I didn't mind being upstaged by her creative streak all that much, but being flat-out ignored all the time was really starting to piss me off. The least she could do was answer.

I did my best to shake off the feeling, though. After all, I'd probably been right earlier when I assumed she was asleep, so I kept my voice cheerful and gave it another try. "Hey, Mom! I'm gonna make something to eat. You interested?"

More silence, and I was about to go up and wake her when her voice came drifting back down, sounding distracted. "No," she called back. Then, as if it was an afterthought, "...thanks anyway."

I shrugged, my irritation fading. *Fair enough,* I thought. At least she was noticing me enough to answer, and since that had been kind of hit or miss lately, I was willing to take what I could get.

I was anxious to get back to the diary, so after rummaging around in the pantry, I poured a can of chili into a pot and then fed Moe his dinner while it heated on the stove. When the chili was bubbling, I stirred in a good handful each of corn chips and shredded cheddar, and ate while standing at the counter.

Back in my room, Moe lay down on the bed, watching as I sat at my desk and reopened the diary beneath the light of my camping lantern:

> *Tue, 22 Apr '46*
>
> *I'm beginning to think that Philip really might be stuck on me, which is perfect because I think he's absolutely swoony! Today he was on the front steps when I got to school and went out of his way to hold the door for me. Not only that, but he asked to sit with me at lunch, and we talked so much that I forgot to eat! He always looks so spiffy (shirts and slacks pressed and such nice neckties), and when he sat next to me I could smell Bay Rum aftershave. He's a perfect gentleman, too! Could a girl ask for more? What will I do if he asks me for a date? Oh my goodness, what will I do if he doesn't?!*

Aunt Claire went on like that for another couple of pages, and I had to shake my head. It was hard to believe that the girl who thought some guy was "swoony" was the same stern old lady who used to scare the crap out of me when I was little. The way she wrote reminded me of the dialogue from all those old horror and sci fi movies that I'm prone to watching, and I had to make myself stop reading and remember that I was there on business. I flipped back to the start of the entry, this time relaxing and reading it slowly while occasionally glancing out of the corner of my eye to see if my room had shifted back to 1946. Nothing happened.

Hmm.

Was I doing something wrong? I thought back, trying to remember how it all had worked before, but nothing came to me. Sure, my last vision happened when I was lying on the bed, but I'd been sitting right there at the desk the first time, so I was pretty sure that wasn't it. I read on, stopping to inspect the little drawings made in the margins and examining the photos stuffed here and there. Still nothing. Her doodles weren't magic runes for time travel, and most of the photos were just anonymous faces in black and white. The old-fashioned clothes and hairstyles made the kids look older to me than they probably had been, and of all the captions that were sometimes written on the backs of the photos, only one had any meaning to me. The photo was of two girls in skirts and sweaters, the one on the left smiling radiantly while the other wore a knowing grin. Written on the back was "Mary Lou and June, 4/14/46." Well, well. Aunt Claire's besties.

I read on, taking my time and thoroughly examining each page to make sure I didn't miss anything, but the next dozen pages were all about Philip Garret's wonderfulness. It was funny at first (and, okay, *kind of* sweet) but it got a little tiresome after a while. You'd think she'd find something else to go on about. But no, aside from being swoony, Philip was apparently "the cat's meow," a "dreamboat," and "heaven sent." Way to go, Phil. I wondered offhandedly if he was related to my pal the quarterback, but then I decided I didn't really want to know—it would spoil it somehow.

The closest I came to experiencing another vision was when Claire suddenly burst into my room and collapsed face down on the bed, weeping bitterly into the pillow. It was totally unexpected, and I bolted to my feet with a yelp, not sure if I was going to pee myself or have a heart attack. Luckily, neither one happened. It was right after I'd read how Alice (Philip's ex—I had to page back to make sure) had cornered Claire in the bathroom at school and called her a "share crop." I wasn't sure what that was, but I had a pretty good idea.

Alice. You bitch.

The vision faded to nothing almost as soon as Claire hit the pillow though, and the excitement appeared to be over. Except for my heartbeat, anyway—that took a while to calm down.

It wasn't long after that that I started yawning and my eyes began to feel grainy, and I was surprised to look at my watch and see that it was nearly 11:00. I wanted to read more, but I didn't want to miss any important clues either, so I figured I'd be better off tackling it again with fresh eyes in the morning. Besides, Ab would probably kill me if I got too far ahead without her, so I closed the diary and switched off the lantern.

Moe was snoring and never woke up when I crawled into bed.

I'm running barefoot between rows of grapevines, grinning with the exhilaration of secret freedom. The dirt is cool and soft beneath my feet, each stride sending up the rich smell of summer-tilled earth. It's twilight and almost too dark to see, but this place is as familiar to me as the inside of our house, and the gray light from above is enough to guide me through the lush growth looming high above my head on either side.

A detached part of my brain is dimly aware that this is a dream, but the realization is overwhelmed by vivid images and sensations: the sound of my breathing, the cool brush of air on my bare legs, the leaves and sinewy vines that blur past in my peripheral vision. The scene around me is every bit as real as my dreams about the tidal wave but with a crucial difference: this time I know *I'm dreaming. Before, I had simply been the guy in the dream, with no sense of my own identity or realization that I was experiencing visions of the past. Now I'm slightly more removed, caught up in the scene around me, but with just enough of myself along for the ride to be able to make observations. But even those fade to the background as thoughts that are not my own fill my head.*

I've slipped out without anyone knowing, but I don't have much time. It won't be long before Claire…

[Thump-THUMP…]

…comes looking for me. She'll be mad and probably will scold me like anything, but at least…

[…Thump-THUMP…]

…she won't tell Daddy. It's just not fair that I'm always being left out! Nobody lets me do anything! *Maybe if I hurry, I can be back before…*

[…Thump-THUMP…]

Moe whined, crawling up from the foot of the bed and worming his way between my chest and arm. I blinked groggily in the darkness, my brain still more than halfway attached to the dream and not quite tuned in enough to figure out what was wrong.

Thump-THUMP…

Moe growled, staring across the room toward the open door even as I recognized the sound that had woken both of us. It was the same sound that I'd heard my first night in the house—the noise I first thought was a banging shutter but wasn't.

Thump-THUMP...

Sudden cold washed into my bedroom as the heavy tread of someone limping moved past my doorway, the temperature slowly returning to normal as it continued down the hall. I fumbled on the nightstand for my flashlight, clicking it on as I threw the covers aside and ran to the door.

The hall was empty. For a second, it looked like the stairwell door was moving, as if swinging open the final inch or two, but that could have just been because the flashlight was shaking in my hand. I held my breath, listening, but the only thing I heard was my own heartbeat.

Between my fear and the cold that lingered on the air, I was trembling like crazy, so I ducked back into my room and quickly pulled on sweatpants and a hoodie. While stepping into my slippers, I paused for a second to aim the flashlight down at my watch on the nightstand: *03:54.*

I frowned. Something about the time bothered me. I couldn't figure out exactly what, though, and when Moe whined, I dismissed the thought with a shake of my head. "Stay, boy," I muttered, heading back out into the hall. "You don't want any part of this."

I moved silently to the attic stairwell, clicking off the flashlight when I saw a faint glow filtering down from above. I began to climb the stairs, stepping on the sides of the risers so they wouldn't creak. I wasn't exactly sure what the hell I was doing—trying to sneak up on a ghost, maybe?—but it didn't matter. The only thing I was certain of was that Gloomy Gus had been prowling around the house and I needed to make sure that Mom was okay.

The stairwell seemed to get colder with every step, and by the time I reached the attic, I could see my breath. That worried me. So far, the chill had been confined to the cupola. Now, not only was it tagging along with the ghost as he wandered around, but also it seemed to be spreading beyond its original boundaries. How long would it be before the cold spread through the entire house? And did that mean the ghost was becoming more powerful? More importantly, if the ghost was becoming more powerful, *what was it feeding on?*

I crossed the floor to the cupola stairs and began to climb gingerly. I expected the door to slam shut in my face again, but it remained open as I mounted the last few steps and emerged into the light. The room was like an ice cave, and the sorrow all around me was nearly overwhelming, but either I was getting used to it or I was just too worried right then to care, because what I saw made me mentally shove it all aside.

Mom was seated at her easel, painting by the light of a kerosene lamp that she'd found somewhere. She was still wearing the jeans and green tank from two days before, but now it was spotted with paint and streaked with pencil charcoal where she'd absently wiped her hands. Her hair hung lank and oily, half held back by a rubber band, but with stray hairs escaping here and there and one heavy lock swinging in front of her eyes. She didn't appear to notice it, though, and worked with a faint, dreamy smile pulling at one corner of her mouth. As I watched, she paused, staring intently out the window into the darkness for a long moment, and then returned to her work.

If she'd noticed me standing there she gave no indication, so I cleared my throat nervously. "Uh…hi, Mom," I began. "Burning a little midnight oil?"

She continued working, now beginning to hum a tuneless melody I didn't recognize.

"That was a joke," I offered.

No response. Was she sleepwalking…or maybe sleep-*painting?*

"Mom, it's nearly four a.m.," I said, now starting to feel really uncomfortable. "Don't you think it's time you called it a night?"

She gave another glance into the blackness outside the window and then hummed some more as she dipped the tip of her brush into the paint and began to dab it lightly on the canvas in front of her.

I stepped forward, noticing for the first time that there were a lot more drawings and even a couple of new watercolors on the shelves. I could see right away that they all had a common theme. I couldn't help myself, and I examined each in turn as my fear and dread wrestled with breathless fascination.

Bonnie in her overalls, chasing a butterfly at the edge of the vineyard.

Bonnie hosting a tea party for a doll and a stuffed rabbit beneath the vines.

Bonnie grinning as she crouched in leafy shadows, watching while Claire stood looking for her in the wrong direction.

Bonnie with juice all over her cheeks as she sat eating grapes in the shade.

There were maybe a dozen more, all of them incredibly detailed, and I turned from them to see what Mom was working on. It was an oil painting, and she was just getting started. It was going to be a fairly big one—twenty-four by thirty-six inches—and she was working down from the top on what looked like a twilight sky. Below that I could see rough pencil lines that would later be the rows of the vineyard. I wasn't sure, but from the perspective of the painting, it looked as if it was the view from the cupola window, and I wondered what it would show when she was done.

Mom sighed, dropping her brush in a jar of turpentine and getting awkwardly to her feet. She turned, her gaze passing over me without recognition, and I wondered what she was seeing behind that wide, glassy stare. I stepped back, my heart turning to ice as I watched her limp slowly to the rocker, favoring her left leg. Curling up in the chair, she pulled the quilt over her as her eyes drifted closed.

I was shaking again, but it had nothing to do with the chill. All I could do was stand there helplessly, the sound of Mom's footfalls as she had crossed the floor echoing over and over in my mind. Her tread was much lighter, which is maybe why I hadn't noticed up until then, but the lopsided rhythm of her steps was exactly the same:

Thump-THUMP...

Thump-THUMP...

TWENTY-ONE

I STOOD THERE FOR A LONG TIME, NOT SURE WHAT TO do next. Eventually, I took a deep breath and stepped over to kneel beside the rocking chair. "Mom?" I said gently, shaking her arm. "Mom, are you okay?"

She made no response, sleeping deeply with her mouth open. The dim glow from the lantern threw shadows on her sunken cheeks, making her appear ancient. The shock I'd felt a few minutes before was replaced, first by concern, and then by fear bordering on panic as I continued trying to bring her around. "Mom, wake up!" I urged. The room seemed to be getting even colder, and I could feel the beginnings of a dull headache from the tension in my shoulders and neck. *"C'mon,* Mom…we need to get out of here!"

Then I scrambled to my feet, turning a slow three-sixty as my gaze swept the shadows. Another presence had just entered the room, and the temperature wavered uncertainly as the atmosphere seemed to gather close and thick around me, like there wasn't enough space in the cupola to contain it all. I figured that this was what sitting in a diving chamber must be like, only with conflicting emotions instead of air pressure. I half expected the walls to start bulging outward under the strain, and even the flame in the lantern seemed to grow dim. Then, just when I was sure all the windows would shatter any second, the freezing air tore savagely around the room in a sudden whirlwind. Mom's drawings tumbled though the air like falling leaves before the cold presence retreated down the stairs, slamming the cupola door shut as it fled.

The sound nearly made me jump out of my skin, and long seconds ticked by as I stood trembling, waiting for something else to happen.

Nothing did.

At last I let out a long, shaky breath. Tentatively, I reached out with my gift, but the chill and depression that had been so overwhelming a few moments before were completely gone. For now, anyway. The air felt considerably warmer, and the only feelings I could detect were comfort and reassurance. The lamplight brightened, pushing the shadows back toward the corners.

It was the other ghost, I realized, and it was still in the cupola with us, keeping the cold and gloom at bay. I glanced down at Mom, who was sleeping peacefully. Her mouth was closed, lips turned slightly upward as if she was having a good dream, and the more cheerful light had erased the age from her face. Relief washed over me, and could I feel the tension in my shoulders and neck start to ease.

Then Mom's eyelids blinked open, and her gaze traveled contentedly around the room for a moment before it found me. "Benny," she said, brightening. "It feels late, hon. Why aren't you in bed?"

I swallowed, struggling to keep my voice from cracking. "Can you come downstairs for a while, Mom? I need to talk to you about something."

Her smile seemed to dampen a little, and she gestured to the chair by her easel. "Have a seat," she offered. "We can talk right here."

I chewed my lower lip, seriously considering her suggestion, but then shook my head. Even with the comforting presence of the ghost watching over us, I was sick of the cupola and sick to death of being scared. I wasn't going to spend one more second of the night up here if I could help it. "Let's go to the kitchen," I insisted. "C'mon, Mom... please?"

Her eyes narrowed, and she let out a sigh of irritation before throwing the quilt aside. *"Fine,* Ben—have it your way." She let me help her to her feet but then shook off my hand and limped to the stairwell on her own. Obviously, she didn't want me touching her, and the rejection was like a slap in the face. I stepped forward, intending to take her arm again anyway, but then I thought better of it and followed her instead. She was angry, but I'd gotten what I'd wanted. There was no sense pushing it. I watched as she made her way down to the attic, leaning awkwardly on the bannister but otherwise doing okay, and I paused at the top of the stairs for a final look around the cupola.

"Thanks," I whispered.

Downstairs, she slouched in a kitchen chair and watched me in silence while I started water heating in the kettle and slid a bagel into the toaster. I was feeling more and more like my old self the longer we were away from the cupola, and I used those few quiet moments to think about what I wanted to say. I could feel Mom's sullen glare boring a hole in my back, and I didn't need my gift to sense that she was getting angrier the longer I let the silence drag out. But by then I figured we both were aware that a fight was coming, and I knew from long experience that things would be more likely to go my way if I took control right from the start. So I took my time, letting her fuse burn while I slathered the bagel with cream cheese and her favorite peach preserves, dropped an herbal tea bag into a mug of hot water, and slid both in front of her on the table.

"Did I *ask* for that?" she snapped.

"No," I shot back. "But you haven't eaten in days, and you look like shit." I could tell by the way her eyes widened slightly that my words had stung, so I pressed my advantage. "I love it that you're drawing again, and it's great that you're so happy here, but you need to come down from that goddamned room once in a while and take care of yourself. Eat and drink something. Sleep in a real bed. A shower would do you a lot of good, too."

She continued to glare at me for a moment and then picked up one half of the bagel, took a single bite, and set the remainder back on the plate. Her gaze never left mine while she chewed and swallowed, and then chased it down with a sip of tea. "Happy?" she asked at last.

"No," I told her. "Finish it."

She crossed her arms instead. "You want to tell me what this is really about?"

"I'd love to," I replied, "but judging by the last couple of days, you don't think I'm worth talking to anymore." Another subtle flash of hurt in her eyes, and I felt like I was getting through to her. "Now, can you please tear yourself away from your hobby long enough to pretend like you care?"

"Hobby?" she spat. "As I remember, my *hobby* didn't bother you when it was putting food on the table. Or when you needed shoes. Or when you were hitting me up for money so you could go to the movies. No, back in Vacaville you seemed to think my *hobby* was pretty damned convenient."

Yeowch, I thought, feeling guilty. That wasn't what I'd meant and not at all the direction I'd wanted the conversation to take. I took a deep breath, choosing my next words carefully in an effort to get the conversation back on track. "Mom, I didn't mean it that way. I know that your art is important to you..."

"Just not when it means that Ben isn't the center of the universe every second of the day," she finished scathingly, cutting me off. "Our inheritance has given us a chance for a new life—a life where I don't have to worry about where our next dollar is coming from. A life where I don't have to choose between paying the power bill or paying the rent." Her voice rose to a shout. "A life where I don't lay awake at night worrying how I can send *you* to college!"

"Don't change the subject!" I hollered back, angry that she'd put me on the defensive so easily. "That's got nothing to do with..."

"It has *everything* to do with it!" Mom rose shakily to her feet, her face white with rage except for two red spots high on her cheekbones. "The whole drive up here all you did was whine about having to leave that cracker-box apartment. You've whined about the house, whined about the town, and now you're whining because I finally get to spend some time doing something I love instead of..."

"YOUR'RE NOT *LISTENING* TO ME!" I yelled. "There's something going on here, Mom, and it's *affecting* you! Can't you see that?" She said nothing, allowing me to take a deep breath before continuing. "It's the cupola...or what's *in* the cupola. There are *ghosts* in the house, Mom. One out in the vineyard, too. But the one up in the cupola...it's like it's *seeping into you!* Ab has been helping me figure out the history of this place, and if you only knew some of the stuff that has happened since we got here, maybe you'd understand!"

She watched me for a long moment before speaking, and when she did her voice was cold with anger. "Ghosts, Ben? *Really?* That's the best you can do?" She shook her head. "You couldn't whine us back to Vacaville, so now we're down to ghosts." She was wearing an expression of contempt that I'd never seen on her before—an expression that made me feel utterly alone.

"Mom..." I began.

"I'm done talking about this, Ben. We live here now, and you'd better get used to the idea." Turning her back, she shoved her chair aside and began limping slowly toward the shadows beyond the kitchen archway.

This had been a complete disaster. I thought hard, trying to figure a way to reach her. "How have you been sleeping lately?" I called out. "Any dreams about tidal waves? Or running around in the vineyard?"

She ignored me, now halfway across the floor.

"And what about that limp of yours?" I pressed, starting to feel desperate. "How come *that* hasn't gotten better?"

She might have slowed for half a second, but I couldn't be sure. "It's a pinched nerve," she said, not looking back. She was almost to the archway.

I tried a last-ditch effort. "Who's the *girl,* Mom? The one in all the pictures. Who is she?"

That one got her. She paused with her hand on the archway molding, half turning to stare back at me with uncertainty in her gaze. Uncertainty…and maybe just a little fear.

"It's Bonnie," I accused. "…Isn't it?"

My question hung in the air for a long moment before she gave a slight shake of her head, her uncertainty disappearing and being replaced by a guarded expression. "It's just a girl," she muttered at last. "I told you before. I made her up. I don't know any Bonnie."

And then she was gone.

I stood there, unable to do anything but listen to the retreating sound of her limping footfalls until they faded away somewhere on the stairs. I felt deflated and useless. The whole thing had turned into a complete train wreck, and all I had done was drive an even bigger wedge between us. Two things I knew for sure, though. First, I had to find a way to get rid of the ghost in the cupola.

And second, my mother was lying to me.

I dropped into a chair and sat there for a long time. How long, I had no idea. Moe eventually found me and kept batting at my knee with a forepaw until I pet him, after which he curled up contentedly at my feet. All I could do was stare at the half-bagel with the bite taken out of it, feeling lost and alone.

It was just after dawn when I heard a muted thump on the front porch, bringing my head back into reality. Moe was on his feet at once, growling as he trotted to the entry hall, and I hurried to follow. I pulled open the front door, glancing left and right at the empty porch, and then recoiled when I looked down.

A dead raccoon lay on the welcome mat. For a second, I wondered if the cupola ghost was ratcheting things up a notch, but then the smell hit me and I wrinkled my nose, realizing the thing had been dead for a while. Moe wanted to sniff it, but I pushed him behind me and squatted down for a closer look. Its skull had been crushed, and I'd spent enough time on my bicycle to recognize roadkill when I saw it. Gross.

I stood again, glancing around the yard even though I knew whoever had left it there was already gone, and then closed the door long enough to retrieve a garbage bag from under the kitchen sink. I put my hands inside the plastic to pick up the carcass, and then turned the bag inside out so that I wouldn't have to touch it. No fuss, no muss. I briefly considered burying the raccoon but then tossed it into the trash bin instead, not wanting Moe to dig it up later.

I shook my head while walking back to the house. What the hell was *that* all about?

The grisly chore finished, I went upstairs to shower and dress. So far the day wasn't shaping into one of my all-time favorites, and I felt restless to be away from the house so I could talk to Ab and find out what she thought. She'd be at the coffee house soon if she wasn't there already, and I could use the ride over to clear my head and hopefully start sorting things out.

I paused on my way back downstairs, drumming my fingers on the bannister. The argument with Mom had left behind feelings of wounded regret that gnawed at my insides, and I didn't want to leave with things unresolved between us. Turning, I retraced my steps, climbing up to the cupola and stopping just inside. I reached out to test the psychic water, but the only presence I could sense in the room was Mom's, which was fine by me. I would have felt better if the comforting ghost had decided to hang around for a while, but at least the cupola's usual resident hadn't found his way back yet.

I stood at the top of the stairs for nearly a full minute, watching Mom as she sat at her easel, painting again. I knew she was aware of my presence, but I wanted to give her the chance to decide if we were on speaking terms yet. The silence in the room stretched out, long and brittle, and I was about to head back down in disappointment when at last she spoke:

"*What,* Ben?"

Relief flooded through me. "I just wanted to say I'm sorry," I confessed, my voice sounding meek in a way that normally would have bothered me but didn't then. "I don't want to fight," I went on, "and I don't want to leave Windward Cove. But when you're ready, I'd still like to talk."

Her paintbrush paused over the canvas while she thought about it. "Not now," she said after a moment. Her tone was less frosty, though, so I took it as a hopeful sign.

"Um…okay. Let me know." I swallowed, knowing that she wanted me to leave, but unable to resist throwing out a final peace offering. "I love you, Mom."

Silence.

Say it back, I pleaded wordlessly, really needing to hear it right then. *C'mon Mom…just say it back. Please?*

"I know, Ben," she said at last, finally turning to look at me. "And we'll get through this. Just not now, okay?"

I nodded, my face feeling hot, and retreated down the stairs.

TWENTY-TWO

THE AIR FELT GOOD ON MY FACE AS I COASTED DOWN TO the road, and between that and the morning sunshine (and maybe just getting out of the house), I was starting to feel a little better by the time I turned toward town.

The day was already warming up, clear with just a hint of breeze blowing in from the ocean. Moe trotted in his usual wingman position, to the right and slightly behind me, his gangly legs carrying him easily along. I forced myself to relax, lulled by the hum of my tires on the pavement and the rhythm of my breathing as I pedaled. A couple of cows grazed in the field off to our right, and a red-winged blackbird regarded us with quick, jerky head movements from its perch on the wire fence as we went by.

The sound of an engine rose up from behind us, and I veered toward the shoulder. Moe, nervous around cars, crossed the ditch to run along the fence line, and I glanced back to see a battered Toyota pickup riding high on knobby, off-road tires. It eased left to straddle the yellow line as it came around me, and I glanced over to give the driver a nod of thanks for sharing the road.

Rick and I recognized one another at the same second. He sat behind the wheel, his left arm hanging out the side window, and probably would have passed without realizing who I was if I hadn't looked over. He wore dark sunglasses, and his lips curved in a predatory smile as soon as our gazes met.

This day just keeps getting better and better, I thought.

Rather than passing, Rick slowed down to match my speed. He stayed there for maybe fifty yards or so, smiling the whole time, and then veered suddenly right as if to sideswipe me. It wasn't a serious try, though, and still left me with plenty of room, but I didn't know it at the time. I overreacted, going off the pavement and nearly ending up in the ditch. "Knock it off!" I shouted, steering back onto the asphalt. I knew he was just screwing around, but that didn't make me any less nervous about playing tag with a ton of rolling metal.

I had just recovered when he swerved again, his smile widening to a grin. I did better that time, gauging his path correctly but still gritting my teeth as his right side mirror swung dangerously close. I looked up to throw Rick a glare, only to see him pointing through the windshield. Shifting my gaze forward, I sucked in a gasp as I saw I was coming up fast on a eucalyptus tree that grew by the side of the road almost directly in my path.

Crap!

I cut hard to the right, jumping the ditch just as Rick tried his most aggressive move yet. There was a narrow space between the eucalyptus and the fence line, and I shot through the gap with Moe right behind me. As it turned out, it was lucky that I did. As he swerved, Rick's rear tires lost traction on the seed pods lying scattered on the road beneath the tree. The swerve became a fishtail, slamming the truck's rear corner against the bole and tearing a deep gash into the wood. Metal crumpled, the right taillight lens shattering and throwing shards of red plastic across the shoulder like a spray of blood. I heard the screech of rubber as I recrossed the ditch and got back on the road, and I looked behind me to see the Toyota stopped diagonally in the middle of the lane. The driver's door was open, and Rick stood by the tailgate with his hands in his hair, surveying the damage.

Karma's a bitch, pal, I thought, grinning as a warm feeling of vindication spread through me. It was only then that I realized just how close I'd come to being seriously hurt or even killed. If I hadn't noticed the gap by the fence or if I'd hesitated even a second or two, I probably would have ended up as just so much jelly smeared on the tree. The grin faded from my face as I felt a stab of anger. That *asshole!*

I was still seething when I pulled up to Tsunami Joe and locked my bike to the post out front. I didn't know why Rick had it in for me so bad. Our face-off a few days before hadn't been *that* big a deal—not to me, anyway. Somehow, though, we'd progressed to full-on *Road Warrior* mode. The other thing that pissed me off was that there was no longer any question in my mind as to who had left the raccoon on my doorstep or who had cut my valve stems, either.

Freaking psycho.

The coffee house was just starting its morning rush when we entered, and I made Moe lie down in a corner where I hoped he'd be mostly unnoticed before I went over to stand in line. Ab was working the espresso machine and was too busy to do more than offer me a smile of greeting, so I ordered a large mocha and a maple bar from the lady at the register. I stood to one side while waiting for my stuff and then looked around the room, hoping to find an empty table.

I noticed Les hidden behind a newspaper not too far from Moe, so I made my way over. He glanced up as I arrived, moving his feet off the only other chair so I could sit down. "Wassup, *hombre*?"

I didn't know where to start, so I just shook my head.

"Uh-oh," Les said, his eyebrows rising in interest. He folded the newspaper and set it aside. "Who pissed in *your* Cheerios this morning?"

I took a huge bite of the maple bar, the taste flooding my mouth as I chewed. "Rotten day so far," I mumbled with my cheeks full. I swallowed and then chased it with a sip of mocha without thinking and scalded my tongue, which didn't help my mood at all. "I had it out with my mom this morning," I explained, "and then nearly got wiped out by a truck on the ride here."

"Yeah?" he pressed, leaning forward. "You okay? Did you see the driver? Maybe I can help figure out who it was."

"Don't worry—I know exactly who it was. Rick Whatshisname. Garrett's pal."

"Rick Hastings?" Les supplied. "Drives a Toyota four-by?"

"That's the guy. He was right alongside me, swerving like he was going to knock me off the road. Then he skidded out and would have squashed me against a tree if I hadn't gone around the other side."

Les shook his head, picking up his coffee mug. "Yep, that's Rick... with a capital D."

I snorted. "Yeah, well that's not all." I went on to tell him about my valve stems being cut and the dead raccoon on my doorstep. I'd hoped talking about it would calm me down, but all it did was make me angry all over again.

Les took it all in, frowning into his coffee mug as he listened. "I dunno," he said when I was finished. "Playing chicken on the road has Rick written all over it, but I'm not so sure about the rest. Hastings is an in-your-face kind of guy. Sneaking around slashing tires and delivering roadkill doesn't seem like his style."

"Oh, it was him all right," I insisted. "I can't see Alan Garrett pulling crap like that. And face it, I haven't been around long enough to piss off anyone else."

"Good point," Les agreed, and then a mischievous glint lit his eye. "Another week and we'd have a lot more suspects."

I snickered, my anger starting to deflate, and then gave my mocha another try. *Much* better.

"So what's up with you and your mom?"

I started bringing Les up to date, but Ab came over a couple of minutes later when business slowed down, and I had to start all over again. They exchanged an excited look when I told them about the diary and visions, and listened intently while I recounted the morning's events in the cupola. I wrapped things up with my fight with Mom in the kitchen.

"You sure keep yourself busy, Wolfman," Ab said when I was finished. "But let's go back to the diary..."

"*Screw* the diary," I interrupted. "I want to help my mom."

"Of course you do," she assured me, "and so do I. But there was never any record of your house being haunted *before* your aunt's time, and the place has been empty ever since. See? Whatever's happening to your mom now must be connected somehow to what happened in 1946, and between the diary and your visions, we have a good chance of figuring it out." Ab stared at me, as if waiting to see if I would object, but I only nodded and waited for her to continue. "So...you say that the visions only appear some of the time?"

"Un-huh." I backtracked, repeating what I'd said about following Claire around while she looked for Bonnie, and about her bursting into my room in tears a while later. "I don't know," I said at last. "It's like the diary lets me tap into the past, but maybe some of the visions are just stronger than others."

Ab had been chewing the inside of her cheek thoughtfully while listening, but then she shook her head. "No…I don't think that's it at all," she said after a brief pause. "You're missing an obvious point."

"Which is?"

She looked at me like I was the world's biggest moron. "*Think*, Wolfman. You were able to see the events that occurred in the house and yard because *you were right there*. To see the rest, maybe you just need to be where they happened."

I settled back in my chair, both stunned by the idea and feeling stupid that it hadn't occurred to me. It made sense, and I was anxious to test the theory. "The next few diary entries happened at the high school," I told them excitedly. "Where was it? Sure, the building isn't there anymore, but I'll bet the visions will still work if we can find the right spot!" I half rose from my chair, ready to head out the door.

"Hold on, big guy," Ab said, pushing me back down. "It's not like that piece of real estate is going anywhere, and you are *so* not doing this without me!"

"She's right," Les agreed. "After all, Ab's the expert on both ghosts *and* the town history, so you need her." He grinned. "And besides, we can't have you stumbling around, visioning away in broad daylight. People will see and think you're some kind of nut job."

I sighed. "So when do we go?"

"Tonight," Ab decided. "You guys meet me here at sunset. Pretty much all of downtown will be closed by then, and no one will be around."

"*Sunset?*" I argued, disappointed. "What am I supposed to do until then?"

Les grinned as he rose to his feet. "I have the perfect idea."

I had to wait a minute or two while Les brought his bike around from where he'd left it by the rear entrance, and then we rode over to his place—a small, run-down house on the southern outskirts of town. He left me to watch our bikes while he disappeared inside, reappearing about ten minutes later wearing his backpack. "Ready?" he asked.

"I guess. Where are we going?"

"You'll see."

We skirted the edge of town, crossing the overpass and heading up a potholed, single-lane road east of Highway 101. The day had warmed rapidly into the nineties and was getting even hotter the further inland we went. *Didn't we just have a rainstorm a couple of days ago?* I thought, amazed at how fickle the days were on the coast. It was nothing like the weather I'd grown up with in Vacaville. It was almost as if Windward Cove had to decide each morning which season it wanted to be in.

The road climbed steeply as it wound into the thickly wooded hills, and I was breathing hard by the time we'd climbed only three quarters of a mile. "Let me know when we get to the top of Mount Doom," I called ahead of me, where I could see Les pedaling with seeming effortlessness up the switchbacks. "I need to throw this ring into the lava!"

He grinned back over his shoulder. "Aw, quit being such a wuss," he shouted back. "Your dog isn't sniveling, is he?"

I glanced over at Moe, who was trotting happily up the grade like it was the most fun he'd had in a while. "You could at least *look* like you're working hard," I grumbled.

Thankfully, the terrain leveled out into a wide clearing not long after that, halting abruptly at a graffiti-covered guardrail at the edge of the forest, with a "Road Ends" sign hanging in its center. Looking around, I thought the sign was only stating the obvious, but maybe that was just me. Les was already off his bike and nodded toward a bright yellow Nissan XTerra pulled off to one side. "Looks like we're not the only ones with the same good idea."

"*We*?" I retorted, and followed him as we pushed our bicycles around past the guardrail, stashing them in a thicket not far off and securing them together with our cable-locks. There was a well-worn trail leading roughly northeast, and Moe and I trudged along behind Les for another mile or so as it wound its way up and down through stands of cedar and pine, past ferns, snarls of blackberry, and the occasional shiny three leaves of poison ivy. At first I wondered why we hadn't just taken our mountain bikes, but after crossing three dry creek beds by picking our way down steep inclines, hopping from rock to rock and then scrambling up the other side, I realized it was a good call.

I was starting to get irritated. Sure, part of me was really into the hike, but the rest was overshadowed by worry over what was happening to Mom. I wanted to be back in town figuring out how to help her, not off playing Davy Crockett. "The minute I hear banjo music, I'm gone," I called out to Les.

He just chuckled, apparently not bothered by my testiness one little bit.

After another half-hour or so, the trees began to thin out as the terrain became more rock than dirt. Large boulders dotted the landscape, the air above them distorted by shimmering waves of heat as they baked in the sun. The dust from our footfalls seemed to hang in the thick air, feeling gritty and sticking to the darker spots on my chest and armpits where sweat had soaked through my shirt. Tiny insects buzzed in front of my face, evading my hand easily when I tried to wave them away, then immediately returning to fly in lazy, maddening circles right in my field of vision.

About the time Moe was starting to run out of gas and I figured I'd give twenty bucks for a Gatorade, Les stopped at the top of a rise and turned, waiting for us to catch up. "We're here," he announced.

"Here" turned out to be a wide, more or less level area stretching from the spot where we stood to the base of tall, vertical cliffs that rose maybe sixty or seventy yards off. Cottonwoods shaded the banks of a creek that started out as two or three feeder springs that emerged from the base of the cliff. It wound around boulders and tumbled down short falls, splitting now and again only to rejoin itself further on. Along its meandering path were half a dozen natural depressions that had filled into pools of clear, inviting water—some heavily shaded by the trees while others sparkled in the sun.

And that wasn't all. Three girls in bikinis were lying out on beach towels, tanning by the side of one of the larger pools. Hiking clothes and boots lay neatly folded out of splash range, and a small cooler sat half submerged where the creek gurgled over a bed of rocks. I barely registered those details, though, as my gaze was immediately drawn to a mass of auburn hair that was all too familiar.

"I take it all back," I confessed to Les. "This is *so* worth it."

He clapped me on the shoulder. "This is Hermit Springs. Pretty cool, huh? C'mon."

The blonde in the middle noticed our approach first. "Hey, Les," she called out as we made our way over, shading her eyes and giving my friend a hundred-watt smile. A girl with dark brown hair to her left turned her head, regarding us over her shoulder as she lay on her stomach with her top unfastened, avoiding those unsightly tan lines. Kelly Thatcher rose to prop herself up on her elbows, bending one knee in a relaxed pose that belonged in the *Sports Illustrated* swimsuit edition.

"*Behold*, Ben," Les said dramatically, stopping and spreading his arms. "The Promised Land of Hot!"

I felt myself flush in embarrassment, but the blonde only laughed, kicking water in our general direction from where her foot trailed idly in the pool. The girl on her stomach frowned, lowering her head back down onto her folded arms, obviously unimpressed. Kelly, though—she just kept staring at me, smiling.

I wondered what to do about that—wave, say hi, whatever—but ended up doing nothing.

We passed them on our way to one of the pools upstream, Les exchanging friendly, teasing banter with Jessica, the blonde, while I just concentrated on trying to look casual under the weight of Kelly's stare. Considering how sweaty and gross I probably looked right then, it wasn't easy. I relaxed after we passed from their view, though, arriving at an unoccupied pool beside a boulder roughly the size of a city bus. Les dropped to his knees and tossed me a pair of swim trunks that he pulled from his backpack. "Change up," he ordered.

I shucked my sweaty clothes in record time and was cinching up my trunks only seconds before Les was into his. He grinned, and I raced him around the boulder to the edge of the pool, following his lead as he dove in headfirst. A single thought—*YEAH, baby!*—crossed my mind the instant the water closed over me.

The temperature was perfect, and I pulled myself down to the colder depths before allowing my muscles to relax and drifting lazily up toward the sunlight. Moe was scampering back and forth along the edge of the pool, whining and barking when my head broke the surface. "C'mon, boy!" I called when I'd got my breath back, and after a brief hesitation he jumped in, forepaws sending up great splashes as he swam awkwardly over to me. His mouth was open in a big doggie-smile, though, and after first assuring himself that I was fine, he paddled back and forth between Les and me until he got the hang of it and was able to propel himself smoothly through the water.

It was a great morning. We swam, dove from the surrounding rocks, and generally just goofed around until the sun was almost directly overhead. Les finally pulled himself out, followed by Moe, who shook himself vigorously before plopping down next to him in the shade of an overhang. I stayed put, floating on my back with my eyes closed, feeling really good for the first time in a while. I hadn't realized just how much everything had been weighing on me lately. The break away from Windward Cove was just what I'd needed, and I wondered if Les had consciously recognized it or if things had just worked out that way. Whichever it was, most of my tension and anxiety seemed to have been washed away along with the dust from the trail.

"Hey, Ben!" Les called over. "Ready for some chow?"

I was starving and got out of the water to join him. From his backpack Les pulled a six-pack of soda that had stayed cool wrapped in a towel, along with a couple of monster sandwiches piled high with cold cuts and cheese. I pretty much inhaled mine but stopped in time to save the last few of bites for Moe, who had been staring longingly while I ate.

After that we talked for a while, just relaxing in the shade, but eventually Les dug a coil of fishing line from his backpack and went to try his luck in some of the other pools. I turned down his invitation to come along, feeling tired and drowsy, and stretched out for a nap instead. But I was almost dry by then, and it was starting to get hot again, so I got back in the water, anchoring myself to the edge with my head resting on my crossed arms.

I must have dozed, because I woke up when I felt a stronger ripple on the water's surface. I smelled coconut sunblock a moment later and knew it was Kelly Thatcher even before she glided up next to me. *"C'mon,* Les," I complained with my eyes closed, "I *told* you I just want to be friends."

Kelly laughed, and I opened my eyes to grin at her. She had mirrored my pose, her cheek on her arms and her shoulder against mine. Her hair was a lot darker wet, slicked back and clinging against her head, and the contrast made her eyes seem to glow a bright emerald. "Hey," she said.

"Hey."

"We're taking off soon, so I thought I'd come and check first to make sure you hadn't drowned."

"Nope," I replied, "I managed to stay afloat. So…a hot tub party yesterday; swimming holes today. A regular Aqua Girl, aren't you?"

"I manage to stay afloat," she fired back, smiling. "Where's Les?"

"Oh, he heard the fish taunting him, so he's off drowning worms somewhere."

"Mmm," Kelly said, and then closed her eyes, sighing. "This is nice."

I didn't answer, but I thought so, too. Maybe it was my summer afternoon drowsiness, or maybe the day's bike-hike-swim triathlon had taken the edge off, but the nervousness I normally would have experienced being this close to Kelly had been replaced by a relaxed, comfortable feeling. Like she said…nice.

"Are you coming to my birthday party?" she asked after a while.

I opened my eyes. "I dunno. Am I invited?"

Her hip bumped against mine under the water, so I took that for a yes.

"When is it?"

"Saturday," she told me. "My birthday is really on Wednesday, but Saturday just works out better for everyone. Will you come?"

I thought about it, wondering if I should say yes with everything that was going on at home.

Kelly noticed my hesitation. "You can bring Abigail," she amended, "and Les too…if you want."

It couldn't hurt, could it? After all, even if we hadn't figured everything out, we'd probably deserve a night off by then. "Sure," I told her, easing my head back down to my arms, "why not?" That's me...Mr. Casual.

The smile that lit her face made me glad I'd said yes. At the same time, an inner voice that I had absolutely *zero* interest in listening to right then was already arguing the point. *Dude...what the hell are you doing?*

"Call me, and I'll give you the details," Kelly said, pushing away and swimming over to the far side where it was easier to get out. "Abigail has my number."

This is a really *bad idea,* my inner voice nagged as I watched her leave. *You have WAY too much on your plate for this!* I shook my head. After all, it was just a birthday party, right? A little finger-food, some cake and ice cream, maybe a little dancing. What's the big deal?

No big deal at all. But do you think Alan Garrett will be happy when you show up? Or did the fact that she has a boyfriend just slip your so-called mind?

Nope, it hadn't slipped my mind, I decided. Right then, I just didn't care.

TWENTY THREE

THE FIELD GLOWED DINGY GRAY IN THE MOONLIGHT, the tall, dry weeds crackling beneath our feet as we wound our way past overgrown trees that sagged beneath the weight of their own limbs.

Even though the years had erased all signs that the area had once held a purpose, I realized that I could have found the site even without Ab and Les to show me. The buildings over on Main Street hadn't changed much since 1946, and my gaze immediately found the spot where the high school had burned down nearly three-quarters of a century before. Even though I had never actually set foot there, it was all still strangely familiar. To my right had been the parking lot, while diagonally off to the left had sprawled a football field, track and baseball diamond, the images from the night of the tidal wave still sharp in my mind. On impulse, I veered off a few paces and dug my heel into the dirt, scraping down four or five inches until it jarred against concrete.

"Ben?" Ab called, looking back over her shoulder. "What are you doing?"

"There's a sidewalk buried here," I replied, and then gestured in a sweeping motion ahead of me. "It loops around to the right, past where the parking lot was over that way and then back around to the steps of the school." I pointed to a dark shape on the ground ahead of us. "And you see what's left of that stump over there? That was once an elm tree that was so big it shaded the whole front entrance."

Ab and Les just stared, but I ignored them while I gazed around me, soaking up the atmosphere. In my mind I could see the grounds as they had been, superimposed against the abandoned field that stood before me now, where dry brush shivered in the breeze and the lonely sound of crickets rode the night air. It felt like a graveyard, and I suppose in a way it was, considering the number of people whose lives had ended there. Even though the school had never been rebuilt, parts like the sidewalk still remained, buried like bones beneath the surface.

I led the way further on, feeling more confident as a sense of familiarity that I knew wasn't entirely my own continued to grow, and climbed a gentle rise that ended in a sprawling expanse of concrete at the top. Something didn't feel quite right about it, though, and I turned my gaze toward Ab. "This is wrong somehow," I told her, frowning. "They changed something after the fire, didn't they?"

Ab nodded. "They tore down what was left of the school, and for years this was just an open concrete pit that had been the basement. Then in the 1950s, when everyone thought we were headed for nuclear war any minute, the town capped it with cement and turned it into a fallout shelter." Les and I followed her to the far side, where a concrete stairwell led down to a rusted-over metal door secured with a padlock.

"What's it used for now?" I asked.

She shook her head. “Nothing. They had problems keeping out groundwater that kept seeping in, so it was never a great fallout shelter to begin with. When Russia never got around to nuking us, the town just abandoned it.”

“So, now you’re some kind of Cold War expert?” Les asked skeptically.

“Of course not, silly,” she replied, and then nodded toward the padlocked door. “There’s a ghost down there.”

“Really? Someone who died in the fire? Or was it the tidal wave?”

“Neither. By the late 1960s, kids had broken in and sometimes used the place to hang out and get high. In October of 1968, they found the body of a nineteen year-old girl named Sue Fromkie down there. She wasn’t a local, and she didn’t have any ID on her, so it took a few days to figure out that she’d hitchhiked down from Portland on her way to San Francisco. She’d been seen with two other guys when they wandered into town a couple of days before, but no one knew who they were or how all three had come to be traveling together. Anyway, when her body was found, the other two were long gone. She’d been beaten and raped, but the cause of her death was a drug overdose. The town sealed up the entrance after that, and kids stopped coming out here when Sue would appear, covered in blood and asking directions back to the highway.”

Les whistled and then grinned mischievously and trotted down the steps to the door. “Sue?” he called, knocking loudly on the steel. “You awake in there?”

“C’mon, Les…don’t do that,” Ab called down to him. “It’s not nice.”

“I thought this was a ghost hunt,” he countered, a humorous tone in his voice. “Maybe all the spooks around here get together to swap stories, and she can tell us something. Hey, Sue! Do you mind coming out for a minute? We want to ask…”

A sudden *BOOM!* came from the door, like a fist pounding angrily on the other side of the metal. We all jumped at the sound, and Les scrambled back up the steps to stand beside us, breathing hard. His eyes were wide in the moonlight. "Holy *crap!*"

"Told you," Ab said. "Now will you stop fooling around?"

"Yeah, I'm all done," Les replied, sounding a lot more subdued, and he stepped gingerly back to the edge of the stairwell. "Sorry!" he called down.

We all stood there for a few seconds, listening, but nothing more came from beyond the door. I wondered if that meant Sue had accepted his apology or if she was still pissed but didn't think it was worth any more of her time. I reached out with my gift, but I couldn't sense anything, so I guessed I'd never know.

"Isn't it about time you got to work?" Ab prompted, nudging me.

I nodded, pulling a penlight and Aunt Claire's diary from my coat pocket, and walked off a few paces to give myself room. I clicked on the light, holding it in my mouth while I flipped to the correct page:

> *Fri, 25 Apr '46*
>
> *Oh my goodness! Even now I can't believe it actually happened! Philip asked me for a date! I'm sure I looked like such a fool, blurting out "Yes! I'd love to!" before he'd even finished asking. When I realized what I'd done, I blushed so hard I thought my face would catch fire! He smiled at me, though, so I suppose I didn't ruin the moment too awfully...*

I smiled around the penlight in my mouth and then looked up as I realized I could hear voices. They were faint at first, as if coming from someplace far off, but it was a start. I looked back down and continued reading.

Philip found me at lunchtime and asked if I liked mystery pictures. When I nodded, he told me that The Big Sleep *with Humphrey Bogart and Lauren Bacall was playing in town Saturday night and asked if I'd like to go, and afterward have an ice cream soda. That's when I made such a fool of myself, but I managed to get back under control before I looked too silly (I hope!) I told him that would be fine, and we agreed to meet ten minutes before the picture starts. I was smiling all afternoon and didn't hear half of what my teachers were saying! Thank goodness Mary Lou let me borrow her notes!*

The voices were rising in volume, and I closed the diary as the air grew warmer around me. While I watched, the world began to change like the fade-in of a movie, the moonlight brightening to morning sunshine and the abandoned field dimming around me, replaced by a vivid scene from long ago:

I'm standing beneath the elm tree that isn't there anymore, its sturdy branches covered with the bright green of spring leaves. Kids are swarming up the front steps of the high school, the girls in calf-length skirts and sweaters, the boys all wearing neckties and a lot of them in blue and white cardigans that I assume must be Windward Cove's colors. The first bell rings shrilly, and they all hurry toward the entrance.

It's amazing, particularly since the vision is the most vivid and detailed I've experienced yet. I can only assume that whatever connection I'm able to make through the diary must be getting stronger. I look around, but just like my vision of Claire's morning back at the house, it's clear that I'm invisible—just observing while this echo of the past plays out around me. I tuck the book and penlight back in my coat, and no one notices as I join the stream of kids, careful not to let any of them walk through me as I make my way inside.

Tall lockers line both sides of the ground-floor hall, and I hear the unmistakable sound of their metal doors opening and closing amid the shouts and laughter while I take it all in. Even though everyone is a lot more dressed up, there's the same morning bustle and horsing around that I see Monday through Friday in my time. I guess it shouldn't surprise me so much that teenagers act pretty much the same regardless of when they went to school. If anything, it makes the differences I do *see stand out even more. For one thing, the place seems a lot cleaner. There's no graffiti on the walls or trash littering the corners, the floors are shiny with wax, and the old-fashioned light fixtures in the ceiling glow brightly. Teachers stroll to their classrooms, returning polite good mornings along the way, and everyone seems a bit more well-mannered as the boys move to hold doors open for girls who smile and say "thank you" as they pass. It should seem stuffy and awkward to me, but somehow it doesn't.*

To tell the truth, now that I'm no longer freaked out by the visions, I'm struck my how incredibly cool this all really is. It's like that scene in Back to the Future *when Marty McFly walks into his own high school after traveling back to 1955 (only better, since I don't have to worry about trying to fit in), and I have to remind myself that I'm here on business.*

As I watch, the hallway begins to empty as kids disappear through classroom doors and up a wide flight of stairs to my right, and by the time the tardy bell rings, the last two or three scurry off, leaving me alone. Part of me feels an instinctive, nervous guilt because I'm not sitting at my own desk somewhere, and I look around, half expecting to get yelled at for loitering in the hall. But then I shake it off with a grin and try to decide what to do next.

At first, I'm disappointed that I haven't seen Claire, but after a moment I realize that this makes finding her even easier. I stroll along the hall, pausing at the first classroom I come to and looking through the narrow, wire-reinforced window set into the door. Inside, everyone is standing with their right hands over their hearts, and I watch while they recite the "Pledge of Allegiance" *before sitting at their desks. I watch while the teacher, a skinny guy with salt-and-pepper hair and a moustache, begins scrawling an algebra problem on the blackboard. I quickly scan the faces of the kids while he works, glad that from where I'm standing I can see almost everyone. No Claire, but I'm not worried—this is going to be a piece of cake.*

It takes less than ten minutes to find out she isn't in any of the first-floor classrooms, and I pause at the base of the stairwell, wondering if I'll be able to go upstairs since all of this is really just a vision. Despite how real it seems, I know I'm really wandering around on a concrete slab in an otherwise empty field, so how the hell is this going to work? I put my foot tentatively down on the first stair and am surprised to find that I can still move forward! It takes me a few steps to realize that while it looks like I'm headed to the second floor, my legs don't feel any sensation of stepping up. It's the weirdest thing—my eyes tell me I'm climbing stairs, but my body knows I'm still on a flat surface. The conflicting sensations make it hard to walk, but everything is fine again when I reach the top.

I find Claire in the third classroom on the right. Through the door I can hear the teacher talking about the migration of workers from rural areas to the cities after the Civil War, so it doesn't take a genius to figure out she has first-period history. She's sitting four places back in the second row, and as I watch she sneaks a quick glance at the guy sitting across the aisle on her left. She's already facing forward again when he shoots a glance of his own back toward her, but from the way the corners of her mouth turn upward, I can tell she knows he's watching.

I give the guy a more careful look, and based on resemblance alone, it takes me all of about two seconds to decide this must be Philip Garrett…and yes, without a doubt, he's my buddy Alan's great-great grandpa. The same build, the same general features, particularly around the eyes.

Terrific. Granted, maybe Philip isn't as big a jerk as his grandson, but I'd be lying if I said I'm thrilled.

The two of them exchange covert peeks back and forth for the next few minutes until the girl sitting behind her finally thumps Claire on the back of the head with a pencil. She's smirking while she does it, though, and I recognize my aunt's friend June. After that the two of them settle down and pay attention, and for the next half-hour or so, I have nothing to do but yawn my way through a lecture on the Industrial Revolution.

As cool as it is to be witnessing the past, standing here watching a whole lot of nothing going on eventually causes my mind to wander. As soon as I start to tune out, though, the vision abruptly shifts in a blur of images that are too fast for me to see clearly, and things get interesting again. Suddenly it's midafternoon, and after I get my bearings, I realize I'm back under the elm tree out front. School is obviously over for the day, and I watch for Claire as the kids stream from the front and side exits into the spring sunshine, separating in all directions to head home. I catch sight of her a few moments later, flanked by June and Mary Lou, but the other two hang back when Philip shows up and falls into step beside Claire. Behind them, June casts a short, wistful look toward Philip before Mary Lou offers her friend a sympathetic smile and leads her away with a tug at her sleeve.

Luckily, Claire and Philip are headed right toward me, so all I have to do is wait. He's grinning, gesturing expansively while he talks. Claire hugs a couple of school books to her chest, wearing a faint, almost secret smile as she gazes down at the sidewalk in front of her.

I shake my head. It's hard to believe that this shy, pretty girl will turn into the intimidating old lady I knew when I was little.

"Dick Powell played Marlowe a couple of years ago in Murder, My Sweet,*" Philip tells her, and I fall in behind them as they pass, "but I bet Bogart will be just as good."*

"It sounds wonderful," Claire replies. "And Lauren Bacall has played opposite Bogey before, you know."

"Has she?"

"Oh, yes. They were together in To Have and Have Not.*"*

"I missed that one." Philip confesses, giving his head a shake.

Claire brightens. "I loved that picture! It was supposed to be based on the Ernest Hemingway novel, but it didn't follow the story very well. Still, I…" She casts a glance toward the parking lot and then stops, frowning slightly. "Oh, dear."

Philip and I follow her gaze at the same time. A beige and green Ford pickup pulls up to the curb and sits there, idling. "Windward Inn" *is stenciled on the door.*

"It's my father," Claire says, now sounding uncomfortable as she edges away to put a little more distance between them. "I have to go."

"Sure, I understand," Philip replies. He's still smiling, but from his tone I can tell he's disappointed. "I'll see you tomorrow, then?"

"Oh, yes! I'll be there with bells on. So long!" Claire turns and runs toward the truck without waiting for a reply.

"So long," Philip murmurs, watching her go.

I hesitate briefly and then decide to follow Claire, catching her just as she's pulling open the passenger door. "Hello, Daddy," she says brightly, dropping onto the bench seat and slamming the door shut. "How was your day?"

Roger Black either doesn't hear her question or simply ignores it. He stares through the windshield to where Philip stands fifty yards off, his hands in his pockets. "Was that boy bothering you, Claire?"

"Him? No, not at all," she replies, keeping her tone light, as if she's already forgotten him. "He's in my history class."

"Who is he?"

"Just a boy."

Her father turns, pinning her beneath his gaze, and I realize he's not happy with her answer. "Mister 'Just a Boy' has a name, *doesn't he?"*

Claire's smile fades, and all the brightness drains out of her voice. "Philip. Philip Garrett."

I frown, trying to figure out what's going on and feeling a twinge of annoyance that he's giving her such a hard time. She was talking to a guy—so what?

"And what were you and Philip Garrett discussing?"

"Like I said, Daddy, we have American History together." She chews her lower lip, hesitating a bare second. "Philip couldn't remember if it was Rockefeller or Carnegie who started Standard Oil."

I raise my eyebrows, surprised that Claire is lying to her dad. Well, well…what's up with that? *I wonder.*

Her father snorts dismissively. "Rockefeller, obviously." The tension in the air dissipates, and I get the feeling Claire has just dodged a bullet.

"Philip thought so, but he wasn't sure," Claire says, relaxing a little. "I told him he was right."

Her father smiles at her, dropping the gear shift into first. "That's my girl! Now let's go fetch you sister and go home." The truck pulls away, and as I watch the tailgate recede…

…the vision faded as well. I stood there in the darkness, listening to the wind and the crickets while my night vision slowly returned. I rubbed the back of my neck, thinking about everything I'd seen, and wondering if it all meant anything.

TWENY-FOUR

"FIVE HUNDRED," *MARLOWE SAYS, LOOKING AT THE check Vivian Sternwood just handed him.* "That's a lot more than I expected, but welcome just the same."

"We're very grateful to you, Mr. Marlowe. I'm very glad it's all over." *A Pause.* "Tell me," *Vivian goes on, sipping her drink,* "what do you usually do when you're not working?"

He shrugs. "Play the horses, fool around."

"No women?"

"Oh, I'm generally working on something most of the time."

Vivian smiles. "Would that be stressed to include me?"

"I like you. I told you that before."

"I liked hearing you say it."

"Mmm."

"But you didn't do much about it."

"Neither did you."

It's a pretty good movie, actually—an old hard-boiled detective story from the 1940s. It's not usually my kind of thing, but it beats watching Claire and Philip lurch their way through what looks like the most awkward date ever. They sit in the front row, a bag of popcorn between them and their faces bathed in silver light reflected off the screen. Behind them, the bright eye of the projector glares down from high on the back wall, the light having to force its way through a haze of smoke that drifts lazily in the air. The theater is close to full, and it looks like half the people in the seats are smoking—maybe more. The tips of their cigarettes glow a sullen orange when they inhale, looking like eyes blinking in the darkness. It's a good thing this is just a vision, or I probably would've dropped dead from secondhand smoke by now.

As I watch, Claire and Philip reach into the popcorn bag at the same time, both hurriedly drawing back as their fingers touch. After a short, awkward pause, he tilts the bag toward her, grinning, and she smiles shyly back as she takes a piece. They both face forward again, but now I notice that he's watching her out the corner of his eye, intentionally reaching into the bag again when she does.

Why Philip, you sly dog, *I think. It's the first time I've seen him do anything a nun wouldn't approve of, and I wonder if there's a chance he has a backbone after all.*

["Ben…?"]

This time neither one draws away, both of them are taking a lot longer than is really necessary to fish out a piece of popcorn. Progress.

["Ben, snap out of it.…]

Claire goes for the bag again almost right away. Maybe she's just hungry, but I wouldn't bet the ranch on it. Philip's hand snakes in right after hers, and I roll my eyes, half amused and half exasperated. Oh, will you just get *on* with it? *I think.*

Philip does the stealth-fingers trick one more time before working up the nerve, and when he finally takes Claire's hand, she stares straight ahead, biting her lower lip to hold back a smile.

["Hey, Wolfman!"]

A hand smacked the back of my head, and suddenly the vision was gone. I closed my eyes against momentary dizziness, and when I opened them again, the theater had shifted back to the present. On the screen, Humphrey Bogart and Lauren Bacall had been replaced by a swarm of zombies chasing some college kids across a night-darkened campus. I tried to remember the name of the movie we'd paid to see but couldn't. "*What?*" I asked, annoyed by the interruption.

"Time to go," Ab told me.

"Already?" I looked at my watch. She was right—it was almost 8:30. We were going to be late.

"Shhh!"

"Oh, shush yourself!" she shot back at Les. Since the three of us were the only ones in the theater, we didn't bother keeping our voices down. I guess zombie flicks weren't very popular in Windward Cove. A shame, really, but in this case it was handy. The last thing I needed was a bunch of people watching me during one of my visions, wondering what kind of idiot was bumping into the furniture and reacting to things that weren't there. Les sat three rows back, his feet up on the seat in front of him while working his way single-handedly through a monster bucket of popcorn with extra butter and cheddar salt. "We need to get a move on," Ab called to him.

"Aw, come on," he objected. "Five more minutes. Christie is just about to have her shirt ripped off—I can feel it."

"Who's Christie?"

Les nodded toward the screen. "The hot blonde," he said around a mouthful of popcorn, and then paused long enough to swallow. "She twisted her ankle back in the cafeteria, which is a sure sign she's a goner. These zombies manage to tear away a lot of clothes when they catch hold of someone, and so far I've seen two pretty good sets of boobs. Christie's, though…they're going to be *awesome*."

Ab rolled her eyes. "Gawd, you're such a…"

"*Here* we go!" he interrupted, grinning and sitting up straight. I followed his gaze to the screen. Sure enough, a gorgeous blonde was thrashing in the grip of two zombies, and her top was ripped away a few seconds before they finally took her down.

I had to admit, Les had called it. Awesome.

"Okay, I'm done," he said, getting to his feet. "Time to party!"

We made our way out of the theater, past the old guy who sat on a stool behind the concession stand. He glanced at us briefly over the top of his reading glasses and gave us a halfhearted "Come again soon" before returning his gaze to an issue of *Sport Fishing* magazine. Outside, we turned right to walk the two blocks to the coffee house where we'd left our bikes, breathing in the twilit air as the first stars began to emerge above us.

"So what did you see?" Ab asked excitedly.

"Nothing much," I replied. "Watching people while they sit through a movie is pretty dull, so as stakeouts go, it wasn't a big thrill. I thought I'd die of old age before Phil made a move and actually grabbed her hand. I should have asked you to wake me up if I started snoring."

It must have been the wrong thing to say because Ab stopped, turning with her hands on her hips. "Hold on," she said, glaring at me. "Let me get this straight: you've got a psychic connection to your aunt through a diary she wrote seventy-something years ago. Probably the coolest thing I've ever heard of, and I only *wish* something like that would happen to me. You're seeing visions of the past so vivid it's like being there, and you're *bored*?"

I felt my face flush, and I opened my mouth to argue.

"Yeah, poor you," Les added, trying to hold back a smile. I could tell he was enjoying this. "Do we need to find you a more interesting dead relative?"

Both of them were watching me with expectant expressions, and I shuffled my feet, pinned down by their stares. "There's one thing you just don't understand," I offered after a pause.

"Which is?"

"It's really weird. Sometimes I open my mouth and stupid stuff just *flies* out of it." I shrugged helplessly. "Maybe I'm possessed."

Both snorted laughter, and we all started walking again. We were on our bikes a few minutes later, the streetlights of Windward Cove fading behind us as we pedaled toward Silver Creek and Kelly Thatcher's birthday party. We switched on our headlamps as night descended around us, the narrow, winding road cloaked beneath overhanging branches of ancient cypress trees that looked black in the gloom.

"So," Les began, "a lonely country road…night coming on…great place for a zombie attack, huh?"

"I don't think so," Ab countered. "The big cities always get hit first, right? So we'd have all kinds of advance warning and probably wouldn't be out here in the first place. We'd be at home, boarding up the windows and stocking up on food and water."

He shook his head. "Not me."

"No?"

"*Hell,* no. As soon as I heard about the outbreak, I'd load up a fishing boat and go anchor a couple of miles offshore until it was over."

Part of me wanted to put in my two cents' worth, but instead I fell back and left them to figure out the zombie apocalypse on their own. I needed time to think.

Back in 1946, only a day had gone by since Philip Garrett asked out my aunt, but in my time, it had taken a lot longer. In order for the visions to work, I had to be at or near where the events happened, which maybe half the time I was able to figure out from the diary entries, but after that was all guesswork. It had taken us close to a week, and even then, the details were still choppy. I'd had to wander all around the house and property to catch different scenes of what had happened that Friday night. I didn't see everything, and the separate visions weren't even in order, but I eventually saw enough to piece together what had happened.

Long story short, Bonnie turned up missing at dinnertime. In the end, it was no big deal—they eventually found her watching the workmen building the wine cellar—but Claire had caught hell from her dad over it. It must have been pretty bad, because her diary entry later on that night had been *epic*: a seven-page emotional meltdown in which she raged not only against how much responsibility her dad had loaded on her plate, but also how hopelessly trapped she felt by it.

Between the diary entries and the visions, I was starting to understand Claire's life in a way I never would have thought possible. I wasn't a hundred percent certain, but as near as I could tell, Roger Black saw himself as the idea guy, whose only job was to set the course and then leave all the boring details for Claire to figure out and keep track of. She described how he loved planning changes and upgrades to the Windward Inn, with the idea of turning it back into a place where the rich people would come when they wanted to get off the beaten path, but it was Claire's job to manage the projects, keep the books, track inventory, and do all the rest of the day-to-day heavy lifting. She also described how his latest grand idea was to establish his own winery, but after the vineyard had been planted and he'd roughed out plans for the cellar and overall operation, he left it to Claire to somehow make it all happen.

Throw in the fact that Roger expected her to keep Bonnie in line, which looked to me like a full-time job all by itself, along with his strong feelings about Claire spending "too much" time with friends (let alone boys, which were totally out of the question), and I honestly didn't know how she had put up with it all.

At least she'd been able to sneak out to see a movie, though. That was something.

"So what did you get her?" Ab asked.

I hadn't noticed she and Les had slowed down for me to catch up, and it took me a second to realize that she was asking about Kelly. "Hmm? Oh, nothing…just a card." I unconsciously touched the front of my jacket, feeling the outline of the envelope through the denim to assure myself it was still safely tucked in the inside pocket.

She shot a questioning glance my way and then faced forward again.

"What?" I asked.

"I didn't say anything."

"Yeah, but you're thinking so hard I can smell the smoke," I said. "So come on…I can take it."

"It's just that Kelly is used to getting birthday presents," she explained.

My insides twisted with anxiety, but I shrugged and did my best to look disinterested. "I barely know her," I argued. "How am I supposed to know what she likes?" It wasn't a lie—not technically, anyway—but the truth was I'd spent most of the morning wandering through shops trying to figure out just that. It wasn't a question of what I could afford. Mom and I had inherited more money than we knew what to do with. It was just that everything I saw either looked too cheesy for a girl like Kelly or seemed way too expensive to give to someone I'd never spent more than a few minutes with. After that I went home and spent nearly half an hour formatting and printing out a homemade coupon that said "Good for 1 Lunch with Ben at Your Favorite Place," but then I decided that it made me look like I was asking her out, so I threw it away. Finally, I just wrote,

"Happy Birthday!! Your friend, Ben" inside a card and figured it was good enough.

A heavy silence passed between us while my brain wrapped itself around the axle second-guessing my decision and thinking back on all the gift ideas that I had rejected. Was I going to look like a dork for showing up empty-handed? And anyway, she had a boyfriend, so what difference did it make? But if I really felt that way, why did the whole idea bother me so much?

I'm nothing if not clear-headed.

Finally, I sighed, mentally tossing the question on the "Too Hard" pile. "So what did *you* get her?" I asked.

"Nothing."

I turned to Les. "You?"

He shook his head. "*Nada.* I'm not the one trying to get in her pants."

"Oh, *c'mon*...I'm *so* not doing that!" I knew he was just trying to get a rise out of me, but I couldn't help it. Les just snickered, and I grit my teeth in annoyance while turning back to Ab. "So *you* didn't get her a birthday present, but you're saying that *I* should have?"

"Oh no. Not at all."

My frustration went up another notch. "Then what the hell was that look you gave me a minute ago?"

Ab laughed. "You're *killing* me, Wolfman! For someone who's not into Kelly, you're sure doing everything just right to get her attention. If I didn't know better, I'd *swear* you were doing this on purpose."

I was totally lost as to what she was talking about, and I would have pressed her further, but I was distracted by the heavy bass beat of music that swelled as we turned right into a neighborhood of custom homes on the outskirts of Silver Creek. Cars were crammed tightly along the street on either side, and as we pedaled the hundred yards or so to Kelly's driveway, my jaw dropped in amazement.

This was a birthday party? Wow.

TWENTY-FIVE

THE THATCHER HOME SAT ON AN ACRE, MAYBE A LITTLE more, that was mostly trees and wide swaths of lawn that probably took forever to mow. Walkways bordered by lights ran from the house to a fountain and a couple of decorative ponds. Off the drive was a detached four-car garage, while around back a fire pit blazed beside a pool with a waterfall at the far end. The house itself was large and stately—two stories of brick with ivy climbing the north wall. Kids streamed in and out, clustering around tables and an outdoor bar, beneath strings of Japanese lanterns that lit the grounds in blue, yellow, green, and red.

"Fancy-shmancy, huh?" Les asked.

I shrugged. "It's okay. The Empire State Building has more windows."

As we strolled up to the double front doors, I felt a sinking feeling as I noticed that almost everyone was dressed up for the occasion. Most of the girls wore dresses and heels, and while the guys were generally dressed a little more casually, almost all at least had collared shirts on. I'm not usually one to pay much attention to that sort of thing, but it was enough of a contrast to make me a little embarrassed that the three of us were showing up in run-down jeans and T-shirts. I thought about suggesting that we abort the mission and go track down a pizza instead, and then maybe catch the last showing of the zombie movie. After all, with a crowd like this, it wasn't as if Kelly would even notice if we never showed. But Ab walked through the doors like she owned the place, and since the only reason she was there was because I'd talked her into it (which was a lot harder than I thought it would be), there was nothing to do but follow her.

The music was even louder inside, and the first thing I saw when we walked in was a mound of wrapped gifts stacked high on a table in the entry hall. Looking at all the bright paper and ribbons, I couldn't help but think how pathetic my card was by comparison. Just the same, I added it to the pile, hiding it between two of the larger boxes near the bottom where it couldn't be seen.

"Abigail? Is that *you*?" called a woman standing in a small cluster of adults to one side. She was slender and looked to be in her forties, and from her green eyes and dark auburn hair, I took her for Kelly's mother. She glided over to Ab and gave her a quick, one-armed hug, bending slightly at the waist while holding her wine glass carefully to one side.

"Hi, Wendy," Ab replied, stepping back. Her voice had a cautious note that I hadn't heard before, and I wondered what that was all about. "It's nice to see you."

"It's wonderful that you came—it's been simply forever," she gushed, pitching her voice so it would carry over the music. "And you've grown into such a *lovely* young lady!" She turned toward Les and me. "Won't you introduce me to your friends?"

"This is Les Hawkins and Ben Wolf," Ab reported. "Guys, this is Wendy Thatcher, Kelly's mom."

She shook hands with Les first, and when it was my turn, I noticed that behind her smile was a look of cool appraisal that made me uncomfortable, like I was being judged against some unspoken standard and had come up short. Instinctively, I reached out to probe her emotions and was stung when I sensed a disdain that bordered on hostility. I couldn't tell if it was directed at all three of us or just at me, but it put me on the defensive right away. "Nice to meet you, Mrs. Thatcher," I said, trying to make up for lost ground. I figured that being extra polite couldn't hurt.

"Call me Wendy," she corrected, still giving me the tight smile. She released my hand after the barest of shakes and then abruptly turned in a way that made me feel like I'd been dismissed. "Now, before you go in," she instructed, "you'll have to leave your car keys in the basket by the door. I won't have you driving home if you have anything to drink."

My eyebrows went up. Was she *serious*?

"We didn't bring a car," Ab explained quickly.

"Better still," she said, stepping aside to give us a clear path. "Make yourselves at home!"

Ab led the way, followed by Les, and as I brought up the rear, I offered Wendy a smile that she didn't bother to return. I looked back over my shoulder as we entered the living room, and she was still standing there, arms crossed, staring after me with an unfriendly gaze.

As first impressions go, I guess I hadn't exactly batted that one out of the park.

The living room was wide, stretching thirty feet to the far wall where the furniture had been shoved aside to make room for dancing. Even that hadn't been enough, though, as couples moving to the beat overflowed through a double set of French doors and onto a brick patio outside. To our left, a buffet had been set up in the dining room, while to our right a DJ danced in place while manning a gigantic sound system.

Les clapped me on the shoulder. "Catch up with you guys later!" he called cheerfully. He struck out into the sea of dancers, weaving his way toward the far side of the room. After a moment, I figured out where he was headed, and I watched with a smile as he pulled up next to Jessica, the blonde we'd seen at Hermit Springs. She'd been standing near the wall, looking bored while a tall guy in a sport coat leaned in close to her while going on about something. In the time it took Les to reach them, I noticed the guy never paused to let her say anything; he just kept droning on and on. Jessica's face lit up when Les slid an arm around her waist, and I almost felt sorry for Mr. Talkative when his words trailed off as Les drew her away.

He was definitely going to have to teach me that.

I turned to tell Ab about it but then realized she was no longer beside me. Looking around, I finally saw her on the other side of the room, working her way through a plate loaded high with hot wings, pot stickers, and deep fried cheese sticks while chatting with Nicole and a burly guy I didn't recognize.

So much for not leaving your wingman. It looked like I was on my own.

I was getting hungry, so I followed Ab's lead and wandered over to the buffet table. The food was all under hinged, silver domes, and I was about to swing the first one back to see what was inside when a voice rose urgently beside me. "We're out of crab cakes!"

I turned, meeting the gaze of a woman who looked to be in her thirties. She had cheekbones a lot like Kelly's, so I guessed she was a relative—an older cousin, maybe an aunt. "Excuse me?" I asked.

"Crab cakes!" she snapped, as if saying it louder would make me understand. "We've been out for nearly an hour! Are any more on the way?"

Her tone irritated me. "How should I know?"

"You *are* with the caterer, aren't you?"

Understanding flooded over me. I looked down at myself, wondering how jeans and a black, V-neck T-shirt were supposed to make me look like the hired help. "No, I'm a friend of Kelly's," I told her. "Sort of, anyway."

"Oh," she said, the venom draining from her tone. "Well, someone should tell them." She turned, stalking away still in a huff.

Sure, lady, I thought. *I'll get right on that.* I shook my head. Those must have been some crab cakes. That, or maybe there was just something about me that pissed people off tonight. Suddenly I wasn't hungry anymore, so I put my plate back on the stack. I'd been there less than ten minutes, and already the party was getting on my nerves. I turned, heading through the French doors toward the less crowded terrace outside.

As I stepped out onto the fresh air, I could see a vacant outdoor sofa and chair arranged beneath a tree about thirty feet beyond the fire pit. It looked like a perfect spot to chill for a few minutes and get my sense of humor back, so I headed that way, weaving and dodging around couples and trying not to get my feet stepped on or catch an elbow from the more enthusiastic dancers. I'd only made it partway across the patio, though, when a couple of girls nearly slammed into me, stopping right in my way.

"I don't know…it just *snapped*," one girl was saying, sounding on the verge of tears. She was pretty, with wavy brown hair that fell halfway down her back. She was holding the front of her dress up, and I could see that one of the thin shoulder straps had broken where it attached to the back.

"Just hang *on,* Lisa, and let me see!" said her friend, and I recognized the brunette from Hermit Springs. "Here, hold this" she said, distractedly shoving a red plastic cup into my hands so she could inspect the damage. "It's not so bad," she told Lisa, "we just need a safety pin. Come on." The two hurried inside, forgetting about me entirely. I watched them go and then glanced into the cup I was still holding. Beer. Over three-quarters full, too.

Things were looking up.

I finally made it across the terrace and could feel the tension between my shoulder blades ease as soon as I left the press of bodies behind me. The air was cool but not cold, so I passed the crowd clustered around the fire pit without stopping. It was a relief to enter the shadows of the overhanging tree, and I dropped gratefully onto the sofa. A low concrete table in front of me held a few empty cups and a chip and dip set. The dip bowl held only a few faint streaks of salsa, but there were still plenty of tortilla strips left, so I helped myself to a handful and then put my feet up on the table as I settled comfortably back against the cushions.

Forget all that back at the house —I have everything I need right here.

I ate a couple of chips and chased it with a sip of beer, puckering at the slightly bitter taste but liking it too, mostly due to memories. Back when I was nine or ten, Mom came home one day super excited because an art consignment place had sold one of her paintings for $600.00—three times more than she'd ever gotten for a piece before. Money had been especially tight for the previous couple of months, and I could tell she was relieved as well as happy. Anyway, as soon as she was done squeezing the stuffing out of me, she took a bottle of beer from the fridge, poured it into two glasses, and we toasted our good luck.

The tradition stuck. After that, every time something big happened for either of us —Mom selling a painting or landing a new job, me getting mostly A's on my report card, that sort of thing—we'd always share a beer and toast the occasion. Mom hardly ever drank, and champagne was way too expensive (back then, anyway), but she believed in celebrating the good things, so we did what we could. Usually, it also involved her making a special dinner, a trip to the movies, or some other treat we couldn't afford all that often, but we'd always split a beer and drink to Team Wolf.

Of course, thinking about Mom depressed me, as it had a lot lately. We still hadn't really talked since the morning of our big fight. Okay, sure, we *talked*...but only when absolutely necessary, and then only in brief, carefully polite exchanges. Over the last week, most of our discussions had gone like this:

"Good morning."

"Good morning."

"I brought you some breakfast."

"Thank you."

"Is there anything else you need?"

"No."

We hadn't made peace or even called for a truce. It was just a cease-fire. Both of us knew the big battle was still to come, yet neither of us was able to get past our hurt and anger enough to be the first to wave the white flag. Just the same, I still brought her food, morning and night. Maybe half the time there were signs that she'd at least nibbled at it, but the rest of the time the food was untouched when I arrived to deliver her next meal. At least she was still drinking, and I made sure that the pitcher of water I'd left where she could see it was always full.

Worse still, Mom was still losing weight, still sleeping way too much, and still spending close to twenty-four hours a day in the cupola. It scared me. The only thing I could think to do was to keep following Ab's theory that it was all somehow connected to whatever happened in 1946. I'd just feel a lot better if figuring it all out didn't have to take so long.

"Need a refill?"

The unexpected voice surprised me, and I turned to see Kelly standing behind the sofa. She looked beyond hot in a short, clingy black dress, with a cluster of three or four thin silver bracelets on one wrist that looked good against her tan. "Thanks," I said, draining the last swallow of my beer—mostly so I'd quit looking at her legs. I was surprised when she handed me another. "I can't believe your folks let you have a keg at your party."

She shrugged. "Mother says that if we're going to drink, she'd rather we do it where she can keep an eye on us. Can I sit with you?"

I waved toward the spot beside me. "Help yourself."

She moved around to the front of the sofa, slipping off one shoe and tucking her leg beneath her as she sat down, facing me. Kelly moved with the controlled grace of an athlete, and it was fun watching her. "Happy birthday, by the way," I said.

She smiled in a way that made my chest feel tight. "Thank you. And thank you for the card."

"You opened all those presents already?"

"No. Just yours."

That made me a little self-conscious, but the feeling didn't stay long. "Sorry I didn't get you anything," I went on. "What do you buy for the girl who has everything, right?"

She gave me more of the smile. "You're here—that's enough for now."

"For now?"

Her voice took on a playful tone. "Maybe I'll ask for something later."

I tried to think of something cool or funny to say but couldn't. It was hard to hear myself think with my heart sledgehammering the inside of my chest. I noticed that her eyes looked like emeralds as they reflected the firelight behind me. I took another drink when I realized I was staring again and then frowned into my cup. Half gone already. I should probably slow down.

"I like your shirt," Kelly said when the silence started to drag out. "It makes your chest look nice."

"Thanks," I replied. "That dress does the same for you." *Holy crap! Did I actually* say *that?* My face grew hot as I blushed furiously. Kelly just laughed, though, so maybe I hadn't crossed any lines. Just the same, I set what was left of my beer on the table, out of easy reach.

"So, are you planning to just sit here by yourself all night? I was hoping we'd dance."

"It's nice out here," I explained, doing my best to sound relaxed and confident. "Trees, stars, firelight—it's like camping out."

"Have you seen our koi pond?"

I shook my head.

Kelly stood, sliding her foot back into her shoe as she held out her hand. "Come on. I'll show you."

I let her pull me to my feet, thinking she'd let go as soon as I was standing, but she didn't. Instead, she laced her fingers into mine and walked close enough for our shoulders to touch as she led me into the trees out of sight of the house. After ten yards or so, we emerged into the clear again and stood beside a rectangular pond that was maybe four feet wide by twelve long. Peering down, I could just make out an occasional flash of orange or red as fish cruised under the black water. "Nice, but I can't really see much."

Kelly laughed. "You don't really think that's why I brought you here, do you?"

"It's not?"

She moved in front of me, her arms encircling my neck. "I've wanted to kiss you ever since the night we talked on the beach."

That sledgehammer started battering the inside of my chest again. Right then kissing her sounded like the best idea I'd heard all day, but still I hesitated. "I don't know. Seems to me Alan wouldn't be too happy about that."

"Really? Well it seems to *me* that Alan isn't here." She stepped closer, close enough to where I could feel her breath on my neck and the way her breasts brushed maddeningly against my ribcage. "Come on, Ben," she murmured. "Just a little birthday kiss—it's not like I'm saying we should get a room or anything. Besides, you owe me a present, remember?"

I had no answer for that, so I nodded, swallowing. *Okay,* I thought. *A nice, friendly, G-rated birthday kiss. No big deal.* I leaned in, angling for her cheek, but before I got there she drew my mouth down to hers. For a fraction of a second I almost pulled away, but then I just gave in, losing myself in the warmth of her lips and body. I shifted my hips back, not wanting her to feel what was going on south of the equator, but she pressed herself firmly against me. A soft moan escaped her as her tongue brushed lightly against mine.

And then she was gone, stepping back to straighten her hair and dress as we heard her Mom calling from the house. "Kelly? Kelleee! It's time to blow out your candles!"

"Wait five minutes, then you can come out," she ordered, and then turned without waiting for an answer and disappeared back into the trees.

I stood there for three or four seconds, stunned and a little dizzy, and then followed. I stopped before exiting the far side, remaining hidden by the foliage but able to watch as she appeared near the fire pit. She stepped quietly from concealment, joining the group clustered around the fire like she'd been there the whole time, and then walked back toward the house with them as they headed in for cake.

I had to admit, the girl was smooth.

Alan saw her from where he stood at the outdoor bar and went out to meet her halfway across the lawn. She squealed with laughter as he picked her up and spun a three-sixty, smiling down at him like he was the pagan god of awesome. It was the same smile she'd given me just minutes before, and I felt a hot stab of…

Of what? I asked myself. Was I jealous? Hurt? Confused? All of the above?

I shook my head, realizing I didn't have a clue what I was feeling right then. I just knew it was a hot stab of *something*, and I didn't like it.

Screw this, I thought, doing my best to shake it off. *This crap I just don't need.*

I gave Kelly her five minutes and then made my way back to the house. I found Ab sitting on the patio railing, still talking to Nicole and her date.

"Hey," I said, joining them. I glanced down at a plate of bones on the rail. "Is that your second helping of wings?"

"Third," she said proudly, patting her stomach. "Belly full—must sleep. How much longer do you plan to hang around?"

"I'm ready to go whenever you are. Where's Les?"

She jerked a thumb over her shoulder. I craned my neck around to see him making out with Jessica in the shadow of a wall. "Hey, Les," I called over. "We're taking off. You good?"

He gave me a thumbs-up. Multitasking.

We said our goodbyes, but as I started to follow Ab inside, Nicole stopped me. "Hold on," she said. She plucked a napkin from a nearby table, wet it with her tongue, and used it to wipe the corner of my mouth. "Lip gloss," she whispered, and winked at me.

Terrific.

"Thanks," I muttered back. For whatever reason, the idea that Kelly had branded me made my mood darken again, and I couldn't wait to get out of there.

Inside almost everyone was crowded around the dining table singing "Happy Birthday," leaving a more or less clear path to the door. I was halfway there when a guy put a hand on my shoulder to stop me. "Is the music going to start again soon?" he asked.

I shrugged his hand off, irritated. "Don't ask me—I'm just the caterer."

TWENTY-SIX

"BENJAMIN SHOWS TREMENDOUS POTENTIAL. HIS TALents should be cultivated. Honed."

The voices in the other room had been incoherent murmurs a moment ago—background noise that had no more meaning for me than the sound of the rain outside. I was still too warm and sleepy from my nap, still too comfortable beneath a knitted throw blanket on Aunt Claire's sofa. It was that point at the edge of waking when my dreams still made sense and it was up to me whether to open my eyes all the way or let them drift back closed. But my ears zeroed in on the sound of my name, and I concentrated to hear what Aunt Claire was saying.

"Don't you think it's a little early for that?" Mommy argued. "Christ, he's not even four yet!"

"I'm aware of his age, young lady. And I'll thank you not to take that tone with me. But think of the gifts he's already demonstrating. His ability to sense emotion is extraordinary, let alone his flashes of precognition and clairvoyance. My concern is that without exercising

those talents, they may atrophy. Can you see what a terrible loss that would be?"

"No, not really. As far as I'm concerned, if those gifts stay with him and continue to grow, then wonderful. But if they don't, that's okay, too. Have you stopped to consider how much more difficult those abilities could make his life? How hard it will be for him to always be different? Honestly, if he turns out being just a happy, normal kid, I'm fine with that." She paused. "What I'd like to know is why you're so anxious to see him manning a phone for the Psychic Hotline. Or would you rather see him wearing earrings and a bandanna in a carnival—The Amazing Zoltar Who Sees and Knows All?"

It was Aunt Claire's turn to pause, and when she spoke again, her voice was softer—so soft I had to strain to make out the words. "No, Connie, I don't want that. I'd never *want that. But just think: what if there was a way for him to use those talents to genuinely help people? How remarkable and fulfilling would his life be then?"*

Their conversation went on, but I had already lost interest. I had decided I wanted to go back to sleep, and even if they were talking about me, they were using too many big words I didn't understand. I sighed, letting their exchange fade to just sounds as sleep crept back to reclaim me...

Moe twitched in his dreams, and I opened my eyes, half expecting to see the high ceiling and woodwork of Aunt Claire's mansion. But it was just my room, where moonlight slanted bluish white through the open window and the far-off crash of the surf sounded restless and lonely. *Well, how about that?* I thought. *Finally, a dream about the past that was actually* my *past. A nice change of pace.*

I smiled in the darkness, reaching down to stroke Moe's head while thinking about that rainy afternoon in San Francisco. It had happened so long ago that I'd all but forgotten it, and I wondered how my mind could dredge up stuff like that when most of the time I couldn't tell you what I had for lunch yesterday. Then I wondered what other memories my brain might have squirreled away, so I thought back, poking around in the dusty corners to see what else might be there. After a minute or two, I began to come up with bits and pieces: my favorite shirt with the race cars on it, the time I drank so much chocolate milk it kept me on the toilet half the night, Mom introducing me to old reruns of *Lost in Space* and how they made me want to be Will Robinson and have a robot for my best friend.

But for whatever reason—maybe just luck of the draw, maybe because she had seemed so intimidating when I was little—memories of my talks with Aunt Claire came to the surface more readily:

"So, Benjamin...have there been any more times when you knew something was going to happen before it did?"

"Uh-huh," I said, nodding.

"When was that?"

"I knew Mommy would make pancakes this morning."

"Did you? And that just popped into your head all by itself?"

"No. We always have pancakes on Saturday."

She sighed. "That's very good, Benjamin, but what about other things? Things that you knew but didn't know why *you knew them?"*

I thought hard. "You mean like Scooter?"

She looked confused. "You saw a scooter?"

"No, silly," I said, giggling. "Scooter – Mrs. Whitley's cat."

"Oh, I see. Well why don't you tell me about him?"

"He was really old, and he was going to go to Heaven soon and make her sad. So I went next door to say goodbye to him and to tell Mrs. Whitley it would be okay." I frowned. "She didn't believe me."

"And did Scooter go to Heaven?"

I shrugged. "I guess. That's what Mommy said. But it looked to me like he just took a nap and never woke up." I met her gaze. "Is that what going to Heaven is like?"

"I don't know, Benjamin. That's really the question, isn't it?" Aunt Claire blinked several times, swallowing, and I could sense her sadness. Funny, I didn't think she even knew *Scooter.*

I let out a breath. Wow...I probably hadn't thought about that since the day it happened. I shook my head, amazed at what I could see in hindsight. I couldn't be sure, but I'd bet real money that while I'd been talking about Mrs. Whitley's cat, Aunt Claire was thinking about Bonnie.

Once again, I wished I had known her better. Looking back, once I got past Aunt Claire's sternness, I could see now that she'd never been anything but nice to me. But I hadn't realized it then, and it made me feel sad to know that I'd missed out.

[Benjamin shows tremendous potential. His talents should be cultivated. Honed.]

It was a shame that we'd stopped going to see Aunt Claire before we got around to that. If we had, then it would probably be a lot easier to figure out what was happening with Mom, the cupola, Bonnie, and everything else. But the fact was, I didn't have a *clue* how to get more out of my abilities.

An idea suddenly occurred to me, and I sat up in bed, my heart thudding with excitement. Sure, maybe I didn't know how...but I bet I knew someone who did!

I tried, but there was no getting back to sleep that night. I was too anxious. Just the same, I tried different positions, searching for one comfortable enough to let me drift off while doing my best to think about something else. But I was too keyed up to lie still for long, and the only thoughts that could distract me were ones of Kelly and the way it had felt to kiss her. Of course, thinking about that brought a vivid mental replay of how she'd gone right back to Alan, which stirred up a cloud of conflicting emotions that only annoyed me.

What the hell had that been about, anyway? Did she like me or not? "I've wanted to kiss you ever since that night on the beach," she'd said. Okay, mission accomplished. So was that all? One taste of Ben, and then off to the next item on her bucket list? If that were true, then I guess I was lucky. As attracted as I was to Kelly, if I was just a passing distraction for her, I was better off knowing that before I got in too deep.

Great logic, Ben, a snide inner voice told me. *Spock would be proud. But there's more to it than that, isn't there?*

The voice was right. All the logic in the world didn't stop the way my heart and body went six different kinds of haywire whenever I got within ten feet of her.

I sighed, shaking my head. This would be *so* much easier if I could make sense of all the feelings that swirled around inside her. But I had no idea how she felt, and I was beginning to suspect that she didn't, either. The bottom line was that I couldn't trust that she wouldn't stomp on my heart if it came down to it, and no matter how astronomic her hot factor was, I'd be stupid to let her get that close. And anyway, she had a boyfriend. That made things clear-cut all by itself. I nodded, my decision made. Until Kelly decided which way she wanted to roll, I'd just avoid her. Ignore her. Done deal.

Sure, big guy, the snide voice piped up again. *Let me know how that works out for you.*

"Oh shut up," I muttered, smiling a little in spite of myself. "Whose side are you on, anyway?"

First light eventually came, and I got up to make oatmeal for me and Mom. She was asleep in the rocking chair when I brought her bowl to the cupola, her head covered by the quilt to expose only a tuft of oily, unwashed hair. I realized that she was starting to kind of smell, and I wondered how many days it had been since she'd showered or changed clothes. Worry and fear started to well up inside me, but I shoved the feelings back before they could turn into panic. There was no fighting her on this, so I needed to just stick to the plan.

Outside, the morning looked dreary. Gray clouds hung low, squeezing out a drizzle so fine that it was little more than a mist. I left Mom's bowl on the shelf beside her picked-over dinner plate and then took the opportunity to go to the easel to see how her oil painting was coming along. It was *amazing*—so amazing that I straightened and blinked in surprise. She'd finished maybe a third of it. The twilit sky was incredibly detailed, with stars visible in the half light and a thin line of clouds scudding in from the west. Under that were the tops of the hills just north of the vineyard, stopping abruptly where the paint ended on the canvas below.

I frowned. Something was strange about that, and it took me a few seconds to realize what. Mom was using a different technique. Usually, she'd start with the background colors, adding elements and details in layers. This was completely different. She was working from the top, and the effect looked almost as if she was peeling down the canvas to reveal a finished painting underneath.

Weird, I thought, but then I shrugged. There were probably all kinds of ways to paint a picture. Besides, in looking at what she'd done so far, I figured this might turn out to be her best work ever, so who was I to judge? I'd just never seen her do it that way before, that's all.

I hung around the house for the next few hours, mostly taking care of chores to give myself something to do, and when 9:00 rolled around, Moe and I headed for Silver Creek. The morning still hadn't warmed up, the air chilly against my face and neck as I pedaled. It felt like October or November, even though July first was still a few days off, and I realized that I was learning to enjoy the abrupt changes in the weather. I listened to the hiss of my tires on the damp pavement, feeling my hair and jacket grow slowly heavier from the mist and occasionally glancing over at Moe as he trotted alongside me.

We swung into the parking lot of Autumn Leaves Residential Care Home at a quarter to ten, and I coasted to a stop beneath the awning at the front entrance. Part of me felt guilty that I hadn't asked Ab to come along, and I figured she would be annoyed when I told her later. But I knew she was working, and besides, this felt kind of personal. I tied Moe's leash to the post and hooked him up, and then gave his ears a good scratching before going inside.

The chubby lady I'd seen before was working the front desk again, still wearing pink scrubs. I wondered offhandedly if she always wore that color. "Good morning," she said, dimpling. "I remember you—you're Ab's friend. Ben, right?"

I nodded, glancing quickly at her name tag and hoping she wouldn't notice. "Hi, Nancy. I came to see Mrs. Gautier. Is that okay?"

"Sure, sweetie. Lisette said you'd be coming by." She indicated the left hand hallway with a nod of her head. "She's in the dayroom. Do you remember the way?"

I nodded, smiling my thanks as I moved past her and started down the hall. Lisette had known I was coming! A hopeful sign, but I tried not to get too excited. I still didn't know for sure if she'd be able to help.

The dayroom was empty except for Lisette and Carl. Both sat in what I suspected were their customary places on the couch, Carl dozing with his chin on his chest while Lisette watched an episode of *I Dream of Jeannie.* The kerchief she wore on her head was blue today instead of yellow, and she was crocheting something out of dark green yarn. *"Mon cher!"* she said, brightening when she saw me come in. She patted the arm of a chair drawn up at right angles to the couch. "Come sit down with me, now. I been waitin' for you."

I did what I was told, the plastic cushion wheezing as I dropped into it. "When did you know I'd be here?"

The old woman laughed, the sound as rich as warm honey. "Knew as soon as I woke up this mornin'. I say to me, 'Lisette, you hurry along, now. That frien' of Abby's comin' by to see you today, an' he got some troubles that need talkin' about.'"

I nodded, fascinated with how at ease she was with her abilities and wondering if I'd ever feel that way. "I hope I'm not bothering you, Mrs. Gautier."

"Oh, *foo*—you jus' call me Lisette," she interrupted, waving a hand dismissively. "An' it ain' no bother at all." She smiled, the wrinkles in her ebony skin deepening as she patted my knee. "You don' know it yet, *cher,* but you an' me...we gonna be frien's."

I believed her and returned her smile. "I wanted to ask you about the things I...*we*...can do. Our abilities. What did you call it? 'The sight?'"

"Tha's right, boy. The sight runs strong in my family. Yours, too. Knew that as soon as I touched your hand."

Mom had it, too? I wondered but then stayed on point. "So, I was wondering...how can I get better at it?"

The old woman's eyebrows went up. "*Better?* Boy, you a pistol already....hell, you a *cannon!*" She chuckled, picking up her crochet project. "You jus' need control, tha's all."

"So, how do I get that?" I pressed.

"Same as anythin' else, *cher.* You good at what you practice. It jus' the way of the world."

I frowned, staring at nothing for a long moment. I didn't know exactly what I'd been hoping to hear from her, but it wasn't that. My gaze drifted to her crochet hook, dipping and pulling with mechanical precision. It was almost hypnotic.

"Take your time, boy. You tell me the res' when you ready to."

I looked back at her, realizing that yes, there was more I wanted to say. I wasn't sure where to start, though. Or, for that matter, how much she already knew. "Lisette," I began finally, "do you believe in ghosts?"

Her crochet hook stopped moving as she met my gaze. "Oh yes, *cher.* They real enough."

It took over an hour to tell her everything; from the first moment I'd felt something wrong in the cupola, to Bonnie's laughter in the vineyard, my flashbacks of the tidal wave, and everything else. Her eyes narrowed slightly when I told her of Mom's obsession with the cupola and the unexplained limp she kept insisting was a pinched nerve, and the old woman nodded thoughtfully as I wrapped up with the visions triggered by Claire's diary. "Everything seems to point back to what happened in 1946," I finished at last. "But my mom keeps getting worse, and I'm afraid…" I paused, swallowing nervously, but there was no turning back now. "I'm afraid that she may *die* before we figure it out." It was the first time I'd said it, even to myself, and it turned the anxiety I'd felt into cold, steel-hard dread. "Can you help me?"

The old woman studied me for a long moment. "Could be," she said at last. "But I need to know the res' before I can tell for sure."

I felt my eyebrows come together. "The rest of what?" I asked, confused. "I told you everything."

"No, boy," she corrected, "you tol' me all you *know.* I need to know what you *don'* know."

I shook my head. "How can I tell you what I don't know?"

Lisette smiled. "Well now, if you was anyone else, I'd have a look at your hand. Or just chit-chat a while. Or maybe read the cards. But you got the *sight,* so all you gotta do is reach out to me."

I shrugged, extending my arm toward her, but she just looked at it and shook her head.

"Oh," I said after an awkward pause, finally realizing what she meant. I took a breath to relax and then reached out with my gift. I gasped immediately, experiencing something I'd never felt before. It was like my mind had been seized...!

"Easy, boy," Lisette assured me, her eyes closed. "It's alright."

I stopped struggling, and at once I felt the spider-sense thing again—a prickly sensation that began at the base of my skull and steadily worked its way to cover my entire scalp. It was followed by what I could only describe as like the vibration of a dentist's drill. You know, when it hits that spot that makes your ears ring. The seconds ticked by as I winced, hoping the feeling would end soon...

And then it was gone.

I opened my eyes and looked toward Lisette, alarmed to see her slumped against the back of the couch taking rapid, shallow breaths. "Mrs. Gautier...*Lisette!* Are you okay?"

She nodded weakly, patting the air in my direction. "Fine... Jus'...give me a minute."

I watched her with concern until, gradually, her breathing returned to normal. At last I let out a grateful breath of my own. "You had me scared for a minute there," I confessed. "I thought you were having a heart attack or something."

She smiled at me, looking tired. "I knew you had the sight strong, boy, but I didn't think *that* strong. *Hoo!* You 'bout took my fool head off! I'll be lots more careful next time, I can tell you *that.*"

"So...?" I asked.

"There's a little girl who wanna be foun'," she told me. "I 'spect that be your Bonnie. She both sad and scared, thinkin' no one ever going to know her secret."

I tried to swallow, but my throat was dry, so I settled for a nod instead.

"Then there's the man in your attic. He lookin' for her, but he ain' lookin' in the right place. He sad, too, and angry. Nothin' gonna change that but findin' the girl."

My heart was thudding in my chest.

"Finally, there's that girl you been watchin'. She want you to find Bonnie, too."

That one I hadn't seen coming. *Oh my God…so Aunt Claire* was *the other ghost in the house!*

"But tha's not all," Lisette went on gravely. "An' what's left ain't the easy part. You need to hear this, *cher,* but I wanna make sure you ready."

I nodded again. "Go on."

"*Votre mère*…your mama…she in real trouble. Her sight made her latch onto the man in the attic. His anger and hurt been flowin' into her…'long with his need to fin' the little girl. Now *votre mère,* she pretty far gone now. 'Less somethin' change soon, she gonna be too far gone to fin' her way back."

My eyes felt hot and dry, and I clenched my fists, taking deep breaths until it passed. The last thing Mom needed was for me to fall apart now. "Anything else?"

She shook her head. "Nothin' clear."

I settled back, staring at nothing while I thought over everything she'd told me. "There's one thing I don't understand," I said at last. "You said my mom has the sight, too, but she's never had flashes or feelings like I have. Nothing even close. How come *she* connected with the ghost in the cupola, but I didn't?"

"I think I might know," said a voice, and we both looked over at Carl.

"How long you been playin' possum over there?" Lisette asked suspiciously.

"Long enough. It was too much fun eavesdropping, and I didn't want to spoil it." He grinned. "You get to be my age, and you've earned the right to a few bad manners."

"You got somethin' *useful* to say, ol' fool?

"Sure." He turned his attention to me. "Ever work with electricity, kid?"

I shrugged. "Mom and I wired in a light fixture once."

Carl nodded. "Okay, so you don't know squat. But we're in luck, 'cause I was an electrician for over forty years, so we don't need another expert. Let me ask you this—what's more dangerous to work with: a hundred and ten volts or two hundred and twenty?"

The answer seemed obvious. "Two hundred and twenty."

He shook his head. "Nope. Sure, two-twenty is a higher voltage, but nine times out of ten that much juice'll just knock you on your ass. Hell, one day when I wasn't paying attention, a two-twenty line threw me clear across a *room*." He leaned forward. "One-ten, though...that's just enough to get you. Grab a one-ten line, and the first thing that happens is all your muscles contract. You fry because you can't let go."

I glanced over at Lisette, but she just shrugged. "The man know his 'lectricity."

"Yeah, but what does that have to do with my mom?"

"Think about it, son. The way I see it, *you* can sense the spook in the attic—enough for it to repel you. That makes your sight-thingy two-twenty." He leaned forward. "But your mom's sight is more like one-ten. *Just enough where she can't let go.*"

I exhaled a long, shaky breath. It made a kind of sense, and the knowledge made me anxious to be on my way. "Thanks," I said. "Both of you." I shifted my feet, preparing to get out of the chair, but Lisette stopped me with a hand on my knee.

"You got a hard row to hoe, boy, an' that's the plain truth," she told me. "But you got it in you—I can tell. You got it in you, *but you got to hurry,* hear?"

TWENTY-SEVEN

THE MORNING DRIZZLE HAD TURNED TO RAIN BY THE time Moe and I headed back, the drops stinging our faces due to a stiff breeze that made the ride home ten different kinds of suck. We were both soaked and nearly frozen by the time we made it to the house, and my hands were shaking as I rubbed Moe down with a towel. After that I shucked my wet clothes, leaving them on the floor of my room as I quickly toweled myself off before crawling under the covers to warm up. Moe jumped onto the bed, stretching out beside me, and after a minute or two, my shaking began to subside.

Thunder rumbled in the distance as the wind intensified, pelting raindrops against the windowpane so hard that it sounded like thrown gravel. It looked like Moe and I had made it home just in time. Cold and wet as I was, I realized it could've been a lot worse. I listened to the storm for a while, my eyelids feeling heavy as I finally started to feel warm again, and…

...and I'm running barefoot between rows of grapevines, grinning with the exhilaration of secret freedom. The dirt is cool and soft beneath my feet, each stride sending up the rich smell of summer-tilled earth. It's twilight, and almost too dark to see, but the gray from above is enough to guide me through the lush growth looming high above my head on either side.

I've slipped out without anyone knowing, but I don't have much time. It won't be long before Claire comes looking for me. She'll be mad and will probably scold me like anything, but at least she won't tell Daddy. She's nice that way. Maybe if I hurry I can be back before anyone knows I'm gone...

I awoke with a twitch, surprised that I'd drifted off and wondering how long I'd been out. It didn't feel like long, although since my hair was dry, I guessed it must have been at least half an hour, maybe forty-five minutes. The short nap had done me good, though. I felt a lot more relaxed and ready to plan my next move.

I rolled onto my back, lacing my fingers behind my head while mulling over what I had come to think of as the "Bonnie Dream." This was the second time I'd had it, so between the repetition and the fact that the details stayed with me instead of fading as soon as I woke up, I was pretty certain it wasn't something conjured up by my own imagination. "Okay, Bonnie," I said out loud, talking more to myself than actually believing she could hear me. "So, you've got my attention. Now show me what I need to *know.*"

I thought back to my dreams of the tidal wave, my heart wrenching at the thought of Bonnie and all those other people being dragged out to sea. I wondered how many of them were already dead by the time they were swept offshore and how many were still thrashing in the freezing water, fighting desperately to stay alive. I shuddered.

It must have been terrifying—watching the light from the burning school fade as they were pulled down into darkness. *How long does it take to drown?* I wondered. *And how much does it hurt while it's happening?*

I shook off those thoughts. They weren't helpful, and I needed to keep my head in the game. Bonnie wanted to be found, Lisette had said. But why? So she could be buried? I shook my head, frowning. That didn't seem likely. I mean, really, what could be left after all this time? Would bones hold up that long in salt water? Teeth, even? I had no idea, and even if there *was* anything left of her, I didn't have a clue where to begin looking. The breakwater was the first thing that came to mind, but then I shook my head again. No, Ab said that hadn't been built until *after* the wave. So what could her body have stuck to for so long? An underwater rock? The dock pilings? I supposed it was possible, but there was no way to tell without looking, and I wasn't even sure how to go about doing that.

At last I threw the covers aside. Whatever I decided, it wasn't going to get done by wallowing around in bed all day. And besides, I was starving.

Moe watched as I pulled on fresh clothes and then followed me down to the kitchen. I rummaged around, frowning when I realized I had a more immediate problem—the oatmeal I'd made earlier was pretty much the last of our food. All I could find was a can of mushroom soup looking lonely by itself in a cabinet, along with half a bag of uncooked rice in the pantry. The fridge was a disappointment too, holding only a bottle of French's Mustard and the last two or three slices of packaged turkey that didn't look all that trustworthy anymore. Aside from that, the cupboard was bare.

I drummed my fingers on the butcher block, thinking. I wondered how many plastic shopping bags I could hang on the handlebars of my bike, but a single glance through the window at the rain pelting down outside was enough to kill that idea. One drenching a day was more than enough for me, thanks. I looked up at the ceiling, trying to figure my chances of prying Mom out of the cupola long enough for a trip to the market, but then I realized the last thing I felt like doing was having *that* fight. I sighed, frustrated. So my choices were either another bike ride in the rain or listen to my stomach rumble while waiting for the storm to pass. Neither one thrilled me.

I straightened. Unless…

Unless I took the car and drove myself.

I chewed my lower lip, thinking it over. I'd had my permit since before we left Vacaville, and even though I hadn't been behind the wheel since the couple of hours Mom had let me drive during our trip north, it wasn't like I'd forgotten how. But what if I got pulled over? How much trouble would I be in? Sure, it wasn't like driving without a license was a hanging offense or anything, but the idea of trying to explain what I was doing—or worse, why they couldn't get hold of Mom to come get me—made me nervous. Then again, Windward Cove didn't have a police department, and I couldn't remember seeing a sheriff's cruiser come through town more than two or three times since I'd been there, so I figured my chances of getting there and back without getting caught were pretty good.

Of course, if Mom could hear the car start from upstairs, the trip might end before it even began. Normally, she'd have a total meltdown and ground me for who knows how long. But normal was pretty far behind us now, wasn't it? And anyway, she'd have to come out of the house to yell at me, right? That would at least get her out of the cupola for a few minutes, and while the hollering was going on, I'd stand a good chance of talking her into a trip to town. Getting her away from the house for a while would do her a lot of good, and I didn't really care how it happened.

I nodded, my decision made. Mr. Toad's Wild Ride was on.

Upstairs, I snagged Mom's keys from the top of her dresser and then ducked into my room for something warm to wear outside. My denim jacket wasn't even close to dry yet, so I pulled on a hoodie instead, pausing as soon as I stepped back into the hall. As usual, the door to the attic stairwell was standing open, and I briefly considered yelling up to tell Mom my plan and see what would happen. After all, I hadn't actually *tried* to take the car yet, and the threat alone might be enough to bring her downstairs. I stood there, my resentment over how she had been treating me lately battling with the knowledge that it really wasn't her fault. And okay, to be honest, part of me was also excited by the idea of my first solo drive, though I don't know how much that swayed my decision. Anyway, I didn't stand there long before I turned and went back downstairs.

Outside, Moe and I trotted from the porch steps to the car. He jumped in when I opened the back hatch but was already on the front bench seat by the time I slid in behind the wheel. "Okay, you can hang out here," I told him. "Just don't freak out, okay?" He looked at me with his big doggie-grin and tail wagging furiously. Obviously, he didn't care if I was about to kill us both or not—he was all in.

The car had been sitting for a long time since Mom had last driven it, but the engine finally started on my third try. I sat there, letting the motor warm up while giving Mom all the time in the world to come bursting out of the house to ask what the hell I thought I was doing. I fiddled with the seat and mirrors, getting everything adjusted just right before I finally decided that she wasn't going to show. *Here goes,* I thought.

With all the rain, I was nervous that the car might get stuck in the mud just off the gravel drive, so getting turned around took a lot of back and forth. After what felt like a twenty-seven point turn, I looked back over my shoulder at the house, giving Mom one final chance to stop me if she was going to.

No sign of her.

"Hang on, Moe," I said, facing forward again, "and keep your paws and arms inside the ride at all times."

I was halfway down to the road before I remembered the lights and windshield wipers, but I got those going and pressed on, taking my time down the grade and easing the station wagon around the switchback corners. It was funny how a car in which I felt so comfortable in the passenger seat seemed to grow to the size of an aircraft carrier once I was behind the wheel. But I got us to the bottom without incident, and I stopped and looked both ways before turning left onto the road.

The rain and wind made me a little more cautious than usual, but all in all, I was starting to feel pretty comfortable by the time we rolled into downtown. A Toyota pickup was stopped in the middle of the entrance to the grocery store parking lot, so I put on my turn signal and was motioning for the driver to pull out in front of me when I realized it was Rick Hastings. His little brother Scott was in the passenger seat, and he scowled as he recognized my face. Rick must not have, though, and even tossed me a wave as he pulled into the street. Scott continued scowling and offered his own little single-digit gesture as they pulled away. It wasn't a thumbs-up.

Nice.

I managed to center the car between the parking space lines on my first try and sighed with relief as I put the transmission into park and switched off the engine. "Okay so far," I said. Moe licked my face, his tail whipping from side to side. He seemed disappointed when I made him stay in the car, watching as I ran across the street to the bank. There was an ATM just inside the vestibule, and after a moment's thought, I pulled the maximum daily limit from our checking account before recrossing the street and grabbing a cart on my way into the store.

I paused just inside, realizing for the first time that I had no plan at all as far as what to buy. Sandwich stuff was always a safe bet, and, of course, I should pick up some of Mom's favorites, but I guessed I should have made a list. I cruised up and down the aisles, making the best decisions I could off the top of my head: bread, pressed turkey and ham, eggs, assorted frozen dinners, hot dogs, cereal and milk. I was loading up on canned soup and chili when a voice sounded behind me. "You're looking lovely today, Mrs. Wolf."

I turned to see Ab grinning at me. "Hilarious," I said dryly. "What brings you out on a day like this?"

She held up a ten-pound sack of sugar. "Running low at the coffee house." She looked around. "Where's your mom?"

I snorted. "Right where she *always* is these days. It was either come to the store myself or eat my own foot."

Ab eyed the contents of the shopping cart. "You expect to lug all that stuff home by yourself?"

"I brought the car," I told her, doing my best to sound casual—like it was something I did all the time.

"Check *you* out, Mister Resourceful," she said, looking impressed. "But you're not really going to live on all that processed food are you? The salt alone will kill you."

"I don't have much choice. Mom's the real cook, and she's been off duty." I narrowed my eyes. "And anyway, who died and made *you* the food critic?"

"Are you kidding? Even if Aunt Abigail couldn't turn me into Martha Stewart, my mom would never let me get away without knowing a thing or two. Besides, it's not like cooking is all that hard, Wolfman. You like spaghetti?"

I shrugged. "Sure."

"We'll start you out on that, then. Come on."

I didn't remember actually signing up for lessons, but I let it go. I needed to talk to her, and the kitchen was as good a place as any. I followed Ab as she started tossing stuff in the cart—pasta, parmesan cheese, assorted spices and whatnot—moving around the store with purpose and authority. I liked that. I thought she'd grab some sauce in a jar, but she passed that section without even slowing down and headed for the canned tomatoes instead. We ended up in the produce section, where she chose stuff for a salad. "How many people are you planning to feed?" I asked finally. Between what I'd already grabbed and all the new stuff Ab kept throwing in, my cart was nearly overflowing.

"Ab's first rule of cooking: always make enough for leftovers," she told me. "This'll be plenty to see you and your mom through the next couple of days." She used her cell phone to call her folks while we stood in the checkout line, explaining that I'd asked her over for dinner and she'd be home later on. I considered mentioning that the whole thing was really more her idea but then decided it didn't matter. After all, it was her story—she could tell it however she wanted to.

We dropped off Ab's sugar at the coffee house and then headed for home, Moe lying contentedly between us with his head in her lap. I was secretly pleased with myself for getting us there without doing anything stupid, and if I didn't look quite as confident behind the wheel as I tried to, Ab was nice enough not to mention it.

Between the two of us, we managed to bring in all the groceries in a couple of trips. "You chop an onion," she ordered. "I'll put the rest of this away."

It sounded like a fair deal to me, so I found a knife and got to work over at the butcher block. It felt nice to be in the warm glow of the kitchen lights while the weather threw its soggy tantrum outside, and I realized that I was glad to have Ab's company. The afternoon would have been depressing without her, not to mention that it gave me a chance to tell her about my morning. “So I went to see Lisette today,” I began.

Ab stood by the open freezer door and paused from stacking microwavable dinners to look at me. “Yeah?”

I tried to read her expression, but if she was annoyed that I’d gone to Autumn Leaves without her, it didn’t show. “Yeah,” I said, nodding, and then stepped aside to give her a view of my work. “Is this small enough?”

She glanced down. “Smaller—about half that size. So what did you talk about?”

I finished with the onion while telling her about the dream that had woken me and the memories of Aunt Claire that followed. Ab listened quietly while showing me how to break off a garlic clove from the head. She smashed it with the flat of the knife to remove the outer skin and then neatly minced it, making it look easy. “Do two more just like that,” she instructed. “Keep talking.”

I went on, explaining how I thought Lisette could help me, and described as best as I could how we had joined our abilities. Ab sat on the counter by the stove, supervising as I browned the onion and garlic in a pot along with Italian sausage and hamburger. When it was ready, she had me drain off the fat and then told me from memory which spices and how much to stir in, along with fresh mushrooms, canned tomatoes, and tomato paste.

“Got any wine?” she asked.

I seemed to remember that we’d brought a bottle of red with us when we moved—a gift from some art dealer who had sold one of Mom’s paintings a while back. After a brief search, I found it lying on its side in a lower cabinet. I hunted around in the silverware drawer until I found a corkscrew and even managed to get the bottle open without help. “How much do I put in?”

"A pretty good slug." She watched me pour and told me when to stop. "Congratulations. You just made meat sauce," she said at last. "Give it a stir now and then, and let it simmer for about an hour."

Wow...she's right, I thought. *That wasn't hard at all.*

I sat next to Ab on the counter, wrapping up my story with Lisette's visions and Carl's theory about what was happening to Mom. "So, anyway, I think Lisette is right," I finished, my anxiety returning now that my hands didn't have something to do. "We need to hurry up. My mom is getting worse every day, and we don't have time to go through every vision for every diary entry."

Ab nodded. "Okay. We'll try it that way and only go looking for the visions that might lead us to Bonnie." She frowned. "Here's the part I don't understand, though. How does she expect anyone to find her body? Even if we did find some remains, how would we even know they were hers?"

"I don't know," I admitted. "That occurred to me, too. I don't even know how we're going to look."

"Oh, that's not a big deal," Ab said, brightening. "Les can help us with that. He dives for abalone every year, so he knows the cove inside and out."

I smiled, feeling encouraged. "I'll get the diary. We can start right now!"

"Easy Wolfman," Ab soothed, stopping me with a hand on my arm. "Survival first. You've got a salad to make and pasta to boil, remember?" She reached for the wine bottle and took a sip. "Get to work. I'll watch you from here."

The sauce was ready by the time I finished everything else, and Ab followed me as I carried a plate upstairs. The chill from the cupola hit me halfway up to the attic, but I shook it off, hoping Ab's presence would bring out more of a reaction from Mom than I'd been seeing lately. It was worth a try, anyway.

She was painting by lantern light when we reached the top of the stairs, a cocoon of yellow surrounded by the gray of the storm outside. Drawings and watercolors were everywhere, piled on the shelves and scattered across the floor like fallen leaves. "Knock-knock," I said as cheerfully as I could. "You've got a visitor."

Mom looked up, and it did my heart good to see her brighten a little. "Oh, hello," she said, and I frowned. Her voice carried a dreamy, slightly distracted tone that I immediately didn't like.

"Hi, Connie," Ab said. "Ben and I made dinner together, and I wanted to see how you were doing."

Mom only nodded, dabbing at a spot on the canvas with her brush.

I remembered the plate in my hands. "It's spaghetti, Mom. Ab showed me how to make sauce from scratch. Do you want some?"

"Too much garlic," she murmured, still concentrating on her work.

"What's that?"

"Garlic," she said, meeting my gaze with a stare that looked slightly glassy-eyed. "Flora always uses too much."

Ab gave me a questioning glance, and I swallowed, quickly setting the plate down because my hands were shaking. "Mom…? Are you okay?"

Her eyes seemed to focus. "I'm fine, Ben. Why?"

I opened my mouth. Closed it.

"I love your pictures," Ab said, dispelling the awkward silence. "Especially the little girl."

Mom's eyes glazed over again. "She's only hiding," she murmured, turning her attention back to the canvas.

"Come on," I whispered, taking Ab's arm.

"Bye, Connie," she called over her shoulder as I led her toward the stairwell. "See you soon!"

"Goodbye, Mary Lou," Mom replied behind us. "Nice of you to come by."

Ab was silent until we reached the attic floor. "Remind me again," she whispered. "Who's Flora?"

"She worked here when Aunt Claire was a teenager," I replied. "The housekeeper, I think."

"And Mary Lou?"

"Claire's best friend."

A long silence.

"This is really bad."

"I know."

TWENTY-EIGHT

...AND HER EXCUSE WAS THAT SHE CAN ONLY KEEP SO much in her head at once, so every time she makes a new promise, she forgets an old one. Unbelievable! As if Lee or I could have ever gotten away with saying something like that! But Daddy only laughed and asked her to do her best, and Bonnie got away with misbehaving again. To be honest, sometimes I feel sad and even a little resentful that she is so clearly Daddy's favorite, especially when I remember back when he used to treat me that way. But can I really blame him when she's my favorite, too?

"Done with this page?" I asked.

"Almost," Ab murmured, and I waited for her finish. We sat at the kitchen table, our shoulders touching as we poured over Aunt Claire's diary, and I turned to look at her in profile. Ab frowned when she read, I realized, and wondered if she knew it. I also realized that she smelled good—not like Kelly with her tropical sunblock or the perfume she'd worn at her party, but a slight fragrance from whatever soap or shampoo she used, along with just a hint of coffee beans. It was nice. “Okay,” she said at last, and I turned the page.

A couple of photos were stuffed between the leaves, so we examined those first. One was of an older lady standing beside Roger Black’s pickup, her foot on the running board. “That’s Flora,” I told Ab. The other photo was of Philip Garret standing at the edge of a sea cliff, his hands in his jacket pockets and the wind blowing his hair to one side. Having seen him in visions so many times, looking at the old black and white reminded me just how long ago it had all happened. I wondered if Aunt Claire had taken the picture, and what they’d been out doing that day. The Pacific stretched out behind him in swells and whitecaps, and I thought I recognized a rock formation about fifty yards out with a natural arch worn through by constant waves battering it for eons. I stared at it, trying to figure out exactly where they’d been standing, but I gave up when it didn’t come to me right away. Rock arches like that were pretty common, and it could have been any of a dozen places.

I was about to start reading the next entry when I felt Ab move beside me, and I looked to see her sitting back, rubbing her eyes. “Need a break?” I asked.

She paused long enough to yawn. “Actually, I think I’ve had enough for one night,” she confessed. “It’s late, and I have to open the shop in the morning.”

I glanced at my watch, surprised to see it was after midnight, and the twinge of guilt I felt for having kept her so long was mixed with disappointment that we hadn’t gotten further into Aunt Claire’s diary. I drove Ab home, my worry over Mom overshadowing any excitement I might have felt about my first time behind the wheel after dark. Luckily, the storm seemed to have run out of gas, the slashing downpour diminishing to a light but steady rainfall that glinted in the glare of the headlights. Neither of us spoke, the rhythmic thump of the windshield wipers sounding oddly soothing as we made our way back to town.

We were at Ab's house a few minutes later, and I put the transmission into park before turning to look at her. Ab was staring at me solemnly, her face half in shadow from the glow of a streetlight slanting down through the windshield. "About your mom..." she began, and then paused for a heartbeat or two. "What's going on with her, I mean. It must be really scary."

I swallowed. "It is."

"If it was happening to my mom, I'd be totally freaking out."

I fished around for a reply but couldn't think of one, so I settled for a nod instead.

Ab unbuckled her seatbelt, and I thought she was going to get out of the car when she surprised me by sliding across the bench seat and reaching over Moe to wrap me in a fierce hug. "We're going to fix this," she whispered in my ear. "Lisette said so, and she's *never* wrong. You believe that, right?"

"Sure," I said, trying to sound more confident than I really felt. Lisette had also told me that we had to hurry, but so far our progress seemed agonizingly slow. Glaciers probably moved faster. Mentioning that probably wouldn't have helped, though, so I didn't. Instead, I shifted in my seat so that I could return Ab's hug, but she was already gone, slamming the passenger side door behind her and running through the rain toward the house. She let herself in, closing the door behind her without looking back.

[Goodbye, Mary Lou... Nice of you to come by...]

The memory of my mother's words sent a sudden chill through me, so I reached over and cranked the heater up to high. It didn't help, but I guess I hadn't really expected it to. The cold I was feeling came from the inside. At last I put the car in gear and headed for home.

Moe was snoring lightly with his head in my lap when the headlights swept across the front porch, the darkened windows looking like eyeless sockets. A dim glow from the cupola was the only sign that the house wasn't some lonely, abandoned relic, and I got out of the car, pushing that thought aside before my imagination had time to run with it. Moe followed me onto the porch and through the front door, and I had gone maybe two or three steps into the entry hall before I realized…

…the living room is lit by the glow of a floor lamp. Its shade is dented, as if it had fallen over and then been set back upright. One door of a glass-fronted bookcase hangs partway open, a pile of hardcover volumes lying at its base. A china cabinet near the kitchen archway lies diagonally against the back of a sofa, shattered dishes and glassware strewn across the hardwood floor. One painting has fallen from its hook, its frame broken, while the rest hang askew on the walls. The room looks like a bomb has gone off in it, and after a confused moment, I realize this is a vision. What's more, I'm pretty sure I know from exactly when.

The murmur of voices drifts down from the second floor, so I turn and make my way upstairs, unconsciously stepping around shards of glass from several framed photos that have broken on the steps. An overhead light illuminates the hall, and I can see Claire standing in her bathrobe, arms crossed, gazing into Bonnie's bedroom from just beyond the threshold.

I step up behind her, looking in over her shoulder. The room is a shambles; desk overturned and a bookcase fallen over to scatter toys and picture books across the rug. Roger Black is seated on the bed, rocking gently back and forth while holding Bonnie in his lap. "Shhhh…It's alright, honey,” he croons reassuringly as she sobs into his chest. “It’s all over now. Everything’s fine.”

“My room moved!” *she cries, her words muffled against the flannel of his pajama top.*

“I know, honey,” Roger says, stroking her hair. “But it’s all done now.”

“I thought our house was falling down!”

“I know...I know. It was scary, wasn’t it? But I already checked, and the house is just fine. A little cleanup, and everything will be as good as new.”

The faint clanging of a bell drifts in through the open window, and Roger looks up to frown at the darkness outside. “A fire,” he says, rising to his feet and turning to set Bonnie down on the bed. “I should go see if they need help.”

“No, *Daddy!” Bonnie cries, clutching his right hand in both of hers. Her face is red from crying, tear tracks shining on her cheeks. “Don’t go! The room might move again!”*

“I told you it’s over with,” he replies, gently pulling free of her grasp. “But now I have to go—someone in town could be hurt.”

Bonnie’s chest hitches with fresh sobs. “But what if our...house falls...down?”

He frowns. “Stop it, Bonnie. You’re perfectly safe, and I’ll be back soon.”

Claire chooses that moment to take charge, bending to heave the bookcase upright against the wall. “Come on, Bonnie. What do you say we pick up this mess and then get you back in bed?”

Roger gives Claire a nod of approval and quickly exits the room. Bonnie watches him go, her chin quivering and fresh tears sliding down her cheeks to drip on her nightdress. After a pause, she begins to absently help her sister, repeatedly looking over her shoulder toward the hall. They’re almost finished when Roger reappears in the doorway, now dressed and pulling on a jacket. “I don’t know how long I’ll be, but

I'll come home as soon as I can. If you decide to go downstairs, put on shoes first—there's broken glass everywhere."

"Yes, Daddy," Claire says dutifully.

He turns to leave when Bonnie runs over to him. "Wait! I'm coming with you!"

"No, honey..."

"I can help! Let me come, Daddy...please?"

Roger goes to one knee in front of her. "I need you to stay here, Bonnie. I know you want to help, but you're too little for that, and you're not even dressed."

"I'll get dressed," she insists. "I'll get dressed, and then run and catch up with you!"

"No," he tells her, his voice firm. "You'll do no such thing. You're going to do as I say, mind your sister, and stay away from town until I know it's safe. Do you understand?"

"Yes," she mutters sulkily, staring at her toes.

"Promise me, Bonnie."

A pause, then, "I promise."

Roger gathers her into a brief hug and then rises and hurries down the hall.

The fight seems to go out of the little girl, and I watch as Claire tucks her back into bed, sitting beside her until Bonnie's eyes finally drift closed.

When she's sure her sister is asleep, Claire tiptoes out, leaving the door partway open and the hall light on. I follow her to her own room. She spends a few minutes putting things back in order and is fumbling with the belt of her robe when she looks up, hearing the soft tick of a pebble against her windowpane. She steps over to look through the glass and then hurriedly lifts the sash and pokes her head outside. "What are you doing here?" she whispers...

And with that, the vision faded. I suddenly found myself standing in near-total darkness, staring at raindrops running down the outside of a windowpane. Claire's windowpane, I realized—now mine.

It took a few seconds for my eyes to adjust to the gloom, but then I went and flopped down beside Moe on the bed, staring at the ceiling while I thought it all over. My heart thudded with excitement as two things occurred to me right away. First, up until then, I'd had to hold Aunt Claire's diary in order for a vision to appear, but the book was still downstairs on the kitchen table where Ab and I had left it. Second, every vision I'd experienced so far had been triggered by reading a passage from the diary. But we were still working our way through May, and hadn't even gotten to the night of the earthquake and tidal wave yet—that would be a month further on.

I grinned in the darkness, my spirits lifting. Lisette must have been right—all the practice was making me better!

I didn't have long to enjoy my excitement, though, as I suddenly sat up, cocking my head at a faint sound at the edge of my hearing. Moments passed, and I was just beginning to think I'd imagined it when the sound came again. It was a half-sigh, half-moan that made my chest tight and my scalp prickle in fear, mostly because its tone was familiar.

It sounded like my mother.

I heaved myself to my feet, grabbing my flashlight and hurrying down the hall with Moe at my heels. We were still ten feet from the attic stairwell when we paused, hitting a sudden, penetrating cold that was like running into a wall. Moe lowered his head and growled, his tail creeping up between his legs. I thought he'd stay behind, but when I went on, he was right beside me, his ribs against my calf as we hurried up the stairs.

The moan came again, now louder, when we were still four steps from the top, a mixture of pain and grief that sent me across the attic floor at a dead run. I swallowed back panic as I pounded up the cupola steps, doing my best to fight back the crushing depression that filled the space like some sort of poisonous gas. The air was even colder as I reached the top, stumbling into the lantern glow with my breath coming out in puffs of white.

Mom was in the rocking chair, whimpering in her sleep as she writhed beneath the quilt. Her sunken cheeks were wet with tears, and her face was twisted in an expression of pain and grief that tore at my heart. She moaned again, the sound loud in the confined space, and then twisted toward the far window with her back to me.

I hurried over, reaching out to touch her shoulder. "Mom…?" I said, trying to keep the panic out of my voice. She didn't respond, so I shook her gently. "Mom, wake up. You're dreaming."

Still nothing.

"Mom!" I shouted, not meaning to but unable to help it. I shook her again, harder this time, and then gasped when her head snapped around, one hand striking out from beneath the quilt to seize my wrist painfully. She glared at me in the lantern light, her teeth bared, her face a mask of loathing and rage. I'd never seen her look that way, and it was like gazing into the face of a stranger.

"It's your fault!" she screamed, her breath sour and spittle flying from her lips.

Terrified, I tried to twist free of her grasp but couldn't. "Mom…"

"You were supposed to be WATCHING her!"

TWENTY-NINE

"DUDE...*LISTEN UP*! THIS IS IMPORTANT."

"I *am* listening."

Les looked at me skeptically, and I felt my face flush. He was right—my head wasn't in the game. I tried to focus on what he was saying, but my mind kept drifting back to the night before. Even in broad daylight, the memory scared me, and I'd woken up that morning with bruises shaped like finger marks on my wrist.

It had started and ended so fast. One second Mom was clutching at me, her face twisted in loathing and rage...

[You were supposed to be WATCHING her!]

...and then the frigid air was tearing around the cupola like a cyclone, throwing Mom's drawings everywhere. Moe barked furiously, his hackles raised and teeth showing, and I followed his gaze to where the cold, depression, and anger seemed to be gathering ... *concentrating*. I could feel my hair trying to stand on end as the presence in the room condensed into a mass that I could almost see—a slightly darker shadow among the shadows. It raged once more around the room and then swirled down the cupola steps, slamming the door behind it.

And then it was over.

Two, maybe three heartbeats passed before my legs went all rubbery and I sank to the floor, exhaling a breath. The room felt warmer, the air seeming eerily calm in the lantern's glow, and I realized that Mom's hand had gone slack on my wrist. I looked over to see her sleeping peacefully in the rocking chair, her cheeks no longer appearing so sunken and the hard lines of anger all smoothed out. I didn't remember how long I sat there, gazing at her, but my heartbeat was back to normal and my right leg had almost gone to sleep by the time I got to my feet. Mom's quilt had been mostly pulled away by the icy whirlwind, so I drew it back up, tucking it around her before sitting back down on the floor beside the chair. Pulling one corner of the quilt around Moe and me, I settled down to wait out the darkness…

"*C'mon,* Ben…you're zoning again! Do you want to do this or not?"

I sighed. "Sorry, man. It was a long, rotten night, and I'm kind of out of it."

Les nodded sympathetically, having already heard the story during the drive down to the wharf, but then he grinned. "Well, don't worry. In about five minutes, you're going to be wide awake!"

I nodded and then watched as he pulled the hood of his wet suit down over his head. I tried to copy him, but despite the stretchiness of the foamy material, I couldn't get it past my ears. "It's too small," I complained, pulling it back off.

"I know it's snug—I outgrew that suit two years go—but you need to try harder."

"Can't I just go without it?" I asked. "Is the water really that cold?"

Les shrugged. "It's your call, but I tried going in without a hood once, and it wasn't fun. Imagine the worst ice cream headache *ever.* Trust me, you'll be glad to have it on."

I nodded and tried again, gritting my teeth as the hood almost pulled my hair out, but eventually I got it down over my head. It was tight around my throat, and the hole where my face stuck through was painful around the edges, but it would do. "What now?"

"Booties and gloves. Booties first."

I followed his example and then sat next to Les on the edge of the dock while he instructed me to rub spit on the inside of my mask so that it wouldn't fog up and then showed me how to attach the snorkel. Fins went on last, and then we were ready to go.

The storm had finally passed sometime during the night, leaving behind a high, grey-white overcast—the kind of day that could surprise you with sunburn if you weren't careful. It was nearly noon, and sea birds rode a slight offshore breeze that made the water lap at the pilings below us. It wasn't enough to really cool things off, though, and I quickly started to feel warm in the heavy wet suit.

"Okay, here's what you need to remember," Les said, looking serious. "See that otter out there on top of that brownish-green stuff?"

I looked where he was pointing and found the otter, floating on his back while using a rock to bang away at a clam on his belly. He seemed to be having a fine time. "Yup," I answered.

"That's a kelp bed," Les explained. "Rule number one: stay the hell out of the kelp. If you get tangled up in that stuff, you're *screwed.*"

I nodded, really focusing at last. "Okay…kelp bad. Got it."

"Rule number two: don't freak out. There's lots of critters down there—fish and sea lions and sometimes even dolphins—and they may come and check you out, but they aren't going to hurt you and will generally keep their distance."

I grinned, excited by the idea. "Critters good," I acknowledged. *This was going to be a blast!*

"Rule three: if there *are* any sea lions, it's a good thing. Keep an eye on them. If they get out of the water all of a sudden, that means you should, too."

"How come?"

"'Cause that means there's a shark around." I opened my mouth, but Les stopped me before I could say anything. "Don't worry. It's rare that they'll come into our cove, and they'll almost always leave you alone. It's just never a good idea to test the odds, that's all. I even saw a great white once, although that was way out beyond the breakwater, and even though it scared the crap out of me, the shark couldn't have cared less. So, if you see one, don't panic. Swim calmly over to someplace where you can get out of the water, and it will generally go away after a little while."

I swallowed and then pointed at the diving knife strapped to his right leg. "Is that why you carry that?"

He nodded. "Uh-huh."

"Seriously? You think you could kill a shark with that thing?"

"*Hell* no. What do I look like…Tarzan?"

"Then why even have it?" I asked, frowning.

Les grinned. "So if a shark comes, I can poke you in the leg and swim away."

I felt my eyes widen, but then I heard Ab cackle behind me, so I looked over my shoulder. "He's just messing with you, Wolfman," she said, smiling from behind her sunglasses. Ab lounged beside a cooler in a folding beach chair, feet crossed at the ankles and resting on an old mooring cleat. She looked comfortable.

"Sure you don't want to come along?" I asked.

"I told you already—I don't do cold water." She settled back, opening the book in her lap and reaching out to pet Moe with one hand. "We'll just hang out here and call the Coast Guard if you're not back by dark."

Les chuckled, and I looked back in time to see him pull his mask down over his face. Then, holding it in place with one hand, he slipped off the dock and splashed down into the water.

I did the same, dropping four or five feet before I hit, and then fighting against the urge to gasp at the sudden shock of cold. I drifted downward, forcing myself to relax while my body got used to the temperature change. The water tasted the way it smelled—briny and saltier than I would have thought—and for a moment I was taken back to my vision of being swept up in the tidal wave. The gloom under the dock was almost as dim as that night on Main Street, and in a sudden, vivid flash of memory, I saw the life go out of Margaret Lindsay's eyes just before the receding water pulled her into darkness. I shook it off, kicking my way upward. My head broke the surface and I coughed, wincing at the raw sting of salt in the back of my throat.

Les was grinning at me while treading water five or six feet away. "So...ready for Snorkeling 101?"

"Sure."

It took no time at all for him to teach me how to cruise around with my head in the water, breathing comfortably through the snorkel. Diving was pretty straightforward too, although the first time I came back up, I forgot to first blow the water out of the tube and ended up sucking in what felt like half the cove. It left me coughing and retching for an embarrassingly long time, and for a second or two, I thought I was going to barf it all back up. In the end, though, all that came out was a belch as loud as a moose bellow, and I felt better right away.

I tried it a few more times, and at last Les gave me a nod of approval. “Okay, you’ve pretty much got the hang of it, so we might as well get to work. Tell me again: what are we looking for?”

“Anything,” I said. “Bonnie was dragged out by the tidal wave, so if there’s something left of her out here, we have to bring it up. I don’t imagine there could be much after all these years, but even if it’s just a few bones, it might be enough to have a funeral and put her to rest.”

Les frowned. “Come on, Ben. Do you honestly think there’s anything down there?”

I shrugged. “No idea. But Lisette told me she wants to be found, so there must be *something,* right? Otherwise, why would Bonnie try so hard to get my attention?”

“Okay, okay. Have it your way,” he relented. “So long as you know this is the creepiest thing I’ve ever had to do.”

We took a few minutes to divide the cove into a rough search grid, using the dock, the breakwater, and various trees and rocks on shore as landmarks. It wasn’t perfect, but we had to start somewhere. The cove was close to a hundred yards across, and it didn’t make sense to just swim around randomly, hoping for the best, so it would have to do. At last Les gave me a wave of farewell and moved off to my left, inhaling a deep breath and slipping headfirst under the surface. I double-checked the landmarks for my first search area and then did the same, kicking downward into the gloom and having to pull hard with my arms to overcome the natural buoyancy of the wet suit.

The storm from the day before had stirred up a lot of silt, so the visibility wasn’t great—maybe only four or five feet—and when the bottom came into view about fifteen feet down, it came as a surprise. The light was enough to see by, if only barely, and was tinged a greenish-blue that slowly darkened as I went lower. Details emerged as I got close enough to see: mollusks and sea urchins and other things I half-remembered from science class, along with seaweed that swayed lazily in the current and tiny silver fish that darted away as I drew near. The bottom was uneven, I noticed, all rocks and overhangs and shadowy fissures that looked like chasms, the cove steadily deepening the farther I got from shore. What surprised me most were all the colors—the dark green of various plants, the electric blue of shellfish clustered on rocks, and even a fire-red crab that scuttled sideways away from me, claws raised to warn me off.

I leveled out, pulling myself slowly along the bottom by my hands and gentle kicks from my fins, taking my time and studying details. Whatever might be left of Bonnie had had decades to blend in with the surroundings, and it struck me how easy it would be to mistake a half-buried skull for a rock or to cruise right past teeth scattered among the pebbles. In no time at all my chest began to ache, so I kicked for the surface, doing my best to swim straight upward so that I could find my place again. I took a few breaths, and then headed back down, feeling like some underwater treasure hunter.

It took me over an hour to search my first thirty-by-thirty-foot square of seafloor, and in that time I found four beer cans (three Budweisers and a Coors Light), nine fishing lures, a rotted Giants baseball cap, two pairs of sunglasses, and a wristwatch with Mickey Mouse smiling up at me through the crystal (I couldn't tell how old it was, but it had stopped at 3:17.) Lots of junk, but no sign of Bonnie—or anyone else, for that matter. The artifacts trailed off the further I got from the dock, and I stuffed everything I found into the nylon mesh sack tied at my waist just as Les had told me to.

There was a fun few moments when a sea lion came by to see what I was up to. He was pretty big—a couple of hundred pounds at least—but he moved as gracefully in the water as if he were a part of it. He circled me once and then rolled onto his back as if to see if I looked any more interesting upside-down, studying me curiously with brown eyes. I lifted one hand to wave, and he disappeared with a powerful push of his fore flippers.

By the time I'd finished my second search area, I was tired and hungry, and Les and I flopped on the dock, wolfing down sandwiches and soda from Ab's cooler. After that we rested a while and then agreed that we both had one more zone left in us, so we hit the water again.

The final round of the day seemed to take forever. My arms and legs felt like dead weights, and I could no longer hold my breath anywhere near as long, so roughly the same size area that had taken me about an hour to search earlier stretched out into two. My enthusiasm faded away in the first forty minutes or so, leaving behind only a dogged determination to get it done, to get it done right, and most importantly, to not get out of the water before Les did.

The last high point of the day came when I found a wreck. I had just finished poking around under a promising-looking overhang of rock, sifting through the sand with my hands because it was too dark to see, when I came out on the far side and saw what was left of an old fishing boat. It lay on its side in about twenty-five feet of water near a large kelp bed, its hull covered in barnacles and mossy-looking stuff. It reminded me of the wreck of the *Orca* from *Jaws II*. I went up for a quick few gulps of air and then dived excitedly back down, heading directly for the wreck while promising myself that I'd investigate the area I'd skipped over later.

Approaching it from behind, I rubbed away the algae and mud just below the stern rail, and could just make out *Laura Marie* in red letters that had faded nearly to nothing. I skimmed along its side, wondering excitedly if it had been among the fishing boats dragged under by the tidal wave back in 1946. The windows of the small wheelhouse were gone, and I looked inside, immediately realizing that the boat hadn't sunk that long ago after all. I rubbed my hand across the instrument panel, sweeping away more muck, and I smiled around my snorkel when I saw what was left of a car stereo with CD player. Definitely not 1940s tech.

My chest was starting to burn by then, so I hurried along, finally discovering what had caused the boat to sink. The bow was caved in just below where I figured the waterline would be, as if *Laura Marie* had hit something head-on. I looked around, only then noticing a thick, nearly vertical column of rock not far off, its top lying just below the surface. Had that done it? I didn't know, but the idea seemed reasonable. I would have loved to spend more time figuring it out, but exploring wrecks wasn't what I was there for. And anyway, I was out of air, so I reluctantly kicked my way to the top.

As my head broke the surface, I looked over and was relieved to see Les climbing the short ladder up to the dock. Water streamed from his wet suit and gear, and I was happy to see that he at least *looked* tired. Seriously...the guy was a machine. I allowed myself to savor the victory while I made the long swim back, sorry that we hadn't found anything but really glad that the day was over with. I was worn out.

It seemed to take forever to reach the base of the ladder, and it took me two tries just to toss my fins up onto the dock. Getting up there myself was a whole new challenge—it felt like I'd put on about a thousand pounds. But Les and Ab reached down to help haul me up the last three or four rungs, and I finally collapsed gratefully on the rough planks. All I could do was lie there for a few minutes, getting my breath back while gazing up at the late afternoon sky, too tired to even bother pushing Moe away as he danced around my head, licking my face.

Eventually, I found the strength to sit up. "Find anything?" I asked, reaching up to yank off my hood.

Les shook his head. "*Nada.* Just crap." He shook his own mesh bag, which contained a collection of fishing lures and trash similar to mine.

"How much of the cove do you think we searched today?"

He gazed out over the water, gauging distances. "I'd say ten percent. Fifteen, maybe."

Was that all? I collapsed back to the dock with a groan.

"Cheer up, Wolfman," Ab said. "You're ten percent closer than you were yesterday, right?"

"I guess."

Les began to peel off his wet suit, so I got to my feet and did the same. We gathered up all our gear and trudged to the gravel parking lot, tossing everything into the back of the station wagon. Les and I toweled off and then dragged jeans up over our swim trunks and pulled on T-shirts before we all piled into the car. I had to shake Les awake when we pulled up in front of his house, and I spent a few minutes helping him hose the salt from the wet suits and gear, hanging everything to dry on a line behind his house. "Tomorrow?" he asked tiredly when we were done.

I sighed, not really wanting to think about it. "Yeah. Tomorrow."

"You suck."

I nodded. "I know."

The drive to Ab's house took only a couple of minutes, and as I shut off the engine I noticed her watching me closely. "What?"

"Ready for more of the diary?" she asked.

"Yeah…sure. Let's get to it." I reached behind the seat into my open backpack, but Ab hadn't moved by the time I had fished out the leather-bound book. She was still staring. "*What?*" I asked again.

"Oh, come *on,* Ben. Do you honestly think you're in any shape for this? You look like you're about to drop."

"I'll be fine," I argued, and then yawned.

"Yeah, right." She held out her hand. "Give it to me."

"What?"

"You heard me—hand it over," she insisted. "You've got more swimming to do tomorrow, remember? Go home and crash. I'll read ahead and look for clues, and if I find anything, I'll tell you first thing in the morning. Fair enough?"

"Well..."

"You *know* I'm right, Wolfman."

I sighed, reluctantly handing the diary to her. "Well, okay...if you're sure. But if you find anything, don't wait for morning. Call me tonight, okay?" I hunted around the glove box until I found a pen that still worked and then scrawled my cell phone number on the back of an old gas receipt.

She took it from me. "The coffee house opens at six. Come by any time after that."

"But you'll call me *tonight* if you find something, right?"

"Yeah, yeah...I promise." She gave Moe a quick kiss and then slid out of the car and pushed the door shut. "Get some sleep, Wolfman. I've got this."

I watched as she trotted to the front door, grateful that she was giving me the night off, but feeling a little left out just the same.

I was starving again. The last thing I felt like was fixing something myself, though, so I swung by Hovey's on the way home. I left Moe in the car while I went inside, thinking I'd just grab a burger and fries to go. But the day was cooling as the afternoon waned, and when I saw that the special of the day was minestrone soup, I decided that sounded better. I sat at the counter and ate three bowls. With bread. And two large sodas. Big Mike didn't say anything, but I thought he looked impressed. I ordered a fourth bowl to go for Mom and then waddled back to the car, ready to go home and sleep for a week.

Back at the house I dropped off Mom's soup (she was asleep in the rocking chair—surprise, surprise) and then fed Moe before trudging upstairs. Even showering seemed like a chore, but I made myself do it anyway, getting rid of the sea salt that covered me with lots of soap and hot water. The sun wasn't even down yet when I fell into bed, but I didn't care. Right then my pillow was the best thing in the world.

It seemed like I had just closed my eyes when I sat up again with a gasp, disoriented to find that my room pitch black. I didn't remember much of the dream that had jarred me awake, but what I did remember left me trembling with adrenaline:

A low rumble, then sudden darkness, followed by a scream. The high-pitched scream of a little girl.

I fell back on the mattress, letting out a breath while waiting for my tremors to go away.

"Don't worry, Bonnie," I whispered to the darkness. *"I'll find you. I promise."*

THIRTY

A COLD SNUFFLING IN MY EAR BROUGHT ME AROUND, and I opened one bleary eye. "Hey, Moe," I rasped. I must have been sleeping with my mouth open, and could barely work up enough spit to get the words out. Then I noticed with sudden panic that the light in my room was all wrong, and I rolled over to paw awkwardly at the nightstand until I found my watch. I squinted at the display, realized a second later that I was trying to read it upside-down, and then cranked my arm around so that I could make out the numbers: *0647*.

I'd slept through my alarm. *Crap!*

As I swung my legs out of bed, Moe jumped down and ran to the door, looking back at me with his tail wagging. "Okay, buddy—I'm coming." I limped painfully downstairs after him, picking the dried sleep from the corners of my eyes and wondering how long I would have stayed out if he hadn't needed to pee. My dream from the night before still nagged at the back of my mind, the memory of Bonnie screaming in the darkness sending a cold tingle of anxiety down my spine. She wanted to be found, Lisette had told me, and I was doing my best, but the mental echo of that scream from all those years ago made my best seem pretty pathetic—maybe even hopeless. But then I shook my head, shoving those negative thoughts away. After all, Les and I had only spent one day in the water, and if Bonnie wanted her remains to be found, it must be because there was something still out there. I wasn't about to quit now, especially since putting Bonnie to rest might be the key to releasing the other ghosts in the house and whatever hold they had on my mom. No way was I giving up on her!

Moe dashed out the front door, and I turned to make my way back upstairs. I had only climbed five or six risers, though, when a voice suddenly called out behind me:

"Claire! Would you come down for a moment, please?"

I yelp, spinning around in surprise and nearly tumbling back down to the bottom.

Roger Black and a man I don't recognize stand shaking water from their raincoats just inside the open front door. Behind them, the sunny morning has become late afternoon. Rain falls heavily outside, pummeling the spring grass, and the part of my mind logging details estimates the time frame to be maybe late April or early May.

"Yes, Daddy?" Claire answers. I look back over my shoulder to see her hurrying downstairs, and I unconsciously step aside to give her room to pass. She stops at the landing, one hand resting on the bannister post.

"Claire, I'd like you to meet Mr. William Crenshaw," Roger tells her, and I watch as the new guy takes off his hat to reveal a balding head he's trying unsuccessfully to hide beneath a comb-over. "We just hired him away from the Viscusi Winery," Roger goes on. "He'll be supervising the workmen at the cellar and getting our equipment up and running for the harvest."

Claire nods. "How do you do, Mr. Crenshaw."

"Pleased to meet you, Miss Black," he answers. There's something about either his tone or smile that makes my skin crawl, and I study him more closely. Crenshaw is shorter than Claire by an inch or two and pudgy, with thick lips and a set of jowls that remind me vaguely of a fish. As he reaches out to shake with Claire, I notice that his hands are small, with wiry, dark hair on the backs and dimples where his knuckles should be. He holds her hand just longer than necessary before releasing it, and by the way Claire steps quickly back, I'd bet real money she feels the same instinctive wariness about him that I do.

Claire's dad doesn't seem bothered by him, though, and turns to address the man. "Since I can't spare the time to oversee the project closely myself, Claire will be stopping by in the afternoons to discuss your progress. I'll appreciate you keeping her fully informed."

"Of course," the man assures him.

*Claire straightens. "*Every *afternoon?" she asks. "But, Daddy, I was going to audition for the spring play, remember? Rehearsals are after school."*

He frowns, looking annoyed. "Excuse us, Bill," Roger says, taking her arm and drawing her away.

The man smiles and nods, and I move past him to follow Claire and her dad into the living room.

"Daddy, we talked about this," she whispers when they're out of earshot.

"I know, sweetheart, but things have changed. Mr. Crenshaw brings a wealth of experience from Napa Valley, and we'll need him if we're going to be ready to crush this fall. You can see that, can't you?"

"Yes, but Daddy you promised..."

"Claire, I need your help. I can't do this alone. And besides, we both know your talent for details is far better than mine. There will be other plays...I promise. Maybe next year. But right now I need you. Can you do this for me?"

She opens her mouth as if to protest further but then seems to think better of it and sighs instead. "Yes, Daddy."

Roger smiles, reaching out to stroke her cheek fondly. "That's my girl! I honestly don't know what I'd do without you."

I can see that Claire is still disappointed, but she brightens little at the compliment just the same and follows her father back to the entry hall.

"It's all settled," Mr. Black says to Crenshaw. "Claire has my full confidence and will be speaking for me. Any questions?"

"No, sir."

"That's fine, then. Come on, I'll drive you back to town." He steps through the door onto the front porch.

Crenshaw pauses before following Roger back out into the rainy afternoon, watching with a small smile as Claire retreats upstairs. Curious, I follow his gaze, and it takes me all of about a second to realize where he's looking. A bright flash of indignation floods through me as I turn back toward the door...

But the front door was closed, the windows to either side bright with morning sunshine. Even though the vision was over, and there was nothing I could have done even if it wasn't, it still took a dozen heartbeats or so for my irritation to go away. Part of me knew I was silly to feel so protective, but I still didn't like it that Crenshaw had been checking out my Aunt Claire's butt. Then I remembered how late I was running, so I shook it off, resigned that 1946 must've had its share of pervs, too.

I made my way back upstairs, using the bannister to haul myself up the risers. Everything ached, like my body was one giant bruise. I pulled on some clothes and then ducked into the bathroom to splash cold water on my face and brush my teeth. I'd anticipated being sore after my long workout in the cove the day before, but I didn't think it would be *this* bad. How the hell was I supposed to keep searching for Bonnie when the only thing that didn't hurt was my hair? But by the time I headed back downstairs, my assorted aches were showing signs of easing as my muscles began to warm, so I figured maybe I'd live after all.

I let Moe in, and he had his breakfast while I quickly scrambled some eggs for Mom. I made one final trip upstairs, leaving her plate where she'd see it when she woke, and taking a moment to pull the quilt up around her shoulders. Then I hurried down to the front door, whistling for Moe as I plucked the car keys from the entry hall table.

I was reaching for the doorknob when a jumble of emotions—fear, excitement, anticipation—pinged my mental radar, like the way the smell of maple syrup hits you just before you walk into the House of Pancakes. I paused, knowing what it meant right away. For a second or two, I considered ignoring the coming knock and staying put until she decided I wasn't home, but then I decided against it. I was already late, and chances were the sound of my whistle had carried out to the porch. And anyway, it wasn't like there was some rule that I had to stick around for a bunch of drama. *Might as well get it over with*, I figured, and then took a deep breath and opened the door.

Kelly Thatcher looked up from the porch steps, her expression first appearing startled but then rearranging itself into a tentative smile. A brief silence hung awkwardly in the air between us, and in those two or three seconds, I couldn't help but notice how good her yellow T-shirt looked in contrast to the auburn of her hair. The shirt was cropped to show a few inches of midriff above clingy, dark blue yoga pants that did all kinds of nice things for her. She looked good—and probably knew it—but I didn't have time to be distracted. "Hey," she said at last.

"Hey yourself," I said, and then closed and locked the front door behind me. I moved around her, trotting down the steps toward the car.

That took her by surprise, but she recovered quickly. *"Hey!"* she repeated, hurrying after me, and caught me by the arm next to the station wagon.

I turned to look at her, eyebrows raised.

She paused, chewing her lower lip. "Are you…*mad* at me?"

"No," I told her.

But I sort of was. Mostly I was just irritated at having to deal with her right then. Okay, there was also a touch of pride mixed in that I was able to stand that close to her without getting all nervous and dorky, which was a first. I wondered briefly if that meant her spell was finally starting to wear off. The thought was both satisfying and a little disappointing, but I ignored it, remembering that I didn't have time for any of that. If it bothered Kelly that I wasn't going to stick around for today's episode of Messing with Ben's Head, well, she had it coming. It served her right for ambushing me.

She shifted her feet, looking uncomfortable. "I guess this is a bad time, huh?"

"Yeah, it is," I replied, still not cutting her any slack, but feeling my irritation slip a notch or two just the same. "Sorry," I added. "I'm not trying to be a jerk or anything, but I slept through my alarm this morning, and I have to get a move on."

"No," she offered, *"I'm* sorry. It's a nice day, and I should have guessed that you and Abigail would have plans."

The remark came out of nowhere, and it caught me off guard. "I'm snorkeling with Les today," I blurted out, and even though Kelly brightened, I immediately wished I hadn't said it—or at least clarified that I'd be meeting with Ab first. But still, the fact was I'd be spending *most* of the day with Les, so it wasn't a lie, right?

It just felt like one.

What am I doing? I wondered, but I already knew the answer to that, too. No matter how I felt about her right then (and the jury was still out on that one), part of me still wanted Kelly to know I was available. After all, I *was*. There wasn't anything going on between Ab and me—that was all Kelly's idea. *She* was the one hooked up with someone, and it didn't look like that was going to change any time soon. So, as long as I wasn't actively going after her, what the hell did I have to feel guilty about?

It was just too confusing, and it irritated me all over again.

A lot of Kelly's confidence seemed to return, though, and she closed the distance between us with a step. "I won't keep you, then," she said, smiling up at me. "And anyway, I didn't know you'd be awake this early, so I just came by to leave you a note." Her left hand, which had been behind her back, came around to hold out a pink envelope with *Ben* written on it in purple ink.

"Thanks," I said, accepting it and then taking a step back. "Look, thanks for the note, and it's nice of you to come by, but I've really gotta go. We'll catch up later, okay?" I turned without waiting for an answer, opening the driver's side door and pausing while Moe jumped in.

"Aren't you going to read it?"

"Sure," I said, tossing the envelope on the dash as I slid in behind the wheel. "Just as soon as I have time—I promise." I started the car, and was surprised when I felt a sudden rush of disappointment. It took me a second to realize that it hadn't come from me. It was *Kelly's* disappointment—the first non-jumbled-up feeling I'd even been able to pick up from her—and it made me pause. I watched in the rear-view mirror as she got into her Jeep, backed around in a U-turn, and then disappeared down the drive.

I turned to Moe. "So, do you think that meant anything?"

He met my gaze briefly and then twisted around and started licking his belly.

"Yeah," I agreed, dropping the car into reverse. "Probably not."

I tried to forget about Kelly, reminding myself that so far she'd done nothing but make me crazy, but my gaze kept centering on the pink envelope that reflected dimly on the windshield like a heads-up display in a fighter plane. To be honest, a couple of times I nearly gave in to the desire to pull over and read what was inside. I managed to shake the feeling off, though, and made it to town without touching it. When Moe and I got out of the car and left it behind, I was both a little relieved and secretly pleased by my willpower.

The morning crowd at Tsunami Joe wasn't much to speak of—maybe only half a dozen customers scattered around the room. I ordered a large mocha from the lady working the counter, along with a monster cinnamon roll I noticed in the pastry display that didn't look like it was doing anything important. My order was ready in no time at all, and I made my way to a couple of comfy-looking armchairs that faced one another across a small table near the back wall.

I had just sat down and taken my first bite when Ab emerged from the back and noticed me. "*There* you are," she said, plucking Aunt Claire's diary from behind the counter and crossing the room to flop in the other seat.

"Yup," I answered after I'd swallowed. "Here I are."

"What took you so long? I expected you an hour ago."

I told her about my morning, although to be fair, I might have just touched on the part where I'd overslept, and I didn't mention Kelly's visit at all. After all, the vision was all that really mattered, and I took my time bringing her up to speed.

"Your aunt mentioned Crenshaw," Ab said as soon as I was finished, and she began paging through the diary looking for the entry.

I leaned forward. "Yeah? What did she say?"

"Hang on, I'm finding it. It happened not long after...*here* we go." She set the open book on the table, turning it around so that I could read the page.

> *Tue, 7 May, '46*
>
> *My second week of daily meetings with Mr. Crenshaw, and while he is very courteous and seems to know his business, there's just something about him that gives me the jim-jams. The only thing that makes our meetings tolerable is getting to see Philip for half an hour or so afterward! He comes every day, waiting just out of sight until I'm finished, and while he hasn't said so yet, I'm almost ready to believe he's as stuck on me as I am on him!*

I reached over to pull the diary closer, accidentally dropping a big crumb of pastry glaze on the open face.

"Hey!" Ab cried, slapping my hand away. She wet a finger with the tip of her tongue and used it to pick the crumb off the page. "Watch those grubby paws," she said, and then absently licked the glaze from her finger.

"Sorry," I said, and then found myself staring at her for a couple of seconds.

My gaze must have lingered too long, because she glanced up and caught me. "What?"

"Nothing," I said, flushing and looking back down at the page. She'd just looked sort of...pretty, I guess. For a second there, anyway. Saying so would have been weird, though, so I went back to reading instead:

> *Sometimes we walk along the cliffs, sometimes we'll spend a few minutes beachcombing, but mostly we just talk. I keep waiting for Philip to hold my hand like he did at the movies.*

I think he wants to, but he hasn't yet, probably because he knows how much hot water I'll be in if someone sees us and Daddy hears about it. But a girl can dream, can't she?

"Anything else?" I asked.

"Not as far as I read. I was almost falling asleep when I got to that point. I did skim ahead a little while waiting for you this morning, though. Most of it was all Philip-Philip-Philip, but I did see something about Bonnie." She took the diary and flipped ahead several pages, and then came around to lean over my shoulder so we could read it together:

Thu, 16 May, '46

Oh my goodness! Bonnie knows. I hadn't realized she'd started following me. She's been eaten up with curiosity over the cellar project from the beginning, and about pitched a fit when Daddy told her it was no place for a little girl. But I found out today she's been sneaking after me, watching the men work while I meet with Mr. Crenshaw, and then spying while I meet with Philip! I tried scolding her, but she dug in her heels and threatened to tell Daddy I was seeing a boy if I didn't let her come along. What am I going to DO? Bonnie is just awful at keeping secrets, and I know that sooner or later the cat will be out of the bag. I'm going to be in such trouble!

"Did her dad find out?" I asked when I was done reading. "And does it even matter?"

Ab shrugged. "Dunno. Haven't gotten that far yet. I'll get back to it tonight and let you know."

I glanced at my watch and then rose to my feet while stuffing the last of the cinnamon roll into my mouth. I had just enough time to get to Les's house while only being a couple of minutes late. "Gah-a go," I said, my cheeks bulging with half-chewed dough. "She 'oo la'er."

Ab wrinkled her nose. "Gross, Wolfman."

THIRTY-ONE

THE LIGHT WAS FADING WHEN LES AND I FINALLY dragged ourselves out of the water, the sun dropping behind dark storm clouds that were massing far out over the ocean. We'd decided to change tactics that day, taking breaks more often and swimming side by side as we searched the bottom, and it had paid off. By the time we collapsed on the dock, we'd covered over a third of the cove.

I pulled off the hood of my wet suit, grateful for the release of pressure and rubbing the tender ring where the face opening had dug into my skin. Moe crept out from where he'd spent most of the day napping in the shade on a narrow strip of sand beneath the dock. "We did good today," I said as he trotted over to nuzzle me. I rolled onto my back as I pet him, enjoying the leftover warmth seeping up from planks that had baked all day in the sun.

Les grunted noncommittally, his legs dangling over the water as he tugged down the zipper of his wet suit. He shrugged his upper half out of it and then stretched before pulling off his booties.

"You okay?" I asked when he didn't say anything.

"Yeah," he answered, sighing. "Just wondering if this isn't a big waste of time."

I levered myself up onto my elbows. "What do you mean? Between yesterday and today, we've covered almost half the cove! We're bound to find something of Bonnie soon."

Les looked over at me. "You still think so?"

"What…you don't?"

He shook his head. "Nope." I felt a bright flash of irritation, but Les went on before I could say anything. "Don't get me wrong, amigo. I'm happy to help, and if you're stuck on searching the whole cove, I'll be right there with you. But what have we found so far?" He shook the mesh sack tied to his belt. "Trash. Fishing lures. Beer cans and ball caps."

"So what?" I shot back. "That doesn't mean we won't find Bonnie!"

He shook his head again. "You're forgetting something. The tidal wave dragged twenty-something people out to sea with it. But have we run across anything? A single bone…even a tooth? You'd think that if there were any remains left after all this time, we would have found some—if not Bonnie's, then *somebody's,* right?" He pointed to the breakwater. "Also, remember that wasn't there in '46. Outside the cove, the shelf only goes out a couple of hundred yards before the sea floor drops away to like five, six hundred feet—even deeper the further out you go—and the currents are strong out there. Face it, brother, there are a lot of good reasons why none of those people were ever found."

Seconds ticked by while everything he'd said sank in. Much as I hated to admit it, Les had a point. "But Bonnie wants us to find her," I insisted. "Even Lisette said so, and Bonnie keeps trying to get my attention!"

"Sure...I get you," Les agreed. "And maybe there *is* actually something left of her out there. But has it occurred to you that maybe it's someplace too deep for us to get to?" I opened my mouth to retort, but he held up a hand, stopping me. "And anyway, you're forgetting the most important thing."

"What's that?"

"Your visions. Have you had any while we've been searching? Even one? Think about it: if Bonnie died close to shore, wouldn't you have picked up on something by now?"

My irritation deflated, replaced by a gloomy, sinking feeling in the pit of my stomach. But I wasn't ready to throw in the towel just yet. "Okay," I said after a moment, and got to my feet. Reaching down, I picked up my discarded hood and pulled it on.

"Dude…what are you doing?"

"Going back down," I told him. "You're right—I haven't had any visions. But I've also been concentrating on looking for Bonnie, so maybe I was blocking them out. Maybe all I need to do is open myself to them. It's worth a try, right?" I stepped to the edge of the dock before pulling on my flippers and then grabbed my mask.

"You want me to come with you?"

I shook my head. "Nah, you stay here. It's easier if I have some space." Taking a breath, I dove headfirst back into the water.

The cold came as a shock after the warmth of the dock planks, but I was used to it again by the time my head broke the surface. Rolling onto my back, I put my snorkel and mask on while using my flippers to propel myself to the deeper water out away from the dock. Les watched my progress and then raised one hand in a wave of encouragement. I returned it and then rolled back over and dived for the bottom.

I hadn't been out of the water all that long, but it was already getting hard to see. I was about fifteen feet down when a large rock emerged from the gloom and I swam over, grasping it with one hand to anchor myself in place while trying to clear my mind. I relaxed, listening to the sound of my heartbeat in my ears while mentally reaching out for whatever might be there. Almost immediately, what little light there was faded away...

...and I am plunged into near-total darkness! I almost panic, surprised by both the sudden change and the sound of an air-raid siren that penetrates faintly into the depths. The water swirls and surges around me, and I instinctively shy away from large objects tumbling in the flow that I can sense more than see. I let go of the rock, kicking upward until my head breaks the surface. I suck in a gasp that is as much seawater as air, causing me to cough and retch even as I try to make sense of what I'm witnessing.

The fire on the roof of the high school is still blazing, silhouetting objects in the water all around me. To my left, a fishing boat rolls over and sinks as it's pulled out to sea, its rudder sticking up like a tombstone just before it disappears beneath the waves. Other debris I can't identify bob and jostle and spin around me as everything, including me, is dragged farther and farther away from shore. My head snaps around as I hear a choked cry next to me, and I can barely make out an old man flailing in the water just to my right. I automatically reach out to grab his arm, but my hand passes through him just before he's pulled under. A woman's scream pierces the night from somewhere behind me, almost immediately followed by a man calling out "Oh God... please no!" somewhere off to my left.

I glance back toward shore, terrified when I realize how far away it is already. I'm a quarter-mile out now, maybe more, the fire at the school looking smaller as the distance increases, and I realize there's no help coming—not for me and not for the people dying around me. Desperately, I try to fight my way back, kicking and paddling as hard as I can against the raw power of the ocean that I already know is far too strong. The noises from shore are far off now, even the siren sounding faint in the distance, replaced only by the sounds of my own gasps and splashes. I cry out, watching in horror as the firelight continues to recede...

"*Dude!* Are you okay?"

I blinked, surprised that I could suddenly see again, and it took me a second to remember where I was. The scene from that night in1946 had been so powerful and vivid that I'd been caught up in it, momentarily forgetting that it wasn't real. It was like the first second or two after waking up from a nightmare, when you don't know where you are and the familiar shadows of your room seem alien and threatening. Now that it was over, I was relieved to see that I was only about thirty feet from shore, not the quarter-mile plus from my vision. I normally would have felt like an idiot for letting my mind play tricks on me like that, but right then I was just too grateful to be alive and too anxious to get out of the water.

Les stood at the edge of the dock, looking concerned while Moe paced nervously back and forth beside him. "You good?" he asked as I swam the last few feet to the ladder.

"Yeah. Just had the crap scared out of me, that's all. Here—take these."

He reached down to take my flippers and mask, and then reached down again to help haul me up the rungs. The shakes hit me as soon as I made it to the top, and at first all I could do was sit there, hugging myself as my adrenaline rush slowly subsided. When Moe came over to crawl into my lap, I put my arms around him, glad for both his company and warmth.

Les sat on a dock piling, his elbows in his knees. "I guess you saw something, huh? From the way you were thrashing around out there,

I figured either it was pretty bad or Jaws just swam up and bit your leg off. I almost went in after you."

"It was *horrible,*" I told him. "Those people—what an *awful* way to die." I went on to describe everything I'd seen, glad for the chance to put it into words since I'd have to tell Ab about it the next day. "Anyway, you were right," I finished. "When the wave receded, it dragged everything way out to sea. There was no fighting it."

"Any sign of Bonnie? You said you heard a scream."

"No, it sounded like a woman, and it was too dark to see much of anything. Bonnie could've been ten feet away and I would have missed her." Sighing, I looked up to meet his gaze. "Not to mention I jumped into it right in the middle of things. For all I know, she was already dead by then."

There was a long, empty silence before Les spoke again. "That sucks."

"Yeah," I agreed, and then shooed Moe off my lap and got to my feet. "Let's get out of here."

After stopping at Les's place to clean up our gear, we got back in the car and drove over to Pirate Pizza for something to eat. We were both starving, so we agreed on an extra-large pepperoni and sausage. Between us we killed an entire pitcher of root beer while waiting for our order and then got a second one when the pizza arrived. Neither of us said much of anything, and I guessed that Les was as frustrated and bummed out as I was.

Despite how hungry we'd been when we came in, I was only able to eat a couple of slices and Les was only good for three or four before we both ran out of gas. Maybe it had been all the soda, but I doubted it. I'd been so certain that we would find what was left of Bonnie somewhere in the cove. I guess in my mind I had already planned that we would arrange some sort of burial, and then all the ghosts in my house would rest easy and leave my mom alone. Now that it looked like we had done nothing but waste two days getting waterlogged, I had no idea what to do next. The longer I thought it over, the more my insides twisted themselves into knots of worry, and Les and I ended up sharing a long, brooding silence while two-thirds of our pizza sat cold and untouched on the table between us. Night had fully descended when at last we had the leftovers split between two boxes and we left.

"So, what's next?" Les asked as we pulled up in front of his house and I shifted the transmission into park.

"No clue," I told him. "I guess the only thing we can hope for is that Ab finds something in the diary we can go on. Unless that happens or unless I get a fresh clue in a vision or dream pretty soon, I think we're screwed."

Les nodded. "You meeting Ab tomorrow?"

"Yeah. Seven-thirty at the coffee house."

"Okay. See you there." He opened the passenger door and got out.

"You don't have to, you know," I called after him, and Les turned, stooping to look through the open window with his pizza box in one hand. "So far, all I've done is waste your time," I went on. "So if you want to bail off the crazy-train, I totally understand."

"Are you kidding? I'm *way* too into this to quit now. If it hadn't been for you, this would be just another boring Windward Cove summer. Besides, what kind of friend would I be if I left you to play Ghostbusters with Ab all by yourself?" Les grinned. "Go get some sleep. We'll figure out something tomorrow."

His optimism made me feel a little better, and between that and the way Moe rode comfortingly with his head on my thigh, my spirits actually improved some—until I got home, anyway. When the station wagon's headlights swept across the front of the house, at first it didn't register with me that something was wrong. But then it hit me, and I put the car into reverse to light up the porch.

A window was broken. A gaping hole nearly three feet in diameter yawned in the big pane to the left of the front door, an irregular circle of darkness surrounded by jagged edges that glinted in the light of the high beams. "What the *hell,*" I murmured, wondering briefly how it had happened, but then it occurred to me that maybe someone had broken into the house.

Worse, they might still be inside!

Panic seized me, and I scrambled out of the car, leaving the engine running and the driver's door open. Moe was right beside me as I leaped up the porch steps, fumbling in my pocket for my house key. It took me two tries to get the key into the lock, but then I threw the door open, hearing it bounce against the wall behind me as I took the stairs three at a time. It didn't occur to me until later that I might have been charging into all kinds of trouble. Right then, all I cared about was making sure my mom was safe.

I sprinted down the second-floor hallway to the attic stairwell, bounced against the back wall because I was going too fast, and then scrambled up the stairs in pitch darkness. I could sort of see again when I got to the top, though, because the soft glow from the open cupola door helped me to navigate to the stairs, and I pounded up the last flight to arrive sweaty and out of breath.

Mom sat at her easel, painting by lantern light. The corners of her mouth were turned slightly upward in a dreamy smile, a lock of hair swinging listlessly in front of her eyes as she worked. The cupola was bitterly cold, but it didn't look like she felt it.

"Mom…? You okay?" I asked, still gasping.

She didn't seem to hear me and began to hum absently. I recognized the song right away. "Blue Skies"—Bonnie's favorite—and hearing it made my scalp prickle.

"Mom?" I repeated, more urgently.

A couple of heartbeats passed before she looked up, her gaze finding me at last. “Yes?” she asked distractedly.

I paused, wondering if I should ask if she'd heard the window break, but then decided not to. “Just…wanted to know if you need anything,” I lied.

She shook her head, her eyes going distant again as she returned to her work.

I shifted my weight from my left foot to my right, wondering if I should try to keep her talking, but then I remembered that the important thing was that she was okay. *Well, okay enough for now,* I amended inwardly. She was still freaking me out, but at least Jason Voorhees or Michael Meyers hadn't chopped her into little bits. I let out a breath, relieved.

Now all I had to do was make sure Jason wasn't in the house.

I retreated back down the stairs, moving quietly now while listening for any sounds that shouldn't be there. The logical part of my brain realized that if anyone had been there when I came home, they probably would have been scared off when I came charging in like a buffalo and would be long gone by now. Just the same, I couldn't relax without first checking to make sure, so I began a cautious, room-by-room search. I reached out mentally, trying to detect any stray feelings that would give away someone lurking in the shadows, but all I could pick up was Moe's curiosity mixed with uneasiness, probably because he didn't understand what was bothering me. That was good, I realized, trusting his ability to sense a stranger before I could. I considered grabbing the flashlight from my room as we passed but then decided not to. The last thing I wanted was a beacon showing exactly where I was, and anyway, I'd gotten used to moving around the house at night, and there was more than enough moonlight glowing through the windows to help me find my way.

When I was sure the second floor was clear, we moved quietly downstairs. I breathed silently through my mouth, straining to hear or sense anyone who might be there, but all I heard was the *ree-ree-ree* of summer crickets through the open door, along with the sound of the station wagon's engine where it still idled outside. I turned right at the bottom of the stairs, sticking my head through the archway where the living room was bathed in the glow of the car's headlights. Broken glass covered the floor under the window, but aside from all the new furniture that had been sitting there since its delivery, the room was empty.

Okay so far.

I trotted into the yard just long enough to shut off the car, not wanting to be backlit by the headlights while I searched the rest of the house. I was able to hear better without the engine noise outside, and I moved with more confidence as Moe and I glided through the dark family room. I paused at the hearth and felt around until I found the fireplace poker, feeling better still with its comforting weight in my hand.

We finished checking out the ground floor, although I decided there was no *way* I was going down into the basement that night. That's where the psycho would be hiding in every slasher movie I'd ever seen, so I just made sure the door was locked instead. Mrs. Wolf's favorite son might be dumb, but he wasn't *that* dumb. At last I turned on the kitchen overhead light, blinking gratefully in the sudden brightness. "Nobody here but us chickens," I said to Moe, and felt the tension between my shoulder blades start to ease.

Moe yawned and then walked over to sniff at his food dish, looking back at me with a hopeful wag of his tail.

"Coming right up," I told him, setting the poker down on the butcher block while I got him his dinner. Now that the excitement was over, I was beginning to feel hungry again myself and remembered the leftover pizza in the car. *Cold pizza is just the thing after chasing Jason Voorhees around in the dark,* I thought, and went to go get it.

I walked back into the darkness of the family room, stopping to return the poker to the stand with the rest of the fireplace tools. I was just turning away when flames suddenly leaped in the hearth…

…bathing the family room with a warm, flickering light. I step back, momentarily confused. The mantel that was empty a second ago is now dressed with a holly garland and topped with ceramic snowmen and figurines of carolers, with knit stockings that look well used hanging on either side. In the corner of the room to my left is a huge Christmas tree, lit by big, old-fashioned colored bulbs and decorated with tinsel and ornaments. Presents wrapped in bright paper lie clustered around its base, while a lit angel backed by a wreath of red, reflective metal smiles serenely down from the top. It looks familiar, and after a second, I recognize the same angel that topped the tree every year in Aunt Claire's mansion.

"The moon on the breast of the new-fallen snow," comes a man's voice, "Gave the luster of mid-day to objects below."

I turn to see Roger Black sitting in a big, upholstered armchair behind me. Bonnie is on his lap, wearing her pajamas and robe while he reads to her from an oversized picture book. A Visit from St. Nicholas, *is lettered on the cover in gold calligraphy that reflects the firelight, and my heart twists with memories as I hear the same words that my mother used to read to me over and over again when I was little:*

"When, what to my wondering eyes should appear,
But a miniature sleigh, and eight tiny reindeer!
With a little old driver, so lively and quick,
I knew in a moment it must be Saint Nick."

"Santa Claus!" Bonnie whispers, her eyes huge, and then she stifles a yawn.

Claire smiles from where she's seated on the sofa, a scattering of schoolbooks lying forgotten on the coffee table in front of her. She watches them closely as their father reads aloud, seeming to enjoy Bonnie's reactions more than the story itself. It's like she's part of the closeness in the room but removed from it, too—like an outsider looking in—and it makes me feel badly for her.

"As dry leaves that before the wild hurricane fly," *Roger continues,*
"When they meet with an obstacle, mount to the sky,
So up to the house-top the coursers they flew,
With the sleigh full of toys, and St. Nicholas too."

But Bonnie falls asleep before Santa even makes it down the chimney. As her eyes drift closed, the room seems to grow dim as well...

...until I found myself once again standing in the darkness of the family room. The sofa and armchair were gone. Beside me, the hearth was empty and cold, and I wondered offhandedly how many decades had passed since a fire had burned in it. I slowly eased myself down to the floor, looking around the room. For a moment, I wondered if the vision had contained some clue that would help me find Bonnie, but after replaying the details in my mind, I decided they hadn't. I'd witnessed dozens of scenes from the past since finding Aunt Claire's diary, and almost none of them had anything to do with the things I needed to find out. The visions just came a lot more easily the more I practiced tapping into them, that was all. The one I'd seen was just another psychic echo that had soaked into the walls of the old house.

Just the same, my memory kept replaying the scene with Claire and her family. *My* family. Watching that scene from a Christmas so many years ago made me feel even more connected to them, and the frustration and gloom I'd felt back at the cove faded. There *had* to be something I was missing. Maybe something in the diary I hadn't read yet. All I had to do was figure out what it was.

"I'm going to help you, Bonnie," I called out to the empty room. "You *and* my mom. But I need your help, too, okay?"

My words seemed to hang in the dark, still air, and I wondered if anyone had heard them.

Then I decided it didn't matter.

THIRTY-TWO

I SLEPT LIKE THE DEAD THAT NIGHT, WORN OUT BY TWO long days searching the bottom of the cove, and if I had any dreams, I didn't remember them. When my alarm went off at 6:00, my first thought was to give myself another twenty minutes or so before getting up. The room was chilly, a stiff breeze that smelled like the ocean causing my curtains to writhe and billow as it came through my open window. But it was nice and warm under the covers with Moe stretched out beside me, and getting out of bed was the last thing I felt like doing right then. I opened my eyes partway, squinted painfully in the brightness, and then shut them again. I reached for my wristwatch, guided by its insistent beeping, but before I found it, my hand hit something that fell to the floor with a clatter and I came fully awake.

I rolled onto my side, saw the fireplace poker lying on the floor, and then remembered bringing it upstairs with me. Even after making sure that no one was lurking in the house, I'd still been a little jumpy about the broken window and had felt more secure with the poker near the bedside table. It all seemed a little silly now that it was morning, but there you go.

I yawned, reaching for the ceiling as I stretched, and then scratched my scalp with both hands. *Ugh...gross,* I thought when I felt the stiffness of my hair, and I regretted not showering the night before. My skin felt tight with dried salt, and I realized that wallowing around in bed wasn't an option. Moe's tail thumped on the bedspread as I first hurried to shut the window and then crossed my arms over my bare chest, looking around for a shirt while shifting my weight from foot to foot on the ice-cold floorboards. I found my T-shirt from the day before lying wadded near the foot of the bed, right next to my slippers, and I felt better as soon as I put them on.

Downstairs, I let Moe out the front door and then went to the living room to survey the damage in the daylight. Shards of glass lay scattered on the floor in front of the window, along with a rock about the size of a softball that I hadn't noticed the night before. Cold anger welled up inside me when I saw it, but at least the mystery of how the window had broken was solved. A low, moaning sound rose and fell from the gaping hole as the breeze came in to swirl around the room, and I realized that figuring out what to do about the damage was at the top of my to-do list for the day.

I took a long shower, letting the hot water chase the chill and lingering soreness out of me. As I was toweling off, though, I paused when I noticed an odd, arched shape drawn into the fog of the bathroom mirror:

I smiled, thinking for a brief, crazy moment that Mom was up and feeling good enough to goof around. Back when I was little, she would sometimes sneak into the bathroom while I was showering to surprise me with pictures drawn in the fog. Jack-o-lanterns and ghosts that said "Boo!" around Halloween, snaggletoothed monsters that said "Brush your teeth!"—that sort of thing. She'd stopped doing it when I was five or six, but even so, my first thought was that it had been her. My smile faded, though, when I glanced at the door and saw that it was locked. And anyway, the shape was nothing like my mother used to draw, so I figured it had to be something else.

I thought about it, remembering that things like soap film or oil from your hands could sometimes keep fog from sticking to glass, and I tried to remember if the shape had been there the last time I'd showered. I shook my head, realizing that it hadn't. Just to make sure, I leaned in, breathing hot air onto the lower left corner. The lines disappeared right away, merging with the rest of the fog, so it definitely wasn't soap or oil. I stepped back as gooseflesh broke out on my arms. Someone—some*thing*—had drawn on the mirror!

The fog was quickly evaporating, so I reached out, putting my own mark on the mirror next to it. The lines of the shape were narrow compared to my own…as if they had been drawn by a tiny finger.

"Bonnie? Is that you?" I called out, quickly wrapping the towel around my waist while scanning the room in a slow three-sixty. Not that I'd really expected to see her, of course, but my heart was beating fast, and some primal part of me needed to make sure. "Are you here?" I urged, reaching out mentally to see what I could pick up but not sensing anything. "Come on, Bonnie. What are you trying to tell me?" At last I faced back toward the mirror, half-hoping that something new had appeared while I wasn't looking, but there was only the strange shape, slowly fading as the fog dissipated.

A few seconds later, it was gone.

I was still thinking about it down in the kitchen fifteen minutes later. I ate the last slices of cold pizza while making eggs, toast, and coffee for Mom and then hurried up to the cupola with her tray before everything got cold. As it turned out, I could've taken my time. Mom lay sleeping half on her side, curled up beneath her quilt in the rocking chair. The best I got after nudging her three times were some murmured words that I couldn't make out, so I gave up and left her food in a sunny spot where I hoped it would stay at least partially warm.

I was about to leave but then turned and crossed to the far side of the room instead, wanting to see how her painting was coming along. It took a second or two before I realized what I was looking at, but then I felt my eyes widen as I recognized the familiar scene...

[I'm running barefoot between rows of grapevines, grinning with the exhilaration of secret freedom. The dirt is cool and soft beneath my feet, each stride sending up the rich smell of summer-tilled earth...]

My legs went all rubbery, and I reached out to steady myself against the nearest window frame. It was the scene from my Bonnie dream! She was only about three-quarters finished, but it was all there: the twilit evening, where stars emerged faintly at the top of the canvas, Bonnie sprinting through the vineyard in a white dress, *everything!* I took a moment to soak it all in: the detailed work she'd made of the vines, the painting's perspective—as if she'd seen it from the cupola window—and even the dust rising from Bonnie's footfalls. Exactly like my dream!

I looked over toward my mother, open-mouthed in admiration, and then back at the canvas. Without a doubt, it was the best work she'd ever done. I stood there for a long moment, torn between my appreciation of her talent and the uneasy suspicion I had over what was driving it. Was Bonnie reaching out to Mom in her dreams, too?

And if so, exactly what was it about that summer evening that was so important?

At last I forced my gaze away, remembering that I had a lot to do that morning. I started for the stairwell but then stopped after taking only three or four steps. *No,* I decided, frowning as I looked back over my shoulder. Something was wrong, and I returned to the painting for a second look. For almost a minute, I scanned the canvas, trying to figure out what was bothering me, but nothing jumped out. It was *amazing,* with depth and a level of detail that I hadn't even known Mom was capable of. Just, well...something wasn't right. Not quite, anyway.

After a while, I decided that staring wasn't doing me any good. Whatever it was about the painting that bugged me would occur to me later when I wasn't trying so hard or I'd change my mind about it and quit being so critical. Either way, I didn't have time to worry about it then, so after a final check to make sure Mom was covered up, I headed downstairs.

"You're sure it was just like your dream?" Ab asked me forty minutes later. She and Les had been waiting when Moe and I walked into Tsunami Joe, and it had taken a while to bring them up to speed.

I nodded. "I've had the same dream two or three times. It *has* to be one of Bonnie's memories."

"But you don't know what it means." It was a statement rather than a question.

I shrugged, shaking my head. "Well, I know that she loved playing in the vineyard, and that's where I first ran into her ghost. Also, everything Mom has drawn since we got here has had something to do with it. I dunno. Maybe it's just the place she's most attached to. Could it be that simple?"

Ab settled back in her chair, frowning. "If it is, then it doesn't help us much."

"I'm still wondering what *this* is all about," said Les. He was studying the paper napkin where I'd drawn the shape I'd seen in the bathroom mirror. "Is it an A, maybe? Like someone's initial?" He grinned suddenly toward Ab. "That's it…you were the killer all along! Admit it!"

She gave him a disgusted look but then brightened. "Actually, that gives me a pretty good idea. Maybe we should give her something to draw on."

"What…like a pen and paper?" I asked.

Ab shook her head. "I was thinking something easier, like the fog in your mirror, but something that would last." She thought the idea over for a few seconds. "Why don't you try sprinkling some flour or sand on a flat surface and see if she does anything with it?"

"Good idea," I said, nodding, and made a mental note to set something up when I got home. "But how about you? Since the cove turned out to be a bust, I was hoping there was something in the diary we could go on."

Ab frowned thoughtfully. "Well, there was something I read last night. Mostly her entries were all about finding ways to meet up with Philip without her dad finding out, and she was worried sick that Bonnie was going to tell. But she mentioned that guy Crenshaw a lot more as she went along, too. He really started creeping her out." Ab pulled the diary over from where it had been sitting on the table.

"Creeped her out how?" I asked.

"Hang on…I'm finding it." She opened the book to where she'd left a sticky note as a marker and then flipped back three or four pages until she found the entry she wanted. "Here," she said, sliding the diary over, and Les leaned in so that he could read it, too:

Tue, 21 May, '46

I'm not sure how much more of Mr. Crenshaw I'll be able to stand! He insists that we meet in the little trailer he uses for his office at the work site, but he keeps the windows closed and it's always sweltering inside! He can't be comfortable either, but nevertheless it seems as if he's doing his best to make our meetings drag out. I can't be certain, but I have a sneaking suspicion that he enjoys watching me sweat. Worse, he keeps staring at my chest while we talk. I'm used to that, of course. Boys and even men sometimes can't seem to help themselves, but they usually look away quickly, as if they're trying not to. Mr. Crenshaw, though…he stares openly. It's as if he knows he's doing it…and he knows that I know it.

Today he showed me a change he wants to make to the cellar's wiring and stood close behind me as he pointed it out on the blueprint he keeps on the wall. I could feel his breath on my neck as he explained the modification, and I could swear that he was trying to smell my skin and hair. I couldn't get out of there fast enough!

What am I going to DO? I've asked Daddy to take over the meetings himself, but he won't hear of it. I have to do something. But what?

"What a pervert!" I said when I finished reading. I must've been too loud, because Ab shushed me. "What did she do about it?" I asked in a lower voice.

"Your aunt was pretty smart. Since Bonnie was still following her to the cellar every day, Claire just started bringing her to the meeting, too. She said having Bonnie there made Crenshaw mind his manners."

"So what?" Les asked. "I mean, no offense, but what does any of this have to do with putting Bonnie to rest?"

Ab sat back in her chair, thinking. "Bonnie still wants us to find her, right? And all this time we've been assuming that she was dragged out to sea. But what if she wasn't? What if she never made it that far?" Les and I exchanged a confused look while Ab went on, seeming to grow more excited as the idea took shape in her mind. "Think about it, guys! Depending on how long she waited before following after her dad, she could have been hit by the tidal wave anywhere between Ben's place and here. Now, remember, the damage the wave caused in town was only part of it. The force of all that water uprooted trees, moved tons of dirt around, and even washed out big chunks in the base of some of the hillsides. What if somewhere in all that mess her body got covered over?"

I brightened at the idea, but Les was still frowning. "Okay, so maybe it happened that way. But what does any of that have to do with Claire and this guy Crenshaw?"

Ab shrugged. "Nothing, probably. But we need a fresh trail to follow…" she tapped the diary entry for emphasis "…and at least here's a place where we can pick it up. As much as Bonnie keeps trying to get Ben's attention, his connection to Claire is a lot stronger. But now we know that the two of them went to those meetings at the cellar together. If Wolfman here can scrape up a few of those visions, and if doing that will help his connection to Bonnie, then maybe we can finally get this thing figured out."

"Sounds like a lot of ifs," I said skeptically.

"You got a better idea?"

I didn't. And anyway, even an iffy idea was more that we'd had ten minutes before. "Okay," I agreed. "So does Claire say where they were building the cellar?"

Ab's smile dampened a little. "No. I figured you knew. Your house, maybe? It has a big cellar, right?"

"Yeah, but the ceiling is super low, and there's nothing down there but an old washer and dryer."

"How about your barn?" Les suggested.

I turned to him. "There's a tractor and some equipment in there, along with a big case of empty bottles and some other stuff, but that's all. And anyway, the floor is dirt. We can check it out, but I don't think the cellar was there, either."

"Are there any other buildings or ruins anywhere on your property—even just a foundation?"

"Not that I've seen."

"That leaves only two places I can think of," Ab decided. "Either they built the cellar right next to the vineyard, and whatever's left has become overgrown by all those vines…"

"Or?" I prompted when her pause ran too long.

"Or the cellar was going into the basement of the inn!"

I thought about it. "That's not a bad idea," I said, remembering that the inn was even pictured on the wine label I'd found. To be honest, I was a little embarrassed that it hadn't occurred to me first. "I mean, it kind of makes sense, right? They'd need stuff like water and electricity, so why not just modify space they already had?" Then I frowned. "But what about all the noise? Wouldn't that bother anybody who was staying there? And even after it was set up, they'd have tractors hauling in loads of grapes, along with whatever racket the machinery made. Could you run both operations out of the same building?"

Ab shrugged. "No idea. But there's an easy way to find out, right?"

I nodded. At the very least, it sounded better than trying to find what was left of a building somewhere in the vineyard. I pictured ruins covered over like the Lost City of Opar. "Okay, so what time are you done here?"

"Three o'clock," Ab said, looking excited. "But I might be able to leave earlier if things slow down."

"Nah, three is good," I assured her. "It'll give me time to do something about that window." I turned to Les. "You have anything going on today?"

"Nope. I'm good with whatever."

"We're on, then," I said, getting to my feet. "We'll be back to pick you up."

THIRTY-THREE

"SO WHERE ARE WE HEADED?" LES ASKED AS WE STEPPED out into the breezy morning.

"The lumber store, I guess. I need to find something big enough to cover that window until Mom and I can get it fixed." I rubbed my arms as we hurried to the car. The wind seemed to be falling off as the morning warmed, but still, I wished I'd brought a sweatshirt.

"Any idea who threw the rock?"

I stopped before getting in, looking at Les across the roof of the station wagon. "Rick Hastings. Who else could it be? I guess roadkill on the front porch wasn't enough for him, so he decided to ratchet things up a notch."

Les shrugged, getting in.

I opened my door and slid behind the wheel. "What?" I asked when he didn't say anything.

"Nothing. Just..." He paused, frowning. "I'm just surprised, I guess. Rick's never been the sneaky type. He's got too big a mean streak for that. If he doesn't like you, he'll just kick your ass behind the gym."

I started the car. "Yeah, well you'd think differently if you'd seen the look on his face the day he almost wiped me out on the road. The guy's a freaking psycho."

"Yeah, maybe so—I'd forgotten about that," Les conceded. "So what are you going to do about it?"

"I dunno. It's not like I can prove anything. I need to wait until I catch him in the act, I guess." I pulled away from the curb, intending to head for Silver Creek, but then I noticed that the needle on the fuel gauge was hovering just above *E,* so I headed for the Texaco station a block over.

"And then what?" Les prompted. "No offense, but I don't see you mixing it up with Rick."

"No, that wouldn't be such a great plan. If—*when*—I catch him, I figure I'll just call the cops." The thought made me smile with a grim kind of satisfaction. "We'll see how much of a badass the thinks he is when he's in handcuffs."

"Um, yeah," Les said after a pause. "About that...have you met Sheriff Hastings?"

It took a second for his question to sink in. "Rick's dad?" I asked.

"Yup."

Perfect, I thought, sighing, and then pulled under the awning at the gas station.

I checked the oil while the car was filling and even glanced at the tires to see if any of them looked low, the actions making me feel all kinds of grown up and responsible. When I got back in the car after paying, the first thing I noticed was Les reading Kelly's letter, its pink envelope open and lying on his lap.

"Hey! Who said you could read that?" I asked, feeling indignant and embarrassed all at once. To be honest, I'd forgotten all about it, but that didn't give him the right to go through my stuff.

"There was nothing else to read," he replied absently, not looking up. He took his time finishing the page. "So...you and Kelly, huh?" he asked finally. "Now, I could've *sworn* you said nothing was going on there."

"Nothing is," I insisted, still trying to figure out if I was angry that he'd opened the letter. After a second, I realized that I wasn't. Not really, anyway.

"No?" he asked, an evil grin spreading across his face as he held it out to me. "You might want to tell Kelly that. I don't think she got the memo."

Annoyed, I snatched the sheet of paper from his hand and began to read:

> *Dear Ben,*
>
> *As much as I've been trying, I haven't been able to stop thinking about you since you kissed me at my birthday party.*
>
> I seemed to remember the kiss had been her idea, but it probably wasn't important right then.
>
> *What are we going to do?* Kelly went on. *I can't just leave Alan. We've been together so long, and if he found out I was falling for you, it would crush him. But I can't lie to myself about what I feel, and it's all just so confusing! All I know is that I can't be with you right now. Not yet. But I can't stay where I am, either.*
>
> *We need to talk. My parents are going out tonight, so we can have some privacy. Come over around 8:00, and I'll cook dinner. Together we can figure out what to do next. I know we can.*

-Kelly

There was a bunch of X's and O's below her signature, but in spite of that, I slumped back in my seat with a sigh. This was the last thing I needed right then.

"What's the matter?" Les asked, still grinning. "She's into you. That's what you wanted, right?"

"Well, yeah, but…" I began, and then paused. "*No,*" I amended. "I mean, I like her and all—like, *like* her, you know?—but she's got a boyfriend."

"So what? Seems to me she'd be trading up."

"It's not cool," I said. "She needs to make up her mind which one of us she wants to date, and I don't like being jerked around while she figures it out. Besides, if she's the kind who'd hook up with me behind Alan's back, then she's the kind who'd hook up with someone else behind *mine,* right? I mean, who wants to be the flavor of the week?"

Les seemed to consider the idea but then shrugged. "I've always been good with that, but it depends on what you're looking for, I guess. Anyway, I guess you didn't make it to dinner, huh?"

I shook my head.

"Have you thought about what that means?"

"Not really," I admitted with a shrug. "I guess she's probably pissed off."

"Yeah," Les agreed. "Maybe even pissed enough to put a rock through your window."

I thought about Les's suggestion on the drive over to Silver Creek. Would Kelly really do something like that? The fact was I had no idea. She'd been disappointed the day before when I hadn't dropped everything to read her letter right away, and not showing up at her house probably made her feel like I was blowing her off. But would that make her mad enough to break a window? I shook my head as

I noticed the entrance to the Home Depot coming up on the right, and mentally tossed the question on the "Too Hard" pile for now. I had more immediate things to worry about.

I bought a sheet of plywood, along with some nails and a package of tie-down straps, and Les helped me secure the wood to the roof rack of the car. I pulled and pushed at it after it was strapped down, satisfied that the sheet wouldn't fly off between there and home, and was about to get in when I noticed Les standing by the passenger door, staring across the mostly empty parking lot toward the street beyond.

I followed his gaze. Across the street to the left I could see a tiny strip mall with a laundromat, a fish and chips place, and a storefront under a sign that read "Checks Cashed." Only the laundromat looked like it was open. On the right was a coin-operated car wash where a bearded guy with sleeve tattoos on both arms was rinsing off a big Chevy pickup, the morning sunlight glinting off the chrome and creating a rainbow in the misty spray. But Les was looking between the two, where a modest, old-fashioned looking church sat well back from the street behind a wide lawn. A gravel parking lot separated the church from the car wash, behind which I could make out headstones in a small cemetery surrounded by a low, wrought-iron fence.

"What are you looking at?" I asked, turning back toward Les.

He raised his head slightly to point with his chin. "The church," he said. "Notice anything about it?"

I looked again, trying to figure out what he meant. The paint on the walls was bright white, with a sign that was too far away for me to read posted beside the front doors, and a row of tall, stained-glass windows running down either side. A steeple rose above the surrounding trees, topped by a metal cross that could've been either gold or silver—it was reflecting the sunlight, so I couldn't tell. The lawn was lush and neatly trimmed, with flowering bushes lining the walkway to the parking lot. All in all, it reminded me of something you'd see on a Christmas card, making the businesses on either side look shabby by comparison. Nice, but I still couldn't see what Les was getting at.

"The shape of the front door," he told me when I didn't say anything. "The windows, too. Isn't it kind of like the drawing on your mirror?"

I looked again. The door and window frames were uniformly tall and narrow, coming to a pointed arch at the top. I frowned, comparing the shape to my mental picture of Bonnie's finger tracks in the steamed-over glass.

"What do you think?" Les asked.

"I don't know," I confessed, and then looked back at him with a shrug. "Maybe?"

"Worth checking out, don't you think?"

I nodded and then fell into step beside him was we made our way across the parking lot. We waited at the curb for a rusty Volkswagen bug to pass in front of us and then crossed the street and went up the front walk.

"St. Agnes Catholic Church," read the sign beside the front doors. Below that were times posted for an 8 a.m. Daily Mass, four separate times under Sunday Services, and Confession from 3 to 4 p.m. The arched doorway was split down the middle, with the right one propped open. We stepped through a shadowy vestibule, past where a shallow basin of water stood on a marble pillar, and went into the church itself.

A double row of pews created three aisles leading up to the raised altar, the walls and the wood of the benches glowing softly in the colored light coming through the windows. We stood there studying the designs in the glass for maybe half a minute before a deep voice called out to us, sounding slightly echoey in the deserted hall.

"If you came for mass, you're late."

We turned to see a priest making his way down the side aisle toward us. He was a big man—six-two, maybe six-three—and burly, with biceps as big as hams and shoulders like a linebacker. His thick hair and mutton-chop sideburns made him look like he should be riding a Harley-Davidson, but the white tab on his shirt collar stood out in the dimness, giving him an air of authority that made me wonder if we'd be in trouble for barging in the way we had.

He carried a coffee mug in one hand, a rag and what looked like a bottle of wood polish in the other. When he stopped in front of us, I noticed his shirt had short sleeves, and he was wearing faded blue jeans, and I relaxed when his face split into a wide, friendly smile. "What's up, guys?"

I was still trying to figure out what to say when Les stepped forward. "Mornin', Padre," he said cheerfully, sticking out his hand. "I hope we're not bothering you."

The priest set the rag and bottle on the pew next to us and then transferred his mug to his left hand so he could shake. "Not a bit. What's your name, son?"

"Leslie Hawkins." He pointed a thumb toward me. "This is Ben Wolf."

The priest turned to shake, his massive paw engulfing my hand. "Father Pete," he said, introducing himself. "I don't recognize you boys. What brings you in?"

"Your windows," Les told him, still barreling on way ahead of me, and I was happy to let him take the lead. I'd set foot in a church maybe four or five times in my whole life, and then only for weddings, and I wasn't sure how you were supposed to speak to a priest. But Les went on talking to him like he was a more or less regular guy, and the awkwardness I felt started to fade away.

Father Pete raised his eyebrows. "Windows?"

“Yeah. I mean, is there something special about the designs or all the colors?”

The priest studied first Les’s face and then mine, as if trying to see if we were serious, but then he shrugged. “That’s a question I don’t get every day, but okay,” he said, half-sitting on the back of the pew as if settling in for a long chat. “The Church has been using stained glass since the Middle Ages. Back then, most people couldn’t read, let alone understand Latin, so they’d work pictures of important Biblical events into the glass—called it the ‘poor man’s Bible.’ The different colors all had their own significance, too—blue for the sky and Heaven, green to symbolize growth and rebirth, what have you—but over time people lost touch with most of the specifics. Modern churches generally just go with pretty designs now. Does that answer your question?”

“Is there anything special about that shape?” I asked, finally joining in.

Father Pete glanced over at the windows, seeming to think it over. “Not that I know of,” he said after a pause. “It’s called a Gothic arch, and it also dates back to the cathedrals of the Middle Ages.” He shrugged. “Back then it had something to do with structural integrity, but now it’s just tradition, I suppose.”

Les glanced at me, his eyebrows raised questioningly, but nothing the priest had told us really meant anything that I could think of. I was about to say thanks and goodbye, but then an idea occurred to me: “How long have you been here?” I asked.

“Me? Let’s see…it must be going on six—no, seven. Seven years.”

“Do you know if the Black family went to church here?”

“I know at least one did. Stella Black. Died in childbirth back in 1940.”

“Wow,” said Les. “You know that off the top of your head?”

Father Pete grinned, jerking his head vaguely behind him. "She's buried out back. Who do you think cuts the grass around here? And besides, Stella has a surviving daughter who's been very generous to us over the years." He looked back at me, his expression curious. "Why do you ask?"

"Stella's daughter…that would be Claire, right?"

"You know her?"

"She's my great aunt," I told him. "Or she was, anyway. She died a little over a month ago."

The priest's expression softened. "I'm sorry for your loss, Ben. We'll remember her in our prayers this Sunday."

"Thanks."

"Would you like to visit Stella's grave?"

I was about to say no, but then I changed my mind and nodded instead.

Father Pete led us out back, through a small gate in the fence and to a tall headstone set near the base of a walnut tree.

Stella Fitzgerald Black

Called to God Jan. 8th, 1940

Bringing a daughter into the world

Gone from this life, but never from our hearts

I reached out with my gift, trying to sense if there was any presence from the grave. There were a couple of faint pings from the back of the cemetery, along with a feeling like old sorrow coming from somewhere off to my left, but nothing from where Claire and Bonnie's mother lay buried.

The priest stood with us a moment and then patted me on the shoulder before turning and walking back toward the church, leaving Les and me alone. "Thanks for everything," I called over my shoulder to him.

Father Pete turned and waved. “Any time, fellas. Feel free to come back and visit. We’re always open—even on Sundays!”

THIRTY-FOUR

"READY?" AB ASKED EXCITEDLY, OPENING THE DOOR behind me and sliding into the back seat.

"We've *been* ready," Les complained, looking over his shoulder. "C'*mon*...all that money you make and you don't own a watch?"

"*You* try running a business and see how much free time you have!" she shot back.

I pulled away from the curb, only half listening to their good-natured bickering. Ab had told us she'd be done by 3:00, and it was only a little after 3:20, so it was close enough as far as I was concerned.

After leaving St. Agnes, Les and I had gone back to my place and spent an hour or so first nailing the sheet of plywood across the window frame and then cleaning up all the broken glass inside. Moe had whined and scratched at the front door, wanting to be let in to see what was going on, but I left him outside to make sure he wouldn't pick up shards in his foot pads while we worked. After that, Les had suggested we do some exploring in the vineyard to see if we could find any remains from the wine cellar hidden in there, and that had taken up the rest of the morning and early afternoon.

It was tougher than either of us had thought. The day Moe and I had chased Bonnie through the vines, zigzagging around guided by the sounds she made in front of us, was a lot different than trying to make a detailed search. I'd almost forgotten how wild and tangled everything was in there, nearly three-quarters of a century of growth winding around itself, layer upon layer, into a massive green maze. The bases of some of the vines were nearly as big around as tree trunks, sometimes giving us a clear passage for ten or twenty feet, but mostly the old and new vines wound together to block our way like a springy brick wall. In no time at all, it began to seem less like an old, overgrown vineyard and more like Mirkwood Forest from *The Hobbit.*

We started on the east side, trying to search south to north, north to south in a back-and-forth pattern so that we wouldn't miss anything, but that plan fell apart almost right away. I went from wishing we had a couple of axes or machetes to help us hack our way through the brush to deciding we'd actually need a bulldozer in order to cover all the ground. We kept having to change directions when our way was blocked, and several times we got all turned around in the darkness only to emerge more or less right back where we'd started. Just the same, we kept at it for over three hours, not making much progress, and with me imagining the whole time that I'd find the cellar by crashing down forty feet into an open pit. It was possible, I realized—a Klingon Battle Cruiser could have been covered over in there, and we would've walked right past it.

We finally gave up a little before 2:00, driving over to Hovey's to wolf down burgers and fries with our arms covered in dirt and scratches, and with bits of dried leaves stuck in our clothes and hair.

I was tired, hot, and discouraged, but mostly grateful that the rest of the afternoon would be easier.

Les and Ab's verbal sparring trailed off as the Windward Inn came into view. "Wow," Ab murmured softly. "I forgot how big this place is." I pulled up to the chain that stretched across the entrance and shut off the engine. The same feeling of quiet watchfulness I'd experienced the day we'd first arrived struck me all over again, the boarded over windows seeming to stare blankly, like blind eyes.

"Well…what are we waiting for?" Ab asked, opening her door, and Les and I exchanged a humorous glance before grabbing the flashlights we'd brought along and following her.

We ducked under the chain, the temperature dropping noticeably as we stepped into the shadows of overgrown cypress trees that whispered and creaked above us. The wind hissed softly through the knee-high weeds, making me shiver as we made our way up the drive, and I was glad when it lessened as we stepped onto the porch. Still, there was enough of a breeze left over to swirl in ahead of us when I opened the front door, stirring up old dust inside and ushering in dead leaves to spin and tumble across the floor. I had just crossed the threshold when everything abruptly changed:

"Quickly—bring them in!" Claire orders, standing right in front of me. I recoil, for a panicked second thinking that she's talking about Ab and Les. Then she steps to the side and I feel the familiar prickly, chilling sensation as two men with a stretcher pass through my body, carrying an unconscious woman with blood covering half of her face. Hurriedly, I get out of the way, turning to watch as a couple of teenage boys haul in a man using a two-person seated carry, followed by a woman with a look of exhausted determination on her face, who half-supports, half-drags another man in with his arm across her shoulders. The man is

groaning, his free hand pressed against a wound in his side that dribbles an alarming amount of blood on the floor.

The lobby of the inn is crowded, with uniformed employees passing out blankets and showing people to chairs, drenched townspeople giving first aid to their neighbors or crying out for a doctor, and Claire standing in the middle of it all, giving directions and slowly turning chaos into order. Through the archway into the dining room, I can see people stretched out on tables, some struggling in pain or crying out while being tended by family or friends, others lying stone still, their faces covered by blankets or tablecloths. At the front desk, a man and a woman work the telephones, the man shouting that they need doctors and medical supplies, while the woman explains calmly that yes, their money would be returned to them, but they need to pack their things and leave as quickly as possible because the room was needed for survivors.

Hotel guests wearing bathrobes line the second-floor railing, some being urged back to their rooms by a couple of bellhops, others simply staring down at the scene with expressions of fright and confusion. Against the far wall sits an old man on a sofa, looking around dazedly as if trying to make sense of it all. A woman I assume is his wife sits slumped against him, and he's holding her left hand in both of his. The woman's mouth is slack, one eye open and unseeing, the other half-closed, and I don't think he realizes that she's dead.

"We're out of bandages and antiseptic!" reports a young woman in a waitress uniform, running up.

Claire thinks quickly. "Start tearing up clean bedsheets," she instructs, "and use alcohol from the bar for now. Hurry, *Claudia!"*

The woman scurries off, but Claire has already turned to grab the sleeve of a young man as he goes by. "Fred! Tell whoever's in the kitchen to start making coffee—lots of it. And some hot food, too. We need to get these people warmed up." He looks like he's about to ask a question, but Claire's attention has already moved on. "No, no, no—don't leave Mr. Davis on the floor! There are still some empty tables in the dining room!"

I watch as Claire continues to get the situation under control. She's wearing a purposeful, no-nonsense expression that I recognize from the older version of her I knew when I was little, and my heart swells with pride and admiration. She's in her element, I realize—a rock in stormy waters that the people around her cling to for direction and reassurance. She surveys the room, ensuring that everyone has something to do, and only then seems to relax slightly. "Mary Lou!" she cries as she sees her friend coming through the front door.

The girl looks over when she hears her name and rushes to her. "I heard everyone was coming here!"

"We're on the highest ground," Claire tells her, "and luckily we still have power. Is your family alright?"

"Yes. They're shaken up, but everyone is fine. Mother and Dad are in town looking for survivors. How can I help?"

"I'm so glad you're here!" Claire says. A crack appears in her commanding presence, and she looks vulnerable for the first time. "I need you to go to my house and look after Bonnie. She's there all alone!"

"Isn't Flora with her?"

Claire shakes her head. "She was due at the house early this morning, and Bonnie was fast asleep, so when the night clerk called to say that people were frightened by the earthquake and the smell of smoke, I came up here to reassure everyone. I thought I'd only be gone a short while, but then things started happening so quickly. I didn't think about Bonnie until they brought in Flora's body ten minutes ago, and that's when I realized she's been alone this whole time! Please go, won't you? I don't have anyone else to send!"

"Of course! Do you want me to bring her here?"

"No…I don't want her to see this. Can you just stay with her unt…"

At that moment, the ground lurches violently, sending people to the floor or careening into walls. Claire and Mary Lou go down together in a tangle. Screams erupt all around as dust drifts down from the ceiling and chandeliers swing crazily overhead. Several people scramble back up, only to run into one another or be thrown sideways as they try to head outside. The heaving of the ground only goes on for four or five seconds, but the screams and panic continue for several more until a voice carries out over the din. "Settle down, ladies and gentlemen!" I look over by the elevator, where a tall man is pressing a handkerchief against a cut on his scalp while trying to calm the crowd. After a second or two, I recognize him as Claire's history teacher. "It's just an after-shock, people! We're all perfectly safe!"

The panic dies down as, tentatively at first, everyone begins getting back to their feet. Mary Lou helps Claire up and then hugs her fiercely before heading back out into the morning.

At the front door, a man carrying a black leather case pauses to let her pass and then comes in and scans the lobby. He's tall and slender, with a full head of silver-white hair and a moustache.

"Doctor Napier—thank God!" Claire cries, and he crosses the floor to her.

"How many are here?" he asks.

"Forty, maybe fifty so far," she replies. "We're trying to get everyone warm and make them comfortable, but..." Her voice trails off as she looks past the doctor's shoulder and then her eyes go suddenly wide. "Daddy!" She rushes past him to where her father is being brought in on a door that three men are using as an improvised stretcher.

"Don't worry, he's alive," one of the men tells her. "We would have brought him here sooner, but his leg was trapped under a car."

The doctor moves in, leaning over to inspect Roger Black's knee. I follow his gaze, noticing what looks like a splinter of bloody wood poking out of his pants leg, but then my stomach lurches as I realize I'm looking at bone. "Get this man to a bed," he orders calmly. "This needs to be set immediately."

Claire straightens. Her eyes are brimming, but she wipes them with the back of her hand, all no-nonsense again. "Don't you want to..."

"In a moment," he says, cutting her off. "If I don't set this, the exposed bone will die and he'll likely lose the leg."

"Paul!" Claire snaps over at the man behind the front desk, and he looks up. "I need a vacant room!"

Paul frowns hurriedly down at a clipboard, but the woman working the phones beside him answers before he can. "202 is open," she reports. "The Burkes just checked out. But the room hasn't been made up yet."

"Never mind that. Show these men upstairs, will you Adele?"

"Just set the door down on top of the bed," Doctor Napier instructs the men. "I'll be up shortly. In the meantime, get him out of those wet clothes and under some blankets. Don't try to move the leg—just cut his pants off, understand?" The three men nod, starting for the elevator as the doctor turns back to Claire. "Now let's see what else we have, shall we?"

Claire turns to lead him toward the dining room, and as I move to follow...

...the scene shifted back to the present.

I spun around, surprised that the room was suddenly deserted except for Ab and Les watching me from the doorway. Where a crowd of frightened, injured people had been pressed together a second before, now only dust and silence remained. I shuddered, dropping onto a tarp-draped sofa and taking deep breaths with my head in my hands.

"You okay, Wolfman?" Ab asked, coming over to sit beside me. Les and Moe followed her over, and Moe pawed at my knee, whining softly as he sensed my distress.

"Yeah, just…give me a sec." I waited for my heartbeat to slow while trying to process everything I had just witnessed.

"Tell us what you saw," Les urged, leaning on the back of the sofa. "You were out of it for at least three or four minutes. Was there anything about the wine cellar?"

I shook my head. "No, nothing like that. It was what happened here the morning of the tidal wave." I went on to describe my vision, giving them every detail I could remember.

"Well, at least we know one thing we didn't know before," Les said after I finished. "Depending on how soon Claire left after her father did, Bonnie had time to get away."

"That poor little girl," Ab added solemnly, her eyes moist. "Waking up to an empty house and the sound of the fire alarm in the distance. No wonder she got scared and went looking for her daddy."

A long silence stretched out between us, and I guessed Ab and Les were imagining the same thing I was: Bonnie, alone and frightened, swept up by the tidal wave somewhere on the dark road. I hoped it was over quickly and that she hadn't suffered much.

At last Les straightened, clearing his throat. "I don't know about you, but all this makes me want to find her even more. But it's not going to happen unless we can get Ben out of Claire's head and into Bonnie's. C'mon, guys...let's do what we came here to do."

We made our way deeper into the inn, our footfalls sounding loud and hollow in the stillness. Now that the vision had passed, all of the assorted feelings and psychic echoes in the old hotel began seeping into my mind. It was like a crowded room where everyone was whispering, and it made it hard to concentrate. Lisette had been right—all my practice lately had made my gift a lot stronger, but there was a downside to that as well. Now the volume was way too high, and I wanted to cover my ears even though I knew it wouldn't do any good. Instead, I focused on the images I was looking for, trying to shut out everything else, and after a while I was able to shove a lot of it to the background. It wasn't perfect, but at least it was manageable, and I figured I'd need to put in some practice on perfecting that skill, too.

At last we arrived at the basement door in the service corridor behind the kitchen. Moe stayed close beside my leg as we carefully descended the concrete stairs, the beams of our flashlights swallowed up by the darkness. I looked behind us when we reached the bottom, half-expecting the basement door to slam shut, followed by a peal of maniacal laughter. Nothing happened though, and I realized the dim light drifting down from above would act as a beacon to guide us back when it was time to leave.

It didn't take us long to figure out we'd been wrong about the cellar, but we explored it from one end to the other anyway. Although it was cavernous and separated into a warren of storage rooms and alcoves, there was nothing that looked like a setup for making wine. The closest we got to it was an excited moment when we discovered a deep niche lined with wine racks, covered in cobwebs and holding a few scattered bottles that glinted dusty green in the glare of our flashlights. But that was as far as it went. We discovered furnaces positioned next to bins still holding a few scattered pieces of coal. A couple of steam boilers rusted away in the darkness, looking like mini submarines, along with a bank of industrial washers and dryers. Pipes crisscrossed overhead, some dripping into puddles of standing water, running alongside air ducts and old wiring conduit. One storage room was full of old decorations: Fourth of July banners and Japanese lanterns and even a three-foot clown's head that leered at us from the shadows, all covered in dark mold. We also found half a dozen other stairwells leading up to other parts of the inn, as well as two that were for access doors to the outside, one of which had a colony of bats nearby that Les noticed in time for us to avoid.

But that was all. We didn't find any equipment that looked like it could be used for crushing grapes or filling bottles or anything else. Worse, I didn't pick up anything at all from the basement—not a vision, not a feeling—nothing. At last we reached the far side and climbed the nearest stairwell, forcing the door open to emerge in a first-floor hallway. We made our way back to the lobby covered in dust and cobwebs, and none of us had much to say when I locked the front door behind us and we all trooped back to the station wagon.

"I guess all we have left is the vineyard," Les said as I guided the car down the switchbacks to the road.

I grimaced, not really wanting to try to fight my way around in there again. But what choice did we have?

"Oh, my god!" Ab cried suddenly. "I'm such an *idiot!* Why didn't I think of this before?"

"Think of what?" I asked.

"City records! I bet we can find what we're looking for there!"

I regarded her in the rearview mirror, my eyebrows raised.

"*Think* about it, guys. A big construction project like that—there'd have to be things like licenses and plans and building permits, right? Maybe even an area map showing where they were going to put it. It could all still be on file!"

I brightened at the idea. It was sure worth a try. Even if the only thing we turned up was confirmation that it was covered over somewhere in the vineyard, at least we'd know we were looking in the right place.

I followed Ab's directions to city hall, pulling up in front of a blocky, art deco-style building that seemed out of place in Windward Cove. The directory inside listed "Records" on the third floor, and we hurried up the stairs to arrive at a counter separating a small waiting area from a single room that took up the entire floor. Only about half of the ceiling lights appeared to be working, casting a feeble, yellow glow down onto tall, industrial shelves filled with boxes that created narrow aisles stretching back into the darkness.

"Isn't this where they stuck the Ark of the Covenant?" I asked, looking around. Les snickered, so I guessed he'd seen *Raiders of the Lost Ark*, too.

Ab ignored us both, stepping forward to ring the bell that was the only item on the countertop. The single ping sounded pathetic as it echoed back into the massive room. We waited for what seemed like a long time—long enough make me wonder if anyone was even back there—and Ab was about to hit the bell again when an older man wearing a sweater buttoned over a flannel shirt finally shuffled out from between the rows. He had a shock of unruly silver hair, and his eyes narrowed in a suspicious gaze behind reading glasses perched on the end of his nose. "Yes?" he asked.

"Hi," said Ab, smiling brightly in the way I'd seen her do at the old folks' home. One look at the old man, and I was immediately glad she was there to turn on the charm. "I was wondering if you could help us," she went on. "We're looking for any records you can find for a wine cellar that was being built by the Black family back in 1946."

The man glanced at a clock high on the wall, its minute hand hanging at two minutes to five, and his gaze went from suspicious to unfriendly. "We're closed. Come back Monday."

"Please?" Ab urged. "It's really important."

He looked at the clock again, pursed his lips as if he'd just bitten down on something sour, but then he sighed and reached under the counter, drawing out a form that he slid across to us. "Fill this out, and I'll get to it when I can."

“Thanks!” Ab said. “Do you have a pen?”

The old man glared but fished out a ballpoint from his shirt pocket. “Do you just want to view the documents, or do you want copies?”

Ab looked at me questioningly, and I cleared my throat. “Uh, copies, I guess.”

“It’s a ten-dollar fee. Covers up to the first fifty pages.”

I paid him, and he wrote me out a receipt while Ab worked on the request form. It was only 5:01 when she finished, but the old man still didn’t look happy. “You’ll get a call when your copies are ready,” he told us. “Pick ’em up at the first-floor reception desk. Bring your receipt. If there are more than fifty pages, you can pay for them then.” With that, he turned and stalked down the same aisle from which he’d emerged.

“Thank you!” Ab called at his retreating back. She looked disappointed when he ignored her.

I didn’t want the old man to hear me, so I waited until we were back downstairs and out on the sidewalk before speaking. “Cheerful guy,” I observed.

“I put my home phone on the form,” Ab said. “I’m just three blocks away, so I thought it made sense.”

I shrugged, handing her the receipt. “Sure. So, what now? Anyone up for some hot wings or something?” Despite the burger I’d eaten at Hovey’s, I was hungry again.

Les seemed to consider the idea but then shook his head. “No thanks,” he announced, yawning. “I don’t know about you two, but I’ve had about enough for one day. I’m going home for a shower.”

“I think I’ll go home, too,” said Ab. “Mom asked me to do a few things, and then I think I’ll see what else I can find in the diary.” She turned and started for home. “Later, guys,” she called back over her shoulder.

I dropped Les off at his place and watched him retreat up the front walk. I felt tired but a little lonely, too. Even though a lot had happened, it felt like the day had ended too suddenly.

Moe watched me expectantly from the passenger seat, his tail swishing. *So what's next?* his expression seemed to say.

"Looks like it's just you and me, buddy," I told him, and we headed for home.

THIRTY-FIVE

I WAS STILL FEELING KIND OF LONELY BY THE TIME I GOT home, so after giving Moe his dinner, I went up to check on Mom. I climbed the stairs slowly, thinking about my vision and the way Aunt Claire had taken charge in the aftermath of the tidal wave. She'd been amazing, directing everyone with sureness and authority as the survivors made their way up to the inn. I especially admired the way she had pulled herself back together so quickly after her father had been brought in. I tried to put myself in her shoes, imagining Mom unconscious with a mangled leg, and realized I would have been a panicked mess.

I crossed the attic floor, listening to the breeze moan softly in the eaves. When the light in the cupola stairwell changed from gold to gray, I didn't think anything of it, figuring that a cloud had passed over the sun, but as I mounted the final steps and emerged into the room above…

...I discover I'm looking out on winter. Dark, brooding clouds hang low in the overcast sky, spilling fat raindrops that are hurled against the windows by a gusty wind out of the north. Outside, the bare branches of the elm trees lean southward, as if drawing away from the thunder that rumbles threateningly in the distance, and even through the downpour dashed against the panes I can see the vineyard below is nothing but barren rows above a carpet of drenched brown leaves.

"Daddy, it's freezing!" Claire says, passing me from behind to set a tray down on a shelf. I notice offhandedly that it's not exactly the same spot where I leave Mom's food, but it's close. She then hurries to close a window that's standing wide open behind her father.

"Don't," Roger orders, looking over his shoulder, but there isn't much authority to it. "I can't hear her if it's closed!"

Claire ignores him. Even though the window is on the leeward side of the room, a quantity of water has pooled on the windowsill and the shelf below. Claire uses the hem of her apron to wipe it up before moving back around to address her father. "Sit down, Dad. Doctor Napier says if you don't stop overusing that knee, it will never heal. Anyway, it's time for supper. You haven't eaten today."

Looking at the two of them, I realize the season isn't the only thing that has changed. Claire's hair is pulled back from her face, making her features look severe in the gray light. The brightness in her voice has been replaced by a direct, businesslike tone, and every movement she makes seems controlled and efficient. I can see a lot more of the stern old woman she will eventually become, and it makes me sad.

Even so, the changes in her father are far more dramatic. His hair has both thinned and grayed noticeably, retreating even further back from his forehead and making the wrinkles at the corners of his eyes stand out. He's lost so much weight that I'm reminded of a scarecrow, his rumpled clothes sagging on his frame and covered in food stains. Roger pulls back reluctantly from where he's been gazing through the telescope and throws his daughter a sullen glare that she meets with an arched eyebrow. Pushing away from the telescope frame, he lurches slowly across the floor, the thump-THUMP of his gait making me shudder with its familiarity. His left leg is fitted with a metal brace that is hinged at the knee, restricting his movements enough to make walking awkward. At last Roger makes it to a rocking chair next to the shelf where Claire left his tray, and he drops gracelessly into it with a grunt of pain. Part of me is not at all surprised when I recognize the very same chair my mother sleeps in, although the green upholstery is far less faded and threadbare.

Claire walks over, first draping a napkin across her father's lap and then sliding the tray directly next to him. There's a large bowl with a spoon in it, along with a coffee mug and a plate of sliced bread. "Split pea with ham," she tells him. "Your favorite. Hurry while it's still hot."

"I'm not hungry."

She sighs. "You need to eat, Dad. Doctor Napier says you're only making things worse by not eating."

"To hell with Napier." He gazes up at his daughter with an expression of barely contained desperation. "How can I think about food when she's lost out there in the storm? How can you*? We need to find her before she gets sick!"*

Claire sighs again, her expression softening as she kneels beside the chair and places a hand on his arm. "Daddy…we talked about this. Bonnie's gone. The wave took her, remember?"

Roger's eyes lose focus as he stares into the empty space between them. "They never found her body," he murmurs, a tear escaping the corner of his eye and sliding down his cheek. "She's only missing."

My heart twists as I watch their exchange, and I wonder how much time has passed since the disaster. A few months at least, by the look of it. What's happened to him? Was it the shock and grief of losing Bonnie? Or was Roger under water too long, and the lack of oxygen affected his mind? Whatever the reason, he's apparently not all there anymore, and I feel sorry for him.

"A lot of bodies were never recovered," she replies, then pauses. When she speaks again, her tone is even softer. "It's time to face the truth, Daddy. You and I…we're it. We're all that either of us has right now. I need *you. I don't know how much longer I can carry on with everything by myself!"*

His gaze comes back into focus, and he places his free hand on top of hers. "You don't understand," he tells her, not unkindly. "Bonnie's still out there somewhere. She was frightened by the earthquake and ran outside, that's all. I see *her, Claire. In my dreams…"*

"You're sleeping much too much. It's not good for you."

"But it helps," he says, offering a bleak smile. "Until Bonnie comes home, it's the only way I get to see my little girl."

"I know," Claire concedes. "And I dream about her, too. But that's all they are—just dreams."

"But I hear her!" he insists. "Even when I'm not asleep! Haven't you? Haven't you heard her laugh…and that song she loves so much…?"

"No. None of it is real. Can't you see that?"

His expression hardens to a glare. "She'd be inside, safe and dry, if it weren't for you!"

A pained expression briefly touches her features, but it disappears as she rises to her feet. "I know," she says. "And I've told you I'm sorry. I've told you a million times." She turns and starts across the floor.

"She's out there!" Roger shouts at her retreating back. "She's out there somewhere, and I'm going to find her!"

Claire doesn't turn. "Eat your soup," she calls back over her shoulder. And as her footsteps fade down the stairs…

…the vision faded as well.

I was left standing in the center of the cupola, staring at the area where Roger had been sitting—the spot currently occupied by Mom's easel. I turned, relieved to see her sleeping peacefully, the barest hint of a smile on her face. The room was stuffy, giving Mom a light sheen of sweat on her forehead and creating darker patches on her shirt at the chest and armpits. That was a relief, at least—the warm air meant that the ghost of Roger Black (I had no doubt about that now) was off being miserable someplace else. I opened a couple of windows to let some of the breeze in, reminding myself to come up and close them again later when things cooled off.

After that I just hung around for a few minutes, wondering what to do next. I briefly considered trying to wake Mom, to see if maybe I could get her to talk for a while, or better still, coax her downstairs for something to eat. In the end, though, I decided not to, partly because she looked so relaxed, but mostly because I didn't want to take a chance on being disappointed again, which I figured was more than likely.

The clicking of toenails drifted up from the attic below, followed by a whine from Moe. I realized that he was probably just reminding me that he'd finished eating and needed to go outside. "Just a sec, boy," I called out, deciding at the last minute to have another look at Mom's painting before going downstairs. I went over and stood at the easel for a long time, comparing the details on the canvas with my view of the vineyard below. Sure enough, something about it still bugged me. It was as close to perfect as I'd ever seen her paint, but still…something was wrong. And the longer I stood there playing *Where's Waldo* with the thing, the more annoyed I felt when I couldn't figure out what it was.

At last Moe barked, sounding urgent, and I headed for the stairs.

I leaned against the porch railing while Moe took care of business, and afterward we just wandered around. The breeze felt good after the stuffiness of the cupola, so we strolled around the outside of the house, my hiking boots crunching through the dry weeds as the afternoon waned. I was caught between feeling restless and having no idea at all what I wanted to do, so I ended up just following where my footsteps led me. We walked a long lap entirely around the vineyard, looking for any evidence of a building, but I came up empty. I kicked myself for not looking for the wine cellar during my vision in the cupola, realizing that it would have been the perfect time to note its location while the vines were bare. But the fact was it hadn't occurred to me at the time, and the opportunity had been lost.

Maybe it was because all the visions I'd seen that day were still rattling around in my head, or maybe it was just my gift guiding me on a subconscious level, but whatever the reason, I was both nervous and a little excited when Moe and I started up the road to the inn. By the time we got there, I was glad to see that some space still remained between the ocean and the cherry-colored sun, and for a while I sat on the chain stretched across the entrance, idly swinging back and forth while gazing at the shadowy, looming silhouette of the old hotel. Behind it, the horizon went from burnt orange to peach to shades of steadily darkening blue further up, with the first stars beginning to emerge directly overhead. An old rhyme…

[Star light, star bright, first star I see tonight…]

…sprang into my head, and I suppose it was only then, sitting there with the ocean breeze blowing my hair back, that I realized I was there for a reason.

I'd seen a lot that afternoon, but not enough. I needed to know the rest of what had happened that day.

I rubbed my palm against my right thigh, feeling the outline of the brass key in my hip pocket, and my heart began thudding heavily in my chest. I wished…

[…I may, I wish I might…]

…that Ab and Les were there, too, but I knew they actually wouldn't be able to help much, if at all. Besides, it wasn't as if anything in there had tried—or even seemed able—to hurt me. At least so far, right? Everything I'd experienced in there amounted to nothing beyond echoes and shadows—no more threatening or real than my visions. The evidence supported my conclusions, and the logical part of my mind was all ready to rock. There was just one problem, though: the other 98 percent of me was scared silly.

I looked down at Moe, who was now just a shadow sitting beside me in weeds that were becoming more gray than gold as the light faded. "You up for this?" I asked.

His tail wagged.

"Even if I'm just being stupid?"

His tail wagged some more.

Fair enough, I decided, standing up.

Game on.

The hinges complained bitterly as I pushed the front door open, echoing back into the darkness with a squeal that was loud enough to make me cringe. The light from a three-quarters moon forced its way through the trees as it rose behind me, throwing a dim wedge through the open door and lancing through the cracks in the boarded-over windows.

I stood there for a while, letting my eyes adjust to the gloom and bracing myself against all of the assorted feelings and images that immediately crowded in on me from everywhere at once. Instead of trying to block them out the way I had that afternoon, I relaxed, allowing myself to get a feel for what was there. I remembered my first visit with Mom, and the handful of things I was able to pick up then, but with the way my gift had grown and strengthened in recent weeks, I was now able to sense *so* much more. It was as if something of the people who had worked or stayed as guests in the Windward Inn had been left behind, the wood and stone soaking up all of that energy like a sponge. I realized there were all sorts of visions I could tap into if I tried, scenes imprinted permanently into the place by the strong feelings of those involved, now just waiting to be revisited like stories in old books. I sensed a handful of active presences as well, some of which were even aware of me on different levels, but most of which were lost in memories of the past, reliving them over and over like psychic reruns.

A woman's laugh drifted faintly down from somewhere upstairs, bringing me to within a hair's breadth of bolting back outside and putting an end to my solo adventure right then and there. But Moe didn't react and, instead, just looked up as if curious about what was wrong, and I knew then the sound had only been in my head. Just the same, it took a minute or so for my heart to stop trying to batter its way out of my chest. At last I took a deep breath, deciding that my eyes had adjusted all they were going to.

Time to get to work.

I ventured inside, looking around nervously for anything that might rush at me out of the darkness, and then eased myself down onto the same tarp-draped sofa I'd sat on just a few hours before. Moe jumped up and curled himself beside me, his chin on my thigh. Closing my eyes and forcing myself to relax, I began trying to mentally block out the stray images and feelings that had nothing to do with what I was looking for. I wasn't sure how to do what I wanted to do or if it was even possible. The fact was that I'd never tried anything like this before. For most of my life, other than reading people's surface emotions, everything I'd experienced with my gift had been completely random, images or flashbacks or the occasional premonition that my mind would just stumble across, like bumping into things in the dark. Aunt Claire's diary had acted like a flashlight, providing focus and allowing me to see more, and even as I'd grown beyond the need for it, the things I was able to see still came as a surprise. But this was a whole different ballgame. For the first time, I was reaching out to find something specific.

For a long time, I thought it was hopeless. I would succeed in shoving some feeling or image to the background, only to have three or four I'd already blocked off come rushing back. Or, I would be making progress, my mind beginning to quiet as I cleared space for myself, but then the dam would break, everything would come rushing back, and I'd have to start over again from the beginning. It was frustrating, and half a dozen times I was on the verge of giving up and going home. But then I'd think of Mom, wasting away just like Claire's father, and I'd tackle it again.

I don't know how long I kept at it—an hour at least, maybe even two. After a while, I lost track of time. I lost track of all the fleeting visions I glimpsed, as well—images from different decades and flashes of people I didn't know who were feeling happy, excited, furious, or any of a number of varied emotions. I kept trying different approaches, guided only by instinct and whatever luck I may have stored up, failing over and over again. Eventually, though, I stumbled across a technique that seemed promising. I pictured myself in a room surrounded by TVs—dozens, maybe hundreds of them—with each one tuned to something within range of my mind's antenna. Some of them were like old black and whites from before I was born, with hazy, weak images that were easy to shut off. Others were more modern—big plasma flat screens that were way too vivid and powerful for me to do anything about except turn down the volume.

It was slow going at first, but after time I began making progress switching off, tuning out, or turning down images, eliminating each of them one by one. Picturing things that way also helped me to focus, and at some point I began to grow confident that what I wanted would be there if I kept at it long enough.

Then, all at once, I found it! The Claire channel.

I open my eyes to find that a vision has materialized around me.

If anything, the Windward Inn is even more crowded, as most everyone in town seems to have made their way there for shelter. It looks less like an inn now and more like a refugee camp. Through the doors on the far side of the room, I can see that people are stacked three deep at the bar, while perhaps thirty or forty more are seated in dining room chairs arranged in concentric arcs around a massive console radio in the lobby.

"Reports continue to come in from Windward Cove," announces a tinny voice from the speaker, "where the tidal wave that struck at 3:54 this morning has left devastation in its wake. Hundreds are homeless, with current reports listing seventeen confirmed dead and over twenty still missing. Search efforts are ongoing and are expected to continue throughout the night. The Coast Guard has dispatched two cutters to look for survivors in the water, although the chances of anyone remaining alive at this hour are slim. Area hospitals have opened their doors to the injured, with many being transported to centers as far south as Fort Bragg and as far north as Crescent City. Stay tuned to this channel for updates as they become available, and contact your local Red Cross if you have the means to help. Now, back to our regularly scheduled

programming." Music swells into a Bing Crosby song, and conversations rise up among the listeners.

Behind me, the front door bangs open, and I turn to see a couple of men in white uniforms hurry in, wheeling a gurney between them. It's obviously not their first trip there, as they turn into the dining room without directions and load up the first patient they find. Behind them, I can see Dr. Napier bustling here and there, his jacket and tie missing, his shirt unbuttoned at the collar and streaked with dried blood. He tends to patients who seem mostly at ease now, assisted by a couple of nurses in white uniforms and starched caps. I watch as the men with the gurney wheel a man past me, heading back out the door to a waiting ambulance that idles in the blue of early evening.

Most of that day has passed, I realize. A baby wails somewhere at the edge of my hearing, but it's a soothing sound compared to the screams of the injured and dying that had filled the Windward Inn that morning. The air of panic that had filled the place is gone too, the townspeople warm and dry, calmly shuffling around in the hotel in robes and mismatched clothes.

I rise from the sofa as Mary Lou and June come bursting through the front door, leading half a dozen men and a couple of other women. They all look dirty and worn out, but Claire doesn't seem to notice as she rushes in from the dining room to meet them just inside. "Did you find her?" Her eyes are wide in an expression of desperate hopefulness.

Mary Lou shakes her head. "Not yet. We've looked everywhere."

"The radio said that a body washed up a couple of miles south! Did you..."

"We checked," interrupts June in a soothing tone. "It wasn't Bonnie, dear. The body was Mrs. Lindsay's."

Claire nods, shifting her weight nervously as tears spill down her cheeks. "I'll check the house again," she declares suddenly. "Maybe she's come home!"

She starts for the door and then stops as Mary Lou places a hand on her arm. "We just came from there."

"WE HAVE TO FIND HER!" Claire shouts suddenly, flinging off the hand as the last of her self-control crumbles away. She's visibly shaking with panic, and conversations go silent as everyone within earshot looks over. "IT'S GETTING DARK OUTSIDE! BONNIE HAS TO BE SCARED AND... HUNGRY AND...AND COLD AND...!" Mary Lou steps forward to take her in her arms, and Claire breaks down, sobbing hoarsely into her shoulder.

June exchanges glances with some of the other searchers, and four of them turn to follow her back outside. The room darkens...

...and I found myself by the open front door, looking out to where the moon had climbed well above the treetops. I went out to sit on the porch steps, thinking about everything I'd seen and feeling so sorry for Claire that it was almost overwhelming. Moe came over to flop down beside me, and I stroked his fur, grateful for his company.

We sat there for a long time, listening to the wind in the dry grass and the restless pounding of waves against the cliffs.

THIRTY-SIX

THE MOON HAD RISEN EVEN HIGHER BY THE TIME I finally got to my feet, rubbing my temples with a wince. My head ached dully, though whether it was from built-up tension or some aftereffect of straining my gift so hard that day, I couldn't tell. In any case, I'd seen everything I came to see, and since I couldn't detect anything else of Claire from the lobby, I figured it was time to go.

I was pulling the front door closed, feeling the first glimmers of relief at having the creepiness of the place behind me for the night, when it struck me that I was wrong. *No,* I realized. I *hadn't* seen everything. Not yet. There was still one place that might have stored up memories from that day.

Room 202…where they'd taken Claire's father.

I took a nervous, involuntary step back from the door, wiping palms that were suddenly sweaty on the thighs of my jeans. *Dude… are you seriously thinking of doing this?* the voice in the back of my mind asked. I swallowed, realizing that I was. After all, I'd just spent

God knows how long inside the Windward Inn already, and nothing bad or scary had happened. Just echoes and shadows, right?

Yeah, well hanging around just a few running steps from an open door is one thing, the voice argued back. *Going all the way upstairs and fumbling around in the dark is something else.*

I stood there for a minute or so, going back and forth in my head, but at last I shook it off. The things I'd experienced back at the house were a hell of a lot more frightening than anything I'd run into so far in there, so it was time to quit being such a wuss. Straightening, I pushed the door open and stepped back into the darkness, heading purposefully toward the stairs.

I was two thirds of the way up to the second floor when I heard a whine behind me, and I turned to see Moe staring up from the base of the stairs. "Here, boy," I urged, trying not to think of what his hesitation meant. "There's nothing up here that can hurt us, buddy. C'mon…we've got this."

Moe paced nervously back and forth in front of the first step but then seemed to make up his mind and dashed suddenly up to huddle next to my leg. From then on he stayed close beside me, and I could feel him trembling as we finished the climb to the second floor.

Luckily, most of the guestroom doors were standing open, and the moonlight filtering in between the gaps in window boards was just enough to create a pattern of dimly lit rectangles along the hallway. It was enough to navigate by, though just barely, and I wished I'd thought to bring a flashlight. I stepped to the door directly across from me, feeling around until my fingers found and traced the shapes of the room numbers: *213.* We turned right, making our way to the next door and repeating the process: *215.*

Wrong way, but no big deal. I'd broken the code and now knew that 202 lay behind us, way down at the end and on the opposite side of the hall.

We were about halfway there when Moe growled, shrinking against the left-hand wall. I was about to ask what was wrong when suddenly a woman wearing an old-fashioned nightgown rushed out from the darkness of the room to my right. She was lit by an internal glow that radiated slightly outward from her body in a white nimbus, giving her skin and the blue of her gown a sort of washed-out look, like an old photo that had been too long in the sun.

"Call someone!" she shrieked hysterically, her eyes wide in a terrified expression. Moe put himself between us, barking furiously, but she didn't notice. *"He's not breathing! Do you hear me? HE'S NOT BREATHING!"*

I sucked in a breath that surely would have been the granddaddy of all screams, but just like that, the woman was gone. Instead, I exhaled slowly as a violent case of the shakes hit me. Moe was still barking, the sound reverberating hollowly through the old inn, and I reached down with a trembling hand to quiet him. I blinked in the darkness, trying to clear the greenish afterimage of the woman that was burned into my vision, and by the time it faded away, my shakes were mostly gone, too.

"This was a *really* stupid idea," I said, but Moe just looked up at me with his tail wagging, as if proud he'd scared the ghost away. I glanced wistfully back down the hall toward the stairwell, wanting nothing more than to abort the mission and get our asses out of there. Then I looked toward room 202, now only three doors down from where we stood. Close. So close...

Which way, big guy? my inner voice asked.

I hesitated a moment longer and then pressed on.

Room 202 was better lit than most of the rooms, a couple of offset knot holes in one of the window boards looking like eyes peering in. I stepped across the threshold, tentatively reaching out with my gift…

...and I cross over into the past.

Roger Black lies unconscious on the bed. His left leg lies on top of the blanket, splinted and wrapped in bandages, and I can see that someone has cleaned him up and put him in pajamas. A dim lamp burns on a table beneath the window, through which I can see that the sky above the ocean has lightened to a predawn gray. Near the bed, Claire sleeps in a wingback chair, still wearing the clothes I'd last seen her in, so I guess it's early morning on the day after the tidal wave.

Roger stirs as I watch, blinking while muttering words I can't make out. The sound wakes Claire, who sits forward to place a hand on her father's arm. "Daddy...?"

His gaze finds her and then travels around the room. "Where?" he croaks, his voice raspy.

"We're at the inn," Claire tells him.

He nods weakly and then begins coughing. Even that little movement causes him pain, and both his hands clutch at his left thigh, trying to keep it still. He grits his teeth in agony, still coughing hoarsely, the tendons in his neck standing out and beads of sweat appearing on his forehead.

Claire is on her feet, leaning over the bed as if unsure what to do, and when his coughing finally subsides, she holds a glass for him filled with water that he sucks through a straw. It's nearly empty when he nods that he's had enough, and he settles back on the pillows with a sigh. "How many are dead?" he asks.

"Twenty-two the last I heard, but that was more than an hour ago. People are still out searching." She sinks back into her chair, reaching out to take his hand. "How do you feel?"

Either he doesn't hear the question or he ignores it. "And the town?"

"They say there's a lot of damage, but I haven't been there myself. There was too much to do caring for the injured, and most everybody is up here while we get things sorted out."

He squeezes her hand. "Tell me."

"Daddy, all that can wait. You're badly hurt, and the doctor says..."

"No," he insists. "Tell me now. Tell me everything."

Claire does, and it takes a long time. She reports what she's heard about the condition of downtown, the names of the dead she remembers, all the efforts they'd made at the inn, and what they had left in the way of food and supplies. As she speaks, I find out that volunteers have been coming into town all night, supported by a mobile soup kitchen run by the Red Cross, and that so far the Coast Guard has pulled four bodies out of the ocean. She tells him everything but the hardest part of all, and I cringe when I finally sense it coming.

"Daddy," She says at last, and then pauses, swallowing as tears well in her eyes. "Daddy, there's one more thing. Bonnie. She's...missing."

Roger stares flatly at her as Claire explains how she'd left Bonnie at the house, thinking that either she'd be back not long after or that Flora would be there before she woke. He listens without speaking as she explains how survivors flooded the inn after the disaster and how she hadn't realized that Bonnie had been alone until Flora's body was brought in. She goes on to insist that there was still hope and that searchers could find her any minute, but Roger only turns his face to the wall, his shoulders shaking in silent sobs.

At last Claire runs out of things to say, and I watch as she sits helplessly while her father cries, refusing to look at her. After a long time, he goes still, and I guess he's fallen asleep. Claire must think so, too, and she rises from her chair, walking quietly toward the door.

"You knew," Roger says, the emotionless tone of his voice causing Claire to turn. "You knew she wanted to come with me. You were there. She begged me to take her along. And you know how stubborn she is... how fearless *she is. You know how she always has to have things her way. But you still left, Claire. You left her all alone."*

She moves back to the bedside, leaning over him as she tries to see his face. "Oh, Daddy… I'm so, so sorry," she says, starting to cry again. "I wish that…"

Her father whips back around, his hand striking out to grasp her arm as he glares at her, his expression a mask of loathing and rage. "YOU WERE SUPPOSED TO BE WATCHING HER!"

Moe and I tramped down from the Windward, the moonlight that dappled the road in front of us seeming bright after the darkness of the inn. I listened to my footfalls, smoldering away in a high state of pissoff. Maybe it was my lingering headache, or maybe it was all the visions I'd overloaded my senses with that day. But all at once I was pissed at Roger Black for blaming Claire the way he had, mad that whatever was left of him was taking over Mom, and furious that the words he'd used when lashing out at Claire...

[YOU WERE SUPPOSED TO BE WATCHING HER!]

…were the same ones Mom had screamed at me. For that matter, I was pissed at Bonnie for not doing what she'd been told, pissed at Flora for getting herself killed in the tidal wave, and even pissed at Aunt Claire for leaving us all that money and making us move to Windward Cove. Right then, the scope of my pissoff was epic. Mostly, though, I was pissed that a big freaking mess that other people had made decades before I was even born had somehow become my problem. Bottom line: I'd had more than enough for one day.

We got back to the house, and I was fumbling in my pocket for my keys when I stopped, realizing that I didn't want to be there. Not right then, anyway. The last things I needed were any more ghosts ruining my life or visions turning my brain into mush, and I decided I needed to be around people. *Live* ones. In fact, right then it seemed like the best idea in the world.

I looked at my watch. *11:23*. Would Ab or Les still be up? Maybe, but I doubted if their folks would be thrilled if I rang the doorbell. Kelly? Worse idea—I still hadn't gotten around to deciding what to do about her, and anyway, I'd had enough drama for one evening. Then a thought occurred to me, and I smiled, quickly calculating which day it was just to make sure. Yep, it was definitely Saturday, and I knew just where to go.

"C'mon, Moe," I said, heading for the car. "Time to hit the beach!"

THIRTY-SEVEN

MORE THAN HALF THE FIRES THAT HAD DOTTED THE beach earlier that evening had been abandoned by the time Moe and I made our way down to the cove, reduced to piles of smoking ash or embers that glowed sullenly in the darkness. The rest were still crackling brightly, though, and I felt my spirits climb a rung or two as I counted thirty or forty diehard partiers still hanging out. A few were down by the water or strolling around visiting friends, but most just sat clustered around the scattered fires, enjoying the closeness and warmth.

A German shepherd wearing a bandanna around her neck trotted over to greet Moe, accompanied by a pit bull who grinned up at me with his tongue lolling out and tail whipping back and forth so vigorously that his whole backside swayed with it. I petted each of them briefly and then left them behind to play, confident that Moe would come find me when they were done sniffing butts and chasing one other around.

I wandered aimlessly, sticking to the shadows just beyond the firelight while looking around for someone I knew. After a few minutes, I spotted Nicole, sitting alone by a low fire a bit removed from the others, hugging her knees as she stared out toward the ocean. "Hey," I said, smiling as I drew near.

She looked up at me, her eyes large and glassy, and it was a second or two before I saw recognition in her gaze. "Oh…hey, Ben," she said at last, giving me a smile that looked more sad than anything else. I noticed a monster-sized can of beer stuck in the sand beside her, with a couple of empties lying beside it, and I guessed she'd been there a while.

"Can I sit with you?"

She shrugged. "Sure. If you want. But I'm probably not great company right now."

I dropped down beside her, crossing my legs. "You okay?"

Nicole just shook her head, her gaze returning to the moonlight reflecting on the water.

"Bad day, huh?"

"Yeah. Broke up with Adam."

I remembered the burly guy from Kelly's party. "Sorry," I offered. "We're you together a long time?"

"Not really," she said. "Five, six months, maybe."

"Yeah, but it still sucks. What happened?"

She made an irritated sound. "Turns out one girlfriend wasn't enough for him. I guess he keeps them in twos and threes."

"Wow…what a dick."

"Uh-huh. I thought so, too. Hence the breakup." She took a drink from her beer. "Story of my life," she muttered. "I'm never good enough."

"Hey," I said, putting an arm over her shoulders. "That's *so* not true. The guy's just a douche, that's all. I mean, who in their right

mind would cheat on you? You're fun, super nice, smokin' hot—a total package deal. Just ask anyone!"

Nicole snorted laughter, bumping against me. "You really mean it?" she asked, sounding hopeful.

"Absolutely." I probed her feelings, noting that she was still feeling down, though maybe a little better now. I felt badly for her but happy that I could help, even if just a little. If nothing else, it was nice to take a break from my own problems for a while.

She took another pull from her beer and then held out the can to me.

I hesitated and then took it. "Here's to putting a rotten day behind us," I toasted, and then took a swallow.

Nicole looked at me, her eyebrows raised. "What made your day so bad?"

I considered sharing some of what was going on but then decided it would take too long. And anyway, I didn't feel like getting into it right then. "Just…family stuff." I said at last, handing the can back to her. "I'm working it out."

"Sorry. Family troubles can be rough—I know." Nicole didn't press me for details, and I was grateful for that. We sat together for a while, sharing a companionable silence while she worked on her beer. She offered the can to me a couple more times, but I waved it away. Driving around without a license was dumb enough. No *way* was I going to cross over into the stupid zone.

Moe found us a little while later, and I sensed Nicole's spirits rising as she gushed over him and he wallowed around on her lap, soaking it up. As for me, I just enjoyed being able to shove my anxieties about Mom and Bonnie and everything else to the background for a while. It was nice to be there, not having to say or do or worry about anything. I could just breathe and enjoy the night.

Finally, Nicole sighed, pushing Moe gently away and finishing the last swallow from the can. "I guess I should go home," she announced.

I rose and helped her to her feet. "Why don't you let me give you a ride?" I suggested, noting that she was swaying a little—not bad, but enough where I didn't feel right letting her go off alone.

"Would you? That would be great."

I nodded and then crushed her cans and stuffed them in my jacket pocket before kicking sand over what was left of the fire. "Let's get out of here."

Nicole leaned against me as we walked back to where the trail met the sand, and I guessed all the beer was taking effect. "Hold on a sec," she said before we started up. "I gotta pee."

I nodded as she released my arm to make her way unsteadily to the bushes at the base of the cliff. I turned to make sure she had privacy and was immediately startled to see the silhouette of someone standing only six or eight feet behind me.

"So…it's you and *her* now, huh?" I recognized Kelly's voice as she stepped up to confront me.

"No, it's not," I said. It was too dark to see her expression, but I didn't need to. Anger, hurt, and jealousy radiated off her like heat. Normally, it would have put me on the defensive, but then again, it hadn't been a normal kind of day, and all I felt was a sort of weary irritation. Just the same, I tried to smooth things over. "Nicole just had too much to drink, that's all, and…"

"I *waited* for you," Kelly interrupted, her voice cracking a little. "I waited three hours—after making food and *everything*—but you never came!"

"Look, I'm sorry about that," I said. "I didn't get a chance to read your note until this morning, and by then it was too late."

"This *morning*?" she asked, wiping at her eyes. "I thought you liked me!"

"I did. I *do*..." I stammered, searching for the right thing to say but not finding it. "I just..."

"You just *what*?" came a second voice from the darkness, and I looked past Kelly's shoulder to see two more silhouettes approaching from the beach. As they got closer, I recognized Alan and Rick.

Perfect.

"Come on, new guy...you just what?" Alan repeated. When I didn't answer, he turned to Kelly. "Is this asshole bothering you? *Please* tell me he is, and I'll take care of it right now."

"No," she answered quickly—a little *too* quickly, it seemed, but maybe that was just me. Either way, we probably both realized at the same time that neither of them had overheard us. Not that I particularly cared at that point, and I was happy to keep my mouth shut and let her handle things on her own. "It's nothing," she assured him. "We're just talking."

"Talking about what?"

An idea suddenly occurred to me and I seized it. "Broken windows," I blurted out before she could say anything, and Kelly turned back toward me. "Last night some asshole threw a rock through a window at my house," I went on, letting the anger I still felt about it come through my voice. "I was just asking Kelly if she knew anyone who'd be that chickenshit."

They all glanced at one another, and I quickly reached out to sense their feelings:

Mild surprise from all three...

...disdain from Alan...

...hostility from Rick...

...concern from Kelly, with her other feelings changing to a mixture of relief and sympathy.

But no guilt at all, I realized. Not from any of them, and it surprised me. I'd expected a guilty pang to give one of them away, but it just wasn't there.

"Are you saying it was *us*?" Alan demanded.

His tone made my anger flare up again, and my face grew hot as some part of me knew I was about to lose control of my mouth. But what the hell—after all, just because they didn't feel guilty about it didn't mean it wasn't them, right? "Why not?" I snapped. "You're supposed to be the guy with the golden arm, aren't you? And since all you've done since I moved here is get in my face, why *wouldn't* I think so?" I turned to address Rick next. "Or maybe it was *you.* What…leaving a dead raccoon on my porch wasn't enough, so you decided to bust up the place?"

"Ben? What's going on?" Nicole asked, returning to draw up beside me.

"Nothing," I said. "I've just had it with all the bullshit around here!"

Alan and Rick exchanged a glance and then moved threateningly toward me, but Kelly turned, putting her arms out to bar their way. "*Stop* it! All of you!"

"I'm not gonna let this guy accuse me of things I didn't do!" Rick snarled.

"Come *on,* Ben," Nicole urged, sounding scared. "It's time to go…please?" Beside her, Moe lowered his head and began to growl, his lips drawn back to show teeth.

"Yes, go!" Kelly agreed, looking back over her shoulder. "Get him out of here!"

"Oh, don't you even *start,* Kelly!" Nicole shot back, sounding angry. "You're more to blame for this than anybody!"

Her head whipped around. "What's *that* supposed to mean?"

"Ben, come *on*!" Nicole ordered, ignoring the question as she tugged at my arm. At last I let her pull me toward the trail, and I tramped angrily alongside her as we climbed toward the top of the cliff.

Below us, Alan's voice rose from the darkness. "Yeah, Kel…what *did* she mean by that?"

We didn't speak during the hike up to the car, but that was good. It gave me time to think, and I could feel a little of my anger dissipate with each step we took. It bothered me that I'd let my feelings take charge of my mouth. While it had felt good to take out my frustrations on Alan and Rick—in that moment, at least—the fact was that I still had no idea which of them was screwing with me. Granted, my money was still on Rick, but if I were being honest with myself, I'd have to admit that I wasn't nearly as sure about that anymore as I had been. But confronting them that way had only made my situation worse, and not just in the short term. It was a safe bet that going to war with the quarterback wouldn't make my life any easier when I started at Silver Creek High that fall. Worst of all, I'd very nearly landed in a fight that was pretty much guaranteed to end with my ass being handed to me.

Not my best example of tactical thinking.

I opened the passenger door for Nicole, and by the time I let Moe in the back and came around to slide behind the wheel, she was slouched with her knees up on the dash. Moe hurdled the seat back and curled up between us, and Nicole entwined her fingers in his fur. "I'm really sorry," she said as I started the car.

I paused, looking over curiously. "What for?"

"For going off on Kelly like that—telling her she was to blame." She smiled, her face bathed in the soft glow of the instrument lights, and I thought again how pretty she was with her girl-next-door looks, nose ring and all. "I can get a little bitchy when my friends are being picked on," she continued. "I didn't mean to, but I guess I got you in trouble."

I shrugged. "It's fine—I was in trouble already. And anyway, I didn't really understand what you meant."

"No, you really didn't, did you?" Nicole said after a pause, and then she shook her head, chuckling softly. "You can be such a *dork,* Ben."

I didn't know what to make of that, so I let it go. I put the car in gear and pulled away, heading toward the lights of downtown.

We'd gone maybe a hundred yards when she spoke again. "So… don't you want to know *why* you're a dork?"

"Not really." All at once, driving Nicole home seemed like a bad idea. Not that I would have chosen differently, but I wished she'd leave it alone. It had been a long day, my headache had never really disappeared, and all I wanted to do was go to bed. The last thing that sounded like fun right then was to hear about my shortcomings.

"Okay," she conceded. "Totally your call." Three or four seconds passed, and I was just starting to relax when Nicole turned toward me, tucking one leg beneath her. "But let's just *pretend* you said yes, okay? 'Cause I'm just buzzed enough to tell you."

I groaned.

"See, Kelly isn't all that hard to figure out," she told me, reaching out to pat my arm. "You know what her problem is? She wants what she can't have. Get it?"

I tried to see where she was going but couldn't. "No," I told her at last. Maybe I was just dense.

"Let me break it down for you. She's grown up with it all—smart, popular, rich parents, the hot boyfriend. She's also gorgeous, and she knows it. Because even *before* her boobs grew out, every guy around would just about trip over himself trying to get her attention. You with me so far?"

I shrugged. "More or less."

"Turn right at the stop," she instructed. "Anyway, perfect world, right? But then *you* roll into town, a cute guy she hasn't been running into every day her whole life, which makes you exciting and mysterious. A guy who *obviously* likes her but doesn't try to do anything about it. As far as Kelly's concerned, that's just not the way her world works, and it's been driving her crazy." Nicole settled back, grinning at me. "Everyone can see what's going on, and we've all been talking about it. The only dorks who haven't figured it out yet are you and Alan. Oh, and Rick too, I suppose, otherwise he would have said something."

I thought about everything she'd said as we rolled through downtown, dark and deserted at that hour, and then I filed it under "Random Info" when I decided that none of it changed anything. I followed Nicole's directions to a small home on the eastern side of town. "You good?" I asked, turning to her after pulling up to the curb.

"Me? Oh, sure. I'll get over Adam soon enough, I guess. Thanks for being there for me."

"Any time." I waited, but she just looked at me, making no move to get out.

"So…?" she said at last.

"So what?"

"So what are you going to do about Kelly?"

I shrugged. "Not a thing. At the end of the day, she and Alan are still together. Whatever goes with that is her problem. I'll worry about what to do with Kelly if she ever actually goes back on the market."

Nicole smiled. "I figured you'd say something like that. You're a good guy, Ben." She then leaned across Moe and kissed me before getting out of the car—not in a way that meant anything, but a good, solid kiss on the lips just the same. I sat back, surprised and pleased, and watched as she made her way up to the front door and then turned and waved before going inside.

I grinned as I pulled away from the curb, heading for home.

As good guys went, I must have my moments.

THIRTY-EIGHT

I WAS ROLLING THROUGH DOWNTOWN, STILL THINKING about the kiss and wondering why I didn't have the good sense to have a crush on someone like Nicole, and I almost didn't notice Claire standing in the mouth of an alley next to the theater. When I realized what I'd just seen, I slammed down the brake pedal, sending Moe sliding off the front seat to the floor as we screeched to a halt. I almost forgot to put the transmission into park, but then I scrambled out of the car, leaving it idling in the middle of the street…

…that was like a ghost town a second before, but is now busy with summer evening traffic. Parked cars line both curbs, and music issues from the open door of a bar across from me. Inside, I can see a man and a woman swing dancing in front of a jukebox that plays a tune I partially recognize—the one about the boogie-woogie bugle boy. A couple of cars crisscross unhurriedly in front of me, and since I don't

see any signs of damage anywhere around, I figure it's sometime before the night of the tidal wave.

I cross to the other side, looking both ways first even though I know in real life Main Street is totally deserted, and walk three doors up to the theater. I glance at the marquee just before I pass beneath it, seeing that The Big Sleep *has been replaced by* The Time of Their Lives *starring Abbot and Costello. The smell of popcorn wafts from the entrance, making my stomach growl, but I ignore it as I step up to where Claire looks anxiously out at the street. She's standing mostly in shadow, as if trying not to be seen, and just as I arrive she smiles and waves toward someone behind me. I turn in time to see Philip wave back from behind the wheel of an old Ford coupe, and then he continues past, searching for a place to park.*

"Here to meet your boyfriend?" comes a voice from the alley. Both Claire and I whirl around, startled by the unexpected sound. William Crenshaw smiles from the shadows, and there's something about his expression that makes me uneasy. He leans casually against the theater wall, his hat tipped back on his head, with his shirt unbuttoned at the collar and his tie tugged partway down.

"No," Claire replies, recovering quickly, but I can tell that she's nervous. "Just waiting for some friends so we can see the picture together. They should be along any minute."

"Nice try, Miss Black, but I know better. Do you really think I didn't see the boy who just drove by? The one you meet every afternoon?" Claire's eyes go wide as Crenshaw utters a low laugh. "Ah, secret love and stolen moments. The stuff poets write about. And I've got to hand it to you…you've been very discreet in your sneaking around. Just not discreet enough. You see, I notice things. I'm very good *at noticing things."*

Claire swallows.

"Yes, I've seen you, Miss Black. I've even followed you. The question is what am I going to do about it?" He frowns as if carefully considering the issue. "Does your father know you're sneaking around with boys?" he asks after a second or two. "No... No, he doesn't, does he? I can see that much in your eyes." Crenshaw chuckles. "There I go, noticing things again. So what do you think would happen if he found out? And what would happen to me *if he discovered that I knew all along but didn't say anything? Why, I could lose my job. This puts me in a very difficult position. You can appreciate that, can't you?"*

Claire opens her mouth and then closes it. I can see her trembling.

"Say *it." The man orders, his smile disappearing. "Say, 'I appreciate the difficult position I've put you in, Mr. Crenshaw.'"*

"I...I appreciate the difficult position I've put you in, Mr. Crenshaw."

His smile reappears. "Good. That's very good, Claire. I can call you Claire, can't I? And while we're at it, why don't you just call me Bill. Wouldn't that be nice? After all, here we are, working out a sticky problem between us. That should make us friends, don't you think?"

Claire remains silent.

"Say, 'I'm happy to be your friend, Bill.'"

"I'm happy to..." Claire swallows again. "...To be your friend, Mr. Crenshaw."

"Bill," *he insists.*

A brief pause, then, "Bill."

"Very good." He nods, straightening. "So now that we're such good friends, and since you appreciate the difficult position I'm in, I think the best thing right now would be for me to drive you home."

Claire takes a nervous step backward, but the man's hand shoots out, roughly grasping her arm before she can escape into the light. Her eyes widening, she draws in a deep breath...

"Go ahead," he challenges her. "Make a scene, and the first thing I'll do is tell your father everything. But if you come with me now, you'll

have the chance to convince me to keep your secret. How's that for a square deal?"

My heart rate increases as every alarm in my head goes off at once. I wish she'd just kick him in the balls and run out of the alley where there are lights and people. Instead, Claire looks over her shoulder just in time to see Philip half a block down on the opposite side of the street. He's out of Crenshaw's line of sight, blocked by the corner of the building, and his steps slow as he looks over. From the angle, I figure he can probably see the man's hand grasping Claire arm, and when his face registers anger, Claire stops him in his tracks with a tiny shake of her head.

"JESUS, CLAIRE! WHAT ARE YOU DOING?*" I yell, horrified that she actually seems to be considering going with the man. Of course she doesn't hear me, and all I can do is stand there, bouncing lightly on the balls of my feet in nervous anxiety. Is she really that stupid? Sure, it's a totally different time, and maybe all Crenshaw really intends is to drive her home, but I wouldn't bet the ranch on it.*

Crenshaw releases her arm. "What's it going to be, Claire? Make up your mind."

She turns back toward him, biting her lower lip. "Alright, Mr. Cren...Bill," she amends. "If you'll just hear me out, maybe you'll understand that we're not doing anything wrong. Certainly nothing you need to trouble my father with."

"Come along, then. Convince me." He turns and walks further back into the alley, clearly expecting Claire to follow him. After a brief hesitation, she does."

"No-no-no-no-no!" I say, walking alongside her. "You don't want to go with this guy, Claire! Come on...you're being an idiot!" I realize that talking to her makes as much sense as shouting at a movie screen when the teenager goes to investigate that sound the monster just made in the basement, but I can't help myself. I glance back toward the street,

overjoyed to see Philip silhouetted at the mouth of the alley. "Come on, Phil!" I mutter urgently. "A little help here, buddy!" But he just stands there, watching as Crenshaw leads Claire to a big sedan parked in the lot behind the theater, holding the door for her as she gets in.

Turning, I sprint back to the street out front. It takes me a second or two before I can see the outline of the station wagon, a hazy distortion in the air, but then I dive behind the wheel just as Crenshaw's car emerges and turns downhill. Moe nuzzles my arm questioningly as I start to follow, but I push him back, concentrating on holding onto the vision. I'm pretty sure that the streets haven't changed position that much over time, if at all, and I can only hope that I don't run into anything in the real world. A detached part of my mind registers the weirdness of the moment—driving a car from the late 1960s while looking at 1946 through the car's windows—but I'm too preoccupied to give it more than a passing thought.

Crenshaw's car arrives at the road to Claire's house, and I'm not really surprised when it goes by without slowing. I follow it down to the wharf, where Crenshaw pulls around behind a warehouse standing near the dock where only a parking lot remains in my time. The place is deserted, and as I pull up, I see the passenger door fly open as Claire tries to escape even before the car has come to a stop. She almost makes it, too, but then Crenshaw's arm snakes out after her, grabbing a handful of her dress as he drags her back inside.

"SonofaBITCH!" I scramble out of the car, running over to look in through the still-open door.

Claire lies on her back, struggling and voicing muffled screams while Crenshaw's hand is clamped over her mouth, pinning her head against the car seat. He lies mostly on top of her, using his bulk to keep her from kicking while his other hand fumbles at the front of her dress.

Suddenly, the driver's side door opens and I look up to see Philip, standing with a tire iron in his right hand. His Ford is parked a dozen or so yards away, and I realize that he must have been following them, hanging back in the darkness with his headlights off, and neither of us had seen him. Relief floods through me as he reaches in, grasping Crenshaw by the shirt collar and dragging him out of the car.

The man tries throwing a punch as soon as he clears the door frame, but he's stumbling backward and his fist misses Philip by a mile. The swing throws him even more off balance, and he falls, landing hard on his butt in the gravel. He quickly gathers his feet under him, trying to get up but then puts his hands up protectively as Philip raises the tire iron.

"Stay right there!" Philip snaps, and then he looks over to Claire, who has gotten out to stand on the opposite side of the car. The front of her dress has been torn open, a single remaining button dangling loosely by a thread, and she holds the two sides closed in front of her as she walks around to glare down at Crenshaw. Where he'd seemed so menacing before, he now just looks small and pathetic, like a rat caught in a trap.

"Claire," Philip asks, his voice gentle, "did he…?"

"No," she replies coldly. "But he tried."

"Hey, now," Crenshaw pleads, "just hold your horses a minute, alright?" He forces a smile that I imagine the sleaziest of used-car salesmen would wear. "Let's not be hasty here! If you're smart, we can all walk away from this with something we want." He licks his lips nervously, sweat beading his forehead. "Tell you what: I'll keep your little secret. Hell, I'll take it to the grave, *and your father will never know—not from me he won't." Philip and Claire watch warily as he climbs to his feet. "In exchange for that, all I want is for the three of us to forget about tonight. After all, no real harm was done. Am I right? We all go our separate ways, and nothing like this will ever happen again." He holds up three fingers. "Scout's honor."*

"Honor?" Philip asks, his voice dripping with contempt.

Crenshaw's eyes narrow. "Maybe you think *you have me over a barrel, sonny boy, but you don't. The fact is you really don't have a choice, do you? You can either take the deal or forget about seeing your girl again because I* will *let the cat out of the bag. Don't you doubt that for a second. Go ahead...look in my eyes and see if I'm bluffing." He grins, sounding more confident. "I'll go have a little chat with Roger and tell him* all *about how I found you two steaming up the windows in the back of your car. It'll be your word against mine, won't it? Sure, maybe he'll believe you, and I'll still lose my job, but at least I won't go down with the ship alone." He pauses, letting the scenario sink in, and then offers the car salesman smile again. "But everybody loses that way. I don't want that, and you don't want that. Take the deal, and everybody wins. What do you say?"*

*A brief silence hangs in the air before Claire speaks, her voice carrying a lot of the no-nonsense tone I remember from when I was little. "No, I don't think so...*Bill,*" she says, emphasizing the last word. "For a man who prides himself on* noticing *things, I'm surprised you didn't notice there's another choice—one that I like a lot more."*

Crenshaw snorts, obviously still feeling good about his position. "Is that so? And what might that be?"

Claire turns, her expression calm. "Philip, would you be a dear and beat this man to death for me?"

The question takes me completely by surprise. It must strike Philip that way, too, as a couple of heartbeats pass before he answers. "Glad to," he says at last, hefting the tire iron.

But then Philip stumbles backward as Crenshaw suddenly charges him, knocking him to the ground just long enough to run to the car. He starts the engine and floors the accelerator, the rear end fishtailing and tires spitting gravel as the sedan speeds away.

Philip rolls to a sitting position, grinning. His grin fades, though, when he notices the calm expression on Claire's face crumble, tears welling in her eyes as she raises her hands to her face. She drops to her knees, sobbing into her palms with the front of her dress hanging open. I catch a glimpse of white bra and quickly look away.

Philip hurries over, kneeling as he draws her into his arms…

…and then the light shifted abruptly, the moon taking a different position in the sky. Where the warehouse stood was now just an empty parking lot, sprinkled here and there with bits of trash and weeds growing up through cracks in the asphalt. Claire's sobs seemed to echo in my ears for a moment, though that was probably just my imagination, and were replaced by the sound of waves lapping gently against the dock pilings.

Moe barked from inside the car, probably wondering what I was doing, so I went over to let him out. I sat on the hood for a few minutes, watching him trot around, and wondered how the rest of that night had turned out for Claire. Did she and Philip tell her father about Crenshaw? Did they go to the police? Did they ever see the man again? More questions. Always more questions.

It was a little after 3:00 when we finally got home, and I headed directly to the kitchen. I slapped together a big ham and cheese sandwich, standing at the counter while I ate it and tossing bits to Moe as he sprawled on the floor at my feet. I was about to head upstairs, planning to check on Mom before hitting the sack, when I suddenly realized I'd forgotten something. Opening the pantry cabinet, I looked around until I found the box of Bisquick that Mom liked to use for pancakes and then poured a generous amount on the butcher block. I used my hands to spread the powdered mix around, smoothing it out the best that I could, and then stepped back, deciding it was good enough.

"There you go, Bonnie," I said aloud. "Show me where to find you, okay?"

I put the box away and then went to the sink to wash my hands. Funny—it had been less than twenty-four hours since she'd drawn on the bathroom mirror, but everything that had happened that day made it seem a lot longer. I filled a glass with water from the tap and was drinking it down when Moe whined behind me. "What's wrong with *you?*" I asked, turning. Then I froze when I saw what was drawn on the butcher block:

THIRTY-NINE

IT'S LATE AFTERNOON OR EARLY EVENING—I CAN'T TELL which—and a storm rages around me. I'm down by the dock, hunched against the wind and the slashing rain beside Bill Crenshaw's car, where my mother lies slumped in the passenger seat. I hold a tire iron in one hand, while with the other I pound on the window, trying to get her attention. Crenshaw will be there soon, and I need her to move aside so that I can break the glass and get her out. But she won't wake up, and though I'm yelling as loudly as I can, she doesn't hear me above the howling gale.

"See, Ben? It's coming! And this one's even BIGGER!"

I look over to see Bonnie standing down at the end of the dock. She's pointing toward a massive wave approaching from the west. It's hundreds of feet high and miles across, engulfing fishing boats and sailing ships and even capsizing an aircraft carrier as it rolls in toward shore.

"Bonnie! Get over here now!" I holler, but my words don't carry to her any better than they did to Mom.

"Hurry!" shouts a man, and I turn to see Roger Black lying on the ground beside me. His left knee is a mangled ruin of blood and exposed bone, but his expression as he glares at me shows anger rather than pain.

I turn away, ignoring him, and try using the tire iron to pry open the door. If I can free Mom fast enough, then maybe there's still time to get her and Bonnie to high ground.

"Why haven't you saved them?" Roger screams. "You knew *this was coming! This is YOUR fault! YOU WERE SUPPOSED TO BE WATCHING HER!"*

Moe whimpered, and I slowly came awake, the details of the nightmare already fading away. I blinked toward the window, frowning when I saw the sky was a predawn gray. I'd only been asleep a couple of hours. Seeing me move, Moe jumped to the floor, still whining urgently, and ran to the door. "Okay…okay," I croaked, feeling grumpy and disoriented, but trying not to take it out on him. *He needs to go outside,* I thought, feeling like my head was full of cotton. *Though he never goes out this early, but okay, I should get up anyway 'cause Mom might need help with whatever she's cooking, but that's stupid—Mom hasn't cooked in weeks, but then what's that smell…?*

Moe barked, the sudden sound jarring me enough to throw my brain partway into gear.

Was that *smoke?*

I tossed my covers aside, shivering as I first yanked on my jeans from the day before and then stumbled into the hall, pulling a sweatshirt over my head as I went. I turned left, at first scared that Mom might have knocked over her lantern in the cupola, but then stopped when I noticed Moe was no longer beside me. I looked back just in time to see him charge downstairs, the meager light barely enough for me to make out tendrils of smoke rising up from below. I hurried awkwardly down after him, and as soon as I made it to the entry hall, I saw the smoke was drifting in through one of the open windows in the living room, the gauzy curtains flickering with a soft, orange-yellow glow.

Throwing open the front door, I sprinted left down the porch and vaulted over the rail at the end. I landed badly, my feet slipping out from under me on the damp weeds, but then I was up again, looking around to see what was on fire.

A loose pile of sticks and brush by the foundation was billowing smoke into the air, a yellow eye of flames glaring in its center. It hadn't been burning long, though, and the wall hadn't caught yet, so I ran around the far side of the house where a coiled hose was attached to an outside faucet. It took only seconds to twist the handle and drag the hose around, the fire hissing and throwing up steam as I hit it with the water. Moe was barking annoyingly in the distance, but I ignored him while I concentrated on dousing the blaze.

When I couldn't see any more flames, I relaxed a little, tossing the hose aside but leaving the water running in case I was wrong and still needed it. Reaching in, I grabbed one of the larger sticks and used it to knock the pile apart, looking for embers. The unburned end in my hand was still cool and slightly damp, and it occurred to me how lucky I was that the dew fell so heavily by the coast. I moved in closer, careful of where I stepped and blinking in the lingering smoke that left tiny bits of ash floating in the air. Everything was drenched all right, and I was grateful to see that the side of the house was only lightly scorched. Not too bad.

What I didn't see, though, was a source for the fire. No old wiring, no electrical outlet, nothing, and I frowned. It was about then that my still-groggy brain remembered that brush pile hadn't been there before, either, and I felt a rush of mixed astonishment and anger as

I realized two things at once: first, someone had deliberately tried to burn down our house…

And second, that Moe was still barking.

I straightened, listening to determine the direction, and then took off down the drive. Running in the cool air drove the last of the cobwebs from my head, and pretty soon I was firing on all cylinders again and growing more furious with each step. I increased my pace to a sprint, guided by Moe, and I finally caught sight of him not far from where the road forked to climb to the inn.

Moe stood on the downhill side of the drive, his head low and feet planted wide, snarling and barking at someone standing in the shadows at the base of a tree. I couldn't see who it was because he was facing the other way with the hood of his jacket up, but that didn't matter. What mattered was the gas can that he swung awkwardly with his left hand, throwing splashes that were aimed at Moe but kept falling short. Seeing that, on top of the fact that he'd started a fire that could have killed all three of us, sent a wave of cold rage through me like I'd never felt before.

"Get!" he shouted, his voice carrying a raw note of fear. I saw a glint of metal in his other hand, and I realized a second later that it was a cigarette lighter. "Go away or I'll *burn* you, dog!" He edged first one way and then the other, looking for an opening so he could make a break for it, but Moe wasn't backing down. He snarled, gliding to the right or left to match the movements of his prey, keeping him pinned where he was.

I took a few seconds to get my breathing under control and then moved to the side, using the same tree for cover as I crept up behind him. He was short, I discovered as I got closer—nowhere near my size, which wasn't what I'd expected at all—and I noticed that he was trembling. What's more, I could see why: Moe was growling like a wolverine and looked totally badass with his teeth bared. The thought sent a vindictive thrill through me, and I decided that a certain buddy of mine would be getting a couple of hot dogs with his kibbles that morning. My bare feet were silent on the carpet of fallen needles and leaves, and the boy didn't even realize I was there until I snatched the lighter from his hand and then tore away the gas can when he spun around.

I recognized him right away, and most of my anger deflated into surprise and shock.

"YOU GIVE THAT BACK!" the boy shouted, his face contorted with rage, but I had already retreated even as he moved to rush me. Then Moe charged in with a flurry of barks, chasing him back against the tree. He uttered a shriek of fear. "Call off your dog!" he cried.

"He's gotten bigger since the last time you saw him, hasn't he, Scott?" I asked.

"Call off your dog, or *I swear to God I'LL KILL YOU!*"

Wow. It looked like Rick Hastings's little brother was even more of a psycho than he was. Suddenly, it all made sense. After all, he'd threatened me the day I rescued Moe from him and his friends…

[You're gonna get it!]

…but I hadn't taken him seriously. Obviously, the kid carried one hell of a grudge, and I realized—a little reluctantly—that everything I'd assumed about Rick was probably wrong. Even worse, considering the standoff we'd had the night before, I probably owed Rick and Alan an apology.

"Call him off! I *mean* it!" A lot of the rage was gone from his voice, and he was beginning to sound more scared than angry.

I ignored him, settling down comfortably on the ground with my legs crossed. Moe advanced to within a couple of feet of the boy, still growling threateningly while I took a moment to examine the lighter. It was an old-fashioned Zippo—the rectangular kind with a hinged cover—and it was inscribed with the Marine Corps emblem. Interesting.

"Come on…*please* call him off!" Scott sounded on the verge of crying, which suited me just fine.

"Sure," I said, finally looking back up. "But first…we're going to talk."

When I arrived at Les's house an hour later, he was sitting on the front porch with his feet up on the rail, scanning the paper while working his way through a huge glass of juice. "Look who's all bright-eyed and bushy-tailed this morning," he called as I got out of the car. "What brings you here so early?"

"Come over and see."

Setting the paper aside, he ambled down the steps to meet me at the tailgate. His eyebrows arched when he saw Scott lying in back, struggling against the cargo straps that bound his arms and legs. He glared at us, making angry, grunting noises through a strip of duct tape over his mouth. "Something tells me there's a great story behind this," Les said, grinning.

I nodded. "There is. And it turns out you were right all along. It wasn't Rick who broke my window or anything else. Captain Sunshine here did it all."

"Yeah? How'd you figure it out?"

"He tried to set my house on fire this morning."

His grin faded. "Seriously?"

"Yeah. How batshit crazy is that?"

Is your mom okay?"

"Yeah, we're all fine, and there wasn't even much damage to speak of."

"And Scott *admitted* to everything? Just like that?"

"Well, not right off," I conceded, smiling. "Moe helped convince him."

Les chuckled. "Good dog. So, what now?"

"Well, I can't just turn him loose, can I? I figured I'd take him home and see what his dad has to say about all this. Can you tell me where he lives?"

"I can do better than that. Give me ten minutes, and I'll go with you. No *way* am I missing this!"

The Hastings family lived in a ranch-style home on the east side of town—only a block or so from Nicole's place, it turned out. It sat behind a lawn bordered by a low, split rail fence, with azalea bushes planted beneath the windows. I wasn't sure what kind of house I'd been expecting—someplace with poison oak and a torture chamber, probably—and it surprised me. A tire swing hung from the branch of a mulberry tree out front, and Rick's truck sat in the driveway beside an SUV with sheriff's department markings.

"You go knock," Les suggested. "I'll grab the pyro."

I nodded, heading up the walk. I was about to ring the bell when the front door swung open and Rick stood glaring at me. "What do *you* want?"

"Go get your dad," I told him.

His mouth twisted in a sneer. "What? You're too big a puss to fight, so..." His words trailed off as he looked past my shoulder, his expression changing to shock and disbelief.

I followed his gaze to see Les step onto the porch. He held Scott by the back of his belt, carrying him facedown like a suitcase. The boy was still tied up and squirming, and I had to bite my lip to keep from snickering.

"What the *hell*!" Rick spat. "You put my brother down!"

Les shrugged, letting go and allowing Scott to drop a foot or so to the porch.

Rick tried to move past me, his glare now focused on Les, but I stopped him with an open palm to the chest, knocking him back. Before he could react, I edged right to block his path, catching his gaze with my own and holding it. "Your dad." I ordered. "Get. Him. *Now.*"

Rick glared at me, then at Les, then back at me again before retreating into the house, leaving the door open.

Puss, huh? I thought.

"You're liking this, aren't you?" Les accused me in a low voice.

I grinned at him over my shoulder. "You bet your ass."

"What's going on here?"

I turned, swallowing as I looked up to see Sheriff Hastings filling the doorway. He was six-four, maybe six-five, and he stared down at me over the top of his reading glasses. He wore a robe that hung open to reveal a pair of flannel lounge pants and a chest covered in thick, black and silver hair.

"Hi, Sheriff," I said, plowing ahead before I had time to be intimidated. "My name is Ben Wolf. I need to talk to you about Scott."

The man looked over to where his son lay squirming on the porch. I braced myself, more than half expecting him to fly into a rage. But instead, he just sighed, seeming to deflate a little. I probed his feelings and was a little surprised to find only sadness mixed with a kind of tired resignation. "Won't you come in?" he asked quietly, stepping back to let us pass.

"Dad," Rick started to object, standing behind him, "you don't believe…"

"Richard," Sheriff Hastings interrupted, "go untie your brother and take him to his room. Stay there with him, please."

Rick didn't try to argue, and I began to think Sheriff Hastings might be a pretty good guy.

He offered us coffee and then sat across from us in the sunny kitchen while I told him everything—from the day Ab and I had rescued Moe to the broken window. He listened without speaking, his expression staying carefully neutral, and after a while I began to wonder if he was taking me seriously or even believed me at all. Then I got to the part about the fire, and I finally got a reaction out of him. His eyes widened, and he shifted uncomfortably in his chair.

Long seconds ticked by after I finished, and he frowned, seeming to mull it all over. "Those are serious charges, son," he said at last. "After all, you didn't actually *see* him set the fire, did you?" The flash of anger I felt must have shown in my face, and he held up a hand. "I'm not saying I don't believe you," he assured me. "And this is just the cop part of me talking now. How did you know it was Scott?"

"Well, for starters he admitted to everything," I said tightly, trying to keep my voice calm. "And since he was the only one splashing gasoline around this morning, I figure it's a pretty safe bet. Oh yeah, and there's this..." I dug the cigarette lighter out of my pocket and handed it over. "Have you seen this before?"

The sheriff sighed as soon as he glanced at it, and then he nodded. "Yes. It's mine." He stared at the lighter for a long moment, turning it over in his hands, and then finally looked back up at me. "Alright," he said at last, straightening in his chair. He looked like someone who wanted to get the bad news over with. "If you intend to file a crime report, that's your right, and I won't try to talk you out of it. Sergeant Shelton is on the desk this morning, and she can help you with the paperwork. Is that what you want?"

I could sense sadness behind his question, and all at once I was back to thinking he was a good guy. "No," I said. "That's why I came here—to see if it would be better to let you take care of it." It wasn't exactly the truth—I'd actually gone there hoping he wasn't as big a jerk as his sons were, figuring I could always throw the book at Scott later if I was wrong.

The sheriff nodded, seeming to relax a little, and he let out a breath. "I appreciate that, Ben. I really do. You see, Scott..." He paused, as if deciding what he wanted to say, and I could tell it was hard for him. "Scott has problems. Issues with rage. Since he was a baby, he's always had a hard time controlling himself, and while he's never tried anything like what happened this morning, this isn't the first time he's caused trouble, either." He leaned forward, his elbows on his knees, staring at the lighter he kept turning over and over in his hands. In that moment, he didn't look like a sheriff any more. He looked like just a dad, and I liked him for it. Finally, he looked back up at me. "But I promise you this: if you let me handle things, I'll get Scott some help. And he won't be bothering you again. You have my word on that."

I thought it over, my anger at Scott and dislike for Rick pulling me one way, and my growing respect for their dad dragging me the other. Finally, I decided to let it go, remembering that I had way more important things to do, and it was a relief to put the issue behind me. "That's good enough for me, Sheriff," I told him, getting to my feet.

He rose as well. "Thank you, Ben. I won't forget this."

He put out his hand, and I shook it.

FORTY

I DROPPED LES OFF BACK AT HIS HOUSE AND THEN IMMEdiately headed for home, hoping to crash for three or four hours before meeting Ab. Tsunami Joe closed at 2:00 on Sundays, and I figured the only plan left was for us to spend the late afternoon and evening reading through the rest of Aunt Claire's diary looking for something—*anything*—that would help trigger a connection to Bonnie.

I was still thinking about the diary when the house came into view and I saw Rick Hastings' Toyota sitting in the drive. "Oh, what *now?*" I muttered, feeling irritable. But I kept my expression carefully neutral as I saw him climb out from behind the wheel, watching as I pulled up beside him. Moe must have sensed what I was feeling and gave a low growl that I didn't bother to shush. If Rick had come looking for trouble, I'd probably need the backup.

I got out, and for a few seconds we just stared at one another over the roof of the car. "Scott's bike is hidden in the brush over there," he said at last, nodding toward a thicket on the south side of the clearing. "He left it behind when your dog chased him off, and my dad asked me to come get it. Is that cool?"

I shrugged, feeling my tension start to ease. "Sure."

Rick nodded and made his way into the taller weeds, walking directly to a point near the tree line in a way that made me suspect that he had already scoped it out. I wondered why he had stuck around to ask if it was okay when he could have been here and gone again without me even knowing. He bent, picking up Scott's bicycle, and I circled around to lean against the back of the car with my arms crossed, watching silently while he loaded it into the bed of his truck.

"There's a gas can that belongs to you, too," I offered, suddenly remembering. "You'll see it by the side of the drive just before the split."

"Okay." I figured he'd just leave after that, but I was surprised when he spoke again. "Thanks for what you did. Bringing Scott home, I mean."

I didn't know what to say to that, so I just nodded.

"My dad appreciates it, too. It's an election year, and if word got around that Scott tried to torch your house, it would make things hard for him." He paused, as if reluctant to go on, but then continued. "I know you don't owe me any favors, but it would be really cool of you didn't tell anybody."

Aha. So there *was* a reason he'd waited for me. I thought about it and then gave him a nod. "Okay."

His eyes narrowed in suspicion. "Just like that?"

"Why not? I mean, what would it do other than stir up a bunch of drama?" I shrugged. "I don't do drama. Anyway, it's over, right? I'm willing to let it go if you are."

He frowned. "What about Hawkins?"

"I'll ask him to keep it to himself."

"Yeah, but *will* he?"

“I don’t know,” I told him honestly. “But I’ll ask.”

Rick stared at me for a moment and then seemed to realize that was the best answer he was going to get. “Okay. Thanks.”

He was opening the door of his truck when a thought occurred to me, and I decided to offer an olive branch. “Hey,” I called, and he turned back around. “I’m sorry about accusing you and Alan last night. That was out of line. I just couldn’t think of anyone else around here who might’ve done that stuff. Scott never even crossed my mind.”

He considered that and then gave me a shrug of his own. “I get it. I probably would’ve thought the same thing.” He was about to slide in behind the wheel but then paused again. “Just so you know…this doesn’t make us friends or anything.”

My irritation flared again, but only briefly. “No,” I agreed. “It doesn’t.”

Rick started the truck and began to reverse past me but then stopped as I placed a hand on the driver’s side mirror. “It doesn’t mean we have to keep being enemies, though,” I offered.

He just stared at me for another second or two and then backed into a U-turn and drove away.

Oh, well, I thought. *No loss.*

Turning, I followed Moe over to the front porch, my legs feeling heavy on the stairs. I let myself into the house and was debating whether or not I was too tired to find something for breakfast before heading upstairs when…

Roger Black suddenly bursts in from the living room, headed straight for me! I yelp, instinctively dodging to one side, but of course he’s not after me at all. Instead, he throws open the front door, charging out into late night gloom. “WHAT THE HELL IS GOING ON?”

I follow him outside, my eyes slowly adjusting to the sudden darkness, and I look past Roger to where Philip Garrett is helping Claire toward the porch. His jacket is draped over her shoulders while she holds it closed in front of her. Behind them, Philip's coupe sits out front with the passenger door open, and I figure that Claire's dad must have seen the headlights as they swept across the front of the house.

Claire looks up. Her face is bathed in the glow coming from the open front door, half-dried tear tracks glinting silver on her cheeks, and I realize what night it is.

"What have you done *to her?" Roger hurries to them, pulling Claire away and gathering her protectively in his arms. "Claire, are you alright?" he asks urgently, and then he glares at Philip. "I swear, if he's hurt you..."*

Claire sobs, shaking her head vehemently with her face pressed against his shirt.

Roger looks uncertain, absently stroking her hair while his gaze goes from Claire to Philip and back again. At last he seems to make up his mind. "Go inside, honey," he says, easing her away. "Clean yourself up and wait for me. I'll be in shortly, and then we'll talk."

"Daddy, Philip didn't do anything wrong!" Claire exclaims. She looks alarmed, eyes wide and pleading above her damp cheeks. "He saved *me!"*

Roger nods reassuringly. "Hush now. It's all right. I'm just going to talk with this young man, and afterward we'll get this all straightened out. I promise."

A fleeting, dubious expression crosses her face, but it's gone so quickly that I'm not sure if her father notices it. "Yes, Daddy," she murmurs, and starts toward the house. She takes maybe three steps before suddenly doubling back, moving past him to stand in front of Philip. "Thank you," she says, offering his jacket back to him while keeping the front of her dress closed with her free hand. "You were wonderful and brave, and I'll never forget it as long as I live." Claire hesitates, as if searching for something else to say, but then she quickly stands on tiptoe to kiss his cheek before hurrying inside.

Philip grins, unconsciously raising his hand to his cheek as he watches her go. Then he notices Roger Black's expression, and he straightens, his grin disappearing and his hand dropping back to his side.

"What happened to my daughter?" The man's reassuring tone from a moment before has been replaced by a cold, barely contained fury, and I'm glad it's not directed toward me.

"She was attacked, sir," Philip begins. He goes on to describe how Crenshaw approached Claire at the theater and insisted on driving her home, followed by everything that happened behind the warehouse. He goes through the whole thing from start to finish, all the while looking Roger Black in the eyes, and I realize that he's calmer and more grown up about it than I would have been.

Claire's dad asks him to wait while he goes in to call the sheriff, and when the black and white cruiser arrives a little while later, Philip goes through the whole story again. Roger adds a description of Crenshaw, as well as where to find him at the Redwood Empire Hotel in town, and by the time the deputy finally leaves, nearly an hour has passed.

"This leaves us with just one thing to discuss," Roger says. "What exactly was Claire doing at the theater when she was supposed to be meeting her friend June at the library?"

Philip shifts his weight, looking uncomfortable for the first time. "She was there to meet me, Mr. Black. Claire and I..." He hesitates. "Well, we've become...close."

A long silence stretches out, giving me time to realize that my respect for Philip Garrett is really climbing the charts. It would have been easy for him to evade the question or even outright lie (which I would have found tempting, whether I care to admit it or not, and I feel a stab of shame at the realization.) But no, Philip just stands his ground.

"I see," Roger says at last. "And were you aware that Claire isn't allowed to go on dates?"

"Yes, sir. She told me, but…"

"And just how long have the two of you been sneaking around?"

Philip winces at the question and then swallows before answering. "A few weeks. But Mr. Black, we didn't mean any harm..."

*"No," Roger snaps, cutting him off, "what you meant was to deceive. To betray the trust I have in her—*had *in her. So, as much as I appreciate what you did for Claire tonight, let me make one thing perfectly clear: your sneaking around days are over. She's far too young for dates, and you are to leave her strictly alone."*

"That's not fair, Mr. Black!" Philip objects, straightening. "I stopped Crenshaw and kept her safe! That should count for something, shouldn't it?"

"Yes, it should," Roger snaps. "But Crenshaw wouldn't have been an issue in the first place if Claire hadn't lowered herself to skulking in shadows." He shakes his head. "No…it's over, young man. I can't keep you two from speaking at school, but you'll damned well stay away from her the rest of the time. I've had to call the sheriff once already. Don't make me do it again."

Philip stands there for a few seconds, looking like he wants to say something, but then his hands curl into fists and he stalks to his car without a backward glance.

The vision disappeared abruptly, leaving me squinting in the bright morning sunlight. *So that's how Claire and Philip got busted,* I thought. I shook my head, feeling sorry for them and more than a little outraged over how Claire's dad had handled things. Nothing I'd seen put me any closer to Bonnie, though, so I shook my head and went back to the house.

Moe was still waiting for me just inside, and I stopped to pet him after I shut the front door behind me. I yawned, my eyes feeling dry and grainy and my head so full of cotton that it was hard to think. Maybe it was lack of sleep, or maybe it was because my gift was so much stronger, but when the visions hit me again, one after another, I had a hard time keeping them sorted out.

"Daddy, look at me!" Bonnie shrieks delightedly, racing down the stairs and rushing past me into the living room. She wears a shapeless black dress and pointed hat, with her face painted bright green. Dazed, I turn to watch her, noting the flickering Jack-o-lanterns that grin out into the darkness from the windowsills.

"Bonnie, you forgot your broom!" says Claire's voice behind me, and I half-turn back to see her hurry down from the second floor. Her hair is in pigtails, and she's wearing a blue and white checked dress above low shoes completely covered in bright red sequins. Then it finally clicks: the Wicked Witch and Dorothy.

Claire disappears halfway across the floor, the scene around me changing again as the Halloween vision shifts to a different time. The shift is unsettling. It comes in an abrupt, almost sickening lurch, like when you slip unexpectedly on ice and your balance goes all wonky as you try to keep your feet under you.

The light coming through the windows is now the deep gold of late afternoon, and I can hear a baby crying somewhere further back in the house. I follow the sound to the kitchen, where a tiny girl wails red-faced from a high chair while a lady I don't recognize is frying chicken on the stove. "Roger!" she calls. "Can you help me with the baby? I don't want to burn dinner!" Outside the window, a balsa glider floats past, chased by a little boy wearing overalls that I assume must be my great-grandfather Lee.

A younger-looking Roger (his hair is darker and starts further down on his forehead) brushes past me from behind. "Of course, darling," he says, and I realize the woman at the stove is Stella Black. I should have known it right away, I suppose—both of her daughters have the same chin and cheekbones.

"Oh, Claire honey…what's wrong?" Roger Black coos, pulling her up out of the high chair. "Why is my best girl so upset, hmm?" But her wails are already falling off to soft whimpers and hiccups as she wraps her little arms around her father's neck.

Stella smiles as she watches the two over her shoulder. "She always quiets down for you so easily…"

[Lurch…]

The vision shifts again, Stella, Roger, and Claire swirling away as other people swirl in. The world outside dims to gray, and I see rain pelting down outside the kitchen window. People dressed in dark, formal clothing circulate quietly through the kitchen, serving themselves from platters and trays of food crowding the table and kitchen countertops.

I turn and wander through the crowd to the living room, almost immediately finding Roger Black in a chair by the fire. A half-full glass sits on the table beside him, next to an open bottle labeled "Old Overholt Straight Rye Whiskey" that's maybe two-thirds gone. He stares straight ahead at nothing, an expression of hopeless grief on his face while he cradles a newborn that must be Bonnie. Claire, who is about ten years old now, stands at his other side, weeping silently as she watches him with one hand on the arm of his chair. It's like they're isolated in the middle of a crowd. For the most part, people give them space, although from time to time, someone drifts closer to try to reach out to them:

"I'm so very sorry for your loss," says one man about Roger's age. "They say she didn't suffer, though. That's a comfort, isn't it?"

Black stares straight ahead. I don't think he hears him or even realizes the man is there, and after an awkward silence, the man goes to join a cluster of mourners nearby.

"Come, Claire, you must be hungry," urges a woman who approaches a few minutes later. "Let's get you something to eat, alright?" That earns her only a tiny shake of Claire's head, and after a moment she retreats, too.

More time passes, and then an older, heavyset woman—I guess a relative from her demeanor, but I have no way of knowing—walks purposefully over to address them. "Roger, dear, give the baby to me," she commands in a take-charge tone of voice. "You simply must *see to your guests. The Lonergans and Gardiners have already left, and Henry and Ruth Clarendon have asked for their coats! Lee is being a perfect little host, but honestly, Roger—that's your place."*

It takes a second or two for her words to sink in. Then Roger's gaze slowly travels up to meet hers, his expression changing to one of angry contempt, as if she'd spit on him. The woman pales, her outstretched arms falling to her side as she backs away…

[Lurch…]

Christmas now, a few years later. It's a vision I've seen before—the evening when Roger reads to Bonnie on his lap while Claire watches from the sofa:

"With a little old driver, so lively and quick, I knew in a moment it must be St. Nick!"

"Santa Claus!" Bonnie whispers, her eyes huge, and then she stifles a yawn.

"As dry leaves that before the wild hurricane fly," Roger continues, "when they meet with an obstacle, mount to the sky!"

[Lurch…]

It's midmorning, and the living room is full of little kids clustered into groups playing party games. Colored streamers arc across the ceiling, and a pink layer cake topped with a ballerina doll and three candles waits on a side table. Three or four moms mingle around, keeping order, and I can hear other adult voices in the distance. I don't see either Roger or Stella, though, so I can't tell if the party is Bonnie's or Claire's...

[Lurch...]

"But why, *Daddy?" Bonnie pleads. "I'll stay out of the way! I promise!"*

"Absolutely not! A construction site is no place for a little girl!"

[Lurch...]

"Daddy, we talked about this," Claire whispers to her father behind me, and I turn to witness another vision I recognize.

"I know, sweetheart, but things have changed. Mr. Crenshaw brings a wealth of experience from Napa Valley, and we'll need him if we're going to be ready to crush this fall. You can see that, can't you?"

"Yes, but Daddy you promised...*"*

"Claire, I need your help. I can't do this alone. And besides, we both know your talent for details is far better than mine. There will be other plays...I promise. Maybe next year. But right now I need you. Can you do this for me?"

"Yes, Daddy..."

[Lurch...]

Suddenly it's night again, and I stagger a couple of steps to one side. My head is starting to pound, and all the shifting visions are making me feel dizzy and sick to my stomach.

Headlights sweep across the windows from outside, and the sound of a car engine recedes in the distance as I hear steps in the entry hall. Unsteadily, I make my way there in time to see Roger close the door behind him and then lean his forehead against it with a long, shaky sigh. "God damn *it," he whispers, and then after a pause he straightens, seeming to pull himself together.*

I follow him upstairs.

Claire is sitting on her bed in a nightgown and bathrobe when her father taps on the door frame. The dress Crenshaw tore lies draped across her lap, and she looks up from where she's been sifting through a worn cigar box half full of assorted buttons.

"May I come in?"

She ignores the question, closing the box and setting it aside. When she looks up, I can read a mixture of betrayal and resignation on her face. "I overheard what you said to Philip," she says in a flat tone. "How could *you, Daddy?"*

Roger glances toward the open window, sighing. He crosses to Claire's desk and pulls out the chair, straddling it with his arms crossed over the back. "I knew we'd be having a talk like this one day," he confesses quietly. Then he offers her a sad, half-smile. "I just didn't expect it would come so soon..."

[Lurch...]

It's dark in Claire's room now, and after I get my orientation back, I get the feeling it's late. When my eyes adjust, I see Claire lying curled under the bedcovers with her face to the wall. Enough moonlight filters through the curtains for me to make out details, though, and when I see her desk chair still pulled out with the ruined dress draped across the back, I realize I've only jumped ahead a few hours.

I'm just beginning to wonder if there's anything important about this particular scene when I suddenly stumble off balance again. For a crazy second or two, I assume it's just more vertigo from all the shifting visions, but this time it's not me.

It's the whole house!

I've experienced a California tremor or two, but this is nothing like I imagined a real earthquake would be. I always figured it would be a jarring, up-and-down kind of sensation, like driving over a stretch of bad potholes in the road. But no, this was like standing in a rowboat in choppy waves. The house heaves and sways, like the earth below is trying to shake it off its back, and I careen against the wall as both the desk and the chair fall over with a thump. Outside the room I can hear furniture sliding around on the wood floors, assorted clatters I can't identify, and the almost musical sound of glass shattering. Claire sits up in confusion, her eyes appearing large and owlish as her bookshelf rocks drunkenly three or four times, spilling more of its contents with each undulation before it goes over, too.

"DADDY!" Bonnie's terrified scream comes from the next room. "DAAAADEEEEE!!"

Her screams jar Claire into action, and she manages to get up from the bed and stagger past me toward the door…

[Lurch…]

The house is still.

My heart is still beating fast, which doesn't help my headache and nausea at all. After a few deep breaths, I push away from the wall and make my way unsteadily toward a glow in the hallway and the sound of low voices from the next room.

When I look inside, Roger is on one knee in front of Bonnie—another vision I've seen before. "I need you to stay here," he tells her as the faint clang of the fire alarm bell drifts in the open window. "I know you want to help, but you're too little for this, and you're not even dressed."

"I'll get dressed," she insists. "I'll get dressed, and then run and catch up with you!"

"No," he tells her, his voice firm. "You'll do no such thing. You're going to do what I tell you, mind your sister, and stay away from town until I know it's safe. Do you understand?"

"Yes," she mutters sulkily, staring at her toes.

"Promise me, Bonnie."

A pause, then, "I promise."

Roger gives her a brief hug and then rises and hurries down the hall.

I watch as Claire tucks her back into bed, sitting beside her until Bonnie's eyes finally drift closed.

When she's sure her sister is asleep, Claire tiptoes out, leaving the door partway open and the hall light on. I follow her to her own room. She spends a few minutes putting things back in order and is fumbling with the belt of her robe when she looks up, hearing the soft tick of a pebble against her windowpane. She steps over to the window to look through the glass and then hurriedly lifts the sash and pokes her head outside. "What are you doing *here?" she whispers.*

A low voice drifts up from the darkness below, but I can't make out the words. "No, wait," Claire answers. "I'll be right down!"

I step aside as she hurries past me and then follow her down. As I pick my way past broken pictures on the stairs, it occurs to me that the vision had already faded before I got this far the first time around.

This is new territory, and it looks promising.

Claire rushes out the front door, scanning the darkness left and right. "Where are you?" she hisses.

I follow her out just in time to see Philip emerge from the shadows into the glow of the porch light. "Your father?" he asks, looking concerned.

"Gone to help with the fire." She hurries down the steps to meet him. "You shouldn't be here. He could be back any minute!"

"I know. But after the earthquake, I…" He pauses, looking sheepish. "I needed to know you were safe."

Claire flushes, biting her lower lip, and then shoots a quick, nervous glance down the drive. "Come on—Daddy will be furious if he sees us!" Taking his hand, she quickly leads him out of the light and around the corner to the north side of the house.

"Claire, I'm so sorry," he says when they're safely out of sight. "I hope you're not in too much trouble. I tried speaking with your father—tried telling him that you and I were just..."

"I know, Philip."

"But he wouldn't listen!" Philip goes on. "There was more that I wanted to say, but when he told me I couldn't see you any more, it was like I froze."

"What was it?" Claire asks.

He shakes his head. "Oh, I don't know...he was just so angry, and I must have been a little scared at the time. And I was feeling plenty guilty, too. After all, he was right when he said the whole mess last night wouldn't have happened if you hadn't been there to meet me. And, of course, I was raised to respect my elders, so..."

"No," Claire interrupts. "I didn't mean that." She drops her gaze, hesitates, and then asks quietly, "What was it you wanted to tell him?"

It's Philip's turn to drop his gaze, and long seconds tick by as a heavy silence stretches out between them. I'm pretty sure I know what's coming, and I roll my eyes, feeling weird about seeing such a private moment between them, as well as frustrated that it's taking so long. Come *on*, dude, *I almost say out loud.* Grow a pair, will you? What do you want, an engraved invitation?

"I wanted to tell him..." He clears his throat, bringing his gaze back up to meet hers. "That I've fallen for you, Claire. Honestly, you're all I think ab..."

He doesn't get to finish. Before the last word is halfway out of his mouth, Claire all but knocks him over, wrapping her arms around his neck and pressing her lips against his.

I can't help it. Even with a pounding head and my stomach about to turn inside out, I raise both fists into the air and turn a slow three-sixty. I'd bet real money that first kisses aren't supposed to happen that way in the 1940s, but who cares? It's about freaking time!

They go on that way for a while, which I guess I should've seen coming, and they even start to look less awkward about it with a little practice. After a couple of minutes, though, I start to feel weird about standing so close. I move off to keep an eye on them from more of a distance, and I use the time to rub my temples and concentrate on not throwing up.

As it turns out, I didn't need to bother. After a few minutes, they break off abruptly, stepping back from one another as an eerie wail that makes a chill run up my back sounds faintly in the distance.

"What's that?" Claire asks.

Philip frowns, turning to face toward town. "I think it's the air raid siren."

"We're having an air raid?"

"No. Something's wrong."

A sense of dread settles over me as I realize the tidal wave has just struck Windward Cove, and right then Claire's father is lying unconscious in the street with a mangled leg. Life for everyone has just gotten bad in a big way.

Inside, a phone starts to ring. The sudden sound startles Claire, and she glances quickly at the house before turning back to Philip. "I need to answer that," she says, shifting her weight anxiously. It could be Daddy. Or someone from the inn."

Philip nods. "I should go. Whatever's going on, maybe they need help."

But they just stare at one another, neither of them moving for two or three seconds. Then they come together in a rush, and I watch their goodbye kisses, feeling sad for them. Neither of them knows just how horrible things are about to get.

Then I remember Bonnie. Panicked, I glance up at her window. Of course it's empty, and I'm furious with myself for sticking with Claire instead of watching to see how Bonnie got past her. Not that it would have been hard—she probably scooted right out the front door while Claire and Philip were making out on the side of the house. Deep down, the sensible part of me realizes that I had no way of knowing everything would happen so fast, but just the same, I feel sick that I missed my chance to follow Bonnie and find out what happened to her. Crap!

Claire and Philip are untangling themselves as I turn and run unsteadily past them, swallowing back bile as I round the corner and sprint down the drive. I know it's hopeless—the wave has already come and gone, taking Bonnie with it—but I run for the road anyway. Even if I don't find her, there still might be some fresh evidence – fallen trees, wreckage, washed out earth—something that could help point me in the right direction!

The ringing of the telephone fades behind me as I make it to the tree line, and I'm dimly aware that it's getting brighter around me, but that's weird because it's still too early for sunrise…

Suddenly, it was midmorning again. The vision was gone, and my sprint faded to a jog before I finally come to a slow, reluctant halt.

"NO-NO-*NO*!" I hollered in frustration, but there was no one around to hear me. I closed my eyes, pressing my palms to my temples as I tried to force the vision to return. But then the dizziness hit me again with a vengeance, and I staggered sideways, falling to my knees. Moe came running up just as my stomach finally let go, and I vomited sour, viscous puke onto the dirt road. My head felt about ready to explode as the world started spinning out of control. Moe was sniffing the puddle I'd made, and I had just enough energy left to push him away and scrape dirt over the mess before I collapsed on my side.

I rolled onto my back, taking weak, shallow breaths and smelling trees and the dust of the road as I allowed my eyes to drift shut.

Moe nuzzled me, whining with concern. "S'okay, boy," I told him, although forming words right then was hard. The world was still spinning, but the ground was blessedly cool, and staying put for a while seemed like a great idea. *I'll lie here for a bit,* I decided. *Just until I feel a little better.*

Then darkness crept over me, and I didn't know anything for a long time.

FORTY-ONE

"GET OUT OF THE *WAY*!"

I opened my eyes, confused to see a ragged patchwork of blue sky through interlacing tree branches. It was late afternoon, I realized, the light a lazy gold from the western sun. Rolling my head to one side, I was confused even more when I found myself staring first at a tire tread, and then my vision pulled back to see the front of a maroon Jeep Liberty parked just downhill from where I was lying.

"*Move,* I said!"

I shook my head, levering myself up onto my elbows, and even then it took me a second or two to figure out what was going on.

Kelly Thatcher stood beside the open driver's door, her face twisted in annoyance as she glared down at Moe. He stood between her and me, pacing right and left with his head down, warning her off with soft growls that made her keep her distance.

"Moe," I called, my voice raspy. "It's okay, buddy." Realizing I was awake, he trotted over and started licking my face enthusiastically, and after a moment I sat up and pushed him away.

"He sure is protective."

I looked over to see Kelly standing with one hip against the Jeep's fender. "I guess he is," I replied.

She looked good in khaki shorts, with a sleeveless green top cut low in front and a tiny gold anklet that winked in the sunlight just above her left sandal. A line of concern creased the space between her eyebrows. "I wanted to help you, but your dog wouldn't let me near. Are you okay?"

I took a few seconds to think it over. My headache was still a dull, background thud, but the world wasn't spinning anymore. And although my stomach wasn't ready for Space Mountain, at least it didn't seem in danger of pulling the eject handle again any time soon. "Yeah," I told her, rolling to my feet. "I'm good." I must have gotten up too fast, as lightheadedness forced me to lean against the Jeep's hood for a few seconds. "Good enough, anyway," I amended when it passed.

Kelly looked concerned. "What happened, Ben? Do you need to see a doctor?"

I shook my head, giving myself time to think about what to tell her. Not the truth, obviously. Even if I was comfortable with that idea (and I wasn't), it would take way too long to explain and I just didn't have the energy. A random quote

[He thought up a lie, and he thought it up quick!] crossed my mind, and I wasted a second or two figuring out where it came from. *Oh yeah,* I recalled. The Grinch. *When Cindy Lou Who caught him stealing Christmas. Why do I remember this stuff?*

"Ben..?"

"Food poisoning," I told her, forcing my head back into the game and offering the first idea that occurred to me. "Something I ate yesterday or this morning, I guess. I tried walking it off, but then I threw up and I must've fainted. Maybe I'm dehydrated."

"Food poisoning." She didn't sound convinced. "Are you sure it's not a hangover?" I must have looked confused, so Kelly offered me a wry smile. "Nicole looked pretty hammered last night. I figured you were, too."

That one hadn't occurred to me, but I recovered quickly and did my best to look embarrassed. "I guess I did have a swallow or two. Maybe that was part of it."

That seemed to get rid of her suspicions. Her worry line disappeared, replaced by a smug expression. "Yeah, well I've been there, so I know." She stepped forward to take my arm. "Come on, big guy—I'll help you back home. I'd give you a ride, but it looks like you're carrying half the road with you."

I looked down at myself, discovering that my gray T-shirt was soaked to the point that it was black, with dirt clinging to the backs of my arms. I must have been sweating like a pig all afternoon. I couldn't see what the back of my shirt looked like, but it must've been something.

We didn't speak on the short walk to the house, and I took the opportunity to probe her emotions. As usual, she was feeling a lot of different things at once, but what really stood out was nervousness, and I wondered what it meant. Whatever it was, though, dealing with it was the last thing I felt like doing. All I wanted right then was to wash up and drink some water. After that, I needed some time alone to think about everything I'd seen in that morning's series of visions, and I wanted to do it while the images were still more or less fresh. Kelly's visit stood in the way of that.

I needed to get rid of her.

I stopped and turned after we mounted the porch steps. "Thanks for helping me out," I said, doing my best to sound polite but firm. "It was nice of you, but I can take it from here."

She moved around me, opening the front door and standing just inside. “I’ll help you get settled.”

“That’s okay,” I insisted. “I’m just going to wash and lie down for a while.”

Kelly’s gaze hardened. “I find you passed out by the side of the road, and you think I’m just going to drop you off on your *doorstep*?” She shook her head. “Not happening. I’m not leaving until I’m sure you’re alright. We can argue if you like, but I’m going to have my way on this. Now, are you coming in, or do you want to fight about it here?”

She stared at me for a long moment, her eyebrows raised expectantly, and at last I gave in. *Fine,* I thought, realizing that I was just wasting time. I stepped past her, leading the way back to the kitchen. *She wants to know I’m okay? Great—I’ll give her okay. How long could it take?*

I went to the sink, drew a big glass of cold water from the tap, and drank the whole thing without stopping. Right then I couldn’t remember *anything* tasting so good. I almost followed it up with another but then thought better of it. *Probably should wait and see how the first one sits,* I thought. As much as I wanted to get Kelly out of the house, I wasn’t ready to yak in front of her to make it happen.

She sat on the butcher block, her legs swinging idly and crossed at the ankles, and watched while I turned the tap back on to wash the dirt and bits of leaf from my hands and arms. The cold water felt so good that I took off my shirt and dropped it to the floor, first splashing my face, chest, and armpits, and then ducking my head under the flow, rubbing the back of my neck and using my fingers to comb the dirt out of my hair. When I finally shut off the tap, I felt a lot better and turned back toward her with a smile. “See? I’m gonna live.”

Kelly grinned in a way that made my face feel hot. “Thanks for the show.”

She tossed a dishtowel at me, and I used it to dry my face and hands. The rest I left to air dry—it was stuffy in the house, and the cool water felt great, especially the way the drops from my hair ran down my back. Setting the towel on the counter, I reached into the refrigerator and pulled out a can of Pepsi, holding it up where she could see it. "Want one?"

"Sure."

I handed it over, grabbed one for myself, and then went and dropped into a chair at the kitchen table, watching while she came over to join me. "So," I said, and then paused to take a swallow from my can. "Other than saving me from a horrible, lonely death, what brings you to this neck of the woods?" Right away the soda was helping to settle the last of my upset stomach, and sounding cheerful was less of a chore.

Kelly's smile dimmed. "I needed to talk to you. I really didn't like the way things ended last night."

I felt a twinge of irritation, and it threatened to snuff out what little good mood I'd managed to work up. "That's funny," I said in a flat tone. "I didn't like the way things *started* last night."

She nodded, looking uncomfortable, and that suited me just fine. Her gaze dropped to the tabletop, and she absently ran one finger down the outside of her can, making lines in the condensation. "I'm really sorry about going off on you like that. Seeing you and Nicole together just caught me off guard, that's all. It hurt." She brought her gaze back up to meet mine. "But if you're really into each other, I've got no right to be mad. Just tell me so, and I'll back off."

I rolled my eyes in exasperation. "Kelly, I told you last night—there's *nothing* going on between Nicole and me. We're just *friends*." Then I remembered that Nicole had kissed me before getting out of the car, but I was 99.9 percent sure that didn't count, so I shoved the thought aside. "I ran into her on the beach, we talked for a while, and then I gave her a ride home. That's *all* there was to it."

"Oh, come on, Ben," she snapped angrily. "I saw you two together! She was all *over* you!"

"She was drunk!" I shot back, not meaning to raise my voice but raising it anyway. Even though I kept my volume below a shout, Kelly recoiled as if I'd slapped her, looking down at her lap as tears welled in her eyes. It made me feel like a total dick, so I took a deep breath before continuing, this time in a softer tone. "Nicole was hanging onto me to keep from falling on her ass. She's not into me; I'm not into her. We're friends. End of story."

Kelly drew a deep, ragged breath, wiping her eyes before looking back up. "And Abigail?"

"*Gawd*...will you ever give that a rest?"

"Well, what am I supposed to think? You come into town, and all the girls just *flock* to you. Sometimes I wonder if you really like me at all! If you're always hanging around other girls, what does that say about us?"

"What 'us' are you talking about?" I asked, laughing a little in exasperation. It sounded cruel, even to me, so I decided not to let it happen again. "Last time I checked, you had a boyfriend. Has that changed?"

"That's not fair, Ben. I *told* you. It's...complicated."

"No," I insisted. That's the thing, Kelly—it's not complicated at *all.* You've got a boyfriend, and it's not me. It's as simple as that."

Funny...I suddenly realized that saying this stuff out loud was helping me straighten out my own confusion over the issue, and it felt good to finally figure out where I stood.

Kelly was staring at her lap again, so I paused long enough to reach out and lift her chin. "Look...it's true. I really do like you, and if you ever ditch the quarterback, then maybe we've got something to talk about. In the meantime, I'm not going to be somebody's sneaky thing on the side." She opened her mouth to object to that, but I kept going before she had the chance. "Not that I'm saying that's what you *meant*, but at the end of the day, it amounts to the same thing. It's not fair to me, and it's sure as hell not fair to Alan. Now sure, I don't like the guy—that's no secret—but that's not an excuse to do the wrong thing."

For a long moment, Kelly just stared at me, but at last she reached out to squeeze my hand, saying softly, "Alright, Ben…I understand." She stood, taking a last drink of her soda, and then set the mostly full can on the table. "I should go."

"I'll walk you to your car," I offered, rising.

"You don't have to."

"I *want* to."

A pause, then. "Okay."

We made our way out front, walking side by side down the drive. Moe ignored us, veering off to chase a butterfly flitting just above the dry grass. Apparently, he'd decided that Kelly was okay and that I wasn't in any life-threatening danger.

The silence was awkward, and Kelly's feelings were more jumbled than ever when I reached out to test the water, so I tried to lighten the mood. "You look really good, by the way. You could wear that every day and it wouldn't bother me a bit."

She looked over long enough to give me a weak smile. "Thank you." Then she went back to staring at the ground in front of her.

Some moods must lighten easier than others.

I slowed my steps as we got close to her Jeep, stopping five or six feet from the front bumper and allowing her to go the rest of the way without me. Kelly opened the driver's side and was about to get in, but then she paused and looked silently back at me with her elbow resting on the top of the door frame and her chin on her arm. After a few seconds, she seemed to make up her mind about something, and all at once she was running back toward me. Before I really understood what was happening, she was pressed against me, reaching up to drag my mouth down to hers. I froze at first and was about to pull back, but then her tongue found mine, and every bit of my resolve, my good-guy intentions and all the rest just packed up and went to Florida.

That's me: Mr. Restraint.

We stayed there for a while. The sky was darkening toward twilight when we finally took a break, and she looked up at me with half-lidded eyes. "I've wanted to do this since I first saw you."

"Yeah, me too," I admitted.

"What is it about you? Why am I falling this hard?"

[I've fallen for you, Claire…]

The sudden memory of Philip and Claire's exchange was sobering, and my anxiety flared as I remembered I had work to do.

"You're in my head all the time, Ben. It's like I can't concentrate on anything else."

[…Honestly, you're all I think ab…]

"What are we going to *do*?"

I sighed, gently pulling her arms down from around my neck. "You're going home," I told her, "and I'm going to feed my dog."

She offered a sultry grin. "I can come back later if you want."

"Tell you what," I countered. "Come back when you're single."

It took a second or two for it to sink in, and then Kelly's expression turned to shock. "You mean after all *this*…after we just… *You're blowing me off*?"

I sighed, wondering if she'd paid any attention earlier or if she just didn't care. "Nothing's changed, Kelly. You've got this huge kryptonite effect on me, but I'm not going to do this anymore. Get back to me when you've decided who you want to be with."

Angry tears stood in her eyes. Turning, she all but ran to the Jeep and got behind the wheel, slamming the door behind her. She reversed into a turn and then glared at me through the window as she shifted gears and sped away, leaving me in a cloud of dust.

Moe chose that moment to come over, and we watched her drive away together. "Well…" I said at last. "That could've gone better."

We turned and headed back for the house. I was torn, pretty certain that I'd made the right call but sick at the thought that I might've just killed any chance I had with Kelly, now or ever. Mostly I kept seeing the glare she'd given me, not just because it had stung, but also because there was something familiar about it, although right then I couldn't remember what. I was almost to the porch steps when it finally came to me.

It was a lot like the look Kelly's mom had given me at her birthday party.

FORTY-TWO

NIGHT HAD FALLEN BY THE TIME I GAVE MOE HIS DINner and left food in the cupola for Mom, and after that I was pretty much out of things to do. I made myself a sandwich, realizing that I hadn't eaten all day, but after just a couple of bites I didn't want any more, so I gave it to Moe.

I was restless. I'd lost over half the day lying unconscious, and it felt weird for it to be dark already when my inner clock was sure it was only 3:00 or 4:00 in the afternoon. The house felt huge and empty and lonely, and I wandered aimlessly around downstairs, moving through the darkened rooms by feel. Even though I'd gotten exactly what I wanted—time alone to think—I found myself wishing that Ab or Les were there.

At last I went outside and sat on the hood of the car. A steady, insistent breeze hissed through the grass, cooling the night air but making me feel even more edgy, not less. The visions I'd experienced that morning kept replaying over and over in my mind, but the more I examined them, the more useless they seemed. They were all just shadows of the past, none of which put me any closer to finding Bonnie—except for the last one, of course. I probably could've seen exactly what I needed in that one, but I'd gotten distracted and blew my chance. It was depressing.

I closed my eyes, mentally reaching out to see if I could latch onto the vision again, but aside from some murmurs that were too faint to hear and a few random images that were too dark or blurry to make out, there was nothing I could grab onto. All I succeeded in doing was reawakening a dull headache. I figured my gift had pushed itself too far that morning and still needed more time to recharge.

I half-turned to gaze up at the cupola, hoping that maybe Mom was awake, but the room was dark—just a black shape against a backdrop of stars. Crap.

At last I gave up and headed inside, hoping that a good night's sleep would make things look better in the morning. But even that turned out to be a bust. Between my restlessness and having been out of it most of the day, I couldn't get comfortable, let alone drift off to sleep. Worse, the air was that exact temperature where it was too hot to sleep under the top sheet but too cool without it. And I wasn't the only one who felt that way. Moe would be at the foot of the bed for fifteen or twenty minutes, then jump down to curl up on the floor, and then a little while later jump right back up beside me.

The night felt like it would never end. From time to time I would pick up my watch, convinced that hours must have passed while I'd tossed and turned, only to be surprised to find out that only thirty or forty minutes had gone by. I watched the moon as it slowly emerged at the top of my window, descended with maddening slowness down the panes, and then finally disappeared out of sight below the sill.

At last, sometime around midnight, I drifted into a light, on-and-off doze, haunted by distorted nightmares—mostly echoes from my visions—that kept me twitching awake, confused and scared. Sometime after that, though, I finally fell asleep.

Later.

I came reluctantly to near-consciousness, hearing the click of toenails on the floor, followed by the familiar sensation of Moe jumping up and curling himself up at the foot of the bed. I rolled onto my back, and had almost fallen asleep again when the sheet was drawn aside and a body slid in next to me.

I came awake with a jerk. "Hey…!"

A low, playful chuckle caressed my cheek with warm breath. "Shh… It's okay—I didn't mean to scare you." An arm snaked across my chest, followed by a bare thigh crossing over mine as someone snuggled her head on my shoulder. "Mmm," she murmured. "You feel good."

"Kelly?"

"Mm-hmm," she murmured. "I couldn't wait any longer."

I blinked as the world came into focus. "How did you get in here?"

"Your front door was unlocked. The dog was there when I came in, but as soon as he knew it was me, he didn't even bark." Her hand ran lightly across my ribs and then down the side of my boxers and along my thigh. "You need to wake up now," she breathed. "I've got something for you."

Oh, I was awake alright. Awake enough to realize that Kelly wasn't wearing anything. "No," I said, suddenly irritated and trying to draw away, but I was against the wall already and there was nowhere to go. "*Jesus*, Kelly…did you hear a single thing I said this afternoon?"

"Oh, I heard you," she murmured, giving my earlobe a tiny nip as her hand started up the inside of my thigh. She traced a line along my jaw with the tip of her tongue, sending a shiver down my whole body. "I heard you, and I ended it. That's what you wanted, right?"

"Wait…what?" I asked. It was getting hard to control my breathing, and *way* too hard to think with her body pressed against me. I fumbled for her hand, trying to trap it, but she eluded me.

Thump-THUMP...

"I'm *done* waiting," she breathed, her voice low and husky. "Alan and I are over—I called and told him. Now *stop* telling me no, Ben. I'm tired of…"

She gasped then. We both did.

"Oh, my…I think I found a yes right *here.*"

Thump-THUMP...

(…pause…)

Thump-THUMP...

Kelly froze, looking over her shoulder toward the door. "What was that?"

Thump-THUMP...

"Oh God. Did we wake your parents?"

Thump-THUMP... Gloom and frigid air began to drift in from the hall—both more intense than I'd ever felt this far from the attic. Moe must have picked up on it, too and jumped off the bed, growling as he faced the door.

"Get up, Kelly," I said, trying to keep my voice calm as I squirmed out from beneath her. "Get up *now.*" I was pretty sure I could deal with whatever the spirit threw my way, but considering how strong it had grown, I didn't want to take the chance with Kelly. I needed to get her out of there.

She sat up, pulling the sheet up to cover herself. "Ben...? Why is it so *cold*?" I put a hand on her upper arm, feeling it break out in gooseflesh as she began to shiver.

Thump-THUMP... Close to my door now.

There was no time for anything but the truth. "Kelly, get dressed! It's this house—you shouldn't have come here. Not at night."

She threw the sheet aside as we both stumbled out of bed, pulling on clothes in the darkness. "What are you talking about?" she pressed, pulling her top down over her head. "I mean, people say this place is haunted…

Thump-THUMP...

…but that's just bullshit, right? Campfire stories to…" Then she sucked in a startled breath, her hand clutching suddenly at my arm as she looked past me. Even in the dim starlight, I could read terror in her expression, and I followed her gaze to my bedroom door.

A shadowy figure stood in the hallway—a deeper black in the surrounding darkness. For several heartbeats, it just stood there, staring into the room. At last, though, it turned slowly away, shambling in the direction of the attic stairs.

Thump-THUMP...

(…pause…)

Thump-THUMP...

Kelly screamed.

We stood outside a short time later, and I held Kelly close as she trembled uncontrollably against me. It had taken everything I had to get us all out of my room, her refusing to go near the door and Moe barking his head off, but once she was in the hallway she turned and ran, bounding down the stairs like a deer. I stopped her as she was about to climb into the Jeep, wrapping her tightly in my arms until she finally stopped struggling and her panic began to wear off. I wasn't about to let her kill herself by tearing down the narrow, switchback drive in full freakout mode, and she eventually hugged me back as her breathing returned to normal.

"You good?" I asked at last.

I felt her nod against my chest. "I'm sorry," she said. "I didn't mean to fall apart on you like that. Tonight was supposed to be special, and when that awful cold filled the room..."

"Yeah," I said gently. "I know."

"Let's get out of here!"

Stepping back, I opened her car door, held it while she got in, and then closed it after her. Hurriedly, Kelly got the engine started and only then noticed that I hadn't moved. She rolled down the window. "Ben, what are you doing? Get *in*! Your dog can go in the back seat! Please, we need to leave!"

I shook my head. "Can't."

"Are you *crazy*? Why not?"

I looked up at the cupola. "Because my mother's in there. And I'm not going to leave her alone with that thing."

Kelly began to cry in either terror or frustration—probably both. "I don't want to leave you. But Ben...*I can't stay here*!"

"I know," I told her, trying my best to sound reassuring. "And it's fine—really. I've been dealing with this since I moved in, and it hasn't hurt me yet. But it *is* hurting my mom, and I have to try and stop it."

"At least wait until morning!"

I shook my head.

"Ben, I don't understand..."

"Go on," I insisted. "I'll call you tomorrow or the next day and explain everything. I promise. This isn't something you can help with. So just go home, okay?"

Kelly seemed about to say something but then just nodded instead, and I watched as she turned the Jeep around and drove away. The sound of her engine faded in the distance, leaving only the whisper of the wind in the grass and the far-off pounding of waves against the cliffs.

I took a last look up at the dark cupola before heading for the door. *Okay, Roger,* I thought grimly. *Let's dance.*

It began to feel colder before I'd even reached the second floor, and by the time we reached the attic stairs, it was like being frozen in a block of ice. The gloom and depression were there, too—so thick in the air that at first I thought I might choke—but I pushed back against it with my mind, creating a protective bubble around me so that I could think without being dragged down by feelings that weren't my own.

I looked around when I reached the cupola, and after a moment, I could make out the faint silhouette of Mom's lantern where it sat on the low shelf. Feeling around beside it, I found a box of matches and soon got it going, the flickering, yellow light forcing the darkness to retreat to the far corners of the room.

The painting is what I saw first, but only because it was right beside the lantern. Mom had finally finished it and then had arranged it on top of the shelf where she could see it from her rocking chair. But I didn't waste any time admiring it; instead, I lifted the lantern higher as I used my gift to search for the spot where the darkness and gloom were the most concentrated. When I discovered where it was, though, my heart seized suddenly in my chest.

Mom?

No, I realized a second later—it wasn't Mom. The darkness just occupied the same *space* that she did. She slept in the rocking chair, appearing draped in shadow, but as I drew closer, I realized that it wasn't a shadow at all. It was the dark figure. It sat in the chair with her, duplicating her pose to cocoon her entirely within it.

"Get away from her!"

But the figure didn't move or even show any sign that it had heard me. I reached out with my gift, probing at it. I felt resistance, so I pushed harder, almost managing to see through the fog…

…and then an invisible force shoved me back!

I staggered off-balance, losing my footing but managing to catch myself with one elbow on the shelf behind me. Moe yipped as he dodged out of my way and then turned and growled at the figure, moving to position himself between us with his tail between his legs.

"No, boy," I said, calling him off, and after giving me a quick glance, he reluctantly backed away. I took a few seconds to get my breath, rubbing my ribs where they'd slammed against the shelf and realizing how lucky I was to have held onto the lantern. If I'd dropped it, the whole place might have burned down. I moved three or four paces to the right, setting the lantern safely out of the way in case I got knocked around again.

I stepped closer, until my knees were barely inches from the darkness covering Mom's legs. The dark figure seemed to glance warily right and left, as if it looking for something it could somehow sense but not see.

Cold anger welled up in me. Closing my eyes, I took a deep breath and then hit it mentally with everything I had!

Something happened then that had never happened before. It was as if I'd tapped into not just feelings but thoughts as well, and I wasn't at all prepared for everything that suddenly flooded into my mind. It only lasted a few seconds, but it was overwhelming—blasting through my head like a bullet from a rifle.

And then I was reeling backward again, tripping over my own feet and falling heavily to the floor. A sharp pain hit me—like an icepick being driven through my head—and I screamed, writhing for maybe fifteen or twenty seconds until the feeling passed.

I am never, NEVER doing that again! I thought.

As painful as it had been, though, I realized that it had been worth it. I'd stayed connected long enough to finally understand what I was dealing with. In those brief few seconds, I discovered that the dark figure really didn't have any sort of active consciousness. Oh, it was Roger Black, all right—what was left of him, anyway. But mostly he was somewhere else, a place frozen in the past, where he kept reliving the same pain and grief over and over again. He wasn't aware of Mom or me—not in any real sense—and I didn't think he even knew that he was dead. He was just…stuck. His grief and overwhelming need to find Bonnie had anchored him to the house a long time ago. But then Mom and I had arrived, and that changed things.

Lisette had been right. Mom *did* have abilities, and Roger had been drawn to that energy and had fed off it. He was *still* feeding off it, in fact, but not in a conscious or bad-intentioned way. It was more like how tree roots will crack the side of a swimming pool reaching out for water. But even as Roger grew stronger—strong enough to be seen now and for his gloom to reach well beyond the cupola—my mom was growing weaker. And she didn't have much energy left.

I had to stop him.

The ice pick sensation in my head had all but disappeared, so I crawled to the rocking chair, reaching into the darkness and wrapping my arms around Mom's waist with my head in her lap. The gloom was almost smothering, but I pushed it back with my mind, gritting my teeth as I fought to extend my protective bubble outward to surround Mom.

"Get…the hell…out of my mom's…CHAIR!" I yelled.

Initially, Roger seemed to give ground, which gave me a brief spark of hope, but then he doubled down. All I could feel was the weight of his despair, and I knew at once that he was a lot stronger than I was. He'd tapped into my mother's energy like a battery, pulling more of hers to combat mine, and I realized right then that if I didn't get him away quickly, it could kill her! Straining, I gave it everything I had in a rush, hoping the sudden surge would throw him off, but it was no use. It was like trying to wrench a telephone pole out of the ground. Worse, whatever instinct that was left in Roger now knew that I was there, and I could actually *feel* my own energy dim as he latched onto me...and began to feed.

I tried to pull away I but couldn't. "*Mom...*" I managed to say. All at once it was like I was deep in the ocean—crushing depth—and I had barely enough air to form words. "*Mom...help me...*" I could hear Moe barking in alarm as my vision began to go dark around the edges, and I felt a repeated tugging and heard my shirt tear as he tried to pull me away.

Suddenly, another presence was there! At first I thought Mom had heard me and was adding her energy to mine, but I was wrong. It was the other spirit in the house. *Claire!*

Reassurance surrounded me, warming me, and together we pushed back against the darkness. Nothing happened at first, and for a few seconds I thought that Roger had grown too strong for even the both of us, but then we slowly began pushing him out and away from my mom.

Like that night weeks before when the two spirits had clashed, the energy in the room seemed to concentrate, building pressure until I was sure the glass walls would explode outward. Then, with a ripping sound that I felt rather than heard, Roger suddenly let go! He'd lost his hold, and his dark form hurtled angrily around the room like a tornado before finally swirling down the cupola stairs, retreating into the darkness below.

It took a long time for my breathing to slow down, and for a while all I could do was sit slumped on the floor next to the rocking chair, waiting for my heart rate to go back to normal. I might have even dozed off for a minute or two—I don't remember. But then Moe was licking my face, whining as if to make sure I was okay, and at last I climbed back to my feet.

I looked at Mom, curled up in her usual position in the chair, and I was amazed that she had slept through it all. Even though she'd lost enough weight that her cheeks were sunken, and hadn't had a shower in who knows how long, she looked peaceful in the lantern light. I wondered if I should try to wake her but then decided to leave her alone at least until breakfast. Now that Roger was gone—for the time being, anyway—I figured the best thing would be to leave her to rest and let her body recharge itself. I blew out the lantern and was halfway down to the attic when…

The door at the base of the stairs opens. I scramble backward as Claire begins to climb the risers toward me, her face and shoulders illuminated by a stubby candle set on a tray of food she carries in front of her. She pauses when she's halfway up, looking past me with an expression of alarm, and then hurries the rest of the way.

"Daddy, it's freezing *up here!" she scolds. "What did I tell you about leaving that window open?"*

I step out of the way as she reaches the top, and there she pauses, looking past me with a sharp intake of breath. Just then a breeze blows out the candle, plunging the cupola into near darkness, and I turn to see what made her gasp.

The cupola windows are open. All of them.

Outside, a weak, gray glow to the west is all that's left of a winter sunset. Dark clouds hang low in the sky, threatening rain, and I catch a brief flicker of lightning far out over the ocean. There's just enough light left to silhouette Claire as she sets the tray angrily on the shelf and then goes around the room shutting the windows one by one.

"Honestly, Dad…what are you thinking? The radio says a storm is coming, and here you are, trying to let it in!" She finishes by securing the northernmost window, turns, but then has to double back when the latch slips and the window bangs open again. "I swear *I'm going to nail these things shut," she mutters irritably as she fastens it again.*

Returning to the dinner tray, she digs a box of matches out of her apron pocket and relights the candle. "Now, no complaining," she says, picking up the tray and turning. "I've been practicing, and this *meatloaf may be my best one ye…" She stops in midsentence and stands frozen in place for a second or two. Then the tray slips from her fingers, crashing to the floor. The candle lands on its side, still burning, and rolls to the base of the rocking chair.*

"…Dad?"

Roger Black sits unmoving in the chair, his face turned north in the direction of the vineyard. His mouth hangs slightly open, his eyes half-closed. He isn't breathing.

"Daddy?" Claire cries, rushing over and falling to her knees in front of him. "Dad, wake up!" *She begins to sob, first shaking his arm and then holding his hand to her cheek as she starts to rock. "OH, DADDY, NOOO! NOT YOU, TOO! DON'T…DON'T LEAVE ME, DADDY… PLEASE!…I DON'T WANT TO BE ALONE…I CAN'T DO THIS BY MYSELF…OH, DADDY, I'M SO SCARED…!"*

Claire collapses forward, pressing her face to his chest as wracking sobs shake her whole body. She's still talking to him, but her words are muffled against his shirt and I can't make them out.

All I can do is watch, feeling helpless and miserable. I want to reach out to her, to tell her it's going to be okay. But I can't.

It takes a while, but eventually Claire sits back, sniffing and wiping her red eyes. The candle is almost out, leaving a hardened puddle of wax on the floor. She's reaching over to set it upright when the latch slips and the north window swings open again, sending in a breeze that makes the tiny flame waver and dim. Claire rises, shivering and rubbing her arms while she goes to close it. She is just reaching for the window when a giggle drifts up from the darkness below, making her scoot back with a frightened squeal.

I watch as she stands, eyes wide, with her hands cupped over her nose and mouth. After a moment, she seems to compose herself, exhaling a sigh as she wipes her palms on the front of her apron. "That didn't happen," she whispers, as if trying to convince herself. "Why, the very idea…it's insane. It's just the shock, that's all. Pull yourself together, Claire."

Just the same, after a brief hesitation, she steps gingerly toward the window and pauses before closing it to turn her ear toward the night.

She waits, hearing nothing but the wind and a low rumble of thunder from the approaching storm. With a slight shake of her head, Claire steps back and begins to swing the window shut but then freezes when a little girl's voice wafts in on the breeze, humming a run of notes from "Blue Skies."

Claire sobs once, stepping closer to the open window. Fresh tears stream down her cheeks, and she looks like she's struggling to form words.

"Bonnie…?" she manages at last. "Is that you*?"*

The vision faded, and I stood silently in the darkness for a while.

Eventually, I stepped to the window—the same one where Claire had heard Bonnie's voice all those years ago—and stared into the darkness beyond the glass.

The vineyard, I thought. *Somehow, everything keeps coming back to the vineyard.*

Dawn was only an hour or so away.

When it came, I was going to find out why.

FORTY-THREE

MORNING WAS JUST A PINK BLUSH BEHIND THE HILLS TO the east when Moe and I left the house. I shivered in the chilly air, the dew on the grass quickly soaking through the cuffs of my jeans as I followed the beam of my flashlight the hundred yards or so to the barn.

The wide front doors were just as stubborn as I remembered, the rusted wheels grinding resentfully on the metal track above, and I had to set my light on the ground so I could yank them with both hands. When I had them far enough apart, I used my foot to push against the left door while straining with everything I had on the right. Just when I was about to give it up, the door in my hands suddenly broke free of the rust holding it, and I stumbled to the ground as it rolled aside with a long, high-pitched squeal.

Satisfied, I got to my feet, wiping my hands on my jeans. I bent to pick up my flashlight but then scrambled backward as a loud screech broke the stillness and something large hurtled out the open doors just above me! I landed hard on my butt as my feet slipped out from under me, and I whipped my head around just in time to see the owl bank gracefully left, disappearing into the gloom. Moe took off after it, barking, but gave up after twenty yards or so and trotted back.

I exhaled a long, shaky breath. "Wow…*that'll* get your attention, huh?"

We entered the barn, my flashlight piercing the darkness and reflecting dully as it passed over the ancient tractor's headlights. Old garden tools hung on the left hand wall, dusty and laced together with cobwebs, and I headed that way to see what I could find. I was looking for something I could use to chop my way through the grapevines, and I slowly swept my light from left to right, seeing shovels, rakes, pitchforks, and even a posthole digger. *A machete would be perfect,* I thought, imagining myself hacking through the tangle of vines like Indiana Jones, but there wasn't one. I grinned in surprise when I found a scythe with a blade that was nearly three feet long, but after setting my light on the ground and taking it down for a few practice swings, I put it back. It was heavy, and felt awkward, and seemed more likely to get tangled up in the vines than anything else.

At last I settled for a double-bladed axe, a rusted sickle that looked kind of puny but might get through the smaller stuff, and a kind of digging tool that had a pick on one side of the head and a wide, heavy blade like a hoe on the other. Not ideal, but they were all I could find. Probably my best find was a pair of old leather work gloves, stiff with age, but which I figured would loosen up after I had them on for a while.

It was light enough to see by the time we left, and I stuck the flashlight in my back pocket while I carried the tools back toward the house. The vineyard was still a tangle of black shadows, and I realized that I'd have to wait until the sun crested the hills so that I wouldn't be flailing around in the dark. *That's okay,* I thought. *It won't be much longer.*

I went inside, fed Moe, and then made oatmeal. When it was ready, I carried a bowl to the cupola, frowning when I picked up a faint gloom and the beginnings of a chill in the air. *Damn it!* I figured that Roger Black's spirit would eventually come creeping back, but I'd hoped it wouldn't be this soon.

I closed my eyes, concentrating my mental energy and suddenly releasing it outward in all directions, hoping to drive him away again. It seemed to help—a little, anyway—though I could still feel him out there somewhere, waiting.

"Benny?"

I spun, almost dropping the bowl.

Mom smiled weakly at me from the chair, and I hurried to her side. "Hey," I said, kneeling beside her and reaching out to take her hand. "Good morning, sunshine. How are you doing?"

"I'm...okay," she said. I suspected we both knew it was a lie. "Did you see my painting?"

"I sure did. It's amazing, Mom—the best work you've ever done."

"Thank you. I think so, too. It's like..." She frowned, gazing into the empty space between us. "It's like I had the image stuck in my head, and putting it on canvas was the most important thing in the world. It was all I could think about." Her gaze refocused on me, and she smiled again. "But it's done now, and at last I can rest."

Her words carried a note of finality that made me uncomfortable. "Listen, Mom. You're not well. We need to get you to a doctor. You've barely eaten in weeks, and all you've done is paint and sleep. Something's wrong, and we need to find out what it is."

Of course, I knew exactly what was wrong, but if I could get her out of the house for a few hours—or better still, if she was admitted to the hospital for a day or two—maybe she could shake herself free of Roger. At the very least, getting her away to recover some strength would give me more time to find Bonnie.

"I'm fine, hon. Don't worry."

"But *Mom...*"

Her expression hardened. "I'm not going *anywhere,* Ben. Now will you stop badgering me?"

"Okay, okay," I conceded. "But will you at least eat something? I made you oatmeal, with a little brown sugar, just the way you like it."

The hard lines in her face smoothed out. "That sounds nice. Thank you." She took the bowl, and I watched as she slowly began to eat. "Don't you have anything better to do than stare?" she asked after taking three or four spoonsful.

Actually, I did. Sunlight had fallen on the vineyard, and it was time to get to work. "Sure, Mom. I'll see you later, okay?" I started for the stairwell.

"Benny?" she called after me.

I turned back toward her.

"Open the windows before you go, will you?"

A chill washed over me as I flashed back to the vision of Claire finding her father. *Probably just a coincidence,* I thought. After all, it was summer, and it wasn't like she was going to freeze to death. I went around the room, opening the windows to let in the morning air. "Anything else?" I asked, turning.

But she was asleep again, the half-eaten bowl of oatmeal resting on her lap.

A short time later, I stood just inside the vineyard, as near as I could tell to the spot where Les and I had left off searching a couple of days before. I took a moment to concentrate, mentally casting out to see if I could sense anything of Bonnie, but if she was there, she was out of range. A little disappointing, but it didn't really change anything, I decided. I held the axe in one hand, the sickle in the other.

Ready or not, kid, here I come.

Standing on tiptoe, I craned my neck until I saw a redwood tree with a lightning-blasted top on the hill to the north—a good point of reference I could use to stay on course. Then I plunged ahead, worming and ducking my way into the growth. When the vines got too thick, I tried using the sickle to clear my way. It actually worked better than I'd thought it would, the curved blade slicing neatly trough anything smaller in diameter than my thumb. At last, though, my way was blocked by thicker stuff—older vines almost as big around as my forearm that looped and twisted around one another, barring my way.

Time to try the axe.

I dropped the sickle and then studied the vines until I found a spot that looked like it would open the tangle enough to let me pass. Setting my feet, I swung the axe, annoyed when I overshot and the handle just bounced against the point I was aiming for. On my second try, the axe head actually landed, but it barely pierced the bark when most of the force was absorbed by the springy vines. Annoyed, I tried once more, but just then the axe head flew off the handle, disappearing somewhere deep in the thicket in front of me.

Sighing in frustration, I tramped back the way I'd come, retrieving the digging tool from where I'd left it at the edge of the vineyard. I studied the wooden handle, wondering if the same thing would happen again, but no, the business end was flared outward, and there was no way the head was going to slip off.

Still, the springiness of the vines was a problem, so instead of hacking at the middle of a branch, I traced it back to where it met the thicker bole of the vine and tried hitting it there. It took me another couple of tries, but when I finally hit what I was aiming for, the vine separated easily, the heavy head half-cutting, half-tearing through the soft wood.

Okay, I thought with satisfaction. *That'll do.*

Moe stayed with me as I continued, slowly but steadily hacking and chopping through most of a century's worth of old growth. We were almost to the far side when we both heard Bonnie's playful giggle, and Moe charged off in the direction of the sound, barking as he disappeared into the tangle ahead.

For a second or two, I considered following him, but then I remembered how that had worked out last time. *No way,* I thought. I was *not* going to be distracted again. Come mud, flood, shit, or blood, I was going to find that freaking cellar!

I broke free to the north side of the vineyard a few minutes later, blinking in the sudden brightness. I dropped my tools, leaning with my hands on my knees to rest, and then looked at my watch. Not so bad—it had only taken me about half an hour to make my way through the tangled vines, while without tools it had taken Les and I nearly twice that long. When I had my wind back, I rose and moved ten paces west and then picked out my next reference point—the cupola.

Taking a deep breath, I went back in.

The second leg of my sweep didn't take quite as long as the first. Moe rejoined me about ten minutes later, panting happily while staying well back from my sometimes wild swings. I was getting better with the sickle and digger thing, though, and was able to fight my way through the vines a lot faster the more I practiced. Twenty-six minutes later, I stumbled out again, my shirt soaked through with sweat. I pulled it off and hung it on the fence, and then took a short breather before walking another ten paces west and getting back to work.

We'd only gone a little way when we heard Bonnie again, this time humming "Blue Skies," and Moe was off like a shot, heading vaguely northwest by the sound of it. "You have fun with that, boy," I grunted, slashing ahead of me with the sickle.

It went on like that all through the morning and into the afternoon: south to north, north to south in a back and forth pattern. Even under the heavy gloves, my hands eventually started to blister, but I didn't stop. Whenever I felt like giving up, all I had to do was think of Mom sleeping in the rocking chair while the spirit of Roger Black crept closer, and then I'd plunge back into the vines.

At one point, I thought I'd finally found what I was looking for. I was slashing through a particularly dense thicket when the sickle suddenly hit something unyielding, bouncing back with a hollow, metallic sound. Excitedly, I tore the vines aside, finding a wall of rusty, corrugated metal. Not seeing any kind of opening, I worked my way to the left, rounded a corner to go north again, and then turned east for three or four feet before the wall finally disappeared and I discovered a wide opening curtained off by layer upon layer of grapevines. A few slashes and I was through, looking into a twenty-by-twenty-foot shed containing a rusted-over well pump and, parked alongside it, Roger Black's pickup truck.

It sat on flat tires, the beige and green paint covered in grime and splotched here and there with rust, but the shed and mounds of grapevines had largely protected it from the elements, preserving it. It was like discovering an ancient tomb. I took a step or two inside, wanting a closer look, but then I pulled up short. *No,* I thought, shaking my head. *There'll be time for that later.*

Backing out, I fought my way north for another fifty feet or so before finding myself in the clear. I turned and looked behind me, realizing that the shed had probably been well away from the grapevines originally but that the vineyard's wild growth had expanded a lot between then and now. *It doesn't matter,* I reminded myself. *Keep going.*

Ten paces west, then south again into the vines.

I was almost through another southbound sweep late in the afternoon when a voice called out in the distance, causing Moe to lope on ahead, crashing through the vines. "Ben…? Hey, Ben!" It sounded like Les.

"Yo, Wolfman! You around?" Ab, without a doubt.

"Coming!" I called back, hoping that my voice carried far enough for them to hear. After another twenty feet or so, I finally cut my way free, stumbling out within sight of the house.

They stood by the porch steps, petting Moe as he bounced around in circles, greeting them.

I walked slowly their way, my steps feeling heavy, and I was suddenly aware of how exhausted I felt. Their faces registered shock, and I looked down at myself, seeing that I was coated with dirt and bits of vine and leaves, with a sheen of sweat covering my entire upper body and darkening my jeans in a V below my waistband. Even though I'd been working in the shade of the vines, the skin on my shoulders and upper back had reddened with sunburn, and my hands were cramping from gripping tools all day long.

"You look like crap," Ab said by way of greeting, a backpack over her shoulder.

"Nice to see you, too," I said, and dropped my tools at the base of the steps.

"You're going through all that with just a sickle and a mattock?" Les asked, whistling. "You must be a lot tougher than you look."

I snorted, strolling around to the rear of the house. *Mattock,* I thought idly. *At least it's a better name than digger-thing.* Ab and Les followed, watching as I turned on the hose and doused myself, washing off the worst of the sweat and dirt. When I was done, I felt a lot more human.

"When you didn't show yesterday afternoon or this morning, I got worried," Ab told me. "You okay?"

I had to think about how to answer. "I don't know," I told her honestly. "Come inside and I'll fill you in." They followed me into the kitchen, and I gave them sodas before piling five or six slices of sandwich meat onto a slice of bread, folding it over and cramming in down. I followed it with a big glass of water and then joined them at the table, grabbing my own Pepsi and gulping down a third of it, already feeling better.

"Don't leave us hanging, *hombre*," urged Les.

I nodded, telling them everything that had happened since we'd split up at the town hall, being careful to describe all of my visions in detail. (Well, okay…I sort of glossed over Kelly finding me passed out in the driveway and skipped the whole part where she'd crawled into my bed. But hey, it wasn't like that was critical information.) I finished with my fight with Roger's spirit in the cupola, Aunt Claire swooping in to save me, and the vision of her finding her father dead and then hearing Bonnie's voice in the darkness.

There was a lot to say, and it took a long time.

"Your night was a lot more interesting than mine," Ab said, unzipping her backpack. "All I did was finish reading Claire's diary." She drew it out, setting it on the table and sliding it over to me.

"Did you find anything?" I asked hopefully, leaning forward.

She shook her head. "Nothing that helps us. Her last entry was the day before the tidal wave. She and Philip planned to meet at the movies, and she was hoping he'd hold her hand."

"Yeah, well we know how that worked out."

"After that, she didn't write anymore," Ab went on. "The last thirty or forty pages are all blank." She shrugged. "Sorry, Wolfman."

I nodded, trying not to feel too disappointed. After all, I wasn't any worse off than I had been ten minutes before, and I'd already made serious progress searching the vineyard. Something was keeping Bonnie out there, and sooner or later I was bound to find out what it was.

We sat together in silence for almost a minute before Ab brightened. "Oh God, I'm such an airhead!" She reached into the backpack again and drew out a thick manila envelope. "I almost forgot—the clerk from city records called this morning. Here's everything they had on the cellar project."

"Yeah?" I asked excitedly, bending back the metal tabs that held it closed. "Anything good?"

She shrugged. "Dunno. I was running late and only had time to duck in and grab it on my way to work."

All three of us leaned in together as I pulled out the stack of documents. The top page was a copy of the request form that Ab had filled out, followed by a multi-page building permit that was stamped "Cancelled by Owner." Following that were notarized deeds proving that the land where the construction was happening was owned by Roger Black.

The cellar plans were down toward the bottom of the stack, and I had to study the overhead view closely for a few seconds before I understood what I was looking at.

"They were excavating a hillside," Les said, recognizing it just before I did. "It wasn't a building at all. They were digging a cave!"

"Yeah, but where?" I asked. The next page was an architect's drawing of the entrance, and as soon as I saw it, I jumped to my feet, the chair I'd been sitting in falling over with a crash.

A massive set of double doors were set in a concrete frame on the side of the hill, twenty-four feet high by sixteen wide, according to the scale.

They were shaped in a Gothic arch!

I pawed through the rest of the drawings, looking for an area map that would show the location. When I found it, I ran outside, comparing the shape of the surrounding hills to the map to make sure I was reading it correctly. *I was!*

"Ben?" asked Ab, standing next to Les on the porch.

Then, all at once, a shiver shook my whole body as I made the final connection, though I needed to go and check, just to be sure. I dropped the map, darting past Ab and Les back into the house.

"Wolfman, hold up! Where are you going?"

I could hear them running after me as I pounded up to the second floor, flew along the hall, and then ran up the attic stairs. I was shaking with adrenaline when I finally reached the cupola. The cold and gloom of Roger Black was seeping back in, but I ignored it as I skidded to a stop in front of Mom's painting.

There it was—the detail that had been bothering me. It was so obvious, but I'd missed it completely.

The shadows were on the wrong side!

All this time I'd thought it was a picture of Bonnie running through the vineyard in early evening. But the shadows were all to the left, which meant the sun was in the east—*morning!*

At that moment, Ab and Les arrived in the cupola, out of breath and looking at me with confused expressions.

"I know where she is!"

FOURTY-FOUR

"HEY!" AB CRIED AS I RAN PAST THEM AND BOLTED DOWN the cupola stairs. "Ben, *wait!* Where are you going?"

But I couldn't wait. After all this time, after all the uncertainty and running into dead ends, I couldn't wait a minute longer.

I could hear Ab and Les pounding down from the second floor after me when I leaped down the porch steps, snatching up the mattock as I went. Moe loped alongside me, grinning his doggie-grin as if he was excited by the adventure of it all. I increased my pace to a sprint for the first hundred yards or so, but then my adrenaline began to wear off as the long day caught up with me, and I eased my pace back to a jog. I veered right to go around the vineyard, and Ab and Les finally caught up to me as I rounded the corner by at the eastern edge.

"Are you…freaking out?" Les puffed as he pulled up alongside me. "'Cause it looks like you're...freaking out."

"C'mon, Wolfman," said Ab, just a step or two behind. "Stop and take a breath!"

I realized they were right, so I stopped, letting the mattock fall to the ground beside me as I sank to my knees, breathing hard. I sat back on my heels, rolling my head back toward the sky, and after a few gulps of air, I began to get my wind back. "I've been so *stupid*," I began. "The day Moe and I chased Bonnie around in the vines—remember? I thought she was leading me away—that there was something in there she didn't want me to see. But then Lisette told me that she wanted to be found, so how would that make sense? And anyway, if Bonnie was killed by the tidal wave, what would the vineyard have to do with *any* of it?"

Ab looked confused. "But the wave *did* take her."

"No," I said. "It didn't!" I scrambled back to my feet and started running again, trusting them to follow. When they pulled up alongside, I went on. "Bonnie had begged to go with her dad, so when she came up missing, everyone just *assumed* that's what happened. As far as anyone knew, she was just one more body dragged out to sea." We swung left, heading northwest toward the wide, level expanse between the hills and the cliffs above the ocean.

"Yeah?" Les panted. "So?"

I halted again, turning to face them. "So, when you're a willful kid, and your dad looks you in the eye and makes you promise not to do something, you can either go ahead and do it anyway—and risk getting caught—or go do something else!

"You mean…" Ab began.

"The cellar!" I finished for her. "Even though her dad had told her not to, Bonnie always kept finding ways to go there. Picture it: she wakes up at dawn. Her dad's still gone, Claire's gone, and there's no one to stop her. She has no idea what's happened in town, so why wouldn't she make the most of her chance?" I started running again, swinging north along the cliffs.

"But, Ben, that still doesn't explain the vineyard! Why does she haunt it? And why did she try so hard to keep you away?"

"She didn't!" I called back over my shoulder. I kept running until I saw the wide gap to my right, and I swung into the box canyon before finally coming to a stop. "I thought that was what she was doing, but I was wrong! She wasn't trying to get me out of the vineyard. She was trying to lead me *here*!"

We stood there, letting our breathing slow down and listening to the sound of the waves as they echoed against the barren cliffs.

"Dude, I don't see any cellar," Les remarked at last.

"Oh, it's there alright," I assured him. "It just got covered. A good part of the hillside must've come down on it that morning." I plunged ahead into the box canyon, running the hundred feet or so to the end.

"You mean when the earthquake happened?" Ab pressed, running up beside me. "Then how would Bonnie have gotten inside?"

"No, not the earthquake," I said, scrambling up the steep incline until I figured I'd gone high enough. "The quake probably got things loosened up, but there was that big aftershock later, remember?" Balancing myself awkwardly on the grade, I swung the mattock, the wide blade biting deep and dislodging a bowling ball-sized clod of earth that tumbled down to the base of the hill.

There was a long pause as the realization of what I was telling them sank in.

"Hey! You don't have to do this alone, you know!" Ab called up to remind me. "How can we help?"

"There are more tools in the barn," I hollered, not looking back as I took another swing. "Go and help yourself!"

They took off, Moe staying behind to pace back and forth, barking up at me and occasionally having to dodge big chunks I kept cutting out of the earth. Bits and pieces of images popped into my head as I hacked away at the hill—brief images that were not quite visions:

Bonnie running into the box canyon, grinning when she realizes she's alone…

Bonnie grunting with effort as she pulls the right-hand door open just enough to squeeze through…

Bonnie terrified when the ground begins to shake, hearing a rumble and turning just in time to see the landslide push the cellar door closed. She screams…

I shoved the images away, not wanting to see any more.

By the time Ab and Les got back, carrying shovels, I'd carved out a ledge deep enough to stand on. They scrambled up, and Les put a hand on my shoulder between swings, gently pulling the mattock out of my hands. I'd left my gloves back at the house, and I never even noticed when my blisters had broken, the softer skin below wearing down until I'd left bloody hand prints on the handle. I accepted his shovel in trade and then watched as he swung the mattock with practiced ease, his big shoulders driving it deep and sending explosions of sand and dirt that rained down as he cut out chunks of earth even bigger than mine.

We kept at it until the sun was low in the west, Les swinging the mattock tirelessly while Ab and I used our shovels to clear away the rubble.

Then, all of a sudden, the mattock bounced back against something unyielding, and I had to grab Les's shirt to keep him from tumbling backward down the hill. Then we scraped away the dirt, and I realized what it was: the concrete frame around the doors!

Ten minutes or so later, we'd cleared away enough soil to reveal the top two feet or so of the arched doorway. "Stand back," Les said, and then swung the mattock, tearing out a big chunk of the rotten wood. He swung again, sending pieces flying into the gloom and leaving a gaping hole behind—ragged splinters surrounding only darkness.

I dropped to my belly, squirming forward until my head was through the breach.

It took nearly a minute for my eyes to adjust to the darkness. Even then, I could just barely make out the small, curled-up form of Bonnie, her nightdress a dingy white in the meager glow leaking through the hole around me. Now little more than a skeleton, she lay on her side, her face pressed up against the doors beneath what remained of her blonde hair.

"Wolfman," Ab said, poking me in the ribs. Then, when I didn't respond, "Ben…!"

Irritated, I wormed my way back out on my elbows to glare up at Ab, but then I saw her expression and followed it down to the bottom of the hill.

Bonnie stood there. Her nightdress was fresh and white, and Moe sat beside her with his tail wagging as she looked up at us.

"Is that…" Les began.

"Yeah," I breathed, "it is."

She only remained there for a second or two longer, and then she turned and ran toward the mouth of the canyon.

Without thinking, I leapt after her, landing hard in the loose soil that we'd piled at the bottom of the incline. My feet were behind the rest of me so I automatically tucked my head, rolling in a somersault and coming back up at a run, following her.

No matter how fast I ran, Bonnie always seemed to be fifty feet ahead of me. My shoes pounded the earth, my gasps sounding loud in my ears as Moe flew along beside me. We veered left as Bonnie disappeared into the vineyard, taking the longer route around and hoping to pick her up on the far side. When we finally made it around the vines, though, I could see her well ahead of us, already running up the porch steps and into the house.

It took us nearly a minute to get there, my legs feeling like rubber when I finally staggered into the entry hall, and I collapsed to my knees, sliding to the base of the stairs.

Movement. To my right.

I looked over, blinking sweat out of my eyes and then suddenly forgetting to breathe as I saw Aunt Claire, old and hunched over her cane, emerge from the family room. As I stared, she made her way slowly over toward me, stopping near my feet and only then turning her gaze up the stairwell with a look of satisfaction on her face.

I twisted around just in time to see Roger Black slowly descend from the second floor, Bonnie in his arms. He appeared the way he had been just before the tidal wave had struck—not the ruin of the man in the wake of Bonnie's loss—and I could feel my heart swell as he reached the landing, turning and reaching out for Claire.

I watched as they touched hands, and the years seemed to melt away from my aunt all at once. In the space of a heartbeat, she had straightened, her cane disappearing as she became the teenage Claire I had come to know from my visions.

Just then Ab and Les stopped near the base of the porch steps. They stared, open-mouthed, as the three went out the door together. Then they paused, Roger gazing down at Claire beside him as she turned to look back over her shoulder at me.

She smiled.

Then they continued forward again, fading away as their feet touched the dry grass.

For a few seconds afterward, Ab and Les remained frozen in place, taking in everything they'd seen. Then they raced forward, pulling me to my feet.

"Dude, you good?"

"You okay, Wolfman?"

I shook them off, turning and staggering up the stairs. The climb to the cupola was the hardest I'd ever made, my dread so heavy that it was like I was pushing a piano in front of me. At last I fell to my knees beside the rocking chair, taking my mother's right hand in both of mine. "Mom…?" I asked. "Mom, are you there?"

After a long moment, her eyes fluttered slowly open. "Benny?" she asked, sounding unsure, as if waking from a deep sleep. Then her gaze focused, and she offered me a half-smile, half-frown. *"Oh, baby…*why are you crying?"

I smiled, letting go a breath as I sagged against the side of the chair. "Are you okay?" I asked, feeling hot tears on my cheeks.

"Sure, honey…I'm good," she replied, reaching out to stroke my cheek. "Just…*starving!*"

EPILOG

WE BURIED BONNIE IN WINDWARD COVE CEMETERY LESS than two weeks later, in a tiny grave right next to her father. A cool, offshore breeze stirred the leaves around the headstones, but the sun was warm, the sky was clear, and the smell of the ocean and eucalyptus was pleasant in the air.

Only a handful of us were there to see her laid to rest: me and Mom, Ab and Les, and Eleanor Markham in her wheelchair, flanked by Lisette and Carl. Not much of a send-off, I suppose, but Father Pete's eulogy was really nice, and at the end I don't think anyone's eyes were completely dry.

Afterward, Mom treated everyone to an early dinner at DeMarino's, an Italian restaurant in Silver Creek that was only a half-mile or so from Autumn Leaves. I had the sausage tortellini, and it was good. Carl finally got his bourbon and spent a good part of the time joking around with Father Pete, while I watched from across the table as Mom and Lisette sat with their heads together, chatting like old friends. Mom still looked too thin, but she was starting to put some weight back on. She had even been running a couple of times—only short distances, of course—but every time she went out, I was glad to see her move without the limp. Even Eleanor was having a good day and tried sharing a few stories about what Bonnie was like when they were little. She got distracted, though, never finishing one story before starting a different one, but that was okay. All in all, everyone had a great time, and it felt the way I'd always imagined a family get-together would be like.

When Nancy showed up with van from the retirement home, I was disappointed, and I walked out with them while everyone else waited for their leftovers to be boxed up. I was watching Carl push Eleanor onto the wheelchair lift when I felt a tug at my sleeve. "You come with me, now," Lisette said quietly, and we walked a few steps away to stand in the shade of an olive tree.

"You done good, *cher,*" she said, smiling up at me. "That li'l girl, she finally restin' easy. Not many in this world could'a been a help to her, and I'm proud of you."

I grinned. "Thanks, Lisette."

"And don't you be worryin' 'bout *votre mère.*" She went on. "I give your mama a good lookin' over while we was havin' supper, and there ain't nothin' of that ol' man left in her. She gonna be jus' fine, and I 'spect your house gonna feel pretty quiet from here on out."

"Yeah," I admitted. "I guess it will." *It would have been nice if Aunt Claire had stuck around, though,* I thought, but I supposed that was selfish of me.

"Hol' this," said Lisette, handing me her cane, and when I took it, she reached up and grabbed me by both ears, pulling me down to plant a kiss on my forehead. "Time for me to go, *cher,*" she said, winking, and then started toward where Carl and Nancy waited by the van.

"I'll come by and see you soon, okay?' I called after her.

Lisette paused, looking back over her shoulder at me with a smile. "Oh, I know that, boy. You comin' to see me even sooner than you think. I got the *sight*, remember?"

I didn't know what to make of that, and was watching the van pull away when Ab and Les came up to join me. "So what's next?"

I shook my head. "No idea. I guess Moe is probably hungry and lonesome back at the house, and I *definitely* want to get out of this necktie. What did you have in mind?"

"Well, it *is* Saturday night," Les offered. "There's always the beach."

I shrugged.

"C'mon, Wolfman," Ab teased, grinning. "Kelly might be there!"

I thought about it, and then decided I was good either way.